"Don't bre...
don't break!"

J.B. muttered the litany as the friends raced through an obstacle course of boiling springs and over ground he knew had to be undermined. They ran on a crust of earth that could give way under their combined weight, plunging them to a terrible death by scalding.

They reached and rounded the muddy shore of an infernal lake, and when J.B. looked up, a black shadow passed across the stars, cutting off all hope of their retreat. The Armorer slowed, then stopped. He stood slope-shouldered, his blasters hanging useless in his hands. The companions closed ranks around him, facing the oncoming assault gyro. Rumbling cauldrons to the rear spit drops of boiling mud on their unprotected backs.

It was the least of their worries.

Silhouetted against the blue-white moon, the aircraft slowly turned its weapons pod toward them.

JAMES AXLER

DEATH LANDS®
Shadow World

A GOLD EAGLE BOOK FROM
WORLDWIDE®

TORONTO • NEW YORK • LONDON
AMSTERDAM • PARIS • SYDNEY • HAMBURG
STOCKHOLM • ATHENS • TOKYO • MILAN
MADRID • WARSAW • BUDAPEST • AUCKLAND

First edition March 2000

ISBN 0-373-62559-6

SHADOW WORLD

Printed in U.S.A.

...my suspicion is that the universe is not only queerer than we suppose, but queerer than we *can* suppose.... I suspect that there are more things in heaven and earth than are dreamed of...

—John Burdon Sanderson Haldane
Possible Worlds, 1927

THE DEATHLANDS SAGA

This world is their legacy, a world born in the violent nuclear spasm of 2001 that was the bitter outcome of a struggle for global dominance.

There is no real escape from this shockscape where life always hangs in the balance, vulnerable to newly demonic nature, barbarism, lawlessness.

But they are the warrior survivalists, and they endure—in the way of the lion, the hawk and the tiger, true to nature's heart despite its ruination.

Ryan Cawdor: The privileged son of an East Coast baron. Acquainted with betrayal from a tender age, he is a master of the hard realities.

Krysty Wroth: Harmony ville's own Titian-haired beauty, a woman with the strength of tempered steel. Her premonitions and Gaia powers have been fostered by her Mother Sonja.

J. B. Dix, the Armorer: Weapons master and Ryan's close ally, he, too, honed his skills traversing the Deathlands with the legendary Trader.

Doctor Theophilus Tanner: Torn from his family and a gentler life in 1896, Doc has been thrown into a future he couldn't have imagined.

Dr. Mildred Wyeth: Her father was killed by the Ku Klux Klan, but her fate is not much lighter. Restored from predark cryogenic suspension, she brings twentieth-century healing skills to a nightmare.

Jak Lauren: A true child of the wastelands, reared on adversity, loss and danger, the albino teenager is a fierce fighter and loyal friend.

Dean Cawdor: Ryan's young son by Sharona accepts the only world he knows, and yet he is the seedling bearing the promise of tomorrow.

In a world where all was lost, they are humanity's last hope....

Chapter One

Beside the deeply rutted dirt track leading to the ville of Moonboy, wedged between a pair of boulders, a warning sign shimmered in the blistering midday heat. Crudely chiseled into the rectangle of rusted car door were two words: NO MEWTEES.

Behind the sign, the good people of Moonboy had left a universal symbol for those travelers who couldn't read. From a gallows made of an old basketball stanchion and backboard hung a naked corpse. Sun-dried, and as hard and brown as jerky, it had a huge head and a misshapen body, its finger bones twice as long as its arms.

Like many of the other small outposts of human survival in Deathlands, the ville had sprung up from ruins more than a century old. On January 20, 2001, a Kamchatka-launched ICBM, part of an all-out, U.S.-Soviet nuclear exchange, had vaporized nearby Salt Lake City. The three-warhead airburst had left behind a radioactive, thermoglass rubble field that covered more than fifty square miles. As in the case of other earthly disasters—tornadoes, hurricanes, forest fires—Armageddon had turned out to be a capricious bitch. Up Highway 15 from ground zero, snuggled in a gap in the promontory ridge of rock, a Salt Lake City bedroom community had taken a less than annihilating hit. What was now the main drag of

Moonboy ville had once been a suburban street in the upscale residential development; it was one of the few blocks left standing in the administrative region formerly known as Morgan County, Utah.

Facing rows of stucco-sided, three-story homes, their windows blown out in the same horrific shock blast, were the underpinnings and center point of the ville. Scabrous add-ons and rickety lean-tos used the outside walls of the original buildings as their main structural support. Rusting sheets of corrugated metal formed a jumble of makeshift shanty roofs. Their orange stains streaked the predark stucco, iron oxide bleeding from thousands of less than mortal wounds. Intermittent acid rains had long since turned the asphalt pavement between the rows of houses to coarse black sand, and had cratered and dissolved most of the broad, curving driveways and concrete sidewalks.

On this cloudless summer day, Moonboy's unemployed residents and visitors sought out the shade of the metal-roofed, ramshackle porches that lined either side of the main street. Steel not only defended them from the brutal sun, but from flesh-etching, sulfuric acid downpours. About two dozen women and men, none particularly clean, most gap-toothed and weathered, sat chewing the fat and sipping air-temperature green beer from recycled, plastic antifreeze jugs. A few lay curled up in the shadows on the hard-tamped dirt, snoozing off the remnants of their market day drunk.

By the standards of Deathlands, where wealth and status were measured in armament, Moonboy was a shitpoor place. Along the main street, there were no weapons that would accept high-power, center-fire brass cartridges. The only firearms of modern design were a handful of single-shot, top-break, exposed-hammer 12-gauges, and every one had a rust-brown barrel, a broken or missing stock and a crudely tied, rope shoulder sling. The rest of the population carried long, razor-honed, chilling knives and cheap, scarred, black-powder revolvers—late-twentieth-century, mass-produced copies of Civil War–era side arms.

There were no cops in Moonboy. Official law enforcement was unnecessary with so many weapons on display. Justice, or what passed for it, was within easy reach of every hand. And God help the rad-blasted mutie who stumbled within range of blade or pistol ball.

Piercing screams erupted from the top floor of the gaudy house in the middle of the block. It was impossible to tell whether the screamer was male or female, or if the cries were of pain or pleasure. The porch squatters ignored the shrill racket. Moonboy's pure norm sluts were well compensated for their time and trouble. After a few minutes, the shrieking stopped and the echoes faded.

None of the drowsy, streetside spectators expected anything interesting to happen until nightfall. The withering heat made a knife fight to the death highly unlikely. The potential combatants were all either too flagged or too hung over to get into a serious beef with anyone.

Then the air in the middle of the street began to shimmer.

It wasn't just heat waves coming off the ruined asphalt.

At head height, dust motes glittered and whirled, quickly turning into a man-sized tornado. The Moonboy folk blinked in amazement, then hurriedly kicked awake their dozing friends. This was no ordinary dust devil. It sparkled as if it held millions of tiny fragments of mirror in its spinning funnel; with each passing second the glittering bits grew more and more distinct.

And brighter.

So bright, in fact, that the residents had to either squint or shield their eyes from the hard glare.

A powerful wind accompanied this apparition. It set road dust flying and scraggly beards flapping. There was a deep bass rumble below the wind's howl, the building growl of some impossibly huge engine.

An earsplitting thunder crack rattled the corrugated steel roofs over the spectators' heads. The shock wave vibrated up through the soles of their feet, through their legs, to their very bowels. In a flash, the tornado flew apart, and before their eyes, at the epicenter of the ville, the seams of reality split and peeled back.

A tall, humanoid figure in black stepped out of nothing and nowhere, out of the ragged slash in space, birthed full-grown into the middle of the road, accompanied by a nauseating, superconcentrated, petrochemical stench. The figure wore a suit of head-to-foot black armor, and the armor gleamed as if it had been dipped in machine oil. Like the carapace of some gigantic, rad-mutated insect, the suit was segmented over arms and legs, overlapping, contoured plates protecting the torso. The boots, shin guards and helmet were of the same material. An impenetrable, smoke-colored, wraparound visor concealed the face.

All eyes locked onto the blue-black blaster the creature gripped in its gauntleted hands. The weapon was of stubby, bullpup design. A styrene stock held three heavy barrels joined in a triangular configuration, and a single, claw-toothed flash-hider crowned all three muzzles. A massively thick, curving magazine extended below the stock just in front of the rifle's buttplate. No one on the street had ever seen or even heard tell of anything quite like it. Though they didn't know what mayhem the wicked-looking piece was capable of, in their hearts every man and woman lusted after it. Whether traded for jack or jolt, or kept as a personal side arm, such a weapon could make life in the hellscape known as Deathlands a whole lot easier to bear.

Before any of the folk could move to appropriate the blaster, there was another boom of thunder and a flash. A second, identical figure stepped from nowhere into the middle of the road. It, too, carried a magical blaster. It, too, was followed by a gust of foul wind.

The appearance of another armed, apparently mutated stranger galvanized Moonboy's idlers, whose rule of thumb was always to kill first and ask questions later. A hodgepodge of handblasters cleared belts and hip leather on both sides of the street. The intruders stood stock-still, at a range of less than twenty yards. There was a rattle of gritty clacks as single-action hammer spurs locked back.

''Yee-hah!'' someone shouted in glee. ''We got ourselves a fuckin' mutie shoot!''

The self-appointed firing squads took positions on both sides of the street. Aiming two-handed, the shooters thoughtfully angled themselves to keep from hitting their opposite numbers with near-misses or ricochets.

The figures in black armor responded by shifting position as well, standing back to back in the center of the road, each staring down a line of blaster muzzles. Oddly enough, the all-over armor plate they wore didn't seem to inhibit their movement. The material bent and flexed with them. The strangers held their own weapons at the ready, but unaimed. As if either ignorant or disdainful of the mortal danger they faced, the pair calmly waited for the ville's welcoming committee to make the first move.

They didn't have to wait long.

No formal signal to fire brought on the withering barrage. When the first shot suddenly barked out, the rest of the blasters followed in short, ragged order. Volleys of pistol balls and buckshot rained on the standing figures. As the massed handblasters boomed and flashed, dense clouds of thick, white gunsmoke rolled from both sidewalks, fogging the street and partially obscuring the targets.

A STROKE OF DUMB LUCK had landed Grub Hinton in the upper floor of Moonboy's gaudy house that same morning.

A scrounger by trade, Grub eked out his solitary living beneath the thick glaze of nuke-melted sand on the outer edge of Salt Lake City's crater. He pickaxed holes through the layers of thermoglass, then crawled in headfirst, searching the narrow, jagged air pockets for anything of value. Prospecting the wasteland was largely unrewarding work, as most of the wealth of the city that hadn't been vaporized had been turned into unrecognizable and immovable

globs of slag. The work was also extremely dangerous, and not just because of the lingering high levels
of radioactivity. Chances were, long before the first
weeping, rad-cancer lesions appeared on Grub's
cheeks and hands, some other scrounger would have
bushwhacked him for his meager bag of booty, or
for exclusive mining rights to some especially prom-
ising hole. On the upside, he always had more than
enough to eat, even if it was just rat-on-a-stick.

Grub Hinton's jackpot find, a 1958 Buick hubcap
slightly scorched on the edges, lay propped against
the filthy, bug-splattered wall of the gaudy crib. He
had traded this singular treasure for a rare, all-night,
green beer drunk, and an even rarer, full three hours
in the saddle.

As Grub's morning of bliss wore on and on, the
gaudy slut in question had cause to rue the deal she'd
struck with him. Even her most enthusiastic faked
screams of passion had failed to make the little man
finish his mechanical rutting and scar-fisted pawing
of her body. The sudden thunderclap from the street
that rattled the building's walls and floor, and
whooshed inward the shredded clear plastic sheeting
that passed for window curtains, accomplished what
her ham acting couldn't.

"Stun gren!" Grub barked as he rolled off the
woman's doughy stomach and pushed up from the
straw-stuffed pallet on the floor.

Still staggering drunk and naked, a sickly pale,
two-legged, potbellied pig, hairless but for the fringe
of reddish fur on his behind, Grub lurched for the
frame of the third-story window. As he reached it,
there was a second, floor-shaking boom, the tattered
plastic curtains fluttering in his face.

He pushed aside the strips of plastic and forced his eyes to focus on the scene directly below. Like a dip in an ice-cold mountain stream, what he saw momentarily sobered him. Grub Hinton had come nose to nose with plenty of nasty, rad-mutated creepy crawlies while rooting in the dark under the dirty glass skin of Slakecity, but nothing like this....

At first glance, the three figures in the middle of the street looked like giant black cockroaches, straight out of a jolt-binge, melt-brain nightmare. But on closer inspection, he saw they had two arms and two legs, like men. And like men, they carried stubby-barreled blasters.

If Deathlands had taught Grub anything in his twenty-three years, it was to expect the unexpected; if you could jolt-dream a living terror, odds were it existed there, someplace. Generations after the nuke-caust of 2001, monsters that should never have been born were born—and once born, bred in awesome profusion. Norms like Hinton, lucky enough to have no obvious outward abnormalities, rationalized the hunting down and indiscriminate slaughter of their less fortunate brethren because some of the mutated human subspecies—known variously as stickies, cannies, scabbies, scalies—had devolved into crazed, senseless killers. As a general rule, mutie bastards didn't pack blasters; they preferred to do their murdering with fang and claw, with club or suckerfist.

From his position at the window, Grub could see the norm folk lined up on the opposite side of the street. A grin spread over his face. The intruders were about to be executed, Moonboy style, and Grub had himself a front-row balcony seat.

"Come over here," he told the woman on the pallet, waving his arm for her to hurry. ''This is going to be some kind of show.''

The gaudy slut stepped up to the window without bothering to conceal her nakedness. But she did cover her ears when, in a deafening thirty-second fusillade, every norm weapon along the street emptied.

As the haze of burned black powder lifted, Grub saw Moonboy's antimutie posse scrambling to rack fresh, preloaded spare cylinders into their revolvers. Amazingly, the intruders still stood, their armor unmarked.

''I could have hit 'em with a rock from way up here!'' Grub snorted. ''How did all those triple stupes miss?''

Then, with cold deliberation, the newcomers shouldered their own weapons. As the homeboys and -girls tried to scatter from the porches, the roachmen opened fire. And it was clear at once that the assault rifles they carried were as rad-blasted queer as they were.

Instead of the crack of single gunshots or the canvas-ripping clatter of high-rate autofire, the weapons gave off painfully shrill, whistling sounds. From out of their flash-hiders shot single, narrow beams of emerald-green light so intense that they could be seen in the midday sun. Everywhere the pencil-thin beams touched, they cut. And the slicing effect was instantaneous. The sprinting residents and spectators of Moonboy dropped, screaming as they were bisected, along with sundry chair backs, stucco walls, rain barrels and porch posts. The row of rickety roofs collapsed. Out from under the rising cloud of dust, human heads, cleanly severed at the neck, rolled downhill like runaway melons, bounding off the curb and into the gutter.

The battle, if you could call it that, was over in a few heartbeats.

Frozen in place, Grub and his female companion stared slack-jawed at the ruination below.

Though every member of the firing squad had been chopped in two, the screaming continued. A few people were still alive down there; Grub could see them thrashing in the dirt beside the collapsed roof. He recognized one of the survivors as Old Rupe, the man who did all the beer brewing for the gaudy's saloon. Old Rupe's detached legs and hand lay on the ground two yards from where he writhed. Despite his terrible injuries, he hadn't bled so much as a drop. The stumps of his limbs looked blackened and scorched.

Grub and the slut flinched as thunder rolled again, and three more of the roachmen appeared out of thin air. They carried a different assortment of gear than their predecessors. Two of them wore heavy-looking, flat-black canisters strapped onto their backs. The third intruder pushed a squat, shiny black cube on big wheels.

With the initial pair providing cover, this new trio moved quickly from the middle of the road to where Old Rupe lay thrashing. Seeing what was coming his way, the brewmaster flopped to his stomach and desperately tried to drag himself to safety with his one good arm. His considerable effort was futile. One of the canister men blocked Old Rupe's path; the other kicked him onto his back, and easily held him there with a boot heel on the throat.

The cube pusher drew something bright and silvery from his belt. It was a cylindrical, latticework metal cage, about two feet long, with a pistol grip. To Grub, it looked like an oversized, predark drill stand, complete with battery-powered hand drill.

Old Rupe flopped around on the sidewalk, trying in vain to get out from under the boot. The cube pusher jammed the business end of the silver device against the brewmaster's chest, securely pinning him to the concrete. Then the device snicked sharply, steel grating on steel, and brutally ended Old Rupe's torment. The mechanical cookie cutter plunged into his torso right over his heart, crunching through breastbone and ribs, and then snapped back with a fruit-can-sized sample of red, dripping meat, which was quickly dumped into the matching hole in the top of the squat cube.

The pusher leaned over the cube, intently studying its LED readout. After a few seconds, the roachman looked up from the machine. Without a visible or audible command, the two with canisters began to move among the debris and the sprawled bodies. From short hoses connected to their back tanks, they sprayed creamy yellow foam over each of the downed human forms. Beneath their mounds of foam, the still-living and the newly dead dissolved, liquefying into sheets of bubbling brown goo that poured off the edges of the sidewalk and into the asphalt sand.

Grub heard a hissing sound quite close, and felt a sudden, warm wetness between the toes of his bare feet. When he looked down, heart thudding, he saw that he was standing in a quickly spreading puddle of urine that wasn't his own. The gaudy slut beside him began to wail at the top of her lungs. He grabbed her by the arm and jerked her away from the window. "For nuke's sake, shut your face!" he said, shaking her by the shoulders as he backed her across the room. "Do you want to put them mutie bastards on us?"

But the poor woman was wild-eyed with fear. If anything, her cries got louder.

Grub took hold of her face, squeezing her jaws shut, and gave her a hard shove that sent her stumbling backward onto the mattress. As she scrambled to take cover beneath it, he pulled on his torn desert camouflage BDUs and raggedy jungle boots.

"Good thinking," he said to the human-sized lump under the middle of the pallet. "They sure as shit won't find you there."

Realizing the slut was in no position to complain, Grub picked up the Roadmaster hubcap on his way out the door.

Chapter Two

The sun's sweltering heat made the empty eyesocket beneath Ryan Cawdor's black patch itch. He shut his one good eye and listened. Hard.

Crouched in the shade of the stand of scraggy, mutant willow trees, the tall, powerfully built man blocked out the sawing hum of insects, the steady plip-plop-plip of his own sweat dripping into the sand and the footfalls of his companions approaching around the bend in the river channel. Though Ryan strained to pick up sounds of pursuit, he could hear nothing.

Out of sight and earshot, faceless, nameless hunters dogged Ryan and his friends across the floodplain of the dried-up river. More than a mile wide, its thousands of narrow willow islands were separated by winding sandy lanes, which, during the wet season, were interlaced stream braids.

It was an evil place, a maze of nearly identical paths bordered by skinny trees ten feet tall, their lower branches creeping along the ground like vines.

The area was full of patches of quicksand, rad-blasted, suffocating heat and dark-scummed puddles of poisoned water—a place made to order for ambush, by both four-legged and two-legged predators. And Ryan and his companions were moving through this no-man's-land at a snail's pace—when they were moving at all.

The sound of a baby fussing cut through the throbbing insect song. Someone made soft shushing noises as the scrape of boot soles on sand grew louder.

Ryan opened his eye and, leaning on the stock of his Steyr SSG-70 sniper rifle, looked over at J. B. Dix, who knelt in a patch of shade on the other side of the wash, his fedora tipped back on his head. Rivulets of perspiration poured around the wire frames of J.B.'s glasses and down the sides of his face. He held his Smith & Wesson M-4000 shotgun balanced between pistol grip and pump slide, index finger braced against the outside of the trigger guard, poised and ready for anything.

The two men had traveled Deathlands together for many years. Both had been in the service of the legendary Trader, J.B. as his Armorer, Ryan as his second in command. In the Trader's employ and in the years after, they had survived more pitched battles than either could begin to count. Long ago, words between them had become unnecessary.

J.B. looked back toward the source of the mewling cries and shook his head.

For what had to have been the dozenth time in their two-hour trek, the two men had had to stop and wait for the main file to catch up to them. Another full minute passed before a tall, skinny man dressed in a dusty frock coat and tall boots rounded the bend in the stream. He carried an ebony walking stick with a silver lion's head for a handle. The cane concealed a steel serpent's tongue: a wicked, double-edged short sword.

Though he appeared to be in his midsixties, Ryan

knew that chronologically Dr. Theophilus Algernon Tanner was closer to 250 years old. He had been born in the small village of South Strafford, Vermont, in the year 1868. One hundred and thirty years later, the first successful experiment in time trawling, code-named Operation Chronos, had plucked him without his consent from his wife and children, from a simpler, if not kinder and gentler world, and had deposited him in a top-secret government laboratory. Because of the physiological and psychological shock brought on by the experience, the Oxford doctor of philosophy had proved a less than ideal test subject. His truculence had caused the Operation Chronos researchers considerable frustration and aggravation. In the year 2000, just before skydark, the scientists decided "Doc" was more trouble than he was worth and sent him forward in time to Deathlands.

Seeing that Ryan and J.B. had stopped, Doc slid a massive black-powder revolver from the front of his frock coat. The gold engraved LeMat was a relic of the decade of Tanner's birth. Arguably the Civil War's most potent side arm, the LeMat fired nine .44-caliber balls through a six-and-one-half-inch top barrel. A second, shorter barrel beneath the first had a much bigger bore, chambered for a single scatter-gun round. The "blue whistler" barrel was currently packed with a mixture of glass and iron fragments. Capable of inflicting devastating damage in close-quarters combat, this particular payload gave new meaning to the phrase "face lift." Doc hand-signaled those walking behind him to slow down and be careful.

Krysty Wroth appeared around the bend, her glorious mane of prehensile red hair cascading around her shoulders, the centers of her cheeks rosy from the riverbed's raging heat. She had tied the arms of her long, shaggy, black fur coat around her waist. In one hand she held a .38-caliber Smith & Wesson model 640 revolver; the other hand shielded a girl child of about seven who stood timidly behind her long legs. The girl wore a faded and tattered dress, and her blond hair was hacked off in a bowl shape just below the ears.

Krysty's emerald-green eyes sought out and locked on to Ryan's face. As with J.B., there was a connection between them, a different sort of connection to be sure, but one that also didn't require words. Though Ryan felt something akin to tenderness at the sight of his woman so fiercely protecting the child, his face gave nothing away. Wrong time. Wrong place. Reading her lover's expression, Krysty lowered the blaster, but didn't reholster it as she advanced.

A second or two later, Dr. Mildred Wyeth stepped into view. The stocky black woman was also a time traveler of sorts. Cryogenically frozen after a life-threatening reaction to anesthetic on December 28, 2000, the medical doctor had been reanimated by Ryan and his companions after a century of near-death sleep. Her hair in beaded plaits, Mildred wore baggy, desert camou BDU pants, and her gray, sleeveless T-shirt was soaked through with sweat, front and back. On her right hip, arms locked around her neck, legs gripping her waist, rode another girl child. This one was frail and about six years old. Mildred carried her Czech-built ZKR 551 handblaster with its muzzle pointed skyward. She was a deadly accurate markswoman. Lifetimes ago, when such things still had meaning, she had won a silver medal in the last ever Olympic games.

Right behind Mildred was the source of all the racket: an infant in the arms of a young mother. The woman wore a shapeless dress made of sewn-together scraps of colored cloth. A broad-brimmed, crudely woven straw hat shielded both mother and child from the sun.

Abruptly, the insect song stopped, and the baby momentarily ceased its fussing.

In the sudden, oppressive silence Ryan could hear the rasp of his own breathing. He didn't have to explain to his companions what was wrong. Sweaty hands tightened on pistol grips as they searched the tree lines for the slightest flicker of movement. Something was closing in on them from all sides, homing in on the baby's cries.

The woman called Uda moved the weight of her infant to her other arm. "Why are we stopping again?" she asked Ryan.

Not wanting to panic the young mother and the older children, and therefore compound their predicament, Ryan told her only part of the truth. "We're going too slow," he said. "We've got to pick up the pace. We'll wait here a couple of minutes and let Jak and your man, Benjy, catch up. Then we'll shift the loads around. The men will carry the girls from here on. And after that, there'll be no more stops. Everybody double-times it until we're out of this hellpit."

The woman nodded. All she wanted was to get her family to someplace safe, and as quickly as possible.

Ryan looked away from her worried but hopeful face. He knew the chances were she wasn't going to make it. Maybe none of them would make it. He looked over at his son, Dean, nearly twelve years old and almost the mirror image of himself, and understood her concern.

Uda and Benjy had been driven from their hardscrabble farm by an outbreak of the bloody flux in nearby Brigham ville. They had abandoned everything they owned in their haste to escape the spreading contagion. Ryan and the companions had learned about the cholera epidemic from some travelers on the road and, accordingly, had given the ville an extra wide berth. On the edge of the desolate floodplain that separated Brigham from the nearest disease-free ville, they had come across the refugee family.

Despite Ryan's warnings about the dangers of traveling through Deathlands, Uda and Benjy had refused to turn back to their homestead, which was understandable. Without antibiotics, the cholera raging through Brigham ville was a death sentence.

At an earlier point in his life, Ryan would have flat-out refused to convoy the young family to safety because of the additional risk to his own crew. In his wild years with the Trader, his first responsibility had always been to himself, to ensure his own survival, and after that, the survival of the people on whom he depended. With age and experience, with his son, Dean, traveling at his side and the steadfast love of Krysty, he had acquired a little bit more compassion for his fellow man. To abandon the young family on the edge of the plain when they had every intention of crossing with or without an armed escort, was no different from murdering them all in cold blood. Though a bullet in the back of each of their heads might have been a quicker, kinder fate, he found he had no stomach for the role of executioner. After a brief discussion in private, Ryan and his friends had agreed to take the family under their wing. None of them liked the idea any more than he did.

Before they'd gone fifty yards along the dry stream channel, they'd come across scattered bundles of fly-swarmed, stiff and bloody rags. It was all that was left of another group of recent refugees from the ville. They'd made easy pickings for the things that lurked in the willows. It had been just the first of half a dozen such unpleasant discoveries.

"How much farther?" Krysty asked Ryan as she shared her purified water with the oldest girl. Mildred moistened a cloth with her canteen and mopped the middle child's heat-flushed face with it.

"Another two hours to the outskirts of Perdition ville, if we're lucky," he said.

Something moved in the brush to his right.

A shadowy form shifted behind the thick screen of branches. Ryan swung the Steyr around, aiming it from the hip. Every other blaster in the arroyo sought and located the target. A mutie deer stood there, frozen for a second before it caught their scent and was gone in a mangy blur. The companions held their fire.

It wasn't a herd of scab-assed deer flanking their every step.

Ryan stared down the riverbed, cursing Jak Lauren for taking so long.

BENJY THUMBED BACK the hammer of his single-shot Stevens 12-gauge. It locked in full-cock position with a butter-soft click—a smoothness that came from age and wear. The weapon was more than 150 years old and had seen much use, passing through many sets of hands before it had reached his. In the shotgun's chamber was a precious, high-brass, three-inch goose load. The red plastic hull represented one-fifth of his ammunition stockpile.

The sound came to him again, a faint moaning, high-pitched, like a woman.

It made the hair stand up on the back of his neck.

Benjy quickly looked around. His backup, the other half of the rearguard, was nowhere in sight. The dirt farmer gritted his teeth; he didn't have a clue where Jak was. The albino teenager moved noiselessly through the bush, like a wild animal. Jak was spooky in other ways, too: he had that long, stringy, dead-white hair, scarred white skin and those awful, ruby-red eyes. Benjy thought about calling out to him, then thought better of it, realizing he would give away his own position.

The question he faced was whether to investigate the source of the sound or to move quietly on. He had about made up his mind to keep going when he caught sight of something small and white moving on the other side of the screen of willows. He stepped closer to the branches for a better look. Through the breaks in the foliage he could just make out the next stream channel over, and a pair of pale hands, waving at him.

Benjy cautiously edged forward, far enough to see the carnage in the sand. Bloody remnants of clothing lay in a heap, bristling with buzzing black flies— more luckless, waylaid refugees from Brigham ville.

"Help me," a weak voice said. "Oh, please, help me...."

Benjy poked through the tangle of branches, 12-

gauge first. It was a woman. She lay on her back on top of a fallen log ten feet from the pile of bodies. Her arms were tied at the wrists with close turns of heavy rope. The same kind of rope bound her midsection to the downed tree. Half her face was smeared with blood. It looked as though she'd taken a terrible beating—and worse. The hem of her long dress was pushed way up over her waist, exposing her naked flesh. Apparently, she had been abused, used and left for the stickies to finish off.

Over the bead sight of his shotgun, Benjy scanned the stream channel and the bordering trees. There was no sign of the coldhearts who had committed these atrocities. Though it looked safe to advance, part of him still wanted to withdraw, to slip silently away, while another part of him couldn't help but think what if it had been his Uda bound there, helpless like that? What would *he* expect from an armed passerby?

Then the woman raised her head slightly and said, "I know you! I know you from Brigham ville."

Benjy didn't recognize her, not with the gore all over her face, but her words made up his mind for him. He could consider turning his back on a total stranger, but not on a neighbor.

The second that Benjy stepped through the wall of willows into the middle of the dry stream channel, he realized something wasn't right. He could feel it, hard and cold, in the pit of his stomach. He started to retreat at once.

"No, don't leave me here," she begged him.

He took a good look at the woman as he continued to back up toward the tree line. Her black hair was cropped so short he could see the white skin of her scalp showing through on the sides of her head; she had huge, coal black eyes. Frenzied eyes.

He knew he'd never seen her before in his life.

As Benjy turned to run, the pack of cannies concealed in the willows rushed him from all sides. His legs felt as if fifty-pound rocks were strapped to them, and they seemed to move in slow motion. At his back came a shriek of feminine laughter, then a heavy cudgel crashed down on his head from behind.

At the stunning impact, the fingers of his right hand clenched reflexively. The 12-gauge fired, blowing a smoking crater in the sand at his feet. Benjy was already, mercifully, unconscious as he sagged to his knees. Before he could slump onto his side, a heavy-bladed machete split his skull down the middle, from the back of his head to the bridge of his nose.

The black-haired cannie female who had lured Benjy to his doom wasn't really tied up, and the blood on her mouth wasn't her own. She was first to reach the cleft skull with an eager tongue.

Chapter Three

Running in an easy, loping stride, Jak moved at right angles to the companions' line of travel. He picked his way through the gaps between willow islands, cutting a wide arc across the river bottom. His goal was to outflank and overtake the invisible hunters, and once he had position, to hit them hard from the blind side. Though the leapfrog maneuver was really a job for two, Jak had left the Brigham ville dirt farmer behind. Benjy was tangle-footed, and he had no fieldcraft. Following the yard-wide trail Ryan and the others had made in the sand was about all he could handle.

As the white-haired teen ran through the blinding heat, he had little doubt who their stalkers were. From the scant human remains he'd seen in the streambed, he figured no way were the sneaking bastards a band of stickies. Stickies liked to tear their victims to bloody shreds, but they rarely ate them. And stickies never bothered to steal personal belongings, either; they had no use for such things. They ran around half-naked and preferred to do their chilling *cuerpo a cuerpo*, using the powerful grip of the suckers and adhesive glands on their fingers and palms to rip away flesh and crack bone.

Cannies, on the other hand, left next to nothing of their victims' bodies or worldly goods behind. They were usually completely norm, both in their outward appearance and in their lust for the things that norms valued, like blasters and gold. Cannies routinely stripped everything from their victims, taking away all but the bloody rags of their clothes. To put it simply, they killed, they ate, they robbed.

Though not necessarily in that order.

As Jak rounded the point of a willow island, he found what he'd been searching for. Even Benjy couldn't have missed it. The sand of the stream channel before him was so churned up by footprints it looked as if it had been plowed. He knelt and examined the riverbed. The freshly turned surface had already started to dry out, but the bottoms of the jumbled, overlaid tracks were still dark with moisture. From this he guessed the cannies were no more than three or four minutes ahead of him. A scan of the footprints gave him a rough head count. On this side of the river alone, there were maybe twenty of them, which was a much larger than usual band. And from the length of some of the strides, they were moving at a dead run.

Jak sniffed at the air. The faint, coppery scent of blood told him these particular cannies had chilled someone, and not long ago. Gore-splattered from the murder, they weren't satisfied. They wanted more.

The other refugees from Brigham ville had been bushwhacked long before they'd gotten this far. As he straightened, Jak realized why the flesh eaters were waiting to attack. Though there were lots of them, they had to be seriously undergunned. They hadn't jumped Ryan and the others because of the quality of the companions' blasters. They weren't eager to face all that concentrated firepower.

Jak also knew that three things had kept the cannies from abandoning the hunt altogether: the three children.

And especially the baby.

Cannies loved baby.

Horrible images flooded Jak's mind—flashback images of his own infant girl after she'd been smashed to death against the side of his homestead barn in New Mexico, of his wife, Christina, brutally raped and murdered on the floor of their homestead cabin. Though he and Ryan and the others had hunted down and chilled the marauders who had butchered his family, it wasn't enough. Revenge could never balance out what had been taken from him. Beneath the deep layers of scar tissue on the teenager's soul, there was a place that would remain forever wounded, bleeding.

Tragedies like Jak's weren't unusual in Deathlands—they were, instead, the hard-and-fast rule. He had learned early on that the hellscape had an insatiable appetite for the innocent, the good and the helpless. To do something about it was to fight against fate, to battle one on one with the nuke wind or the chem rain: sooner or later you were bound to lose. Even Jak, a born warrior, a true child of Deathlands, couldn't protect his own loved ones from its savagery. Though he couldn't put his feelings into words, perhaps more than any of the other companions, he wanted to see the young family make it to the safety of Perdition ville.

He crossed the lane of tracks and moved low and quick through the bordering line of willows. One stream channel over, running full out, he began to parallel the cannies' course. He figured the flesh eaters were trying to reach a place that would give them the greatest possible advantage for their attack—maybe a particularly narrow and steep-sided channel with heavily treed islands on either side, a spot where they could use close quarters and their superior numbers to overrun and overwhelm the companions.

The teen had sprinted about seventy-five yards when behind him and off to the left, Benjy's single-shot 12-gauge boomed sharply. He skidded to a stop as the gunshot echoes rolled over the floodplain. After the echoes faded away, there was silence.

Reload! he thought. Reload!

It was as close to prayer as Jak Lauren got.

The silence stretched on.

And on.

THE SOUND of the lone shotgun blast set Ryan into motion. The one-eyed man didn't have to wave for the others to follow. Weapons at the ready, they fell into a loose skirmish line behind him as he raced back down the stream channel, retreating toward the source of the gunshot.

Under different circumstances, Ryan would have most certainly gone the other way. If he and his friends hadn't been hobbled by the farmers and their kids, their best option for survival would have been to light out for Perdition, to rely on foot speed and firepower as they had so many times before.

But they didn't have that luxury this day.

A running firefight was out of the question with the burden of Uda and the little girls. They really only had one choice if they wanted to live—they had to quickly close ranks with the rear guard, then, with their force maximized, stand and fight.

No more gunshots split the air, the only sounds the tramp of their boots as they ran down the riverbed.

The lack of follow-up shotgun blasts didn't bode well for Benjy. Though there were other possible explanations for his firing just the once, given the situation—and his inexperience—none of the alternatives was very likely. Cannies didn't know the meaning of the word "mercy"; inhuman cruelties were part and parcel of their feasting.

If the dirt farmer was rad-blasted lucky, Ryan thought, he had already taken the last train west.

As was their custom, the companions didn't waste breath speculating about the man's fate; they proceeded in grim silence. Uda had to have figured it out for herself because she put forth an extra effort and, baby and all, somehow managed to keep up.

For Ryan and the others the only question that remained was, what had happened to Jak?

Chapter Four

Jak closed in on the scuffling, grunting animal sounds filtering up the arroyo. Those sounds told him Benjy was already beyond help. With his .357 Magnum Colt Python leading the way, Jak circled downwind. When he was one stream channel away from the ruckus, he crawled through a stand of willows and, keeping to the shadows, peered out through the screen of low branches.

A dozen cannies huddled in the middle of the stream bed, bending over and grabbing at something limp that lay in the sand. Arms pumping, the cannies were fighting like wild beasts over the last gobbets of flesh on Benjy's skeleton.

One look at their weaponry told Jak he'd been right about their lack of firepower. They had a few black-powder handblasters, a couple of homemade crossbows built out of auto leaf springs, but it was mostly knives and clubs. And it was with the knives that they were scraping away at what little was left of the dirt farmer.

All the noise didn't seem to worry the cannies one bit. Maybe they didn't figure their other potential victims would come back for a straggler. Or perhaps they were counting on the refugees to run like hell for Perdition? Any rate, Jak thought, they figured it was plenty safe enough to take the time to make a meal out of poor Benjy.

They were dead wrong.

Knowing that help was fast on the way, and not wanting any of the coldhearts to escape, Jak jumped from cover with the big handgun in a rock-solid two-handed grip. His abrupt entrance went barely noticed.

Only three of the cannies bothered to glance up from their feast, fresh blood smeared over their faces and hands. Perhaps their comrades had been made sluggish by the big meal they were finishing, or they were just too pig-greedy to pay attention. One of the three made a grab for the Colt Third Dragoon strapped to his hip, the cannie's wet fingers slipping on the pistol grip; Before he got the .44's barrel clear of leather, the .357 barked and bucked in Jak's hands.

The Magnum slug sailed through the flesh eater's open mouth. His head snapped back, gory chin pointing skyward, and in the same instant, the rear of his skull exploded, spraying pink mist over his stunned fellows.

They didn't stay stunned for long. A crossbow bolt harmlessly swooshed past Jak's right ear. The teenager shifted his aim point and fired again. The cannibal archer sat hard in the sand, clutching at a small, dark hole along the midline of his chest, three inches below his Adam's apple. Exiting his back, the soft-nosed Magnum slug had taken with it big chunks of his airway and spinal column. The through-and-through had sufficient force to bowl over another cannie, hitting him square in the head as he tried to rise from over Benjy's corpse. There was no wet plume of flying brains this time, as there wasn't enough velocity left in the slug to make an exit wound. Trapped inside the cannie's skull, the flattened, razor-edged bullet ricocheted off the inside of that bony vault, zigzagging back and forth, cutting great swaths through his gray matter, and he dropped as if all his strings had been cut.

Jak caught the bright, white glint of sun on steel and reacted. He fired again before the knife thrower could snap his arm forward. The blade dropped and the thrower crumpled, folding in around the final beat of his shredded heart.

The last shot—and its deadly effect—made the remaining cannies abandon their meal. To Jak, some of the chillers seemed much more lively than others. Surprisingly lively. Before the teenager could fire again, the lively ones took off, scattering in all directions like a clutch of frightened spiders. The not-so-lively ones had difficulty slipping into the willows, thanks to the violent tremors that seized their arms and legs. Three of these horrid stumblers lurched toward Jak with clubs raised, mindless of his death-spitting Python. Gruesome leers twisted their blood-daubed faces, lips drawn and tight on one side, drooping on the other; one eye bugging out, the other narrowed to a slit.

Rather than waste ammo on them, Jak shifted the revolver to his left hand. A flat-black leaf-bladed throwing knife appeared like magic between his fingers, then vanished in a blur. Like magic, the short metal handle of the knife reappeared in the side of a cannie's neck. It was a carotid hit. Blood jetted through fingers clawing futilely at the deeply buried blade, but there was no way to stop the spurting flow. Before the second attacker could take another step, Jak put a black-steel thorn through his right eye to the hilt. The cannie fell to the sand in a shivering, shuddering fit. The third stumbler got the same treatment as the first, but he didn't try to pull the blade free of the arteries in his throat. As if grateful that the horror of his life had finally come to an end, he collapsed and died quietly, taking a slow, almost dignified seat beside the stand of willows before he slumped onto the sand.

Finding himself alone in the stream channel, Jak stepped over to the remains of Benjy's carcass. The dirt farmer's face was stripped to the skull, his jaws gaping in a tongueless, silent scream. The cannies had taken everything from him. His life. His flesh. His scattergun and ammo. His boots, belt and backpack. Left to themselves for a few more minutes, and they would have sucked the marrow from his bones.

Out of sight, the scattered cannies would regroup quickly, and when they realized he was on his own, they would come for him. Jak opened the Python's cylinder and dumped the three empties beside Benjy's corpse. After thumbing in live rounds, he snapped the cylinder shut and set about retrieving his knives.

The teenager had just freed the blade from the dead cannie's eye socket, using a boot sole on the forehead for leverage, when he heard fast-approaching footfalls coming his way. Wiping the knife in the sand before replacing it up his sleeve, he moved quickly to cover.

WHEN RYAN ROUNDED a turn in the channel and saw the patch of churned-up, bloody sand just ahead, he waved for the others to halt.

"Benjy?" Uda gasped.

Ryan tried to keep her from rushing forward, but she was so determined to get past him that he couldn't stop her without risking injury to her or the baby. She slipped under his outstretched arm, but ran only a few steps more, stopping well short of the body that lay twisted on the ground.

Uda's eyes went wide with shock. "No, no, it can't be..." she moaned, drawing the baby more tightly to her breast.

As soundless as a shadow, Jak stepped from the concealment of the tree line, his blaster lowered.

"Is," he said flatly.

A look passed between Jak and Uda, and she knew in an instant that he was telling her the truth. She let out a soft little cry and sank to her knees in the sand.

"How many?" Ryan asked the albino teen.

"Eighteen left. Mebbe more."

The new widow's grieving had to wait. Death for all was very close.

"Everybody into the willows," Ryan said as he helped Uda to her feet. He took hold of her shoulder and guided her ahead of him. "Fan out," he told the others. "We need a perimeter."

At Ryan's direction, they crawled into positions inside the edge of the long, narrow stand of spindly-trunked trees. J.B. and Jak were at opposite ends of the little island; Doc and Mildred were spaced along one side; Krysty, Dean and Ryan covered the other. In a sunken area in the middle of the grove of trees, defended by all seven blasters, lay Uda and the three girls. Together, the companions had a 360-degree view of the surrounding channels and all possible points of cannie attack, but they were spread very thin.

Some things just couldn't be helped, Ryan thought as he scanned the tree line opposite for signs of movement—like Benjy's death; like Uda seeing what had been done to him; like the battle lines being drawn so the dirt farmer's corpse lay in plain view of his family. His mutilated remains were unrecognizable to the six-year-old, who, though terrified, didn't seem to really understand what had happened. The oldest child kept staring wide-eyed, back through the trees at her father's body, tears streaming down her cheeks. She understood, all right.

Ryan watched Uda reach over and touch her daughter's small chin, gently turning her face away from the sight. "Don't look," she said.

Doc's voice filtered through the trees to his back. "If you have formulated a defensive strategy, my dear Ryan," he said softly, "I am sure we all would appreciate hearing the essential details. Or do you intend the impending conflict to be a free-for-all?"

Loud enough for the others to hear, the one-eyed man replied, "When you see the cannies break from cover, give a shout, but hold your fire. We want them to cross the channels. On my signal we pull back to the center of the island. Let them follow us into the bush. That way they'll be backlit and they'll have to fight the tangle of limbs to get at us."

From the trees off to Ryan's right, J.B. said, "Sucker the bastards in, then wipe out the whole bunch."

"You got it," Ryan stated. "Otherwise we'll be swatting them off our tails all the way to Perdition."

"As masterful as ever," Doc pronounced.

Anticipating the fight to come, Ryan hurriedly hollowed out a space in the bed of dry leaves beside him. With its long barrel, the scoped sniper rifle was going to be next to useless in the thick undergrowth at the island's center, and if he tried to lug it with him, it would only hang up in the brush and slow him as he backed into position. After carefully covering the rifle with leaves, he pulled his 9 mm SIG-Sauer P-226 from its well-worn holster. He took an extra full magazine from his pants pocket and set it on the ground close to hand. Then he resumed his scan of the opposite tree line, which was separated from him by seventy-five feet of open stream channel. There was no sign of them, yet, but the branches were so tightly interlaced on the other side that the entire pack of cannies could have been inches back from the edge and still remain invisible to him.

A minute or two passed, and he shifted the pistol to his left hand and wiped the sweat from his right palm onto his pant leg. Ryan knew the all-out attack would come soon. As a rule, cannies weren't big on patience, and they had already waited longer than they'd wanted to. They could probably smell the children.

"Coming at me!" J.B. stated. "I got three, no four."

A feint, was Ryan's first thought. It made no sense for the bastards to hit one end of the island; it meant that they'd have to travel through the maximum amount of brush to reach their victims. "Pull back," he said, grabbing the extra mag.

Even as he started to scoot back from the perimeter, he caught movement in the other tree line. Dark shapes rushed out from cover and into the streambed. The end-on attack was, indeed, a trick. The main force was charging straight at him.

"Got ten on this side!" came Mildred's shout from behind.

Correction, *half* the main force was charging at him.

Fireblast! Ryan thought as he reverse-crawled. There had to be a couple dozen of them. They weren't yelling or whooping it up as they advanced, wanting to get as close as possible without raising an alarm. Backing through the undergrowth as fast as he could, he caught sight of Krysty and Dean doing the same thing on his right. Further over on that side, J.B.'s boot heels and backside came into view. By the time Ryan reached Uda and the girls, Doc, Mildred and Jak had closed in as well, and the children were ringed with outpointing blasters.

The cannies' plan was to drive a double wedge through the middle of the island, to split the companions' force, giving themselves an opportunity to snatch up the children. Mildred and Krysty covered each of the girls with their own bodies, Uda shielded the baby with hers. To get at their intended prey, the cannies were going to have kill them all. And before that happened, Ryan vowed, Uda and the girls would get mercy bullets in the brain.

At the farthest reaches of his sight, almost lost amid the confusion of leaves and branches, which were pierced by narrow shafts of sunlight, Ryan glimpsed moving shadows. No matter how careful the cannies tried to be, they couldn't enter the tightly packed stand of trees without making noise. As they dropped to their bellies and snaked into the bush, branches creaked, leaves rustled. The one-eyed man waited, likewise on his stomach, with the sweat rolling down his face and dripping off his chin. It was hotter than rad-blazes in among the willow roots, and so dusty it half choked him to draw breath.

A twig snapped not six feet in front of him.

Then the backlit silhouette of a head and shoulders popped up. The cannie scout was close enough to spit on.

To Ryan's left, Doc rose slightly, the LeMat's hammer already cocked. It was a fire-at-will situation, and that was just what Doc did. The massive pistol boomed in his hand, sending forth a yard-long tongue of flame and a boiling cloud of white smoke. At such close range, the blast from the pistol's shotgun barrel was nothing short of awesome. Its load of steel-and-glass splinters scoured the flesh and sinew from the cannie, forehead to chin, and emptied his eye sockets, the heat flash turning his hair into a halo of fire.

At the LeMat's roar, the other cannies abandoned stealth, jumped up from the ground and threw themselves headlong into the fray. Knowing their main chance was to overwhelm their quarry, they crashed through the walls of branches from both sides of the island at once, screaming at the tops of their lungs and firing their weapons. Unlike the high-powered, cased-cartridge blasters Ryan and his friends carried, the cannies' black-powder pistols couldn't shoot through tree limbs to reach their targets. No matter how they angled their shots, the maze of intervening tree limbs deflected the flight of their crossbow bolts. To bring knives and clubs into play they had to get within arm's reach.

Which was something the companions were determined to avoid.

Ryan put a 9 mm slug dead center into an onrushing form. When the cannie didn't even slow, he followed up with two more quick shots. The body fell forward, arms outstretched, splintering the frail branches and crashing in a cloud of dust to the ground. Right on the first cannie's heels was another.

Dean, who lay about ten feet to the left, blazed away with his 9 mm Browning Hi-Power as the second cannie leaped over his fallen comrade and drove onward through the bush. Though he hit the man in the stomach and chest, the 9 mm slugs seemed to have no stopping power. Ryan took a careful aim and shot the man through the face, which not so neatly did the trick.

The body had barely slammed to earth when the cannie behind jumped it and threw himself forward. They were cutting a path to their prey, paved by their own corpses. Krysty's blaster cracked twice more, then the hammer snapped softly on a spent primer. Ryan raised up and fired three Parabellum rounds into the oncoming cannie's neck and head. The man dropped to his knees, then his face, falling away to reveal yet another charging figure behind him.

Dean chilled that one, as well as the one that came after, while Krysty hurriedly dumped the spent shells from her revolver, then fumbled with the speed loader.

Before she had the live rounds chambered, Ryan had shot two more cannies, then the SIG's slide locked back. He was out of ammo, too. He thumbed the release button, dumping the empty mag into the dirt. Through the rising clouds of dust, more cannies charged, a seemingly endless wave of them. The path of bodies now ended no more than fifteen feet from where he, Dean and Krysty lay.

Behind them, J.B. was cutting loose with his 12-gauge, firing, pumping, firing into the cannie rush. Double-aught buckshot blasted tree limbs, sending bark, leaves and chunks of cannie flying. Then J.B. let out a startled yelp, which made Ryan glance up just as he was raising the fresh mag to the SIG's butt. The M-4000 dropped on its shoulder sling as J.B. grabbed at his left arm. Something dark protruded from the middle of it, crossways to the bone.

Over the steady firing of Jak's Colt Python, Mildred's .38, and Doc's .44, Ryan heard crashing footfalls. Close. Slapping the full mag home, he turned to find a heavyset cannie shoving a hogleg Remington New Army pistol into Krysty's face.

"Dad!" Dean shouted in panic.

It was a moment frozen in time.

Before he or Dean could do anything, almost point blank, the Remington .44 discharged with a flash and boom.

The cannie jumped over Krysty's slumping form, fell upon Uda's back and tried to wrench the baby from her grasp. Failing to instantly do that, he jerked the woman to her feet, snatched her by the hair and craned back her neck. He held the muzzle of the cocked .44 tight to her throat.

The SIG's slide snapped closed, and a fraction of a second later, the pistol barked once. Shot in the temple, the cannie toppled backward, and, as he fell, the Remington discharged skyward. Ryan quickly turned Krysty onto her back and was relieved to see her green eyes blinking up at him. Black-powder soot dusted one side of her face; her red hair clung tightly to her head. "I'm okay," she said, clutching at the juncture of her neck and shoulder. "Bastard just skinned me."

More shotgun blasts boomed.

By the time Ryan looked up, he had no shot. The surviving cannies were already in full retreat. He leaped to his feet and sprinted after them. As he burst through the edge of the trees, he saw four of them darting into the willows on the other side of the channel. The last cannie in the line, a big guy with stubbly iron-gray hair and beard, was wearing a long khaki duster and carrying a scoped longblaster by its sling.

"Fireblast!" Ryan snarled, raising the P-226 and snapfiring twice as the man disappeared into the bush. The slugs thwacked futilely into the thicket. The bastard had his Steyr! It had to have gotten uncovered during the cannie advance or retreat. Ryan lowered his handblaster, a bitter taste in his mouth. He couldn't go after the treasured rifle, and he couldn't chase down and chill all of their attackers. Uda and her children still needed protection.

Jak stepped up beside him. "Track?" he said.

Ryan nodded. "Just far enough to see where they're headed."

When he returned to the others, Mildred was treating Krysty's wound, a shallow pistol-ball crease where her neck met her shoulder. Though it bled a little, it was barely a nick. Krysty gave him a warm and confident smile, but her mane of red hair, which was still in a state of shock, coiled defensively close to the sides of her head.

"Hey, this hurts bad," J.B. complained. He held up his arm for Ryan to see.

The wooden crossbow bolt was no more than six inches long. The single-bladed, steel broadhead point poked out the underside of his forearm, the fletched tail stuck out the top. Lucky for J.B., the broadhead had slipped between the major blood vessels, bones and tendons.

"Lend me a hand, Ryan."

Ryan decided that snapping off the short bolt would cause J.B. unnecessary pain. He unsheathed his eighteen-inch panga, and with a couple of strokes from the heavy blade sawed through the shaft behind the broadhead. J.B. then jerked out the shaft himself. Bright blood seeped down his forearm and dripped off the tip of his elbow.

While Mildred cleaned and dressed the Armorer's flesh wound, Ryan did a quick survey of the battlefield. Seventeen cannies were sprawled in and among the trees. Overhead, wisps of gunsmoke trapped in the foliage drifted slowly through skinny shafts of sunlight, shimmering like spirits of the newly departed.

"Will they come again?" Uda said to his back.

Ryan turned and shook his head. "We hurt 'em plenty bad."

When her medic duties were completed, Mildred knelt over the nearest cannie corpses, careful not to touch them with her bare hands. Picking up a twig, she took a sample of the thick, sticky gray matter leaking from the ears of one of the dead. "Damn!" she exclaimed, then held up the twig for Ryan to see. "Did you notice this nasty discharge coming from their ears and noses? Some of these sons of bitches have got the oozies, and it looks like third stage to me."

"Yeah, I saw. The whole pack is probably infected."

"That would explain the suicidal frenzy of their attack," Doc added.

"Oozies?" Uda repeatd, putting a protective arm around the shoulders of her older children and drawing them close. "Is that some kind of disease? I've never heard of it before."

"It's a disease of the brain that's transmitted through the eating of raw human flesh, and in particular, the uncooked tissues of the brain," Mildred explained. "If I had time to do autopsies on these bodies, I'm sure I'd find holes threading all through the cerebral tissue."

"And this disease, that's what makes them go cannie?" the young mother said.

"Actually," Mildred told her, "we don't know what the cause of the cannibalism is. It could be unrelated to the oozies. It could be genetic, a failure of hemoglobin metabolism...." Realizing she was talking over the woman's head, Mildred translated the predark medical terminology. "A rad-mutation of the blood, passed on from parents to child," she said. "There's a similar illness called porphyria, which produces an obsessive compulsion to feed on fresh blood and raw meat."

Doc cleared his throat noisily. "Is that your diagnosis, Madam?"

"No, not a diagnosis," Mildred countered. "It was a hypothesis about the origin of their murderous behavior being secondary to infection. I didn't say the oozies and porphyria are one and the same. If anything, the symptomology here is closer to transmittable spongiform encephalopaly, a disease that incubates silently over dozens of years. When the oozies finally start to kick in, its victims first lose control of their emotions, and then, more gradually, of all of their bodily functions. Cannibalistic behavior predates by decades the appearance of all disease symptoms, and by inference, the appearance of amyloid plaque lesions in the brain tissue. As we all know, cannies have the habit, during lean times, of eating their weaker fellows. Because of this, the oozies will eventually be passed on to every member of a band. So the behavior causes the transmission of the infection, not vice versa."

"My apologies, my dear Dr. Wyeth," Doc said, using his cane to sweep a low, dignified bow. "I should have let you complete your remarks. The power of your physician's logic is, as ever, irrefutable."

"Bunch of crazy, sick cannies," J.B. muttered, cradling his injured arm.

"We should really burn the bodies, Ryan," Mildred said.

"Yeah, but how can we do it without some kind of fuel?" Dean piped in.

Jak reappeared in the clearing, stepping nimbly over the string of corpses. "Cannies make run for Perdition," the teenager announced.

"Then they're hightailing it," Krysty said, rising to her feet.

"Question is, are we going to let them get away?" J.B. said, flexing the fingers of his wounded left arm and grimacing. "We still owe them something."

With a twenty-minute head start, and the companions hobbled by noncombatants, Ryan knew the prospects of catching up with the cannies before they reached the ville were slim or none.

"First thing we've got to do is get Uda and the girls safely to Perdition," Krysty said.

Ryan nodded.

"And after?" J.B. queried.

"Cannies got longblaster like yours," Jak told Ryan.

"Yeah, I know."

Then the oldest girl struggled free of her mother's sheltering arm and jumped to her feet. Her angelic face twisted by grief, her lower lip and chin quivering, she advanced on Ryan. In a shrill voice, she cried up at him, "Hunt them, mister! Chill them all, the ones what ate our pa!"

But Ryan had already made up his mind to do just that.

Chapter Five

A tin cup thunked on the long bar top, which was made from five hollow-core doors, lined end to end.

"Just a minute," the bartender said, continuing to sweep around the sawhorses that supported the doors

The cup thunked again, louder.

Somewhat irritated, the bartender of Perdition's finest gaudy house looked up from his broom. The impatient customer was tall, lean and lantern-jawed. The hair on his head was shaved to a gray stubble, which matched the salt-and-pepper scruff that carpeted his cheeks and the front of his neck. His ears were rimmed with what looked like layers of light brown, river dirt. The barman took in the longblaster slung over the guy's right shoulder, a sniper job with telescopic sights. Worth plenty of jack. It was the kind of blaster a fellow could get himself killed dead over, if he wasn't careful.

"Who's the sawed-off little shit running off at the mouth?" the tall man said, hooking a thumb in the direction of the gaudy's only crowded table, where a dude in tattered BDUs was holding court before a spellbound audience of sluts and hangers-on.

The bartender took an involuntary half step backward. This customer had some of the foulest breath he had ever suffered through. And given the gaudy's regular clientele, that was saying something. "Who's askin'?'' he inquired, resting his elbows on his broom handle.

The skinhead female who stood beside the tall guy leaned over the bar. The barman's gaze dropped at once to the low-cut top of her dress and the high, tight cleavage she was showing off, then to the muzzle of the cocked, blue-steel .36-caliber Colt Army blaster half concealed behind her slender, dusty arm. She was pointing the black-powder revolver's muzzle straight at his heart. ''The Right Reverend Gore's asking,'' she said through a feverish smile. ''And you'd best be answerin' right quick.''

''It's no big secret,'' the bartender replied, meanwhile mentally measuring the distance between himself and the sawed off, double-barreled 12-gauge he kept hidden under the bar top. Given that the grinning skinhead bitch had caught him flat-footed, and that counting the tall guy, she was backed by three evil-smelling, road-scum compadres who were lined up on the other side of the bar, he figured the wisest course was to leave the scattergun alone.

''Guy's name is Grub,'' he said. ''He's a scrounger from down Slakecity way. Came in here late last night, tellin' stories about some strange happenings over to Moonboy ville. Crazy stories. Muties in black armor. Blasters that cut through solid walls like they were made of paper. Mass chillings. Lots of other stuff, too, but I can't tell you about it 'cause I wasn't listening real hard. I hear a lot of rad-pure crap around here, usually when somebody's falling off a jolt high. Anyway, some of the customers been finding what Grub's got to say altogether fascinating. He even got a couple of the dumb sluts to give him freebies and the local high rollers been buying him rounds all night. If you want to hear his act, all you got to do is feed him drinks—'' he gave the skinhead female a deadpan look and added ''—or fuck him a few times.''

Though his delivery was perfect, the bartender's remark didn't have the anticipated shock effect. If anybody was shocked, it was he, by the high-pitched, shivery laugh that exploded from the woman's throat. The sound set his teeth on edge, but it was those huge coal-black eyes of hers, absolutely insane eyes, that forced him to turn his gaze from her pretty, dirty little face.

''Give us a bottle, then,'' the Right Reverend Gore said.

''Better take you a jug, or you're just gonna have to come back for more,'' the bartender told him. ''For a stumpy little scab, he can sure hold his 'shine.''

GRUB HINTON WAS in heaven. Never before in his pathetic, shit-crossed life had he been the undisputed center of attention. On either side of him at the table sat two of Perdition's most accomplished and uninhibited sluts, both of whom had already accommodated him free of charge. The sluts hung on his every word, as did the prominent citizens of the ville who filled out the audience and kept his tin cup topped up with white lightning. Four more interested parties, three men in dusters and a skinhead woman in a long dress, started to amble toward him from the bar. Yes, it was mighty fine being the one in the spotlight for a change. A thing to be savored. And all he had to do to keep the ball rolling was talk, talk, talk.

''No, I tell you it was *cleaner* than a knife,'' he

said for probably the fiftieth time, but nobody was counting. "Cut through Old Rupe's arms and legs faster than you can blink. And no blood came from the stumps. Not one drop. Sealed them right up."

"What kind of blaster can do something like that?" one of the citizens asked, shaking his bald, sun-browned head in disbelief.

"Predark, whitecoat secret technology, I figure," Grub speculated at top volume, for the benefit of the approaching newcomers. "Same goes for their body armor. I know what I saw. It's burned into my brain. Hundreds of pistol balls fired at those two muties from rock-chucking range, and not one ball so much as grazed them."

"Sounds bastard impossible," said the tall stranger with the scoped longblaster as he and his friends stepped up to the table. "You wouldn't be shittin' everybody, now would you?"

"You don't know Grub Hinton, mister," one citizen replied. "He could never make up a story like this."

"I'm too fucking stupid," Grub agreed good-naturedly.

Everybody at the table laughed at the joke; so did the skinhead girl, in a kind of hysterical cackle.

Grub liked the look in her eyes. A lot. It was crazy, like her laugh. He figured she was the kind of girl who'd go triple wild if he could just get a leg over on him. And he could tell from all the silky bosom she was showing out the top of her dress that she had a much firmer body than either of the gaudy sluts he'd sampled. He licked his dry lips, then took a deep, satisfying pull of 'shine. In the radically altered universe of Grub Hinton, anything was possible.

The tall, gray-haired man then bent over the citizen and practically nose to nose with him said, "Why don't you folks give us a few minutes alone with this gent?"

The color instantly drained from the citizen's face. Choking, he got up at once and offered his empty chair with a wave of his arm. "Need some water," he said, rushing for the bar.

The other citizens reluctantly rose and followed him, driven from their places by the threatening looks on the strangers' faces. Only the two sluts remained glued to their seats, clinging somewhat defiantly to the storyteller's arms. After all, this was both their primary residence and place of business.

"Out, bitches!" the skinhead female snarled at them. Then she gave Grub a look so sexy and inviting that it made his groin twitch and jerk like a headshot jackrabbit. "We need us some privacy..." she said huskily.

One of the sluts started to protest, but her coworker caught her by the wrist and stopped her, indicating with a nod of her head the cocked, shortbarreled, blue-steel pistol the skinhead held pointing downward, along the outside of her thigh. Without another word, the two women made themselves scarce.

As the four newcomers sat, the gray-haired guy produced a full bottle of booze and topped up Grub's cup. His hand trembled a little as he poured, slopping some 'shine onto the table. "Might as well get properly introduced," he said. "My name's Gore, the Right Reverend Gore. And she's called Giggly Jane."

The skinhead woman sitting next to Grub showed

him her wet tongue. It was quick and pink, and pointed at the tip.

"This here's Spadecrawler." Gore indicated the barrel-chested, round-faced man on his right, who looked as if he'd been caught out in an acid rainstorm without a helmet. A big splatter of dead-white, hairless scar tissue sat on top of his head, the waxy skin dripping down on the right side to a shriveled mushroom of an ear.

"And this is Egregious Jones." The third man was big and powerfully built, with oily, debris-flecked brown hair hanging to his shoulders. Exposed at the open neck of his duster were interlaced, angry red raised scars. The overlaid self-brandings were what in some parts of Deathlands passed for tattoos.

Grub noted that Egregious Jones's front teeth, upper and lower, had been filed to sharp points, but he was far more interested in Giggly Jane, whose amazingly hot little hand was under the table, resting lightly high on his inner thigh.

"Have a drink," Gore said.

Grub drank deeply, slamming the empty cup to the table when he was done. "What do you folks want to hear about?" he said. "The tornado? The blasters? The chilling?"

"All of it, from the beginning," Gore said, refilling the cup.

Grub retold the entire tale once more. His new audience was less intrigued by the flourishes of purely fictitious heroism than by descriptions of the roachmen's gear: their body armor, blasters, cube on wheels and flesh-dissolving foam. Gore asked him pointed questions about the operation of each of these devices, from time to time shooting meaningful looks at his friends.

By the time the story was finished, so was the bottle. After Gore sent Spadecrawler to the bar to fetch another, he said, "I got a real sweet proposition for you, Grub."

"I'm listening."

"If what you're telling us is true—and for your sake it damn well better be—sounds like there's some fine pickings waiting over at Moonboy."

"You could look at it that way, I suppose."

"What if I told you that the four of us are just the advance scouting party for our band? What if I told you we've got a bunch more pals camped just outside the ville? All with good, center-fire blasters like this one. All of them seasoned bush-fighters. Some of us used to be sec men over in the eastern baronies."

"And what are you now?" Grub said.

"Opportunity seekers," Gore replied. "If you lead us to these armored muties, we'll chill them all, then divvy up the spoils, fair and square. Should be plenty to go around. Interested?"

Before he could respond, Giggly Jane's hot fingers crawled into the middle of his lap and, once there, began to rummage around most skillfully. Awash in pleasure, Grub gazed helplessly into the whirlpools of her eyes.

"I've got an idea," Gore said, scraping back his chair. "Why don't we go someplace where we can talk more freely about the details of the job? Someplace where you and Giggly Jane can get much better acquainted."

At this, the skinhead dug her nails into him and, leaning her face close to his, pushed the wet, squirming tip of her tongue deep into his ear. It was all the convincing he needed.

"I love women," Grub confessed as he staggered to his feet.

Chapter Six

The midafternoon sun was still blisteringly hot when Ryan and the companions escorted Uda and the girls into the outskirts of Perdition. Built on a high, tree-less knoll, the ville had an unobstructed view of in-coming trouble, from across the riverbed or across the plain from the range of peaks to the west.

Uda knew right where she wanted to go. She se-lected one of the nearly identical, narrow dirt lanes that ran through the jumble of lean-tos at the base of the hill, and, with her children in tow, started on up. Similar shanties, roofed with car hoods and doors, spilled down the flanks of the knoll, along with drift-ing piles of the inhabitants' refuse.

The entourage drew curious looks from rag-clad, low Perdition dwellers, but no one said anything to them, and no one stared at them for long.

At the top of the knoll, double-wide trailers sat in a circle. According to a huge, electric-powered sign that had been dark for more than a century, they were part of a pre-Apocalypse commercial enterprise called O-Ke Bonanza Manufactured Home and RV Center. The trailers at the hill's summit and the lean-tos at the bottom were separated by a ring of junked and decaying motor homes, all of which had been turned into multifamily apartments. Uda had no trou-ble finding the one she was looking for, a Winnebago

Brave sitting on its rusted brake drums. She knocked on the door and a woman who looked like her twin, only older, appeared at the cracked window.

After a tearful reunion with her sister, Uda said goodbye to each of the companions. "We won't ever forget any of you," she promised.

"Stay safe," Ryan told her as Krysty and Mildred took turns hugging the two little girls.

After Mildred released the older one from the embrace, the girl walked over to Ryan, her back straight, her head held high, eyes shining. She reached up and placed a tiny, perfect Deathlands daisy onto his open palm. Staring up at him, she carefully closed his powerful fingers over it. Ryan basked in the intensity of her gaze, as hard and bright as a diamond. He felt a passing curiosity about who had fathered this child. What coldheart had crept into Uda's bed while poor Benjy toiled in his rock garden? he wanted to ask, but didn't. Better by far to savor such a mystery than to unravel it.

The one-eyed man knelt and lightly touched the girl's cheek. Putting his mouth close to her ear, he whispered softly so no one else could hear, "Consider the bastards chilled."

Straightening, Ryan signaled for his friends to follow him, then continued the short climb to the top of the hill, heading for the circled trailers and the ville's most well-appointed gaudy. The double-wide gaudy in question was painted bright pink, as were the rocks that lined the dirt walk leading up to its doorway.

It wasn't much cooler inside the trailer. A handful of sluts sprawled on a long, broken-down sofa in the foyer, which reeked of once-cheap, now-expensive perfume. The working girls didn't bother to get up as the potential clients filed past, they just flopped open their gauzy robes to show all.

"Hot pipe!" Dean chirped.

"By the three Kennedys!" Doc Tanner swore, averting Dean's gaze by spinning the boy by the shoulder. "In all my years, I have never seen such a row of tangle-matted medusas. If they are the blooming roses of this ville, then I know why the diabolical dung heap is called Perdition."

"Gee, they didn't look half-bad to J.B.," Mildred teased.

The Armorer muttered something under his breath, then spit on the floor.

The gaudy's bartender took one look at the people walking toward him and quickly dipped his hands under the makeshift bar.

"There's no need for that," Ryan assured him, holding both empty palms up for him to see. "We're not here for trouble."

The bartender brought his hands out from under the bar. He held a cut-down 12-gauge. "What can I get you, then?" he said.

"Information." When the man frowned, Ryan added, "We'll pay for it, of course."

"What sort of information might that be?"

"We're looking to catch up with some people who passed through here earlier today. One guy in particular you mebbe remember. He was tall, gray-bearded, carrying a fine bolt-action longblaster."

"These friends of yours?"

"No."

"I seen them. What're you paying?"

"Show him," Ryan said to J.B.

The Armorer stepped forward and rapidly pumped the M-4000's slide, ejecting two red-cased, live 12-gauge shells onto the bar. The barman eagerly scooped them up and stuffed them into his pants pocket.

"Let's hear it," Ryan said.

"The graybeard you're looking for, along with three others, two men and a skinhead witch, left here mebbe twenty minutes ago after talking to a scrounger name of Grub Hinton. Took Grub with them when they went."

"He go along willingly?"

"Looked mighty happy to me."

"Know what they talked about?"

"Had to be discussing Moonboy ville. It's the only thing people been talking about around here since last night. According to this scrounger, some kind of strange things went on there yesterday noon. He claims some muties popped out of nowhere with tricky, silenced blasters and cut just about everybody in half."

"Sounds real unlikely," Krysty said.

"Think your pals had a raid in mind," the barman went on. "They wanted to get their hands on the extra-special chilling gear."

"They're not our pals," Krysty told him. "They're cannies."

"I guessed that something wasn't right with those bastards," the barman said. "Goddamn coffin breath on the gray-bearded one practically knocked me down."

"They've been working the riverbed," Ryan told him, "nabbing the folks trying to cross over from Brigham ville."

The barman narrowed his eyes and said, "You know, I would've chilled them myself if I'd known what they were—"

"Yeah, sure you would," J.B. said dubiously.

"Tell us which way they went," Ryan said.

"Cost you more shells."

Ryan nodded to J.B., but instead of cycling out more live rounds from the tubular magazine, the Armorer swiveled on the bartender and aimed the wide gun barrel at his throat. With his index finger resting lightly on the trigger, J.B. cautioned the man, "Next one you collect is going to hurt some."

"Okay, okay, forget it," the barman said, carefully putting his weapon on the bar top, then raising his hands in surrender. "No rad-blasted harm in trying, is there?"

Doc used the tip of his walking stick like a prod, thrusting across the bar and jabbing the man in the shoulder. "You would be well advised to reveal without further delay all that you are privy to, or make no mistake, you will suffer the consequences."

"The lot of them went due south," the bartender stated hurriedly, "along the main road out of the ville. It leads straight to what's left of old Highway 15. Once they get there, they've got to double back north on the highway for about a mile to get to Moonboy."

"Is there a faster way to get there?" Ryan asked.

"Sure, if you don't mind jumping some rock."

"We don't mind."

"Go south toward the ridge, turn right and follow the base of the ridgeline for five, mebbe six miles. You can't miss Moonboy."

"How's that?"

"It's the only thing left standing for as far as you can see."

THE RIGHT REVEREND Gore caressed the edge of his skinner knife with precise, circular motions of the whetstone. The back of the wide, crescent-shaped blade was deeply notched a half inch from its tip, and the notch formed a razor-sharp guthook that could zip open a body cavity faster than a man could hawk a spit. Gore put the ball of his thumb against the bright new edge, testing it. Plenty good enough, he decided.

"Why are you doing this to me?" Grub bawled at him.

Gore looked up from the boulder on which he sat. Across the small clearing, the naked slag-heap scrounger was strung up by his wrists in the branches of a dead willow. His ankles were likewise tied with leather thongs and his legs pulled out straight and spread-eagled.

"I gave you everything you wanted!" Grub cried.

"Not quite," Gore replied, getting slowly to his feet.

"I don't want no cut of the profit," Grub swore to the four coldhearts who held him prisoner. Giggly Jane was using a yard-long willow branch to test the cutting power of her own blade. It was a predark, made-in-the-U.S.A. treasure: a titanium-nitride black, Edge Tactical One-Hander.

"Don't need none of her, neither," Grub added bitterly. "Just let me loose from up here. I won't tell nobody about Moonboy and spoil your raid."

"You already told half of Perdition about Moonboy," Gore reminded him. "It's time to face facts, little man. You were never gonna get a piece of the job's profit, nor of our funky little gal Jane, neither. And we're not gonna let you go. We're taking you with us, in a manner of speaking.''

Gore shivered, despite the day's oppressive heat. He could no longer ignore the gnawing ache in the pit of his stomach; he had to do something about it. No matter how much he ate, Gore was hungry all the time now. Trouble was, he couldn't keep his meat down, he was always chucking it back up. And the weight was dropping off him so fast the others had started giving him sidelong, measuring looks. His fingers trembled violently on the stag-horn grip of the skinning knife, and for a second it damn near slipped away from him. Gore knew he had the oozies, and that he was on the steep downhill slide. Every time he wiped his nose on the sleeve of his duster, he expected to see the first smear of gray pus that signaled the beginning of the end.

When the leader of a cannie pack faltered, the pack picked his bones.

Gleefully.

There was no telling when he'd caught the sickness. Sometimes it took half a lifetime for the death signs to appear. For all he knew, it could have come from his first bite of manflesh, and that was better than a quarter century ago. Some claimed that cannibalism was an acquired taste, but as soon as Gore got that first lick, he was hooked solid. A young sprout back then, he'd joined up with a band of cannies that was passing through his ditchwater ville one summer night, picking off stragglers and half-wits. He loved the cannie life right off, too. It was like being a wolf cub. Hunting and chilling and eating.

Ultimate freedom, every minute of every day. But it wasn't some hog-slop, romantic philosophy that held him captive; it was the flavor.

The fresher, the better.

At that very moment Gore was thinking about liver. Bloody, still-warm liver. It made his mouth water.

"You're taking me with you?" Grub said hopefully. "Then you're not gonna chill me!"

The triple-stupe bastard still hadn't figured it out.

Giggly Jane playfully poked at his protruding white potbelly with the sharpened point of the willow stick.

"Oh, we're gonna chill you, all right," Gore said. He moved closer with his knife held waist-high and poised to strike. "But first we're gonna gut you, from goobers to windpipe. After you bleed out, we're gonna quarter-saw your pasty carcass and pack it along with us."

Grub's eyes bulged in horror.

Gore grinned at him. "What, you never heard of 'trail mix'?"

Chapter Seven

Krysty matched, stride for stride, her black-haired lover's brutal pace. The path they were taking, at the base of the towering bedrock ridge, was an obstacle course of boulder outcrops in shades of dusty brown and ocher. Some of the rocks were big enough to hide a crouching man; most were mere ankle breakers. No screen of trees shielded them from the sun, and it would be hours, yet, before it sank into the west. The only things growing in the thin desert soil were scattered, stunted bushes and widely spaced clumps of needle grass.

To her left, sweeping all the way to the southern horizon, was a vast depression in the earth. Though she could see for tens of miles into the bowl scoured out by three thermonuclear warheads, Krysty couldn't see the far side of it. This was in part because of the sun's blinding glare off the thermoglass, which looked to her like a frozen, storm-tossed sea, but mostly because the blast crater's diameter was so enormous. At irregular intervals, individual pillars of smoke rose in the dead air, spiraling into the blue sky for thousands of feet. More than a century after the nuclear holocaust, Slakecity still burned. Isolated fires raged beneath the thermoglass skin, fueled by Gaia knew what, plumes of smoke steadily uncoiling from fractures and deep fissures in the surface.

Mildred had told her what this place had looked like before skydark. It was hard for Krysty to imagine a Great Salt Lake stretching off to the west, or a large city framed by a backdrop of hills. Mildred said there had been a huge temple with a gold statue atop it that could be seen for miles around. All that had once been—immense lake, bracketing hills, glorious temple—was gone, vaporized by the fury of man-made suns.

An unseen rock scraped against her ankle, then clattered noisily away. Krysty's attention snapped back to the ground and its hazards. Because of the accumulated stresses of an already long and dangerous day, because of the distance she had already walked, because of the unrelenting sun and heat, it was getting more and more difficult for her to maintain a triple-red level of alert.

Ryan turned his head at the sound the rock made. Seeing that she was okay, he half smiled and turned back without slowing.

Krysty knew he wasn't pushing himself and everyone else to exhaustion just because an angel-faced, seven-year-old girl had asked him to avenge her father's murder. Ryan was far too much of a pragmatist, and far too good a leader, to fall for something like that.

Sure, he had a personal score to settle with the cannie who had stolen his Steyr SSG-70. In Deathlands, a person's main blaster was like a strong right hand; it was the key to survival. It was something that was never willingly surrendered, and always retrieved, if possible.

And there was no forgetting the wounds suffered by his friends during the cannie attack. Krysty's own shoulder and neck throbbed agonizingly in time with her footfalls, a reminder of how close she had come to death. But payback, with interest, for that had already had been dished out in the form of the seventeen enemy they had left chilled in the willow thicket.

A need for more retribution wasn't the demon driving Ryan across the high plains. The one-eyed man wasn't consumed with anger; he was steely calm. He had heard of Moonboy's reputation as a "pure norm" ville, a place where Jak and Krysty were at risk of being summarily murdered, and yet he was resolved, as were Krysty and the rest of the companions, to take the risk and do what had to be done in order to hunt down and exterminate the remaining cannies.

Extermination was standard operating procedure with cannies.

Because of the way they could blend in and mingle with unsuspecting folk, like wolves among the sheep, they were far more dangerous than stickies, scalies or scabbies. The gaudy house bartender had served this particular bunch of flesh eaters without batting so much as an eyelash. They had walked unnoticed through the ville of Perdition and, equally unnoticed, had carried off another victim.

Krysty recalled, word for word, what her uncle Tyas McCann had taught her about them when she was young. "You can always tell a cannie if you get nose to nose with one," he'd said. "Death hangs over them like stink gas in a bog. Trouble is, if you get close enough to whiff that brand of brimstone, it's too late to back away. Smell that smell, girl, and make no mistake, you've got to fight for your life, tooth and claw.''

Tyas had passed on this information after a pair of suspected cannies had been caught red-handed at a slaughter scene in a cabin near their Harmony ville homestead. Subsequent events were forever burned into Krysty's memory. After having been beaten and kicked around by the townsfolk, the two suspects were dragged into the ville's square and staked out on the ground. The men had loudly protested their innocence, and when it had come time for them to get fed they had refused the flatbread and water they were offered. Inside of three days, the pair had gone stark raving mad, eyes rolling, jaws snapping, foaming at the mouth, howling like dogs. Eventually, they swallowed their own tongues and their faces turned purple, then black. Choked to death by their chill frenzy.

To a cannie, Tyas had explained, the taste of human blood delivered a joltlike kick. If a cannie was without blood for too long, he or she went crazy. According to her uncle, that was the reason why, when they couldn't find victims, they chilled and ate each other.

Krysty's thoughts drifted back to the children. And as she remembered holding them in her arms, she felt a sudden, surprisingly painful pang of loss. Though her desire for babies of her own was strong, she had always suppressed the maternal urge. Unlike the world before skydark that Mildred and Doc had told her about, there was no way of increasing your odds in Deathlands. No amount of jack, or of blaster-power, could stack the deck in your favor. Even rich and powerful barons died prematurely and in the same wretched agonies as everybody else. Living a life on the edge of oblivion was a hard enough cross for an adult to bear, let alone a child.

In a flash of pure white light, an image formed in Krysty's consciousness. She saw a snake's flat, scaled head, twice as wide as the back of her hand, with eyes like bulging blood drops, and exposed fangs trailing thick strands of yellow poison. She immediately recognized the image for what it was, a premonition of impending danger. The gift of second sight was just part of the mutie inheritance handed down to her by her mother, Sonja, an inheritance that allowed her to tap into the all-powerful, feminine spiritual force of the planet. Shaking free of the startling vision, Krysty came to an abrupt stop.

Three yards from her right boot, it looked like just another flat rock.

Then the rock moved.

She let out a cry and took a giant step sideways, her hand automatically dropping to the butt of her revolver.

More than seven feet long, and at its widest point two feet around, there was nothing shy about this snake; it was both aggressive and predatory. It rapidly slithered closer to her, then coiled itself. A tail bigger around than her forearm reared up, amber-colored rattles shaking, as the mutie diamondback prepared to strike.

"Hold it!" Ryan shouted back to the others.

The column froze at his command.

"Oh my God!" Mildred exclaimed as she turned and saw, for thirty yards in all directions, the rocks beginning to uncoil. "They're everywhere!"

As if responding to some silent, instinctive call to

attack, dozens upons dozens of rattlers, some of them easily forty-pounders, their backs as big as fire hoses, moved in for the kill.

Krysty unholstered her .38, but before she could aim and fire, the snake in front of her struck, fully two-thirds of its body length extended, its jaws gaping wide. She instinctively twisted to the side and the fangs missed the top of her thigh by less than an inch. With amazing speed, the huge rattler recoiled itself for a second strike, this time point-blank.

Krysty was tightening down on the revolver's trigger when Ryan called out a second warning.

"No blasters!" he said. "We don't want to give away our position. Follow me, I'm going to open up a path."

Krysty held her fire, but kept the snake in her sights and her finger on the trigger as Ryan drew his panga from its sheath. The blade slashed down in a tight arc and under the blade's keen edge, the rattler's head seemed to leap free of its neck. Spurting ten-foot jets of blood, the headless body went wild, thrashing and slapping the dirt.

Ryan grabbed Krysty by the arm and pulled her along after him. "This way!" he called to the others.

No one questioned his choice of direction. There wasn't time for discussion. They all knew that standing still meant certain death.

Krysty followed his boulder-hopping, straight-line dash. Farther out on the plain, she could see more big rocks turning into big snakes, and the big snakes were sliding their way. Whatever path Ryan could clear with the eighteen-inch knife, it wasn't going to stay clear for long.

The panga slashed down again and with a single

stroke the one-eyed man hacked a snake cleanly in two. As they jumped the writhing halves and rushed on, Krysty saw Ryan shift the panga from right hand to left, just in time to flick out his wrist and catch another mutie rattler in midstrike. His left-handed slice chopped off half the snake's head, just in front of the eyes, cleaving its fangs and tongue as well.

Disarmed, its face gushing red, the rattler instantly recoiled and struck at Krysty's shin as she passed by. Forty pounds of muscle and bone slammed against the side of her boot and knocked her off balance. With a crash she landed on her hip on the rocks. When she looked up, still dazed by the impact, she stared into the wounded snake's eyes and saw the hate. Pure unreasoning hate. Blood mist puffed out in time with its breath as the mutilated rattler rewound itself, preparing to hit her harder.

Krysty jumped out of the way before it could strike. Ahead of her, Ryan growled a curse of "Fireblast!" She closed the gap between them while he dealt with the three snakes that blocked their escape route. Forehand, backhand, forehand, the panga's blade screamed through the air, and, severed, outsized viper heads hurtled off across the boulder field.

For a quarter-mile across the desert, the companions ran full-out. Only when Ryan was sure there was nothing but real rocks for fifty yards around them did he signal a halt to their headlong flight. Gasping and drenched with sweat, the companions slumped to seats on boulders. It took several minutes for them to catch their breath enough to drink water.

Lowering his canteen, J.B. jabbed a thumb in the direction they had come and said, "Shame to waste all that good white meat."

"I'll cook it up," Mildred told him, "if you go back and collect it."

J.B. shook his head. "Rather eat my own foot."

A HALF HOUR LATER, and another two miles into their trek, it began to rain. But not raindrops saturated with caustic chemicals.

It rained birds—small, dead birds. A few at first, hurtling down, headfirst, with wings folded, dark brown blurs thudding into and bouncing limply off the rocks.

The drizzle became a shower, and then the shower became a deluge.

There was no cover for the companions. They shielded their heads with their arms, crouching as they were pelted by the hail of little corpses. The full downpour lasted only a few seconds. When it was over, thousands of unmoving bodies darkened the ground and the air was thick with tiny, shredded bits of feather.

The fluff made Mildred sneeze. "Better not touch them," she warned the others. "It's possible they could be carrying some kind of pathogen, a virus that might be contagious."

Undaunted, Krysty picked up one of the broken creatures. "Must've died triple quick—it's still warm," she said, gently turning the bird in her hand. "No sign of any disease. Looks like they were all struck stone dead."

Overhead, the sky was blue, and the blue was endless.

"Where the blazes did they come from?" Mildred said. She shuddered as she brushed the feathers from her face and plaits.

Observing her discomfort, Doc said, "A person given to superstition might well consider it a sign from Yahweh himself. Similar to a rain of live toads or lambs' hearts, an omen of unspeakable evil."

Clearly disturbed by the unusual event, Mildred immediately snapped back, "Is that the kind of unscientific crap the deans taught you at Oxford, Doc? Did you get your doctorate in Victorian nonsense?"

"I am afraid the idea of strange rains goes back a bit further than that, my dear—"

"Question is, what chilled them?" J.B. interrupted, using the toe of his boot to spread out a small heap of bodies.

Before the discussion could go any further, Jak cut in. "Ahead, big danger," he told Ryan. "Feel rumble in feet."

When they were quiet, they could all feel the faint but unmistakable shaking of the earth.

"Shall we proceed on the current course, my dear Ryan?" Doc asked. "Or is an alternate route in order?"

"Don't know what the rumble means," Ryan said. "Could be anything."

"Sure as hell isn't Amtrak," Mildred remarked.

"Until we find out what's going on," Cawdor told them, "let's take it nice and slow. Everybody up, now."

On triple red, they continued following the ridgeline, which began to bend gradually northward. Long before they caught sight of them, they felt the hot wind off the string of lakes—felt, smelled, tasted.

This brimstone was the real thing, giving off a rotten-egg stink that gagged and choked them. The closer they got to the source, the louder the rumbling noise became.

As the companions crested the top of a low rise, they were slammed by a wall of baking heat that forced them to shield their faces with their hands. Below, in a sunken area of the plain, acres upon acres of desert boiled and steamed. The mud-brown lakes were bodies of superheated liquid, erupting from deep in the earth along nukeblast-opened fault lines. Whole trees, uprooted, their upraised branches stripped of leaves and bark and mineralized to a dead white, swirled like drowning men in the violent whirlpools. For hundreds of yards around the lake-shores, there was nothing but peaked piles of sulfur crystals and orange patches of bacteria. Bacteria were the only living things that could survive the combination of high temperature and toxic gases.

In the center of the closest lake, the water's surface suddenly bulged up, then burst with a dull explosion that sent mud flying like shrapnel and a huge cloud of steam skyward. They all ducked and covered.

"There's your answer, Mildred," Ryan said after things had settled down. "Bubble of hot poison gas goes up. Way high, out of sight, the flock of birds flies right through it. Bang, no more birds."

"Dead in midair," J.B. agreed.

"Dead there, too," Dean added, pointing at the ground ten yards ahead.

It wasn't just birds who got done in by the mud-lake gases. Land creatures wandering a little bit closer to the shoreline had been felled by similar, sideways discharges. Dismantled skeletons of animals, large and small, lay scattered about. The bleached bones were scored with fang marks. Something big had been cleaning up after the dead.

"This bad place," Jak muttered.

"If we go around," J.B. said, "it's going to add five, mebbe six miles to the hike. Might be after dark by the time we make Moonboy."

The truth of the Armorer's words was obvious. If they circled the boiling lakes on the plains side, it would take them south, away from their goal instead of toward it.

"I figure we've already covered the distance the barman talked about," Ryan said. "Looks to me like there's a climbable gully over there. Let's follow it to the ridge summit, and have ourselves a look-see on the other side."

Even though the gully was passable, the climbing wasn't easy. The gully bottom was lined with heaps of loose, gravellike rock that had flaked off and fallen from the cliffs above, and the terrain got gradually steeper and steeper until the last thirty feet, which was straight up. The backbone of the ridge was made of crumbling spires of rock, and the clusters of spires were divided from one another every few hundred yards by uncrossable chasms and deep clefts, which was why the companions hadn't tried to travel along it the whole distance from Perdition. Following Ryan's lead, they carefully crept to the edge of the summit and looked over.

The barman had been telling the truth, at least in part. There was no way to miss Moonboy.

Some freak of geologic erosion had created a wide, protected nook in the promontory rock. Below them, the ville lay nestled in a roughly circular box canyon. Even though the actual paving had long since disintegrated, at a distance of one thousand yards Ryan and the others could still make out the mazelike layout of the predark development's streets. They could also see the gridwork of its building lots, though ninety-five per cent of the original dwellings had been reduced to rubble by the trinuke, by the elements and by legions of human scavengers. A few of the light poles stood upright, towering over the spreading shamble of huts and shacks. Because the backsides of some of the surviving three-story buildings faced them, most of Moonboy's main street was blocked from their view.

"Stay low," Ryan warned, "and keep your weapons down. We don't want sun flashing off our gun barrels."

They watched in silence for a few minutes, passing their three pairs of binocs back and forth. Nothing moved below.

"A ghost ville," Dean said.

"I don't see anything but recycled predark wreckage down there," Ryan stated.

"The scrounger might have made up the story about muties with strange chilling gear just to cadge a few drinks," Krysty suggested.

"Yeah, but a ville this size, this time of day should have people walking around," Ryan replied. "There's no sign of life."

At his suggestion, J.B. moved out to scout another angle of view, and he came back, quick. "Better all have a look," J.B. said.

The companions followed him around the far side of the ridge's spires, and, from the new vantage point, got a view straight down the main drag. Something strange was going on there, all right. Something dark stuck up in the middle of the deserted street. They took turns looking at it through the rubber-armored binocs.

"A derrick, maybe," Mildred said. "Plenty tall. On eight wheels. Could be motor-driven."

"It's never seen a nuke attack, or a drop of acid rain, either," Dix said. "Metal looks new."

"Way over to the right," Krysty said. "Is that a war wag?"

Ryan accepted the binocs from her and framed the vehicle in its view field. Painted desert camou, with oversized, all-terrain tires, the squat wag had an enclosed, two-man driver compartment, but there was no armored rear passenger area for troops. "Not like any LAV I ever saw," he said.

What was behind the vehicle was even more interesting to him. On a big-wheeled flatbed trailer, connected to the wag by a tow hook, sat a streamlined black machine on skids.

"Mildred, what do you make of the thing it's towing? Looks like a helicopter," Ryan said.

After studying the object, she said, "Yes. It looks to me like a one-person helicopter."

"Predark flying machine designed for vertical takeoffs and landings," J.B. affirmed.

"Right, only it's all black—there's no window for the pilot to see out of," Mildred went on. "And I've never seen a chopper with a rotor configuration like that. The tail rotor's ninety degrees off line and it's way too big, almost like a rear propeller. All those stubby things sticking out of the nose, that looks like a weapons cluster to me."

"Had to have been looted from a redoubt," J.B. said with confidence. "But what's it doing here?"

Ryan lowered the binocs. It was a good question.

The all-out nuclear exchange of 2001 had produced an electromagnetic pulse that had fried every computer chip and circuit board on the planet, save those buried deep in the fortified, radiation-shielded bunker complexes known as redoubts. Ryan knew that operational flying machines still existed in Deathlands. They'd seen them. But as far as he was concerned, travel by air was nothing more than a fable told by Dr. Mildred Wyeth. Assuming such a machine was found, and that it could be prepped and fueled, there was no safe way to learn how to fly it by trial and error. The only use it could serve was as an ornament in some baron's garden. Armageddon had turned humankind back into a species of flatlanders, of dirt crawlers.

There was a flurry of movement below as five figures in black stepped from the front of a predark structure on the left. They spread out and began to work on the upraised derrick. In a few seconds, they had lowered it, soundlessly, to a horizontal position. For what purpose, Ryan couldn't guess.

Krysty was the first to speak. "So the scrounger wasn't lying about them after all," she said. "Do you think he was telling the truth about Moonboy's norms, too? That they've all been chilled?"

"Either that or they ran away," Ryan answered, knowing the latter wasn't very likely.

"Sure don't look like muties to me," J.B. said, adjusting the focus ring on his binocs. "Look like norms in full battle armor. Remember that Hideyoshi and the other samurai warriors we come across a while back?"

"Yeah, but this gear is different," Mildred said.

"There's no horns on these helmets. The overlapping armor plates appear to be the same material as the helicopter—the same oily black—but look at the way those guys are moving around. The stuff isn't stiff. It flexes with them like a second skin."

"What do you think, Doc?" Ryan asked. "Does it look like any of the whitecoat ultrasecret tech you've seen?"

Doc didn't reply.

Ryan saw the blank stare, the quivering lips, and realized at once that the old man was slipping away from reality. Doc had no power to control the fits of complete disorientation, which were the result of posttraumatic shock from the time leaps he had been forced to take. Leaps that had fractured his mind and broken his heart. In a second or two, he would either be talking aloud to his wife, Emily, and his beloved children, Rachel and Jolyon, at their dinner table, or arguing some unintelligible philosophy with a long-turned-to-dust academic crony.

"Come on, Doc," Ryan prodded.

The lights went back on behind Doc's eyes. He groaned, then shook his head to clear it.

Ryan repeated the question after the man had recovered his bearings. "The black armor, did you see it when you were captive to the whitecoats before skydark?"

The answer was disappointing.

"Sorry, Ryan, I've never seen anything like it."

"The way they're totally encased, helmets to boots," Mildred said, "it reminds me of the suits the NASA astronauts used to wear. They were pressurized for life support in space. Had their own, self-contained air and water supply, and sophisticated biometry and communication systems.''

"Why would they be wearing something like that in Moonboy?" Krysty asked. "Nothing's wrong with the air around here.''

"They'd be wearing it if they couldn't breathe our air or drink our water," Mildred said.

"We've never seen any people like that," Dean said.

"Never heard of anyone like that, either," J.B. added.

"Mildred, are you saying they might not be from Earth?" Ryan asked in astonishment.

"It is a possible explanation, however remote," the physician replied. "They could be extraterrestrials.''

Fully recovered, Doc held up his hands. "My friends, I beg you to take a closer look. Whatever else they may be, these wayfarers are neither little nor green. And at this moment in time their point of origin, whether earthly or not, should be of less a concern to us than the potential threat they present. Have they weapons we cannot defeat?''

The one-eyed man smiled and nodded. "Our cannies might have their hands full trying to make dinner out these pilgrims.''

"Can't count on the folks in armor doing the job for us," J.B. said. "What if the cannie bastards wait until dark to attack and then just get driven off? There's a whole lot of desert out there. We could lose them, Ryan.''

"They're not going to wait."

"How do you know that?"

He pointed toward the entry road that led up from

Highway 15. "I count four cannies, coming on the run."

As the companions watched, low-moving figures slipped around and through the rubble piles on the outskirts of the ville. The cannies split up, working themselves into position to attack Main Street. They crouched in plain view from the ridge top, their stationary heads and shoulders completely exposed to down-angled blasterfire.

They were challenging but not impossible targets.

Ryan gritted his teeth.

That was, if he'd still had a weapon that could reach out and touch somebody at one thousand yards.

Chapter Eight

Giggly Jane's jungle boots made no sound as she scampered over the broken ground of outer Moonboy. What the nukecaust hadn't swept away, human scavengers had long since torn asunder. The concrete foundation slabs of the upscale executive homes—every one a 3,500-square-foot palace fit for a baron—had been painstakingly cracked and plundered for their metal pipes and wiring. The resulting rubble had been left in scattered heaps, or dumped out of the way into the craters of waterless swimming pools.

Giggly Jane and her fellow pack members moved quickly, single file, from rubble heap to rubble heap. Just ahead, beyond the last piles of concrete, shanties of all sizes spilled out from the sides of the handful of surviving buildings. Some were cozy lean-tos for one made of a single piece of corrugated steel; others were flat-roofed and big enough to sleep a dozen or more.

As they drew closer, Giggly Jane could see the rude dwellings were deserted. Though no tangles of corpses decorated their packed dirt floors, the air hung thick with a maddening perfume of death.

Irregularly spaced, six-foot-long blotches of brownish slime stained the earth; in other places, much wider areas were discolored. From these patches rose the dizzying scent. She felt a powerful urge to throw herself down and roll on them like a dog.

The Right Reverend Gore signaled for the group to split up, then moved off to the right with the scoped longblaster. Spadecrawler and Egregious Jones continued straight on, while Giggly Jane turned left, according to plan, cutting through the empty lots until she reached the remnants of a street.

Despite what the scrounger had told them about the chill capabilities of these muties, Giggly Jane had no fear of what lay ahead. Her bravery was due partly to the wormholes the oozie protein had already bored in her infected brain, and partly to her excitement at the promise of blood and booty. She already knew what she was going to do with her share of the spoils. True to the freewheeling, gather-no-moss, cannie lifestyle, Giggly Jane planned to use every crumb of it to trade up for better blasters and bigger knives.

At the edge of the ruined street, she carefully placed her .36-caliber handblaster beside a big chunk of concrete. She wasn't going to need the reproduction Colt to play her role in the assault. Though she was an excellent shot, her real forte was diversion, which would allow her three comrades to get into perfect position for an ambush. She shrugged out of her dress and let it fall around her boot tops. The sun blazed against her bare back, buttocks and legs. As she stepped out of the garment, her dirt-and-sweat-edged breasts swayed, and their silver nipple rings and antiqued death's-head ornaments tinkled sweetly.

Hell's bells.

After fishing the Tactical One-Hander knife out of a dress pocket, she concealed the serrated blade in the top of her right boot. It was the only tool she required—Giggly Jane had never learned to eat with a fork. Naked but for the boots, she set off down the lane of asphalt sand, following its sharp curve to the right until the center of Moonboy came into view.

In the middle of the street, some three blocks away, she saw the collection of strange machines and counted five figures in black. They weren't holding any weapons. Though their eyes weren't visible through the smoke-colored visors, the figures appeared to be looking at her, so she stopped in the middle of the road and did an impromptu little dance. Hands held high over her head, torso wriggling, legs spread wide, Giggly Jane bubbled over with laughter as she pumped her hips enthusiastically.

Of course, her wild, erotic contortions were a total sham. She had zero interest in performing actual sex with anyone.

Ever.

Because cannie girls just wanted to have fun.

THE SUN REFLECTED OFF the nasty, lopsided patch of white scar tissue on top of Spadecrawler's head. The damned gruesome thing looked as if it was getting bigger, Egregious Jones thought as he shadowed four steps behind, spreading like a rad cancer.

Over the years, he'd heard different stories about how the man had come to be so horribly disfigured, with that skanky little ear, all shriveled and puckered like an albino bat's butthole. Some said that his own mother had done it to him, shortly after his birth. Held him by his heels and dipped him into a bucketful of acid rain she'd collected, trying to chill him. Some said that he had done it himself by accident when he was stoned on jolt. Passed out and fell into a bonfire. Some said that norms had caught him bloody-handed and stacked hot coals on his head, trying to melt his murdering cannie brains. For his own part, Spadecrawler never said a single word about it, one way or another. Whatever the ugly truth was, it didn't matter a blood drop. From the nose up, the man was largely fucked, and he'd stay fucked until the day his running buddies ate him, nasty scar and all.

Assuming there were buddies left to do the job.

The way Gore was leading the show, nothing was for sure anymore. He'd started the day with a couple of dozen cannies, the biggest, meanest pack of man eaters this side of the Shens, and in a few hours there were only the four survivors. To Egregious, it was no mystery why things had gone so sour so fast. Terminal oozies had old Gore by the coattails. The way his hands shook, pretty soon he wouldn't be able to keep hold of a blade, let alone use it to cut free a nice loin chop.

He turned his head to the side and spit into the dirt. Thanks to the pecking order of cannie culture, he was going to have to let Gore take the best stuff from this raid, which had the makings of the score to end all. The juicy bits were sorely wasted on the Right Reverend. The kindest thing, to Egregious's way of thinking, would be to put a .58-caliber lead ball through both his lungs, then finish the job with the man's own stag-handled, guthook skinner. Tough, stringy meat, for sure, but while chewing it, at least he'd know that he'd seen the last of Gore. By right of succession, he was scheduled to become the next leader of the pack. Or what little remained of it.

Spadecrawler entered a narrow dirt lane between shambling squatters' huts, his weapon at the ready. Built on an Italian reproduction, the rifle-stocked carbine had an eighteen-inch, octagonal barrel. The extralong barrel added some distance to the .44's range, without making the blaster hard to handle in close quarters.

If the "Cowboy Carbine" was made to order for the job this afternoon, Egregious's blaster wasn't. As he followed Spadecrawler into the shantytown, he thumbed back the twin hammers of his Kodiak Express longblaster to half-cock. The black-powder biggame rifle had enough power in either barrel to bowl over a buffalo at seventy-five yards. The shooting distance would be about a hundredth of that, if things went right.

He and Spadecrawler were supposed to filter through the shacks without being seen, get as close as possible to their targets, and then when Gore opened fire with the scoped blaster, charge in and finish off the wounded at point-blank range. The success of the scheme depended on Gore's accuracy with the Steyr. Egregious would have felt a lot better about the deal if the pack leader's hands had been steadier.

As it turned out, he was worrying needlessly— things never got to the charge-and-finish-them-off part. Neither Spadecrawler nor Egregious saw the minefield until it was too late.

With the sound of rattraps snapping shut, more than twenty dirt-colored spheres the size of hens' eggs leaped from the ground. They jumped to various heights around Spadecrawler, all in a midchest-to-knees strike zone. As the mines rose in the air, they started to spin, and as they spun they chittered like a flock of sparrows. Invisible to either of the startled cannies, around the equators of each of the little spheres were alternating laser firing ports and tiny mirrors. When the mines reached their designated maximum altitudes, the lasers fired in a precise sequence. They weren't targeted at living trespassers; they were aimed at the mirrors of the mines spinning opposite, which created a cat's cradle of zigzagging, reflected green light beams.

Egregious watched as Spadecrawler stumbled through the fluttering, interlacing rays. He might as well have fallen into a web of band saws. Bloodlessly, he sizzled and came apart.

The light show lasted for a second or two at most. As if on cue, all the spheres dropped back to the ground and were still.

Egregious stood rooted to the earth, barely daring to breathe. Spadecrawler lay chopped into hundreds of pieces on the path in front of him. Even though he knew damn well the mines were on the ground around what was left of the man, he couldn't pick them out from the other rocks. He also knew if he didn't figure an escape plan, and quick, he was going to be down there in pieces, too. The only jump-up mines he'd ever seen had had trip-wire triggers. Assuming these chirping bastards were no different, the way he'd come in was clear; if he could just retrace his path, he'd be safe.

But these mines *were* different. There was nothing so crude as a trip wire. And some were set to go off at second, third or fourth contact, instead of the first.

Egregious took one step backward, and it was his last.

As rattraps clattered shut all around him, and the triple-deadly, spinning spheres jumped up, he managed to get one word out.

"Shit!"

And it hung in the air longer than he did.

CROUCHED BEHIND A PILE of rubble about one hundred yards from the mutie camp on Main Street, Gore did a quick inventory through the Steyr's scope.

And he liked what he saw.

By itself, the fully functional, all-terrain vehicle would bring enough jack to spell easy retirement for a cannie with late-stage oozies. No longer would the Right Reverend have to hunt down his own dinner. After today, he could afford to buy his meat, have it brought in live and on the hoof.

He put the cross wires on one of the armored figures. The scope had a built-in range finder—distance could be estimated by fitting the target between the horizontal marks, which were calibrated to the height of an average man at ranges from 100 to 800 meters. At the distance indicated by the finder, the Steyr's 7.62 mm x 51 round was a flat-shooting son of a bitch.

The muties did have a slight numerical advantage, but Gore was counting on the longblaster to change that in a hurry. The scrounger's story about firing squads of Moonboy's finest failing to drop these muties, even if true, didn't really concern him. After all, there was a huge difference in muzzle velocities—and knockdown power—between black-powder pistol balls and a slug fired from a metal-cased, military rifle cartridge. Gore figured that head shots with 173-grain, M-118 boattails would open up the backs of those greasy black helmets as if they were paper bags full of mashed yams.

Because of the view angle he had, which was straight up the street, Gore couldn't see where Egregious and Spadecrawler were hiding, but he had a perfect view of Giggly Jane as she sidled, jaybird naked, down the other end of Main. When all five muties turned to look at her, he had the jump on them, and he took it.

The Steyr bucked hard against his shoulder. He rode the rifle's recoil wave, immediately bringing the scope back on target. The shot was a clean miss! He marked the dirt puff, wide to the right. Cursing, he ejected the hull and chambered another round. Lucky for him, the triple-stupe muties were just standing there, like they didn't get the picture. He was about to give it to them, in full color. Snugging the rifle tight to his shoulder, Gore adjusted his aim point for the degree of miss and fired again.

On the other side of his target, the bullet kicked up dirt.

Gore looked at his trigger hand. It wasn't shaking. It was rock steady. And there was no wind to push the bullets off track. Something had to be wrong with the scope's zero. Maybe the tube got bumped. Glad to see that the muties still hadn't moved, Gore halved the distance of the last miss and squeezed off another shot.

The slug veered to the right again, as if the bullets were being diverted around their intended target.

That couldn't be fucking happening, he thought as he frantically worked the bolt.

As soon as the shooting started, Giggly Jane's job was done. Laughing hysterically, she dashed across the street and down a path between the shanties. She laughed even louder a few seconds later when she stumbled onto the three-dimensional puzzle that was all that was left of Spadecrawler and Jones.

She was still laughing when the rattraps snapped and the jump-ups rose. A beam of green light flicked across her forehead and cut completely through her skull just above the ears, slicing her brain in two. Before her dead body could fall, fifty other laser beams, reflected back and forth off the spinning mines, transsected her torso and limbs in countless, crisscrossing ways.

Most of her hit the ground in neat two-inch chunks.

Chapter Nine

A fine gridwork of lime-green appeared before Colonel Gabhart's eyes.

Though it seemed to be about a foot-and-a-half from the tip of his nose, the map simulation was actually computer-projected on the inside of his helmet's visor. One of the squares at the extreme left side of the grid blinked on and off. They had more company.

"Key nineteen," Gabhart said to his battlesuit. The gridwork display instantly dissolved, and he was looking through the lens of a motion sensor at the edge of their defensive perimeter. Four humanoid figures carrying crude projectile weapons made a stealthy approach from the west.

"Nineteen off," he said.

Before resuming work on the rocket gantry, Gabhart checked the elapsed time, which was projected in the upper-right corner of his field of view. In exactly twenty-two minutes, the launch vehicle was going to pass through the rift. Because there was no direct communication with Earth from the Shadow side, there was no way for him to stop the transfer. No way to speed it up, either. The comm blackout was a function of the structure of the pathway. It dictated that the entire operation be organized around a prearranged timetable. Accordingly, Gabhart and his team were working on a tight and inflexible schedule.

Time was also critical because existing technology and resources were being pushed to the limit. It took an unbelievable amount of power to create the pathway. And once it was in place, it had to be sustained, or there was no guarantee it would terminate in the same location when reconstructed. Each time the Shadow end of the pathway was opened, it caused an even bigger power drain. On the Earth side, in an effort unprecedented in human history, countless millions were sacrificing their own comfort and safety for the sake of this expedition.

Gabhart was grateful for the rigid schedule. It kept his team focused on step-by-step details. There was no time to surrender to the gut-churning agoraphobia that the wide-open spaces produced. No time to stew over the terrible weight of their isolation, or of their responsibility to those who had sent them. No time to consider the danger. Though this wasn't supposed to be a suicide mission, it had plenty of potential for turning out that way, surrounded as they were by a vast uncharted territory full of unknown hazards.

From the base of the mobile gantry, John Ockerman, the systems engineer, and Pedro Hylander, the biologist, had uncoiled the heavy, blast-proof ignition and telemetry cables from their spools, and were dragging them across the street, toward the ATV and launch control. Nara Jurascik, the team biochemist, and Marshall Connors, the geologist, stood beside the ATV, prepping its onboard computer for hookup. All electronic and software systems had to be triple-checked to make sure they had survived the crossing intact.

Like Gabhart, the others were soldier-scientists, line officers blooded in the Consumer Rebellion of 2099, five volunteers selected out of a global human population teetering above one hundred billion. They had been judged the best not just by their academic training or combat experience, but also by their bio-compatibility with the latest generation of Totality Concept technology.

The entire interior surface of the battlesuit was its control panel. Complete mastery of one's physical body—total muscular control—was required to operate the body armor at maximum efficiency. On top of that, few human brains were capable of collating the avalanche of information the battlesuits provided, of shifting back and forth under the most extreme pressure, between complex real and virtual environments, and, in a fraction of a second, making critical and correct decisions.

As Jurascik and Connors ran the launch-sim diagnostics, the colonel helped Ockerman and Hylander examine every bolt and weld on the gantry frame. They had just about completed the painstaking work when a Shadow female appeared at the far end of the street. Naked except for ragged boots, she walked closer, paused, then fell into a wild, hip-churning dance.

Captain Connors's voice filled Gabhart's helmet. "Well, at least *some* of the natives are friendly."

"She does look glad to see us," Ockerman agreed.

"I hope she's got a brother," Jurascik said.

"Yeah, sometimes moves like that run in families," Connors said.

"Or not, as in the case of yours," the biochemist said.

The grid map reappeared before Gabhart's eyes. One of the squares blinked in red. Out of their direct line of sight, a pod of laser mines had been tripped.

"Key 42," Gabhart said.

His battlesuit responded by playing a recording of events that had taken place just seconds before: a lime-green light show, complete with sound. In slow motion, the mines' laser beams passed through the Shadow World humanoids as if they were made of smoke.

Of course, smoke never sizzled like that.

Appearances to the contrary, the laser mine was one of the most merciful killers in the team's arsenal. In about a second, it produced surprise, pain, oblivion. The antipersonnel system subunits launched in unison, flying in precise formation for 1.3 seconds. With perfectly synchronized rotations, their firing lasers and reflectors created a narrow zone of absolute destruction. When the subunits fell back to the ground, the impact automatically rearmed them for the next jump. Once dispersed in the field, the computer-linked mines never needed service or refueling. They operated via their own threat-level analysis program, based on input from automated, sight, chemical and sound surveillance.

In other words, they were perpetual death machines.

Gabhart declined the replay option and the inside of his visor cleared. Down the street, the naked female still gyrated gleefully.

The crack of a rifle shot from behind made the colonel stiffen. Before he could turn to face the source, the bullet had sailed harmlessly past him. Using an infrared scan, he quickly located the shooter crouching in the rubble 90 meters past the end of the street. When Gabhart cranked the visor's magnification up to eight-power, he saw the middle-aged Shadow male taking aim again. He noted the weapon's crude telescopic sight.

Then the muzzle winked at him.

Thanks to the sensory enhancements of the battlesuit, Gabhart could actually see the bullet in flight. In his visual array, it appeared as a bright red dot circled in brilliant yellow. Beside the display, three sets of numbers scrolled.

Projectile caliber: 7.62 mm.

Projectile speed: 860 meters per second, and falling.

Distance to impact: 30 meters, and falling.

Twenty meters from impact, the battlesuit automatically triggered a narrow-band deflection pulse of roughly a terawatt. The colonel felt nothing whatsoever. Like magic, the rifle slug simply seemed to curve around him, and as it did, its whine abruptly dropped in pitch.

As the entire team watched, the shooter fired his weapon again, with the same result. Gabhart wondered how long it would take for him to wise up to the fact that he could fire ten thousand bullets, burn out that rifle barrel and still never come close to the target. Though the artificially intelligent body armor was by no means a perfect defense in every situation, it could handle dozens upon dozens of incoming projectiles at once—projectiles of up to 40 mm.

Evidence notwithstanding, the shooter stubbornly persisted, preparing to fire once more.

"He's outside of our AP perimeter, Colonel," Hylander said. "Should we just ignore him?"

"No, I'd better go collect him," Gabhart said, "before he damages something important."

The colonel trotted over to the windowless black gyroplane. At the touch of his gauntleted hand on its side, a panel slid back, revealing the cramped, two-seat cockpit. Gabhart climbed into the front seat, which immediately inflated and deflated in places, conforming to fit the shape of his body. When that process was complete, the door panel swished shut and red interior lights came on, allowing him to locate the coupler for the gyroplane's onboard computer. Once he connected his suit's umbilical, the red lights and the blacked-out windows vanished. Both pilot and pilot's seat floated in space. Gabhart had an unobstructed view in all directions. An illusion, of course. The world outside the aircraft's black skin was being optically scanned by numerous sensors, and after the irrelevant details were filtered out, the end product was projected onto the inside of his visor.

The colonel felt a slight vibration as the engine started up. He couldn't see the rear propeller building up speed, pushing the main rotor overhead, because the control program determined those details were unnecessary. However, the climbing rpm and thrust levels were displayed inside his visor. When the rotor reached liftoff thrust, Gabhart released the skid clamps and the gyroplane rocketed into the air.

It was like flying an armchair, but an armchair that with a stomach-dropping lurch climbed straight up to three hundred feet. On command, the chair tipped forward, giving the colonel a panoramic view of the terrain below. He located the running man without difficulty. As he banked to intercept his target, G-

force pressed him deep into the contour seat. It was
a max-speed dive. At the outer edges of his vision
the surrounding landmarks—the ridge tops, the rock
walls, the three-story structures—blurred, then
stretched like taffy. Glittering taffy.

Gabhart could have just sat back and watched, letting the computer do all the work, but he enjoyed
hands-on flying, especially in combat. Below him, a
magnified, lone figure ran inside a superimposed red
circle, the gyro's kill zone. He tensed his left index
finger inside the battlesuit glove and the circle shrank
until he had the man's right arm isolated. It was the
arm that carried the projectile weapon. When the
colonel relaxed the muscles of his hand, the fire control system had its target locked in. The circle bobbed
up and down, up and down as the man pumped his
arms, trying desperately to escape onrushing death
from above.

AFTER HIS THIRD SHOT missed, Gore automatically
chambered another live round. Eye pressed to the
scope's rear aperture, cross wires on his target's
black-armored chest, he tightened the trigger to the
break point, then paused. He was rapidly losing confidence in the longblaster, and starting to get spooked
by these muties, who made no move to duck for
cover.

Where were Spadecrawler and Jones? Why hadn't
they backed his play?

Through the scope, he followed his chosen target
as it walked over to the flatbed trailer and climbed
up and into the weird black machine that sat on it.
He stared, fascinated, as the bladed thing in back of
the fuselage began to spin. Then the bigger-bladed

thing on its roof began to spin, too. Gore had no idea what the machine was supposed to do, but he didn't like the look of it one bit. He was about to put a bullet through its middle, just to see what would happen, when it jumped off its trailer and shot high into the sky.

At the sight, Gore panicked. Vaulting over low rubble heaps, he dashed for the base of the ridge, where the boulder fall could provide him some cover. He had crossed no more than one-third of the distance when he sensed the black thing swooping down on him from behind. He felt the terrible pounding of its blades against the air, felt the impacts inside his body and reacted by cutting hard to the left.

The flying machine swept over him, whipping up a cloud of dust. And as it passed by, a pencil line of green light from above cracked a smoking slit in the earth to his right.

For a second it didn't even hurt.

Gore felt a sudden sensation of extreme pressure, of constriction just below his right elbow, and something clattered at his feet. He saw the Steyr on the ground, his severed hand and forearm still gripping the forestock. Staring in disbelief at his brand-new stump, he smelled burning meat, then his elbow exploded in pain. Gore fell to the dirt, squealing.

Chapter Ten

"Kind of a piss-poor shot, isn't he?" was J.B.'s comment after the cannie missed for a second time with the stolen longblaster.

Ryan squinted through one lens of his binocs. "It sure isn't the rifle's fault. At that range, he should be able to drive nails with it."

"Our friends in black down there don't seem to be much bothered by what he's doing," J.B. said. "Either that, or they're scared stiff."

"Don't look scared to me." Ryan said.

"Nah, to me neither," the Armorer admitted. "More like they couldn't give a rusty rad-blast."

"Hey!" Mildred exclaimed. "Did you see that?"

"Where?" Dean asked.

Mildred pointed to the left of Main Street. "A brilliant green flash, over between the big houses," she said. "Just there for a second, bright as day, then it was gone."

"Like stun gren flash, no boom," Jak agreed. "I see."

The Steyr firing a third time brought everyone's attention back to the heart of Moonboy. The gunshot echoed off the walls of the ridge. The five in black armor remained standing, like statues in the middle of the street.

Another miss.

"See where the slug skipped?" J. B. said. "That guy can't hit the broad side of a barn. Kind of humorous...or mebbe pathetic."

"Pathetic is more like it," Mildred said. "He's probably got the oozie shakes so bad he can't keep the sights on target."

"If our cannibal colleague is not cautious," Doc said, "he will anger those black-clad folk."

"Already has, Doc," Dix said. "One of them's moving."

Ryan watched the figure in black climb up on the trailer and disappear into the windowless aircraft.

After a few seconds, its rotors began to turn. First the rear one, then the one on top, both spinning faster and faster, until a dust storm began to fly in the street.

"Got a real bad feeling, Ryan," Krysty said. "Mebbe we should pull back."

"You seeing anything?" The one-eyed man asked. His concern was real. He'd had enough experience with her mutie premonitions to know they had to be respected.

"No," she said. "That thing just scares me."

"It's not after us," J.B. assured her.

"Not yet, you mean," Doc said. "Perhaps we should take a lesson from our flesh-eating friend down there. Discretion is the better part of valor, John Barrymore."

Below them the cannie sniper, valorous or not, was sprinting across the rubble field with the Steyr.

Before the companions could retreat from the edge of the cliff or the fleeing cannie could make good his escape, the aircraft lifted off the trailer.

"Well, I'll be fireblasted," J.B. muttered as it shot

up to the level of the ridge top in the space of a couple of heartbeats.

Browning Hi-Power in hand, Dean stood gaping as the unnatural flying thing hovered high over the ville. His eyes widened in amazement as it abruptly wheeled and dived on its prey like a mutie war eagle.

At the climax of the screaming dive, a bolt of light shot from the weapons pod in the nose and cut a fiery trench across the earth, a line that seemed to graze the running cannie. A graze was all it took to put him down.

"What was that?" Krysty asked.

"It gave off the same green flash I saw before," Mildred said. "If I didn't know better, I'd say it was some kind of a laser beam." For Krysty's benefit, she added, "A laser's a high-energy light that can cut through plate steel like butter."

"This one chopped through solid rock," Ryan said.

"If it was a laser," Mildred told him, "it was a good ten thousand times more powerful than any we had before skydark. None of the really powerful ones back then, the ones that could generate enough energy to create nuclear fusion, could fit into something as small as a helicopter. Took a complex the size of Moonboy to do the trick."

"So you're saying what?" Ryan prompted.

"I'm saying we didn't have the technology to make something like that in 2001. Somebody, somewhere has been pushing the research envelope. Contrary to reports, science isn't dead, after all."

"Lightning without thunder," Doc said, clucking his tongue. "My dear Ryan, this development does not bode well. Sadly, my fear that we are over-matched seems more and more justified.''

The aircraft figure-eighted to come around again. The cannie lay sprawled on the ground and showed no interest in getting up. To Ryan it looked as if he'd dropped the Steyr, and he hoped it wasn't badly damaged. The aircraft made a low pass over the unmoving figure, checking for signs of life, then with a roar of its engine and a blast of dust from its propwash, it rocketed back up to ridge-top level. Hanging in the air directly over the center of Moonboy, it turned a slow, clockwise pivot.

''What's it doing now?'' Krysty asked.

''Looking,'' Jak replied.

''Looking for us,'' Ryan said. ''Nobody move, not a muscle.''

When the nose of the aircraft swung past them, they all breathed a sigh of relief. The machine continued to turn, climbing higher as it did so, then from the peak of its spiraling ascent, it suddenly banked and dived on them at incredible speed.

''By the three Kennedys!'' Doc cried. ''It has seen us!''

Ryan shoved J.B., hard. ''Go! Everybody, head east! I'll make it follow me.''

There was no time for argument. Their last best hope was to scatter. Ryan already had drawn his SIG-Sauer. He led the diving aircraft, aiming well below it, and squeezed off three shots in rapid succession. He didn't expect to down the machine with 9 mm bullets, but he did expect to see them send sparks flying off its black skin.

There were no sparks. The craft had soaked up the slugs like a sponge, or he'd missed it altogether.

The gunfire did draw the attention of the pilot, who immediately angled the craft's dive toward him.

With a glance at the others, who were already taking cover behind the row of spires to the right, Ryan bolted across the jagged terrain, back the same way they had come. As he ran, he fired his pistol in the general direction of the aircraft.

Ryan didn't know what the range of the plane's laser blaster was, but he had a sixth sense when it came to being locked in someone's sights. At that moment, his alarm bells clanged. With a monumental effort he dived headlong, throwing himself behind a man-sized horn of rock. In the same instant there was a blinding flash of light, a wave of intense heat and a rocking explosion, which was followed by the whipping suction of a violent gust of wind. Over his shoulder he saw the black ship zoom past. The stone that had been his cover had been destroyed. Three feet of its tip sliced off clean. Nothing was left of the missing part. The light beam had detonated it like a gob of plastic explosive.

Ryan took a two-handed grip on the SIG-Sauer and, as the airship turned, he punched out four evenly spaced shots. He knew the capabilities of his hand-blaster and the limits of his own skill. At a range of fifty yards, with a steady hold, he could just about guarantee where the bullets would fall. And that was certainly inside a circle smaller than ten feet in diameter.

Yet he scored no visible hits.

"Fireblast!" he snarled, jumping up and ducking between a pair of towering spires.

With the others no longer in sight, Ryan was free to think about his own survival. It was a safe bet that he couldn't outrun the flying machine. Experience had taught him that he couldn't outshoot it, either. His only chance was to outthink its pilot.

The black ship approached his position, then stopped at a distance of seventy feet. Maintaining its altitude, it jockeyed first one way then the other, trying to get a decent shot angle on him.

Ryan pulled back behind cover as the laser cut loose again. This time the flare of light didn't wink out. The beam was sustained. The wave of heat made him groan. Smoke started to curl up from his hair. As the beam gnawed at the rock, it gave off a painfully shrill tone and he could feel the massive monolith vibrating. The rock crag weighed in the vicinity of two hundred tons. At its base, the circumference was probably twenty feet. Ryan was glad to learn that there were some things the aircraft's weapon couldn't shoot through in a single blast.

Then it got noticeably cooler. Shielding his eye from the glare, Ryan saw that the pilot had switched his point of aim to the pinnacle of the spire above him, a place where the rock was much thinner.

Time to move.

As he leaped away from the base, high overhead there was a thunder-crack explosion and the huge pinnacle came crashing down in a golden rain of sparks. The impact raised a cloud of dust that enveloped him.

Since running away from the machine was futile, Ryan dashed toward it. He had to have surprised the pilot as he burst out of the dust cloud, because he ran directly beneath the weapons pod without drawing another burst of green fire. He passed under the sleek belly of the craft and into the confined hurricane of its prop wind.

Fifteen feet below the middle of the aircraft, Ryan raised his pistol high overhead and fired straight into its guts. Though the range was no more than five feet, there was no clank of impact punctuating the flurry of gunshots, only the whine of deflected slugs as they ricocheted on the rocks around him.

Impossible, he decided as he raced onward, out from under the machine's tail propeller. Impossible but true. Bullets had no effect. His hopes for living through this encounter were sinking fast.

Before him yawned the cliff overlooking the mud lakes. He guessed he was very near to the gully they'd climbed in order to reach the ridge top. There was no time left for him to make major adjustments in his jumping-off point. If he had guessed wrong, the drop was going to be a lot longer than thirty feet. The airship wheeled around behind him, swooping down for the chill. Straining, he sprinted for the edge.

As he took the last, desperate stride and his right foot came down on nothing, he thought he'd blown it. Down was a long, long way. Legs flailing, he dropped below the ridge top. Above him there was a flash of light and blistering heat as the laser cannon blasted a new cleft in the bedrock.

Ryan hit the pile of loose gravel at tremendous speed. The impact with the ground knocked the wind out of him, but he didn't stop. He couldn't stop. Because of the gully's steep angle, he continued to fall down the chute, skidding, sliding. He covered his head with his arm as he started to tumble, end over end. With no way to control his descent, he was just another boulder, rolling downhill.

Buffeted, bounced, battered, he came to a shattering stop behind a big rock. Momentarily unable to breathe, he struggled to rise. But as he regained his feet, he found himself face-to-face with the hovering black ship and the multiple barrels of its weapons' cluster. The aircraft was positioned to block any further movement on his part. He had nowhere to go.

Ryan raised his handblaster and opened fire. He didn't have a hope in hell of doing damage to the craft; he was buying a few precious seconds of time for his friends. The pistol spit out several more shots before its slide locked back. Tossing aside the empty pistol, he reached for his right boot and yanked the panga from its sheath.

"Come on, you fireblasted bastard!" Ryan shouted at the windowless craft. He slashed the heavy knife blade back and forth in the air. "Come out of there and I'll cut you a new one!"

Ryan expected the green flash any second.

He expected it to be the last thing he ever saw.

The ship moved in a little closer, as if the pilot wanted to get a better look at him. Without warning, a cloud of clear mist shot from one of the tubes in the aircraft's nose. Ryan gasped in surprise as the mist billowed, wet and stinging, around him. His involuntary intake of breath sucked tiny droplets into his lungs. He tried to close off his throat, but it was already too late. His knees buckled.

Before he hit the ground, he was out cold.

Chapter Eleven

The first thing Ryan heard was the engine's roar and the whipping of the wind. The first thing he felt was the pain in his right ankle, as if it were very slowly being twisted off. Blood throbbed in his face and neck, and the weight of his insides pressing at the back of his throat felt like they were about to jump out of his mouth. He opened his eye a crack, and there was nothing beneath him but air. For hundreds of feet.

Head down, he hung suspended in space.

As Moonboy corkscrewed far below, an awful dizziness hit him. He shut his eye; it was either that or throw up. But before he did, he glimpsed the black expanse of the aircraft's belly above him, and his ankle trapped in some kind of clamp. It was all that kept him from falling to his death.

Then the plane dropped like a stone with him hanging there, helpless, every muscle in his body clenched.

Six feet above the center of Moonboy's main street, the aircraft stopped and hovered. With a clack, the claw around his ankle snapped open, and Ryan fell unceremoniously to the dirt. The propwash lashed his back as the plane turned away and landed on the trailer.

When he sat up, black-armor-clad figures had him

surrounded. He stared down the muzzles of their tri-barreled blasters, then looked from visor to visor, trying to make out the faces behind them. All Ryan saw was his own reflection.

One of the creatures in black gestured at him with its blaster. "Stand up," it said.

The thing spoke English, but its voice was rad-blasted strange, metallic and disembodied.

As Ryan obeyed the command and rose to his feet, a door slid open in the side of the aircraft and the pilot exited, hopping down to the road and walking purposefully toward him. The cannie who'd stolen his longblaster was sitting by the ruined curb on the other side of the street. Beside him was a squat black cube on wheels. The skin of his face under the salt-and-pepper beard stubble looked sickly gray-green. Perhaps, Ryan thought, because his severed right hand was sticking up out of the top of the cube, as if it were waving goodbye. The cannie cradled the scorched stump of his right arm to his chest. The treasured Steyr SSG-70 stood leaning against a piece of corrugated steel, part of a collapsed porch roof.

"I'm not part of that cannie bastard's crew," Ryan said, hooking a thumb over his shoulder at the cannie as the pilot stepped up. "Came here to chill him myself. I have no grudge against any of you."

Ryan didn't expect instant amnesty. He was just trying to draw them out of their black shells, looking for an edge, something he could use. He got no response.

The pilot who faced him was the biggest of the lot. Bigger than Ryan, too. No telling how much of it was armor, of course. Irritated by the silence, determined to show no weakness, the one-eyed man went nose to visor with him.

"Can you hear me in there?" Ryan shouted at his own reflection. "Or are you a bunch of rad-blasted dimmies?"

"This one's quite a specimen," said a scratchy, metallic voice behind him. "Love the eye patch."

"He came after the assault gyro with nothing but a great big knife," the pilot said.

Ryan winced at their peals of laughter, laughter grated through stainless steel. It dawned on him that they all had some kind of amplification system for external communication. "I'm guessing you people aren't from around these parts." he said dryly.

The pilot pointed to the cannie. "Over there."

As he was escorted across the street, Ryan checked out the stubby blasters they carried. He'd never seen their like before. Why three barrels? he asked himself. Unlike Doc's LeMat, all the muzzles seemed to be the same diameter. So what was the point of having three of them if they all fired the same thing? It looked like the barrels were fed from the blocky-looking mag near the stock's buttplate, so they weren't a triad of single-shot breeches, same way a side-by-side shotgun was. He also noticed they had two triggers, instead of one.

Or instead of three.

Ryan wondered if he was going to live long enough to figure it out.

The cannie looked mighty worried as they approached. He shrank against the curb, cowering like a kicked dog.

"How did Reverend Gore check out?" the pilot asked.

"He's a wash," the one with the higher-pitched voice replied. "Standard tests show he's infected with a Shadow variant of Creutzfeldt-Jakob."

"Ice Nine," the pilot said grimly. He leaned over the huddled cannibal. "With the ugly shit you've got in your head," he said, "we can't even use you for fertilizer."

As he straightened, the pilot barked a command. "Foam him. And don't forget his fucking hand."

One of the figures in armor snatched the severed limb out of the hole in the top of the cube—to Ryan, the stump end looked as if it had been gnawed by rats—and unceremoniously threw it to the cannie, while another armored figure unclipped a hose from its hip. One end of the hose terminated at the bottom of the tank on its back; the other in a nozzle. As the hoser advanced on the cannie, the other one moved the cube to the middle of the street. Everyone else backed away from the flesh eater. Ryan followed suit.

"What're you gonna do to me?" Gore croaked, his eyes wide with fear.

"Ever hear of a carniphage?" the pilot asked.

The cannie swallowed hard and shook his head.

Ryan didn't know what it was, either, but he didn't like the sound of it.

The pilot tried another tack. "Well, do you know what bacteria are?" he asked.

Gore looked desperately at Ryan, whose face was a mask of stone.

"That's too bad, because I don't have time to explain it to you," the pilot told him. "Won't say this isn't going to hurt, though, because that would be a lie."

The one with the tank took another step forward, then creamy yellow stuff shot from the nozzle in its gloved hand. Three feet from the tip of the nozzle, the thin line of fluid seemed to balloon in all directions, expanding on contact with the air. Gore let out a banshee shriek as foam splattered his body, head to foot.

Whatever it was, it didn't take long to work.

Ryan could see the clothes melting right off the man. The duster dissolved, then the holey gray T-shirt. As his epidermis dripped from the sides of his face, the cannie did a shivery, heel-drumming, horizontal dance in the gutter. The yellow foam continued to billow up, until it completely concealed him. Ryan heard choking sounds from beneath the bubbling mass.

Then the cannie's good hand thrust up out of the foam, the fingers already stripped of flesh, red bones dissolving from the fingertips down, like icicles held to a flame. Beneath the mound of yellow fluff, brown fluid sizzled forth, pooling then slowly sinking into the asphalt sand.

Ryan whirled on the pilot. "What in rad-blazes are you?" he demanded.

"We'll ask the questions for the time being."

"I don't talk to bugs. I'm not answering any questions until I see your ugly faces. Take off that fucking helmet and look me in the eye. Unless you're afraid."

"We've got nothing to be afraid of, friend. Problem is, these helmets don't come off. Battlesuit isn't designed that way. But we can do something about the tint."

The top of the pilot's helmet started to go transparent, black turning clear, down over the visor, to the neck opening. The head inside had close-cropped dark brown hair in a widow's peak, and hard brown eyes.

"You're a norm," Ryan said.

As the one-eyed man turned, the other helmets went from black to clear. He saw that one of his captors was female. She had pale blond hair cut short, pale blue eyes and a thin, aquiline nose. The man standing next to her had a shaved head and wore a sandy-colored walrus mustache that drooped past the corners of his mouth. The third male was taller than the woman, but only just. He had shoulder-length, curly brown hair, some of it graying.

The last man was the one with the foam tank. He was as big as the guy with the walrus mustache, and sharp-featured. Under his helmet he wore a seamed, red skullcap with an embroidered logo across the crown that read Buy or Die! 759th AirCav. There was a different insignia on his armor's breastplate: the word FIVE in small silver letters. For the first time, Ryan noticed the same design on the breastplates of all the others.

"Hold the foam ready, Ockerman," the pilot said. "If this one's got Ice Nine, too, we're going to need it."

"No worries," Ockerman replied. He looked thoroughly amused.

"I don't have the oozies," Ryan told the pilot.

"That's what you call the disease?"

"Right. I don't have the oozies because I don't eat human flesh. Never have, never will."

"You might think that would make a difference," the pilot said, "but you'd be wrong. Turns out you can get infected from eating an animal that fed on another infected animal. Or by eating a plant that was fertilized with composted flesh from an infected animal. The provirus that causes the infection is almost indestructible because it isn't really alive. It's a kind of chemical. We need a tissue sample in order to test you for it.''

"You're not taking off my hand," Ryan said, retreating a giant step backward, ready to fight.

"No, no, that's not necessary. We used your friend's because it was, well, already available. A tiny snip of your skin will do nicely for our purposes. Or if you'd prefer, we could just forget about the test and carniphage you as a precaution.''

Ryan looked at the yellow curds floating on top of the thin puddle of brown, which was all that was left of the cannie. If the test came back wrong, he was going to be slime in a hurry, too. Ryan thought about making a grab for one of their weapons, but he knew that would draw fire from the others. And even if he got his hands on one of the strange blasters, he didn't know how to operate it. Somehow, he didn't think they'd be willing to give him the time to get up to speed. There was the Steyr, of course, and perhaps it was still loaded, but he'd already seen how ineffective it was. Given his predicament, he decided the best course was to go along with their program, hope his body was disease free, and, if it wasn't, to fight to the death.

The woman gently took his hand, turned it palm up and expertly nicked him with a gleaming silver tool. "Big, brave boy," she said, when he didn't flinch.

A trickle of blood ran down his wrist.

She carried the sample to the cube, deposited it into a clear vial, then inserted the vial into a slot in the side of the machine.

Meanwhile, the others gave ground as Ockerman squared off in front of him, hose in hand. The no-nonsense look in his eyes told Ryan there wasn't going to be time for a discussion if the news came back bad.

"Mind telling me what a carniphage is?" Ryan asked him.

"Flesh-eating, single-celled life-form," Ockerman said. "The carniphage eats, reproduces geometrically, eats some more, then, after a preset number of generations, the whole colony burns out and dies. About the same time as the food supply is gone. Been genetically tailored to have a short life span. We're talking a matter of seconds. Otherwise, it wouldn't be safe to release it into the environment. We use it as a field sterilizer."

"Not on this one, though," the woman said, turning from the cube's LED readout. "He's prion-free. His DNA looks in good shape, too. No sign of radiation-induced mutation in his chromosomes."

"Okay," the pilot said, "the fun's over, Ockerman. Put it away."

"Right, Colonel," the man in the skullcap said. He reclipped the nozzle to his hip.

"You dodged the proverbial bullet, my friend," the pilot-colonel said to Ryan. "If you'd been infected with Ice Nine, or had inheritable damage to your chromosomes, we'd have been forced to destroy you."

"The way you destroyed every person in this ville?"

"That was regrettable, but we had no choice in the matter. Sterilization is part of our mission protocol, to prevent any possible genetic or infectious agent contamination. Everyone living in this settlement was in some way radiation damaged. Either riddled with cancerous tumors or neural-system impaired."

So, Ryan thought, Moonboy ville hadn't been so fireblasted pure after all.

Not until now.

When it was pure dead.

"If I'm not infected or rad-damaged, then I'm free to go?" he said.

Again came the steel laughter, but this time he could see their faces. They were really enjoying themselves.

The one with the longish hair said, "You're good to go, all right, but you're not free."

Ryan glared at him.

"What Captain Connors means," the colonel said, "is that we're taking you back to Earth."

"This *is* Earth, droolie."

"From your point of view, I suppose it is."

"What other point of view is there?"

"You'll find out, in exactly eight minutes. Until then, I suggest you sit quietly on the curb while we finish our preparations."

The impenetrable black tints returned to their helmets, as if they were fishbowls filling from the bottoms with ink.

As he waited for the time to pass and the mystery to be revealed, Ryan scanned the ridge top. His companions were out there, somewhere. Question was, would they do the dumb thing and try to get him out of this mess? He sure as hell hoped not. Considering how hard his captors were to chill, any rescue attempt was doomed to fail.

He'd noticed that they'd addressed one another using military rank. In Deathlands, such things ordinarily had little meaning. People could and did call themselves anything they wanted. Colonel. Archduke. God. But there was something in their voices, as distorted as they were, and in the way they carried themselves that told Ryan the references to rank were real. Perhaps they belonged to some far-flung baron's army? If so, there were no badges, bars or stars; their only insignia was the FIVE on their breastplates, and the word meant nothing special to him.

Ryan took a good, long look at their other gear. All of it was strange. Especially the derrick. It was even more massive than it had looked from the ridge top. It was made up of three interlocking sections that, when extended, doubled its overall length. To what purpose he couldn't guess. J.B. had been right, though. There were no signs of wear on the superstructure or of its having been cobbled together out of recycled materials. No acid rain damage, either. Everything gleamed, as if it had been recently swabbed with oil.

If the others had been captured with him, they might have been able to put their heads together and come up with an explanation for all of it. Of course, an explanation wasn't worth the price of their lives. It was far better for his friends that they weren't here, facing an unknown fate. Ryan hoped they were on their way back to Perdition by now. And that once they arrived there, they had plans to put even more miles between themselves and this place.

Up to this point, Ryan could see no opening for

himself, no weakness in the enemy that he could exploit to either gain control of the situation or make good his escape. Thus hobbled, it suited his purposes to be placid and obedient. When it came time for him to make his move, at least he would have surprise on his side. One thing was certain, however. Wherever they intended on taking him, he had no intention of going along quietly.

FROM A DISCREET DISTANCE, knowing that he couldn't see her face through the black tint of her helmet, Captain Nara Jurascik studied their prisoner. Her interest was neither purely scientific nor purely military. The way he looked, the way he moved, fascinated her. It was more than his apparent natural grace and strength. It was his confidence. The confidence born of a lifetime of freedom. Freedom not easily won. Or held.

He had killed other men, of that she was sure. Probably more men than he could remember. And he had taken the lives of women, too. As a combat vet herself, she could see it etched in his blade-scarred face, a familiar road map of violence.

One-eye was a savage, perfectly matched to a savage land.

And perfectly matched to the needs of the mission.

There was so much to learn about this raw and brutal place, its riches and death traps, and such a short time to do it. What better source for this vital information than a true survivor who'd had the singular misfortune of falling into their net?

Nara recalled how sixteenth-century explorers to the New World had returned to the royal courts of Europe with captured native peoples in tow, as living trophies. The financiers of conquest had no interest in the history, culture and social organization of these prisoners. They had only zoo value. The expedition underwriters were obsessed with the acquisition of a single precious metal, easily mined with slave labor, and transportable in wind-powered sailing ships. While their minions grubbed and murdered for gold, the real wealth of the land lay in plain view before them. The wildlife. The trees. The minerals. Pure water and soil. Vast reserves of petroleum. But above all, the space to grow.

With the advantage of six hundred years of history, of countless bitter lessons learned, Nara considered her colonizer ancestors ignorant, shortsighted swine. A proper job of conquest and exploitation, a job in which not a drop of precious resources was wasted, took scientific and military precision. It took high-tech information gathering and rigorous data analysis. It also took an understanding of the psychology of the indigenous population, of the minds the environment had shaped.

What the Shadow man held in his head, the full range of his experience on this world, was absolutely priceless. If his knowledge was shared among the FIVE, it could maximize the return to all concerned and minimize the elapsed time. It could save, literally, billions of human lives. If, on the other hand, his knowledge was hoarded by just one of the FIVE, it would give that competitor an overwhelming advantage in the weeks and months to come.

A chime tone in her helmet snapped her out of her reverie. The countdown timer in the upper-left corner of her visor showed one minute until the gateway reappeared. Fifty-nine seconds. Fifty-eight.

Nara took a last look around, drinking in the brilliant sky, the limitless horizons, the expanse and emptiness, the unspoken promise of Shadow World. Of all that awaited her back on Earth—a hero's welcome, an honorary CEO-ship, an assured spot in history—the only thing that really mattered to her now was the guaranteed return trip.

A second chime alerted her that there were just twenty seconds left.

"Take your positions, now, "Colonel Gabhart said. "Everyone, stand well clear."

The ground began to tremble underfoot, and once again a glittering tornado appeared in the middle of the street.

Chapter Twelve

When the air in the middle of the street began to shimmer, Ryan had already made up his mind to grab the woman and make her his hostage. But as the earth trembled and the shimmer took solid form, a funnel cloud, spinning, flecked with glittering points of light, his resolve slipped away. It was replaced by awe. Even in Deathlands, tornadoes didn't appear out of cloudless skies. And tornadoes didn't grow brighter and brighter, until the light was like a knife point thrust through the center of his eye. He shielded his face as thunder boomed, and the force of the shock wave jolted him back on his heels.

When Ryan lowered his hand he saw the funnel cloud was gone. In its place, in midair, the fabric of space was unzipping. As the slit widened, he choked on an odor, caustic and vile like burning plastic. In the gap he saw something, a gridwork of black pushing forward, out of nowhere. Ryan held his breath and held his ground. The edges of the opening gaped wider and wider, and the grille, bumper and headlights of a massive vehicle appeared. With a roar of its engine, it lunged forward, and as it did, it stretched and split the orifice to a towering height.

Indeed, it was a monster wag, black, dripping with oil. A helmeted figure, the driver, sat behind the gleaming windshield. As the front wheels appeared out of empty space, so did the nose cone of an enormous red-and-white missile, looming high above the cab. It had the word FIVE written on its side.

With another roar of its engine, the huge truck tractor emerged from the opening with one hundred feet of cargo. As the oil-dripping tail fins of the missile and the rear of the truck bed cleared the slit, it slammed shut with another clap of thunder.

The apparition didn't completely disappear, though.

Ryan could still see something hanging there in space, vague, glittering, a spinning mist. He noticed that all the people in black armor were giving the affected area an extremely wide berth.

His first thought about the wag and rocket was that they had to have come through some kind of mat-trans gateway. He and the companions had uncovered the predark whitecoat technology and used it whenever they could to move around Deathlands. It was part of the Totality Concept, an ultrasecret U.S. program to develop weapons for future warfare. One of the research missions under the Totality Concept umbrella, known as Operation Cerberus, involved the transfer of matter, organic and inorganic, from one remote location to another. Another mission had been the time trawling that had brought Doc Tanner forward from the past.

As far as Ryan knew, the matter-transfer process was confined to gateway chambers that were airtight and lined with armaglass. All transfer was along a network of such chambers hidden around the world in fortified, underground redoubts. There sure as blazes wasn't a gateway chamber in the middle of

Moonboy. And even if there was, he'd never seen one big enough to handle a load this size.

The missile had three stages and sat in a specially padded cradle on the truck trailer's bed. And it came with its own loading crane, which was part of the chassis of the truck.

After conferring with the driver, the colonel stepped over to Ryan, untinted his helmet and announced, "It's time for us to make a deal."

"What do you want from me?"

"Just some cooperation. You know things that we want to know."

"And in return I get what?"

"You get to live, and so do your friends."

Ryan had been wondering when the subject would get around to his companions. "The others are long gone by now," he said. "Vanished into that desert out there like a pack of mutie prairie dogs."

The remark made the colonel smile.

"You think that's funny?" Ryan said.

"See the top stage of the rocket?"

It was conical, like the nose of a bullet. Ryan wasn't impressed. "If you brought that thing here to nuke something," he said, "I hate to break it to you, but you're a hundred years too late."

"It's not a nuke," the colonel said. "That's our eye in the sky, friend. Once it's aloft, we'll be able to use it to count the hairs on a prairie dog's butt, if we so desire."

Ryan shrugged. "Whatever gets you through the night."

"But it's not just a spy satellite," the colonel continued. "The onboard laser cannon has an effective range of five hundred miles and can bull's-eye a target the size of a man's head. After it's in orbit, the laser can be remote-fired from anywhere on the planet. Zap! And your hat size is zero."

The colonel paused for this to sink in, then said, "Are you going to cooperate with us?"

When Ryan didn't answer right away, the man said, "Consider what you've already seen our shoulder-fired pulse weapons do, if you think we're bluffing."

"What sort of cooperation are you looking for?"

"You do what we say. Answer our questions. No resistance. No lies."

"Until?"

"Until we decide we're done with you."

"And the alternatives?"

"Actually, there's only one. We foam you now, and crisp your friends as soon the satellite achieves orbit. Take your time and think about it. You've got fifteen seconds."

Ryan didn't have to think about it. Based on what he'd seen, he was pretty sure the colonel could deliver what he had promised. "Just tell me what you want from me, and I'll do it."

"Good," the colonel said. "Nara, here, is going to escort you back through the passageway."

The woman stepped up behind Ryan.

"Through what passageway?" he said.

"Nara will show you."

The blond woman put her gloved hand to the middle of his back and gave him a push in the direction of the spinning mist. It was no gentle shove. She was a lot stronger than she looked. The push from behind lifted the soles of his boots from the ground and sent him flying forward. He should have regained his balance as his body lost speed and his feet landed. But neither of those things happened because he never lost speed. Gripped by the tornado's suction, he flew faster and faster.

Ryan clamped his eye shut as the glittering light flared in his face, then a thunder clap half deafened him. When he opened his eye, he glimpsed a giant, toothless maw, gaping wide. And inside that, blackness.

It swallowed him whole.

Chapter Thirteen

With the boom of thunder still echoing around the ridge top, the truck and its awesome cargo appeared. Through his binocs, it looked to J.B. as if it were driving out of a tunnel—a tunnel that didn't exist.

"By the Three Kennedys! What a conjuring trick!" Doc rumbled.

J.B. lowered the binocs and whispered, "Dark night, Doc, keep it down!"

Looking into Doc's twinkling, unfocused eyes, J.B. got a sinking feeling in the pit of his stomach. He thought for sure the old man's brain had again come unstuck, and he was afraid he was going to start shouting and clapping for an encore. Something that was bound to give away their position. Before J.B. let that happen, he'd coldcock him. He balled up a fist and held it ready by his side. But Tanner dropped the crazy smile and refocused his gaze on J.B.'s angry face.

"My apologies, John Barrymore," Doc whispered contritely. "I was momentarily overwhelmed."

"Yeah, yeah." J.B. turned to Mildred. "It wasn't magic made that rig appear out of thin air. How do you think they did it? Some new kind of mat-trans?"

"Your guess is as good as mine," she said. "Safe bet, though, that whatever the process is, they used

it to bring themselves, the black aircraft and the rest
of that stuff here.''

''What do you make of the missile?''

''I suppose it could be predark,'' she said. ''From
a distance, one missile looks pretty much like another
except for the external markings. The markings on
that one aren't from any military I've ever heard of.
Either it's a century old and been repainted to look
like that, or it's new gear.''

''The wag that's hauling it is definitely new,'' J.B.
said. ''Never saw a design like that, with a crane
attached. It's meant to move nothing but that missile.
I think you might be right about science still being
alive, somewhere around here.''

''At least we've laid to rest the outer space connection,'' Doc said, referring to the clearing of black
helmets they'd witnessed and the heads visible inside. ''Under that Stygian armor, they're as human
as any of us.''

''And they're using some obviously derivative
technology,'' Mildred added.

''Stone chillers'' was Jak's only comment.

He got no debate there. What little was left of the
cannie sniper lay soaking into the dirt of the street.
Nearby, Ryan stood surrounded by black figures.

''We've got to do something to get Dad out of
there before they hurt him,'' Dean said.

J.B. raised the binocs again. He knew the boy was
right. Trouble was, he couldn't think of a single, rad-
blasted way to save him.

The Armorer watched the black figure step behind
his old friend and give him a push toward the middle
of the road where the truck had appeared. Ryan stumbled forward into a hard flash of light. Thunder

boomed, and the one-eyed man slipped into the tunnel that wasn't there.

"Rad-fucking blast," J.B. swore.

"Where'd he go?" Krysty exclaimed. "Ryan just vanished!"

As they watched, the figure in black who'd shoved him disappeared as well, stepping into a slit in the air. There was another boom as the opening slammed shut.

"They've taken him," Mildred said.

"Well, we're going to get him back," Krysty retorted, pushing up from the rocks.

The black woman caught her by the arm. "Wait, Krysty. We've got to think this thing through."

"Ryan's still alive. We're not going to abandon him. He would've never done that to us."

"No one's suggesting anything like that," Mildred assured her. "We need a plan of attack, some kind of strategy if we're going to have any hope of succeeding. What do you say, J.B.? What can we do?"

"Cannies didn't fare too well against them," he reminded her. "I'd say our odds are about the same."

"That's a big help!" Krysty said.

"I'm just trying to be realistic. Problem is, we don't know how to chill these folks."

"Anything that lives can be killed," Krysty said. "It's just a matter of finding a way."

"A way that doesn't get us all chilled first."

"A plan, J.B.," Mildred prodded.

The Armorer sucked in a breath and let it out slow. Then he picked up a stick and started drawing in the dirt. By the time he was done laying it all out for them, the sun was starting to sink into the bank of purple clouds to the west. Beneath the bank of clouds, chain lightning flashed over the high mountaintops. In the eye of the storm, the earth frothed and boiled under an acid rain downpour.

For better or worse, it was time to make their move.

Chapter Fourteen

Ryan awakened to the sound of his own voice screaming, to terrible pain and pressure below his good right eye. He tried to twist away from the hurt, but he couldn't move his arms or legs.

"Leave the rad-blasted eye alone," someone above him growled.

After a second, the horrible pressure lifted. Blinking away tears, Ryan opened his eye and saw a callused thumb with a filthy jagged nail pulling back from his right cheek.

The owner of the thumb, a man with a round face and dirt-caked black stubble of beard, smiled down at him. There was fresh blood smeared on his cracked yellow teeth.

"Leave the eye, so he can watch," the voice said. "We'll eat that for dessert."

Ryan twisted against his bonds, throwing his head back in a vain attempt to locate the speaker. He did see that the room was smoky and low-ceilinged with heavy wooden cross beams. A fire raged in the stone hearth a few feet away. Another look around told Ryan he was lying on a crude wooden table, and that he had no clothes on.

Beneath his bare back, the tabletop was sticky and wet.

It smelled of blood, and worse.

"The trick, you see," the voice continued, "is to keep him alive and conscious right up until the end. Right up to the moment when one of us takes a big bite out of his beating heart."

A murmur of approval stirred in the hazy, over-heated room. There were others along the walls, many others just out of sight. Ryan strained harder against the ropes that held his wrists and ankles, and felt them give a little. At the edge of his vision, tankards of ale were being passed around. Refreshments for the party.

Then a shadowy form leaned over him. The face was upside-down, the silhouetted hair wild and stiff with grease. "I claim the honor of the first taste," said the now familiar voice.

Breath from the grave gusted over Ryan's face, and something slimy and warm splattered his neck—drool, swaying from the upside-down face.

Clenched in a grubby fist, a long knife reflected dancing firelight. Its blade had been sharpened so many times that it had been reduced to a mere sliver of steel.

Ryan slipped his right hand free of the rope and lunged up from the table, grabbing hold of the cannie's wrist before he could strike. The sensation of grasping a solid form lasted only an instant, then it gave way. As if he had seized a rotten fruit held together by the thinnest of skins, the wrist collapsed with a wet pop under his fingertips.

The cannie squealed and jerked back as the severed hand and knife dropped onto Ryan's heaving stomach. Fat worms crawled out of the hand's gooey stump, white, segmented worms with shiny, blind heads. They wriggled excitedly on his skin.

"Get him back down!" the cannie cried.

Before Ryan could get hold of the knife, a dozen cannies rushed in, grabbed him and pinned his shoulders to the tabletop. The cannie wildman loomed over him again. Undaunted by his injury, he picked up his severed hand and, using his bare teeth, unclenched one by one the dead fingers locked around the blade's handle. When the dead claw dropped to the floor, he took hold of the knife in his surviving hand.

"A bit of thigh for starters," he told the others, "a juicy medallion just here, I think...."

Ryan bucked against the weight that held him down. He couldn't escape the knife. He felt a searing pain inside his left leg, but refused to give his torturers the pleasure of hearing him cry out, biting his tongue to keep from screaming. Above him, the leader of the pack chewed noisily and with obvious relish.

"A most agreeable flavor," the cannie announced to his band. "Just a hint of gaminess that is not at all unpleasant."

Ryan didn't want to die spread-eagled on some cannie's buffet table. Summoning all his remaining strength, he threw himself against his captors. It accomplished nothing. With both ankles and a wrist still tied down, there was very little he could do. They waited until he had exhausted himself before they began to feed.

Securely pinned to the tabletop, Ryan felt pressure and pain from all sides as here and there knife points trimmed away select, bite-sized pieces of him. Even so, he wouldn't surrender his dignity. He chomped down on his tongue until his mouth filled with blood.

Over the guttural, lip-smacking sounds of cannies feasting, he could hear the party music start up. Fiddle and squeezebox played a sprightly jig.

As the blades dug deeper and deeper into him, steel scraping bone, Ryan bit off his tongue. After that, there was no way to hold in the agony. He arched his spine, opened his throat and, spewing blood mist to the ceiling, screamed for all he was worth.

The cannies began to clap and stomp their boots.

The ghastly duet had become a trio.

RYAN CAME TO on his hands and knees, retching.

Jump dream, he thought, as a gray-on-gray world spun madly around him. The same thing happened every time they used the mat-trans gateways—the bad nightmares and horrible nausea.

Only this time it was worse.

It felt as if he were vomiting from the soles of his boots. Just when he thought the wrenching spasms were over, the odor of melted plastic made him dry-heave some more.

When he could open his eye, he looked up from the stinking puddle he'd made on the polished concrete floor. A green bulb in a metal cage overhead blinked on and off; it was the brightest light source in the chamber. The woman Nara stood beside him. Inside her black armor, his keeper showed no signs of postjump distress.

"Are you all right?" she asked with concern.

When he nodded that he was, she used a soft towel to wipe at his mouth.

Only then did Ryan realize he was drenched. Not with puke, not with sweat, but with clear oil. It felt like machine oil. It matted his dark curling hair, soaked through his clothes onto his skin. The corded muscles of his bare arms gleamed, as did his chest at the gap at the throat of his shirt.

"Fireblast!" he groaned and tried to take the towel from her.

"No, let me wipe it off," Nara said.

He gave her a questioning look.

"I want to."

Ryan let the woman mop his face and arms. There was nothing she could do about the rest.

"Where did we jump to?" he asked as he rose to his feet.

"You'll find out in a minute," she said. "But before we go any further and things start to get crazy, I want you to know that I'd like to be your friend. You're going to need someone you can count on from here on out. I'm afraid what you've gone through so far is the easy part."

The nature of her request took Ryan by surprise. He didn't know whether to be irritated or amused. "Either I'm your hostage, or I'm not. Which is it?" he said.

"That was in Shadow World," she told him. "Water under the bridge. Now that we're here on Earth, things are different. Much different."

"You're not making any sense."

"I'm called Nara. What's your name?"

"Ryan. Ryan Cawdor."

"Wait here, Ryan. Try to relax if you can. And don't worry, I'll be back."

She walked away from him, heading for a metal catwalk that bridged a gap in the floor's concrete. On the far side of the bridge, Ryan saw a bulkhead door with a small window in it. Behind the window there was more light, and a press of human faces, fighting for a look inside. Nara opened this door and slipped through it. When the door closed, the faces returned to the window and resumed their wide-eyed gawking.

Ryan pointedly turned his back to them and looked around. Definitely not a gateway, he decided. There was no armaglass, and the distant gray walls were covered with gray pipes, hoses and conduit. Because the huge room was too wide for its height, there was a crushing oppressiveness to it. He stood in the center of a large rectangle painted on the concrete floor. A matching rectangle was in the flat, concrete ceiling just overhead, and it made Ryan feel as if he were about to be smashed flat.

He walked to the foot of the catwalk, where the concrete ended, and looked down. The chasm he faced was hundreds of feet deep, maybe even thousands; Ryan couldn't see the bottom. The concrete pad on which he stood was poised above it, a towering platform. He could see that the man-made canyon's walls were covered with more pipe, hose and conduit. Miles and miles of the stuff.

Standing there, looking over the abyss, Ryan had a momentary lapse of confidence. In his heart, he sensed the truth, that home and loved ones were impossibly far away, a distance beyond his comprehension. Perhaps he would never see them again. Perhaps there was no way home. Perhaps he was forever lost. He tasted his own rising panic, as bitter as gall at the back of his throat. With sheer willpower, he forced the torrent of negative thoughts from his mind. He had taken many hazardous journeys to unknown places; he had countless times allowed himself to be deconstructed and hurled forward at the whim of century-old machines; he had faced dangers larger than life, and no matter where he'd ended up, or what enemies awaited, he had always managed to battle through them and find his way home. Ryan vowed to take this strange twist of fate not as tragedy, but as challenge.

The bulkhead door reopened behind him. When he turned, he saw a jam of people in white lab coats on the other side. He recognized Nara in the front of the pack. No longer in black armor, like the others she wore the uniform of a scientist. However, she wore the military insignia of captain on her breast pocket, just above a badge bearing the word FIVE.

Nara didn't step forward. A tall, lanky whitecoat walked through the door, instead, and advanced onto the catwalk. He had a high forehead, thick brown hair and very long legs.

"Mr. Cawdor, my name is Dr. Huth," he said. "I'm in charge here. I want to make your adjustment to these new circumstances as quick and painless as possible."

"I'm all for that."

Huth waved at the door, and it was pulled closed and sealed. They were alone.

"I will take a moment and answer some of your questions now."

"Where is this place?"

Huth smiled. "You started off with a good one," he said. "No simple answer there, I'm afraid. Do you have any scientific training?"

"I thought I was going to be the one asking the questions."

"I have to know how much to explain. Where to start."

"I know a little of predark science."

"By 'predark' do you mean before the apocalypse on your world?"

Ryan nodded.

"Ever hear of something called the Totality Concept?"

Ryan considered whether to admit his knowledge and decided that it didn't matter.

"I've heard of it."

"The time-trawling mission?"

"Yes."

"That's excellent. Then what I'm about to tell you won't come out of the blue. Please feel free to stop me if any part of my explanation isn't clear." After a pause Huth said, "Where we are at this moment is not the Earth you know. It's another Earth."

"There's only one Earth."

"That's what we thought," Huth said, "until we made a freak discovery while experimenting with time-trawling technology. We uncovered the existence of parallel universes, and with that revelation came the possibility of constructing a corridor between your apocalyptic Earth and our own."

"I don't understand."

"It turns out that both your world and ours exist simultaneously in real time and space. In our world there was no nuclear holocaust. No end of civilization, of science, of humanity. Our world lived on, progressed and thrived."

Ryan scratched his chin, but said nothing. For the first time he noticed the cuffs of the man's coat, how frayed they were. A button was missing, too. Curious, if he was the bigwig scientist he claimed to be.

Huth went on, "We believe that our parallel existences were virtually indistinguishable, exact duplicates until the moment of divergence, which we calculate occurred on January 20, 2001. The day of your nuclear holocaust. After that date, our realities—and futures—veered apart."

"Sounds to me like a great big load of bullshit," Ryan said.

"If you have a question, I'd be glad—"

"My question is, why are you bothering to make up this crap?"

"Ryan, if I may call you that, to convince you of the truth of my words, all I have to do is take you out of this chamber. The proof is there. It is absolute. I just want to prepare you for what you will see. To minimize the shock. Believe me, this is not your Earth."

"Not Deathlands, but somewhere else?"

Huth shook his head. "In this place, the Earth you know is the faintest of faint shadows, only visible under the most intense light imaginable."

"I want to talk to your baron."

"Baron?" Huth repeated, momentarily puzzled by the term. Then he smiled. "Oh, I see. After the holocaust your democratic society devolved into feudal associations. I'm sorry, Ryan. We have no such single authority figure here."

"Assuming for the moment that what you say about this place is true, that it isn't Earth, what do you want from Deathlands? Why have you sent your people there?"

"We want to help you recover from the disaster,"

Huth told him. "To use our century of progress to bring light back to your Earth."

Ryan regarded the man skeptically. "All I've seen of your progress is some ugly new ways to chill. We don't need that. We've got plenty of ways to die already."

"What about those ways of dying?" Huth said. "What about disease? We can put an end to that. And radiation sickness? We can decontaminate your environment. Rebuild your cities. Raise your people up from the mud. You have no idea what our science can do." He looked at Ryan's face. "That lost eye of yours, for instance."

"Yeah, what about it?"

"Surely you would prefer to have stereoscopic vision again. I can make you a replacement eye. The process will take about three hours, and another hour to implant and connect the new organ."

"Why would you do any of that? What's in it for you?"

"In a real way, we have a common ancestry and heritage. You are our flesh and blood. Our Lost Tribe. Ryan, think of it like this. If it hadn't been for the holocaust, you would have a double here on our Earth, an identical twin. We can't desert you now that we've found you. Especially now that we know what desperate straits your world is in. We owe it to you to help, so we can rejoin our futures."

Ryan considered the man's offer in light of the fact that the lives of his companions were being held as leverage to force him to cooperate. Coercion and compassion seemed a highly untrustworthy combination, but he really had no choice but to play along. For now.

From the pocket of his lab coat, Huth produced a cutting tool similar to the one Nara had used on him earlier. "Let me take a bit of skin and I can get started on the eye at once."

"So you can really clone me a new one?" Ryan said as he held out his open palm.

"No, not clone," Huth said. "That is a very inefficient and outdated technique. I'm going to use the DNA code from your skin sample to modify all the cells in an already existing eye. When the process is complete, it'll be as much yours as the one you still have."

"Won't the eye's original owner mind my using it?"

"The owner's dead. Donated his body parts to science."

The doctor took his sample and placed it in a vial, then he gave Ryan a sterile pad to stanch the flow of blood from the nick. After he placed the tube in his lab coat's breast pocket, Huth said, "When we leave this chamber, we will move to another facility for a full debriefing and further medical and psychological testing. As I've tried to explain, our world is different from yours. Much more prolific. Perhaps alarmingly so. If it makes you feel uneasy, I can provide you with a drug to make you more comfortable."

"I'm fine," Ryan said.

Huth signaled and the bulkhead door opened. "Follow me, please," he said, then started back across the catwalk.

Ryan caught sight of Nara in the doorway ahead. She smiled, then turned her back to him, and along with a crew of heavily armed and armored nonscientists, apparently sec men, began to push the crowd of whitecoats out of the way.

The windowless hall beyond the door was jam-packed with scientists, all of them cheering, waving their hands, yelling at him. In the frenzy of enthusiasm, their words were a jumble of ecstatic nonsense. Ryan found himself jostled and pushed through a sea of bobbing heads and outstretched arms. The furor combined with the low ceiling to make the quarters feel smotheringly close. The contingent of sec men kept the whitecoats back with batons, plowing through them in wedge formation. Those knocked to the floor by the sec men were unceremoniously kicked and trampled by their excited colleagues, who seized the opportunity to get a little closer to Ryan.

Following the wedge, with Nara on one side and Huth on the other, Ryan was rushed around a corner and into a waiting, open elevator. Half of the sec men remained outside to keep the whitecoats from pushing into the car. Ryan, Nara and Huth moved to the back wall, their protectors crushing in behind them. The interior of the car was gray, like the concrete walls outside, and well-worn. There was even less airspace to the ceiling. As the elevator doors slowly closed, Ryan noticed the grittiness underfoot.

"Better get used to this kind of attention," Nara told him. "You are a celebrity now."

"Don't know that word," Ryan admitted.

"Means you are famous. Important. People will want to know you, to know all about you."

The elevator started to drop.

"Of course we will have to control the flow of information," Huth said, "and the access. In your initial interview you will only speak to a small, select group, representatives drawn from each of the FIVE. Then we will to see to your medical needs."

"FIVE, like your insignia?"

"That's right."

"What does it stand for?"

"Five global conglomerates," Huth said. "After the Big Shakedowns of the nineties, the controlling international economic powers were reduced to just five—as it turned out, the perfect number for efficient management of Earth's resources. The FIVE are linked by treaties to compete peacefully and provide troops to protect mutual interests and defend individual freedom. This reorganization has allowed us to put an end to war."

Ryan looked around the packed car as it plummeted. "Lot of blasters in here for such a peaceful place."

"Your safety is paramount to us. You've seen how excited people get at the sight of you. I assure you their affection is genuine, but we can't take any chances of your being accidentally injured."

Nara nodded in agreement, but there was something behind her eyes, something cloaked, as if Huth were leaving something important unsaid. When she realized that Ryan was reading her expression, or attempting to, she turned her face away.

Ryan noticed that there was no floor indicator above the doors. "Long way down," he said. "No stops in between."

"That's right," Huth said. "This is an express. It will let us out at road level."

Even without stops, the trip took six or seven minutes.

When the car doors finally opened, it was onto a narrow, apparently dead-end corridor that was practically filled with a black war wag. The fit between wag and hall was so tight that entry to the vehicle's red-lit interior had to be made through its rear double doors.

Ryan was directed to one of the small jump seats spaced along the passenger compartment's side walls. The seats were jammed between the wag's girders. Behind them, the walls were a solid mass of gray pipe and wiring conduit. Inside the compartment, the odor of burned plastic was as sharp as a razor. There were no windows, in either the passenger or driver areas, and it soon became clear there were not enough seats to go around. Some of the sec men had to sit on the floor by the rear doors. They were packed shoulder to shoulder, and shoulder to knee with those who'd found seats.

In the front of the vehicle two men sat facing forward in what looked like much more comfortable chairs. Ryan watched as the one on the left pulled on an opaque visor.

He turned to Nara and gestured with a thumb. "What's that for?"

"So the driver can see outside," Nara said. "It connects him via computer to the vehicle's sensory array."

When the sec man on the right donned a visor, too, Ryan said, "Okay, if that one's the wag's driver, then who's the other guy?"

"Weapons system engineer. That whine you hear is the laser battery powering up."

The engine started with more of a baritone rumble. After a moment there was a loud, grating noise.

"Security gates opening," Huth explained, buckling up his cross-shoulder, webbed harness. He indicated that Ryan should do likewise.

After the one-eyed man had strapped in, the driver called out from the front of the wag, "Brace yourselves, everybody. We are go."

He gunned the engine a few times, then the vehicle shot forward. Almost at once something slammed into the right side of the passenger compartment, metal grinding on metal. Despite the safety harness, the impact twisted Ryan half out of his seat. The wag swerved hard left, then accelerated. A halfsecond later there was an even more powerful impact from the rear, which jolted the vehicle ahead sickeningly.

"Just merging into the traffic flow," Huth assured Ryan. "Nothing to worry about."

Outside the hull of the wag, engines roared, sirens wailed, horns bleated, metal plowed into metal. Never in his life had Ryan been caught in this kind of man-made stampede; to him the chaos and tumult was unimaginable. And everything inside the passenger compartment was rattling loose, as if they were hurtling down a washboard road at an insane rate of speed.

Ryan stared across the compartment at the blurred faces of their armed escort, reading the simple brutality in their big, doughy faces. Their body armor looked like what he'd seen Nara and her friends wear in Deathlands, but it was much more abbreviated. The overlapping black plates protected only the most vital areas, chests front and back, the sides of their necks and their groins. They wore gauntlets made of the same material. Their hairy arms were bare to the shoulder, likewise big and doughy. The red glow of the interior light tinted their pale skins pink, and their battle scars an angry crimson. Their helmets had flanges that protected the backs of their necks and their cheekbones. They also wore armored shin guards above their black boots.

Ryan noticed that each of them carried the same model of tribarreled blaster, and at their belts was a short, double-edged knife with what looked like a knuckle-duster grip.

When he glanced up from the blade, Ryan saw that its owner was staring back at him with a vicious smirk on his face. The sec man leaned forward, puckered up and blew him a big juicy kiss.

The sec men who saw it broke out laughing. They were still laughing when Ryan leaned his face close to the kisser, and, looking straight into his eyes, responded with another universal human gesture. He drew his stiffened index finger across his throat from ear to ear.

The laughter died away.

The kisser pulled back with a snarl, but Ryan could see that his Deathlands sign language had had the desired effect. Behind the little pig eyes there was hesitation, and behind that was fear.

Sec men were sec men, he decided, no matter what world they were on.

Time passed, punctuated only by the occasional sideswipe collision. Ryan had no idea how far they'd traveled when the driver shouted something unintelligible at them over his shoulder.

Braking, it turned out, was also an intense experience.

Tires screeched, and Ryan was hurled forward against his seat harness. He smelled burning rubber, then the wag smashed into something on the left side. Whatever it was, it crunched and gave ground. The impact, coupled with locked brakes, put the wag in a squealing, sideways, four-wheel drift that seemed to stretch on and on. After another grazing impact at the wag's rear left corner, the driver got the machine back under control and gradually slowed to a crawl. He turned left, moved the vehicle ahead carefully, then brought it to a full stop.

Ryan heard the gate sound again, this time barely audible over the howl of traffic. The wag moved forward a bit, then the traffic noise shut off as the gate closed behind them. The engine stopped, but no one made a move to get out. There was a lurch and the vehicle started to rise.

"We're in another, bigger elevator," Nara explained. "It will take us to the top level."

Lingering fumes from the wag's exhaust filtered into the compartment. Evidently the hull wasn't airtight. It took so long for the elevator to reach its destination, Ryan figured that had the driver left the engine running, they'd all have turned purple and suffocated.

Shortly after the upward motion ceased, the sec men cracked the wag's rear exit. Between the back bumper and the elevator doors, there was a distance of about two yards. Huth, Nara and Ryan climbed out of the vehicle, but the sec crew remained inside.

"We don't need protection here?" Ryan asked.

"They have their own," Huth said.

When the elevator doors slid back, they revealed wall-to-wall sec men. The situation was similar to what Ryan had faced outside the transport chamber. The hall was low-ceilinged, windowless and lined on both sides with very excited people. Men and women cheered and waved, pressing against the barrier of sec men as they attempted to reach out and touch him. The people at this location wore different uniforms. Dark blue jackets and slacks for the men, the same jackets and short, tight skirts for the women. All of the garments looked threadbare and shabby.

"Who are all these people?" Ryan asked Nara. "They're not wearing white coats."

"Upper-level management," she replied.

The sec men treated the managers with the same courtesy as their counterparts had treated the white-coats. Using batons and armor-clad elbows, they beat back the throng.

To Ryan's right, a sec man's straight-arm sent a tall woman with brown hair flying back into her colleagues. As she slid off them and hit the floor, her long legs spread wide. The woman wore nothing underneath the tattered miniskirt, and she made no attempt to close her thighs. Ryan couldn't help but stop and stare at what was on offer. Before he turned away, she scrambled to her feet and jerked open the lapels of her worn navy-blue blazer, treating Ryan to an even more startling sight.

Under the jacket she wore a flimsy white plastic bib. On the front of the bib was a full-color likeness of a man with a black eye patch, longish dark hair and a dark shadow of beard. Under the photo were the words Hope Lives.

"That's me!" Ryan said in astonishment. How the image had been produced seemed much less important to him than why it had been produced. "What's going on?" he asked Nara.

"Like I said, you're a celebrity now. The first man

from Shadow World. You've stimulated the imagination of everyone who knows about you. You'll be seeing a lot more of this kind of thing as time goes on. Word hasn't gotten out to the general public yet.''

He noticed many others in the hallway were wearing the Hope Lives shirts. Still others had buttons with his likeness on them clipped to their lapels. It gave him an odd feeling to see his own face looking back at him, affixed to the clothes of strangers.

The sec men cleared their access to a doorway, then escorted them through to an anteroom that ended in another door. Huth ushered Ryan into the room beyond. Inside, there was no crush of people. There were no people at all. Ryan could actually see the four walls, which were gray, unfinished concrete. The room wasn't overly large, and it was made to feel even smaller by the size of the conference table that dominated it, and by the low ceiling and lack of windows. The sense of physical oppression that Ryan had felt since his arrival persisted.

As he stepped farther into the room, a video camera mounted near the ceiling panned along with him. Inset on one wall were five big video screens, and under each screen was a plaque with a name on it. Invecta, Mitsuki, Hutton-Byrum-Kobe, Questar, Omnico.

The screens winked on simultaneously. Four men and a woman looked down at him, each from his or her own monitor. They all wore gold blazers and white turtlenecks.

''Good afternoon, Ryan,'' said the man whose screen was marked Hutton-Byrum-Kobe. He had a kindly face and a leonine mane of white hair. ''I hope you don't mind our getting together in this impersonal and disembodied way. But it really isn't necessary that we all meet you in person today. There will be plenty of time for that later. Right now, we want you to take a seat and relax.'' He pointed at the chair at the head of the table.

As Ryan walked in the narrow space between the backs of the chairs and the wall, he saw that there were panels set in the tabletop in front of all the places, including his. He also saw that the table wasn't new. There were scars on its surface and its edges were chipped. The chair he sat in had an odd but not unpleasant covering, pebbled like animal hide only much thicker. The stuffing was leaking out of one of the arms.

''We only have a few initial questions,'' the white-haired man said, ''then we will let the doctors have a look at you.''

It was the woman who addressed him first. Her plaque said Omnico. Of all the screens, hers was the only one that seemed slightly out of focus, as if she were being videoed through gauze. Her collar-length, auburn hair had been ratted into a bubble shape on top of her head, and it flipped up at the ends. Her lips were exceptionally thin, and the expression they wore was impatient.

''Ryan,'' she said, ''on the table in front of you is a video screen. Please look at it. Good. What you see there is a map of our world. Until a century ago, the major features of your Earth and ours looked exactly alike. We would like to know if the nuclear holocaust you suffered has altered the major land masses. We'd also like to know what areas you have visited on your world. Would you please touch the screen with your fingertip on any places you think you recognize.''

There was only one shape that looked at all familiar. Ryan knew the outline because Trader had shown it to him on a predark map. When he touched the shape with his finger, that part of the screen turned red.

"And you call that…?" the Omnico woman prompted.

"Deathlands," he said.

"The former United States of America," Huth added.

"Any others?"

"I've been outside of Deathlands a few times, but I don't know the places on a map. Russia. Amazon. Japan. I didn't go overland or by sea. Too dangerous. Used the mat-trans system, instead. None of these others look familiar to me."

Deathlands suddenly filled the screen.

"Would you please touch the screen where you know there are cities," the woman continued. "We're interested in locating your largest existing cities. Touch the spots where they are first."

Ryan hesitated. If they did have an eye in the sky, they could do all this by themselves, with whitecoat technology. Why were they bothering to ask him? Was it some kind of test?

"Mr. Cawdor?"

Slightly irked, he put his finger on the screen. "D.C.," he said. "Newyork, and here, Norleans."

"How many people in each?" This question came from the man in the screen marked Mitsuki. He had graying hair, clipped short, and the color of his eyes matched the blazer.

"Couldn't say for sure. A few thousands, mebbe."

"Where are most of the people, then?" the man followed up.

"Scattered around. Outposts and barons' villes."

"Is there much commerce between these villes?"

"A little. Only if they're close enough. Travel is almost always by foot. Roads are bad and dangerous. The people are mostly on their own, grow their own food."

"And is there any industry? Manufacturing?" asked the man whose plaque said Invecta. He was gaunt-faced and dour. The hair that remained to him was shaved down to a horseshoe-shaped shadow that wrapped around the back of his head.

"Scavenging, that's what people do," Ryan told him. "Working over the ruins for things they can use."

"What sort of communication is there between these small, isolated villages?" This question came from the last interviewer, a round-faced man with small close-set brown eyes. His screen said Questar.

"Word of mouth, passed by travelers. There's no other way."

The Mitsuki man asked, "And the military organization is based on these barons, this primitive feudal system?"

"There isn't much of what you'd call military organization. Just the sec men hired by the barons. They're the ones who maintain control around villes and in the barons' outlying territories."

"How do they manage this?" the woman said. When Ryan gave her a blank look, she rephrased the question. "What are these sec men armed with?"

"Blasters. Cased-cartridge models, mostly. Some

grens. Mebbe even some light artillery. Sec men also have knives, clubs, fists, boots. Use all of them to keep people scared. That's how they keep everyone in line.''

"What about the people who aren't part of the security force? Do they have projectile weapons?"

"Mostly black-powder guns in the hands of the regular folk. The other kind are worth a lot of jack. And can be trouble to keep. The barons don't like military blasters outside the hands of their sec men."

"No nuclear weapons?" the white-haired man asked.

"There could be some left in the redoubts, but I don't know where they might be or who controls them."

"How do you think the Deathlands nobility would react if more of our people crossed over?" the Mitsuki man asked. "Would they welcome our help?"

Ryan laughed out loud. "You've got the wrong idea there. Nothing noble about the barons. Most of them are snakes on two legs. Slavemasters. Double-crossers. Rapists. If you send more of your folks across, I think they'd do their best to rob them naked, then chill them for sport."

The sound from the screens went dead as the five interviewers conferred among themselves. Ryan watched their lips move and the shifting play of expression on their faces. The golden-eyed Mitsuki man appeared the most animated; the others seemed to be trying to calm him, which took some doing.

To Ryan, the last few questions they'd asked him seemed much more to the point. They required answers that a satellite recon couldn't supply. He wasn't surprised that these people would be interested in Deathlands' defenses, or the lack of same. From what they had seen of his world so far, they had gotten the impression that its inhabitants were hostile, aggressive and generally murderous.

An impression that was right on the money.

When the sound returned, the white-haired man said, "Thank you for talking to us, Ryan. We appreciate your cooperation and truthfulness. And we hope to spend more time with you in the near future."

With that, the screens winked out.

"You did just fine, for a first go," Huth said as Ryan got up from the table. "I think the CEOs were pleased. You've got to understand that we're all feeling around in the dark at this early stage. Once we have our satellite database to refer to, we can ask you much more detailed questions."

"Sounds like you're planning an invasion," Ryan said.

Huth smiled. "You have to forgive our curiosity and eagerness about the world you come from. You probably feel the same way about this place."

"Haven't seen much of it so far," Ryan said. "Is it all indoors?"

"No, I assure you it isn't. We'll head over to the medical complex now, and get you thoroughly checked out."

Six minutes later, Ryan was once again staring into the pink-tinted, scowling face of his pal, the kisser sec man. Once again they were traveling at a high rate of speed on an unseen road. Though he tried to keep track of the turns, it was impossible for Ryan to maintain his bearings. The occasional collisions that sent his head slamming into the seat back didn't help, either. He had no idea what the world outside the wag looked like, and the only way back to Deathlands was lost in a maze of twists and doublebacks.

Nara read the growing concern on his face and misread the cause.

"Don't worry about the medical tests we've scheduled," she told him. "They aren't invasive, and there's no anesthesia. You'll be awake the whole time. We can do everything we need to do with full body scans. We just want to make sure your health is good."

"Ever get to see the sun?" Ryan asked her.

The kisser glared at him as if he were insane.

Nara opened her mouth to answer but before she could get a word out, sirens started to wail. It sounded as if they were reverberating down a long tunnel. And they were so blisteringly loud that Ryan clapped his hands over his ears.

The driver immediately took his foot off the accelerator and feathered the wag's brakes.

The sec men around Ryan removed their helmets and opened the snap flaps of pouches on their combat belts. They moved deliberately, but in no real hurry. Each took out a green canister the size of a soda can, which had a large, translucent, yellow-tinted plastic bag attached to one end and a metal cap on the other. Nara handed him one of the devices. "You put it on like this," she said. She removed the end cap from the canister and pulled the yellow hood over her head. Then she cinched the throat strap tight. "Breathe through the mouthpiece, like this," she told him, "and you'll be fine."

Ryan donned the plastic hood as she had showed him. The mouthpiece tasted like rubber and charcoal, and it took some effort to draw air through it, which created an unpleasant, dry sensation all down his throat. The colored plastic distorted his vision. It made things look wavy, and the tint turned everything inside the wag a sickly orange. Across from him, Kisser had a face like a two-week-old corpse.

"What's this for?" he asked Nara.

"I'll explain everything after the all clear," she told him. "Too hard to talk with hood on. The inside always fogs up."

In the wag's front compartment, the gunner was helping the driver on with his hood as he continued to slow. Ryan felt a tingling sensation on his bare arms and the backs of his hands, like thousands of tiny pinpricks. The sirens were still howling as the wag came to a halt.

Ryan leaned forward for a better look at Kisser, whose head had slumped to one side. The sec man had his eyes shut. With his lips wrapped around the mouthpiece, he was trying to catch a catnap. Whatever was going on, Ryan figured it had to be fairly routine.

Then something crashed into the right side of the wag, snapping him hard against his shoulder restraints. With the screech of metal on metal still ringing in his ears, there came another collision, same place. Then the wag was being forced to the left by a grinding sideways pressure. Up front, the driver gestured wildly for the gunner to do something.

The head-on impact that came next nearly separated Ryan's neck from his shoulders. Battened-down gear sprang loose, filling the inside of the compartment with missiles. A small metal box fell on

Kisser's head, tearing a foot-long rip in the front of his plastic hood.

Eyes wide with shock and panic, the sec man desperately and futilely tried to hold the lips of the tear together.

"Don't breathe!" Huth shouted at him. "Just don't breathe! I'll get another unit!"

Kisser's panicked expression said it was already too late. His face turned purple and his eyes bulged out as he fought to keep from coughing. He lasted no more than a few seconds before his jaws gaped, his throat opened, and in a single horrendous paroxym his insides came flying out his mouth. Hot blood mixed with shredded lung tissue splattered against Ryan's hood and chest.

Other sec men ignored Kisser's final spasms. They frantically unbuckled their safety harnesses and charged their weapons.

Again the wag rocked, this time by a deafening explosion that lifted the vehicle high into the air. The wave of intense heat that slammed them said only one thing to Ryan: thermite.

Chapter Fifteen

One of two things was going to happen, J.B. thought as he crouched behind a heap of concrete chunks. They were either going to get Ryan back, or they were going to piss off the black-armored people in a real big way. He had easily moved into position in the same general area as the sniper, on the south end of Moonboy's main street. No one had fired on him and he'd seen no sign of antipersonnel trip wires.

Down the road, five people in black were hard at work on the missile. They had unscrewed panels along the sides of the nose cone and hooked up cables that connected it to what had to be a launch-control computer across the street. They were getting the white-and-red bird ready to fly.

Where and for what purpose, J.B. didn't have a clue. Furthermore, he didn't care. He knew the target, if there was one, couldn't amount to much. Deathlands had nothing left worth nuking.

In drawing up his spur-of-the-moment attack plan, he had assumed that the black armor that shielded both the people and their aircraft provided an impenetrable defense against blaster slugs. The cannie sniper might have been the lousiest shot this side of the Shens, but Ryan's skill was triple wicked. And he hadn't been able to do any damage to the aircraft. J.B. had reasoned that if the people in black and their black plane couldn't be hurt by blasterfire, perhaps the white rocket could. This unproved weakness was the basis of his strategy. That and the fact that the missile was plenty valuable. A lot more valuable than Ryan.

J.B. figured they could encourage the bastards to make a trade for Ryan by threatening to ventilate the rocket with bullet holes. In the back of his mind he knew he was grasping at straws, but time was running out, and nobody else had come up with anything better.

The key to running a bluff like that was in making sure the enemy believed you were willing to die in order to win. The Trader had taught him that. He'd also taught him that once you got your edge, once you had the enemy rocked back on their heels, you had to push that advantage to the wall, until the bastards were chilled or otherwise knocked out of the fight.

Sometimes going in like a bunch of crazies was the only way to win.

Sometimes it was just suicide.

None of their short-barreled weapons were particularly accurate past one hundred yards. But the missile was big, and they didn't care where they hit it. Before they had split up to take their attack positions, he had told the others, "If they give us any shit after the shooting starts, aim for the bottom stage of the missile. That's where most of the fuel is. Bastards have to think we're ready to blow them back to where they came from."

J.B. had no idea if Ryan was even still alive—and if he *was* alive, if there was any way to bring him safely back from wherever he'd been taken. It occurred to him that perhaps this was already a lost cause, that in the great scheme of things there was some other field of battle that John Barrymore Dix was scheduled to die on.

The Armorer looked around. This battleground was as good as any, he decided. Flat. Dry. Lots of broken cover. Still plenty of daylight left. And the cause? Friendship. Rescue. Revenge. Success was well worth a seat on the last train west, if that was what it came to.

When he had given the others enough time to get into position, he checked his Uzi, drawing back the charging lever just far enough to catch the glint of brass that indicated a live round in the chamber. Then he cleared out his mind and let his anger build.

Rage was good.

He drew a deep breath, cupped his hand to his mouth and shouted over to Main Street.

"Hey!" he cried. "Hey, assholes!"

SHORT OF THE SPRAWLING profusion of Moonboy's shacks and lean-tos, Krysty paused and crouched behind a chunk of sloping cinder-block wall, her Smith & Wesson revolver in her hand. A step or two back, Mildred dropped to one knee, looking for targets over the barrel of her Czech-built .38.

Twenty yards from the outskirts of the ville proper, the unmistakable scent of death hung heavy in the air. Both of the women had toured the aftermath of massacres before.

They shared a look, steeling themselves for what they expected to find.

Krysty broke from cover, running low and quick to the edge of the ramshackle structures. Doors were a luxury here. The residents used sheets of plastic to cover the entrances or did without. Floors, other than tamped dirt, were a rarity. She looked inside a shack. The reek of death was mixed with something else, a smell so sharp that it made Krysty's throat clamp shut.

There was no tangle of bodies on the ground, only a wide brown patch where some liquid had dried on the dirt. Along one wall was a low shelf made of scavenged brick and a narrow piece of sheet metal. On it sat three crudely fashioned straw dolls, a couple of badly chipped enamel pots, a broken piece of yardstick and a tin measuring cup.

Mildred looked over her shoulder, first at the meager belongings, then at the dark patch. "The foam they used on the cannie," she said softly. "They must've used the same thing on these people after they chilled them. To tidy things up."

"Let's go, Mildred," Krysty said as she pushed on, turning down a well-worn path. She wasn't looking for signs of life, but she couldn't even find signs of death, except for the cloying funk in the air and the earth that seemed to be stained on every side.

As she worked her way down the lane that twisted between the deserted shacks, Krysty avoided stepping on the patches. Though her brain told her what Mildred said had to be true, it was hard for her to believe that all the stains had once been people. Hard for her to believe that in death so many had been so easily disposed of. Even though this had been a pure norm ville, even though these townsfolk would have strung her up from the nearest lamp pole if they had been alive, Krysty felt pity for them.

As they approached a firing position that would

give them the entire one-hundred-foot broadside of the missile for a target, Krysty saw something on the path that made her stop short. She dropped to one knee so Mildred could see what lay ahead.

Not all the corpses had been liquefied.

In the middle of the lane was a scatter of chunked body parts. Krysty had never seen such systematic destruction of human beings. She and Mildred counted the boots; it was the only way they could even guess how many people had died there.

Six boots—four large, two small—equalled three people who had been chopped to bits, yet there was no blood to be seen.

"Either these cannies were hacked up someplace else and dumped here, or this is a spot we don't want to spend much time in," Mildred said.

"Mebbe we'd better go around," Krysty agreed.

She took one step off the track and the rattraps snapped. Dirt-colored spheres jumped into the air and started to spin.

Krysty knew what they were. In that split second, she knew.

No.

The negation was more than a thought. Connected instantly, instinctively to her mutie Gaia power source, it was a tangible and awesome force.

Before the laser mines could fire, Krysty's body unleashed a blast wave of pure energy in all directions. It slammed Mildred to the earth and it tipped the spheres out of synchronization. Laser beams discharged according to their program, but they weren't reflected; they shot off into space or sizzled into the ground. Their cat's cradle broken, in less than two seconds the spheres dropped back to earth.

Krysty was so drained by the sudden all-out effort that she could barely breathe. Her skin was on fire, her heart laboring. She staggered back, fighting to maintain her balance, but her legs were failing and darkness was closing in at the edges of her vision. She couldn't let herself pass out. She had to help Mildred get to her feet. They had to fulfill their part of the plan to save Ryan.

But it wasn't to be.

Close to death, she collapsed in a heap beside her friend.

AT THE NORTH END of Moonboy, Doc, Dean and Jak stood side by side behind the cover of a partially collapsed porch. They had their handblasters drawn and faced the aft end of the ballistic missile and the backsides of the four figures in black.

"You realize, lads," Doc said in a near whisper, "that if we do manage to perforate the hide of that vile projectile, the resulting conflagration could consume everything within this canyon's walls. Which would surely buy us all passage on Charon's barge."

Jak and Dean just stared at him.

"Styx, lads, the River of No Return. Across which the son of Erebus ferries every child born of woman. You must've heard of it."

"Sure, Doc," Dean said, humoring him.

The teenager frowned. "No river here. Chill time, Doc. Blaster up."

"What?" Tanner said. "Blaster what?"

"Up." Jak used the ramp sight of his Colt Python to raise the muzzle of the old man's pistol. "Keep blaster up."

"Oh, yes, up. Up. Yes, indeed. You are suggesting

that I hold a particularly high point of aim, considering the precipitous drop that my .44 will take after fifty yards. A loss of not only altitude but of a good deal of penetration power.''

The teen nodded.

''My dear Jak, what a glorious team you and I make,'' Doc said as he took aim well above the missile. ''The incoherent matched with the incomprehensible.''

At the sound of J.B.'s shouted obscenity, Doc, Dean and Jak thumbed back their pistols' hammers and steadied their aims.

As he straight-armed four pounds of blue steel, Doc said, ''Anyway, past a dozen paces I am afraid these tired old eyes of mine will betray me. Even with your sage advice, I shall be blessed if one of my pistol balls comes within a yard of the target at this distance.''

''Shoot straight, Doc,'' Dean said firmly, ''for Dad.''

''Fear not, my boy. I have the goal well in mind. And even if my shots fall wide, you can be sure that nine bellows of this hoary old cannon will add considerably to the general tumult and confusion.''

HIS CHALLENGE ISSUED, J.B. opened fire with the Uzi, raking the street with a short full-auto burst. The slugs raised puffs of dirt all around the standing figures, but landed well away from the missile, as he intended.

He'd gotten their attention.

The black-armored quartet stopped what they were doing and turned toward him.

''We want our man back,'' J.B. shouted as the

clattering echoes faded away. "Give him back to us safe and we'll leave. Otherwise, that missile is going to get shot up real good."

"That would be a big mistake," said a metallic, amplified voice. "We mean you no harm."

J.B. couldn't tell which of the figures was speaking, but it didn't much matter. He didn't intend to get into a debate. The speaker had just told him what he wanted to know, that the rocket was vulnerable to gunshot damage. It was time to push things to the wall.

"You got to the count of ten," he shouted across the rubble field, "or I'm going to write my name along the side of your rocket with blaster slugs. I got a nice long name, too. You'll want to remember it on your trip to hell. It's John Barrymore Dix."

"Mr. Dix," came the response, "your demand is impossible. We can't possibly produce your friend that quickly. You've got to give us time to work out the details."

"How long?" he called back.

"Until daybreak."

The black-armored folk shifted position on the street, not far, but it was the move J.B. had been watching for. It told him they weren't going to deal Ryan for the missile. The question was, could his threat keep them from going for their blasters? There was only one way to find out.

"Ten!" he cried. "Nine! Eight! Seven!"

On the count of five, the black-armored folk dropped the pretense and lunged for their weapons.

"Shit!" J.B. said, rising above the heap of rubble, pinning the Uzi's trigger and spraying the area downrange with a line of 9 mm slugs.

Before he could walk the autofire to the missile, a green light winked at him from downtown Moonboy. In the same instant, a big chunk of concrete on the pile in front of him exploded like a gren. The thunder-crack shock wave made half his face go numb. As he hunkered back down, three more blocks of concrete on the heap blew up, sending rock shrapnel flying.

J.B.'s bluff had been called, and it didn't take a whitecoat to figure he and the others were overmatched. None of them could help Ryan if they were chilled. The only thing left for them to do was retreat. If they still could.

As J.B. turned to run, he felt the wetness sliding down the side of his neck.

Chapter Sixteen

A second thermite explosion rocked the wag. When the vehicle crashed back down, the wheels on Ryan's side dropped to the rims as the roasted tires blew out. Inside the passenger compartment it was pure chaos. Some of the sec men not harnessed in scrambled to regain their feet, while others—those who had broken bones bouncing off the ceiling and walls—writhed and moaned on the floor. Everything in the wag that could burn—wire insulation, plastic pipe, duct tape—was burning. Dense smoke started pouring up from the floorboards between Ryan's feet. He slapped his harness's release buckle.

"Bail, goddammit, or we're all gonna fry!" the driver shouted through his plastic hood. Beside him, the gunner sat slumped, chin resting on his chest, blood pouring from his ears and pooling at the tightly cinched neck of his yellow breather bag.

There would be no return of fire.

Booting the rear doors open, four of the uninjured sec men jumped out with their weapons raised.

"Go! Go!" Nara shouted at Ryan, shoving him hard in the shoulder. She, too, had grabbed up a tribarreled blaster.

Ryan hopped out onto the tarmac and sprinted after the sec men who were deserting the wag. Nara ran right on his heels.

The world outside was bleak, and it was still *inside*. Bathed in hard artificial light, a vast, tunnellike freeway easily fifty lanes wide, stretched out before him. More than half the lanes were blocked by vehicles obviously wrecked, stripped, abandoned. Other wags appeared to be undamaged except for numerous sideswipes, perhaps left by their drivers because they had run out of fuel. The wailing alarm horns had turned this high-speed obstacle course into a parking lot. The operational vehicles, those with drivers, had stopped, too, waiting for the danger to pass; evidently, there was no way to escape from it, whatever it was.

Most of the wags looked nonmilitary. They had transparent windshields and side windows, and no heavy armor plate. Behind their yellow plastic hoods, wide-eyed drivers sucked on green canisters and stared as Ryan ran between the lines of bumper-to-bumper vehicles.

The sec men paused just ahead, beside an occupied civilian wag. Ryan was closing the gap when the front windshield exploded in hard, bright light and the roof peeled back like the lid of a predark can. The shock wave sent the sec men crashing to the deck.

With bits of metal debris screaming past their ears, Ryan and Nara took cover behind a rear bumper. Then something much, much larger swooshed overhead.

Ryan cranked his head around in time to catch the glint of the freeway floodlights off a thin wire suspended in the air. In the same instant, he saw a guy in a yellow bubble and white coat leap from the wag's rear doors. Huth jumped a fraction of a second before the wire-guided rocket burrowed inside the opening.

No one else got out.

With a terrific thunderclap the wag flew apart. Its dismantled side panels clobbered the vehicles on either side. Before Ryan could blink, there were more explosions, a chain reaction of them as one after another, fuel tanks in the parked vehicles blew. Orange balls of gasoline fire blossomed, blackening the freeway's low ceiling, then dying back to envelop wag roofs and driver compartments.

Beyond the burning wreckage, Ryan got a glimpse of Huth's bobbing yellow hood as he raced in the opposite direction. It was easy to disappear among the thousands of stopped cars. Likewise, it was hard to see where the enemy fire was coming from.

Then the ear-splitting siren stopped. After a pause, it was replaced by a long, steady tone.

"That's the all clear," Nara told him. She stripped off her breathing device and discarded it.

Ryan and the sec men crouched ahead of them did the same. Even without the hood, he couldn't see where the attack had come from. "How about a blaster for me?" he said, pointing at the black grip of the spare side arm she had stuffed in her lab coat pocket.

"No, let's move," Nara said.

Sec men didn't need an invitation from her. Some seventy-five feet away, they were already up and running through the maze of parked and destroyed vehicles. Ryan and Nara ran after them.

After the all clear, the operational wags didn't stay parked for long. Drivers peeled their tires to get clear of the free-fire zone. They had no intention of stopping or even slowing for pedestrians in jeopardy.

As Ryan started across a lane of freeway, Nara grabbed him by the arm, jerking him back as a monster truck roared down on them. The long trailer it towed momentarily blocked their escape route and separated them from their supposed protectors.

"Hey! Wait!" Nara yelled at the sec men as the rear of the truck swept by.

Ryan saw them running down the row of dead wags. They didn't slow; they didn't turn.

The air was split by a loud boom.

Backlit by blooming orange fire, the four small figures disintegrated along with a row of ruined vehicles.

With hot shrapnel pelting down all around them, Ryan turned to Nara and snarled, "Give me a fucking blaster."

The blonde put her free hand on her backup side arm, but didn't pull it from her coat pocket. It was a defensive move on her part, to keep him from grabbing it for himself. To drive home her point, she leveled the longblaster's muzzle at his chest.

"Put your weapons down," a deep voice growled from behind them. "We've got you surrounded."

Ryan dropped down and put his cheek to the pavement, looking under the chassis of the wag they were hiding behind. Past the wheels, on the other side, he could see black boots and black-armored shin guards.

"You want to get your ass cooked?" the deep voice said. "I'm not going to ask you again."

Nara carefully set her weapons on the concrete.

"If you'd let me," Ryan told her angrily, "I would have made a fight of it."

"Then I guess we're lucky you're not the one in charge."

"Stand up," came the command, "hands in the air."

Ryan did so; Nara rose beside him.

Leaning on the hoods and over the roofs of vehicles, black ski-masked figures ringed them with blasters. Ryan counted eleven. Though they wore hoods and body armor, he could tell that two of them were women by the size of their bare arms and their general builds. The armor was battle-scarred, mismatched and in some cases incomplete.

Almost at once, a long metal-armored four-by-four vehicle screeched to a stop in front of them. Like the assortment of body armor, it looked as if it had seen plenty of action. It had a wedge of thick, blast-proof glass for a front windshield and rectangular side windows. Two of the hooded men jumped forward and jerked the side doors open.

"Okay, Jurascik. You and Mr. Wonderful get into the van."

The ski-masked speaker was barrel-chested, with huge biceps and forearms. Stun, frag and flash grens dangled from the straps of his combat harness. Along with the grens was a wicked-looking, ten-inch killing dagger, which hung in a ballistic nylon clip sheath just below his shoulder, with the rubber-clad handle pointing down. He carried a beat-up tribarrel, which he used to underscore his request. "In!" he said.

Ryan got a good look at the dark eyes behind the mask. No fear there. No anger, either. They were all business.

A mercenary.

After he and Nara piled into the van, they were

immediately shoved toward the middle bench seat. He slid in first, all the way to the wall, which had a window, but no door. The only doors were at the side and rear of the wag. Three of the masked mercies climbed into the seat behind them; the rest took the seats in front. The wag was moving before the side doors slammed shut.

"How come he knows your name?" Ryan asked Nara as the van rapidly picked up speed.

She didn't respond.

"And what's with this Mr. Wonderful crap?"

Something hard poked him in the back of the head. He half turned. It was the rainbow-discolored flash-hider of a triblaster. "Look up there," said the mercie sitting directly behind him. The hooded man used the weapon to point out a series of widely spaced, eight-by-eight-foot video screens suspended from the concrete ceiling and hanging down over the traffic lanes. Most of the screens were dark and out of service; a few were lit up in full color.

"Eat FIVES, they're Beefie-tastic!" one of them proclaimed. Under the flashing words, a man and woman, naked to the waist, ecstatically munched sandwiches in a love-tangled bed.

"We call them tell-yous," the mercie behind him said "Because they *tell you* what to want."

As the van zoomed past, the laughing couple on the screen pulled the sheet over their heads. The next billboard said All Good News, All the Time. Your 24-hour Joy Source. Channel 128.

"Up ahead," the mercie told him. "That's the one."

The familiar words Hope Lives filled the screen, along with an image of Ryan's face, scanned from what looked like a sec video shot in the whitecoat hallway. As they raced toward the electronic sign, the catchphrase melted away, and was replaced by another: It Won't Be Long.

The mercie behind him gave him another jab in the back of the head. "No fucking lie," he said.

Ryan looked at Nara. "What won't be long?"

"Milk and honey, motherfucker," the mercie answered for her. "Milk and honey."

The driver of the van veered around a mass of wrecked vehicles and continued to cut left across a dozen lanes of traffic, toward an off-ramp on that side.

Ryan felt Nara tense up beside him as the driver exited the freeway. Until this point, she hadn't seemed very concerned about their kidnapping.

"Why are we going this way?" she asked the mercie leader.

"Relax," the man said, "everything's under control."

There were no overhead lights on the one-lane ramp, so the driver hit his high beams. Ahead of them, the ramp circled down in a broad arc. Outside his window, Ryan saw walls of concrete and concrete block, broken only by small, glassless, gun turret-like slits. A look across the van told Ryan it was the same story on the other side of the ramp—sheer gray walls.

They'd made six or seven complete circles when the headlights flashed on red. The walls from ground level to head height had been painted with a band of color. Then came the warning, in two-foot-high white letters, repeated at intervals along the wall: Danger! You Are About to Enter a No-Response

Zone. No Police. No Emergency Services. No Re-entry without Authorization. Energized Lethal Security Systems.

The headlamps caught the cross-hatching of hurricane fence across the road, floor to ceiling, ahead. The driver leaned on his horn without slowing. Reacting to the sound, automatic gates retracted into the walls. The van rushed past them and continued to spiral down, tires squealing.

Ryan counted eight more complete 360s.

With every turn, Nara looked less and less pleased.

The van stopped at the foot of the ramp. Right away, Ryan noticed how much hotter it was, and how the air was heavy and smelled of open fires and burning plastic.

The driver crept forward onto a flat roadway. He kept his high beams on. Seeping down through the haze of smoke, the light from mercury vapor lamps set in the concrete superstructure two stories overhead was yellow and weak. Likewise dimmed were the flashing messages on more of the huge billboards. The gridwork ceiling appeared to be the underside of an identical street directly above.

Ryan stared out at an endless sea of dirty faces. Dressed in rags and plastic bags, the mass of humanity overflowed the sidewalks and spilled into the wide street, which their sheer numbers had reduced to a single, winding lane. Ryan caught glimpses of still, limp forms on the ground at the forefront. Alive or dead, they were thoughtlessly trodden upon and kicked by those standing—there was simply no room to step around. Behind the encircling mob, both sides of the street were lined with concrete building fronts, and there wasn't an inch of space between them.

There were plenty of windows in the otherwise featureless, gray facades, and every window was lit by erratic strobe flashes.

The mercie tour guide saw his puzzled frown and leaned forward. "The winking lights are from the tell-yous inside," he explained. When Ryan's expression didn't change, he added, "Can't get away from them, and you can't turn them off."

The explanation was cut short by a raucous clatter outside. From the windows on either side of the street, conventional weapons fire rained on them. The hail of bullets pelted into the van's armored roof and sides.

"Welcome to Gloomtown," the mercie said over the din.

Through his window, Ryan could see ragged figures dropping from the ricochets and near misses. No one bent to help them.

As the van rolled along, the blasterfire petered out, but didn't entirely stop. Every once in a while another burst of slugs whacked into them.

"What the fuck is this place?" Ryan said to Nara.

"Hell on Earth," she replied.

"For most people, Jurascik," the leader of the mercies said as he turned around in his seat, "this *is* Earth."

Then he addressed Ryan's question. "We're on Thrill Bill Ransom's turf right now. Turned himself into a self-styled warlord, thanks to FIVE's Population Control Service."

"I hate to break the news," Ryan said, "but your population doesn't look all that controlled."

"Yeah, tell me about it. PCS's approach to the problem has always been consistent. That is, scattergun and harebrained. One of their most brilliant ideas was to pass out free projectile-firing guns and ammunition to the underclasses, who were doing most of the baby making. The idea being, since the FIVE troops protecting the CEOs and upper-level managers were immune to lead poisoning, and since the CEOs and upper-level managers were separated from the masses by miles of concrete, the underclasses could only do the world a favor and kill one another.

"Ransom's just one of thousands of Consumer Rebellion vets who jumped on the PCS gun giveaway as an opportunity to set up private armies and carve out their own kingdoms. Below the red line, warlords like Thrill Bill are the only law." He gestured toward the window. "And what's out there stretches on forever."

Ryan had never seen so many people in one place. Or such uniform expressions of despair and defeat.

"High-list gloomers," the merc behind him said. "Dead before their numbers come up."

An explanation that explained nothing.

The van's driver crept around a semitractor trailer stopped in the middle of the available road. The trailer's side and rear doors were open and mobbed by people with outstretched arms. As they passed, Ryan saw a man inside throwing out armfuls of foil-wrapped packets. Painted on the side of trailer were the words: Eat FIVES Fine Foods. Beefie Cheesie. Tater Cheesie.

"Let them eat rock!" the mercie leader pronounced.

A remark that made all the hooded soldiers-for-hire laugh.

When the driver turned again, heading out of the

center of the street and toward the narrow entrance to another ramp, the tension bottled up inside Nara finally exploded. "This isn't the way to the safehouse!" she yelled at the mercie leader. "What the fuck are you trying to pull, Damm?"

"There's been a change in plans," Damm said as he removed his ski mask. His wiry brown hair was shaved to stubble. What had to be a laser scar wrapped around his meaty chin, like a chunk of twisted purple rope.

The other eleven mercies took their masks off, too. All of them, the women included, had buzz cuts. Their eyes had a look that Ryan had seen before, somewhere beyond exhaustion.

"You can't do this," Nara told him. "We had a deal."

"Considering how important Mr. Wonderful is, it seemed like me and my people were getting the short end of the stick. Why should Mitsuki have the only chance to bid on what's in his head? There are four other Globals who deserve an equal shot at the prize."

"How much more do you want?"

"It's not a question of more, Jurascik. It's a question of different. We don't want drugs, money or guns. We want transport."

"Armored personnel carriers?"

"No. Transport. As in, forget FIVE's fucking fixed lottery, we want immediate passage to Shadow World. As in, today. With weapons, a lifetime supply of power packs, full battle kits...and since you're offering, we'll take a pair of APCs, too."

Nara didn't consider the request for more than a second. "I think all that's doable," she snapped

How To Play:

No Risk!

1. With a coin, carefully scratch off the 3 gold areas on your Lucky Carnival Wheel. By doing so you have qualified to receive everything revealed — 2 FREE books and a surprise gift — ABSOLUTELY FREE!

2. Send back this card and you'll receive hot-off-the-press Gold Eagle® books, never before published. These books have a cover price of $4.50 or more each, but they are yours TOTALLY FREE!

3. There's no catch! You're under no obligation to buy anything. We charge nothing — ZERO — for your first shipment. And you don't have to make any minimum number of purchases — not even one!

4. The fact is thousands of readers enjoy receiving books by mail from the Gold Eagle Reader Service™. They enjoy the convenience of home delivery, they like getting the best new novels BEFORE they're available in stores, and they love our discount prices!

5. We hope that after receiving your free books you'll want to remain a subscriber. But the choice is yours — to continue or cancel, anytime at all! So why not take us up on our invitation, with no risk of any kind. You'll be glad you did.

No Cost!

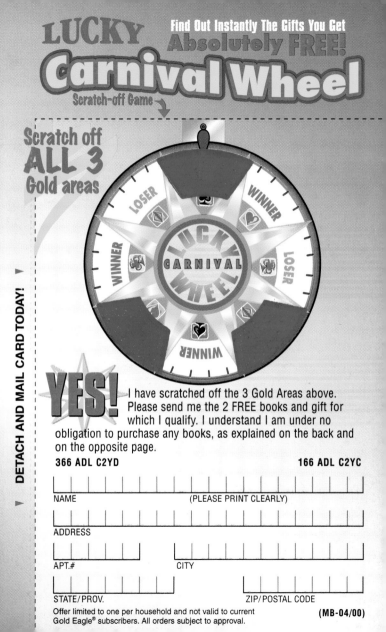

The Gold Eagle Reader Service™ — Here's how it works:

Accepting your 2 free books and gift places you under no obligation to buy anything. You may keep the books and gift and return the shipping statement marked "cancel." If you do not cancel, about a month later we'll send you 6 additional novels and bill you just $26.70* — that's a savings of 15% off the cover price of all 6 books! And there's no extra charge for shipping! You may cancel at any time, but if you choose to continue, every other month we'll send you 6 more books, which you may either purchase at the discount price or return to us and cancel your subscription.

*Terms and prices subject to change without notice. Sales tax applicable in N.Y. Canadian residents will be charged applicable provincial taxes and GST.

If offer card is missing write to: Gold Eagle Reader Service, 3010 Walden Ave., P.O. Box 1867, Buffalo, NY 14240-1867

BUSINESS REPLY MAIL
FIRST-CLASS MAIL   PERMIT NO. 717   BUFFALO, NY

POSTAGE WILL BE PAID BY ADDRESSEE

GOLD EAGLE READER SERVICE
3010 WALDEN AVE
PO BOX 1867
BUFFALO NY 14240-9952

NO POSTAGE
NECESSARY
IF MAILED
IN THE
UNITED STATES

back. "But only if you don't call in the rest of the Globals. You can't play them one against another to get your price. And once the other four find out what's happened, you won't be able to deal with Mitsuki, either. The FIVE will band together and stomp you flat. They'll never allow just one of their member conglomerates to control Ryan. Rather than give up that kind of advantage, they'd prefer to see him dead, his information destroyed and the playing field leveled for all."

The mercie leader rubbed the scar on his chin thoughtfully.

"Damm, stop the van right here," Nara said. "Let me contact my superiors and see what we can work out."

"You can do that once we arrive at our destination. I don't want any surprises from the Mitsuki Tactical Unit."

As the van closed on the ramp entrance, the crowds blocking its path scattered, revealing those who were beyond scattering. Piles of bodies lay on the ground, both around the entrance and some distance down the ramp where they had been tossed.

The driver revved his engine and shifted into four-wheel to plow through the mounds of obstacles. Beyond the mounds, there were no more people, alive or dead, just a long, gray sloping tunnel.

After a few minutes of travel, more red-painted walls appeared in the high beams. This time they were decorated with black and white skulls and crossbones. No security gate blocked their way, just a big sign hanging from the ceiling that warned: Slime Zone 100 Yards.

"You can't take us below condensation level!" Nara protested. "We don't have biohazard suits."

"Relax, Jurascik," Damm said. "We've got an environment already prepared and waiting. As long as we arrive there in under seven minutes, no one will die."

"This is insane."

"Yeah, that's what I'm counting on."

Ahead, a dense white fog filled the tunnel. The driver slowed to a crawl. As he entered the cloud, visibility dropped to zero and the air became so heavy it was difficult for Ryan to breathe. When they emerged on the other side of the fog, the heat and humidity jumped off the scale. As sweat squirted from Ryan's face, he choked on the overwhelming smell of ammonia.

The van's headlamps lit up the end of the ramp below: red walls, gray floor and ceiling turning into a rectangle of pitch-black. As they rolled beyond the foot of the ramp, into a gallery of tremendous width, if not height, the tires made wet, squishing sounds.

The glistening heaps of green-black covered everything.

Bulging masses of it clung to the walls; it hung in colossal drapes from the roof, and between the green on the ground, and the green swaying from the ceiling, airspace was at a premium.

"What is that shit?" Ryan asked.

"It's the only fellow traveler on the planet that we haven't found a way to kill," Damm said.

"It's cyanobacteria, genetically tailored to function in low levels of light," Nara told Ryan. "We've relied on it for food production for a decade, since our other forms of agriculture collapsed. Three years ago, the bacteria got out of control. After it escaped from the processing plants, it spread through all the megacities and we've had to abandon huge areas to it."

"People, too," Damm said. "Sealed them off behind concrete walls trying to stop the spread. Didn't do any good, though. The stuff eventually eats right through concrete. The only thing that kept it from taking over Gloomtown and the CEO level was the condensation layer we passed through back there. Above that, the climate's not optimum for agrobacteria."

Ryan watched a world of green slide by. The van slushed and wallowed through drifts that were four-foot-deep in places. There were no other signs of life. "Pretty deadly, huh?" he said.

"Unprotected out there," Damm said, "you would grow a nice, furry green coat in about half an hour. You would vanish from sight shortly thereafter. Of course you wouldn't notice it because you'd already be long dead. We can breathe the concentrated spores for only a few minutes before lung and heart damage begins. After that, the bacterial reproduction cycle really kicks off. It's pretty hard to suck air with twenty pounds of slime packing each lung."

"After that siren alarm started, a sec man in the first wag coughed his lungs up all over me," Ryan said. "He didn't have anything green in him that I could see."

"Different bug," Damm said. "That was a carniphage. It was developed from a naturally occurring beastie that normally lives in the deep ocean offshore. The species first started showing up in our industrialized salt marshes when I was a kid. Turns out, the carniphage can be either a plant or an animal, depending on the living conditions it finds. It really liked the nitrite pollution from our industrial outflow. Once it was settled in nicely along our coastal shorelines, it started hatching out on a daily basis. And when it hatched out, it killed and ate plants, fish, birds, land animals, everything it came in contact with.

"For a long time, the problem was confined to the Eastern Seaboard. Then the bright boys at PCS decided to make a human population control weapon out of it. They tinkered around with its genetics, and ended up spreading it even further afield. Carniphages are everywhere now. They can't be controlled, so we have to adapt to them."

"And the sirens?" Ryan asked him.

"Only good thing PCS did was to stumble on a way to detect the start of their reproduction cycle. That alert siren goes off whenever cell concentrations reach critical mass. Which is pretty much like clockwork twice a day—it's keyed to the tidal cycle. When the siren sounds, everyone heads for pressurized shelters. Of course, PCS made sure there is never enough shelter space to go around. If you don't get inside, you die. The agrobacteria down here on Slime Level just drown you with their wet weight, but if you suck in a lungful of carniphages, they eat you from the inside out. Takes about a minute to kill you. Then they really get to work. They are busy little fuckers."

Ryan looked at the backs of his hands, which were dotted with tiny red spots.

"That's nothing," Damm assured him. "When they get on the skin surface in low concentrations they can cause rashes and boils, and in some cases, even temporary blindness. All of which goes away in a few hours. Carniphages are really only deadly during the reproductive stage of their life cycle, when there's lots and lots of them. They hatch out, eat, multiply and either die or go dormant, all on their own timetable. The whole thing lasts half an hour, from start to finish.''

"I saw the guys in black armor use something like that in Deathlands, only it ate flesh from the outside in.''

"You must mean the milweapon. Those aren't airborne bacteria. They're held in supersaturated concentrations in a foam suspension.''

The van's high beams caught the outline of something ahead that wasn't all green.

Ryan recognized the rear of a semitrailer, parked in the middle of nowhere. Its silver sides were striped with slimy, wet fronds.

"You've got to be kidding!'' Nara exclaimed. "That's not going to protect us!''

"It's all been taken care of,'' Damm said.

When the driver sounded his horn, the rear double doors of the trailer swung open, revealing a brightly lit interior. The two men waiting inside quickly lowered a metal ramp. The driver turned and reversed the van up and into the trailer.

Ryan and Nara climbed out of the van along with everyone else. The driver and three others donned black plastic boots, rain suits and gauntlets before pulling the protective yellow plastic bags over their heads. Picking up laser rifles, the four of them hopped off the trailer's tailgate.

Ryan got a good look outside before they shut the

doors. Beyond range of the trailer's interior lights, it was blacker than the tenth level of hell out there. The long compartment was lined, floor, ceiling, walls, with an envelope of taped together sheet plastic, which was inflated by air pumps spaced along the floor. After ushering Ryan and Nara to the front of the box, the others completely covered the van with a clear plastic tarp and secured it on the floor with sandbags.

It was even hotter inside the trailer. Through the clear plastic, it looked like the walls were insulated with a silver material.

"The van's contaminated," Nara told the mercie leader. "Covering it over like that's not going to keep the inside of this place—and us—from turning green. And what about the agrobacteria that's seeping in from the outside through the seams in the envelope?"

"You're right," Damm said, "eventually this interior space is going to become a solid mass of slime, but long before that happens we'll be out of here and on our way to Shadow World. In the meantime, don't worry. Pressure from those air pumps should keep most of the spores out. Now, why don't you have a seat and get your thoughts together." He indicated the stack of plastic crates along the trailer wall.

As Ryan and Nara took seats, the mercies started passing around foil packets.

Ryan got three. They were about the size of his palm and warm to the touch. When he opened the one labeled Beefie Cheesie, a puff of steam came out. Even in the ammonia-laced air, the aroma was noticeably sharp and bitter. Inside the foil, a pair of spongy white layers bracketed a densely compacted brown layer. Ryan lifted the edge of the white and discovered a thin coating of orange goo on top of the brown.

"This is supposed to be food?" he said in disbelief. He and Nara were the only ones not eating.

"It's what passes for it nowadays," Damm said as he chewed the round, pale sandwich, "unless you're a CEO."

Nara took the packets away from Ryan and put them on the floor. "If this is what you've been living on, Damm, it explains a lot," she said. "You've got to know better than this."

"A few beefies won't kill us."

"Damm, do you realize you're starting to quote their fucking tell-yous?"

"What is that shit?" Ryan said.

"Stone burger with cheese," Damm said, smacking his lips as he opened a second packet.

"After the collapse of global agriculture," Nara told Ryan, "as a stopgap measure, FIVE tailored bacteria that could turn an inorganic material, in this case rock flour, into a product with some nutritional value. They then reprocessed it to look and taste like familiar foods. It's possible for a person to live on beefie cheesies, but it's not recommended unless you have access to a complete arterial flush. After three days the side effects of some of the component minerals, primarily peridotite and olivine, cause violent mental aberrations and hallucinations."

Damm tossed a small, black plastic object into the woman's lap. "Just make the fucking call, Jurascik," he said, "and don't worry about our state of mind."

Nara stood and walked a few yards away. She pushed a series of illuminated circles on the front of the unit, held it to the side of her face and began to talk in low tones.

Damm said to her back, "Remember, Nara, if we don't get out of here, you don't get out of here."

The blonde moved farther away, so she could speak in privacy.

"This is tough duty for Juracsik," he said to Ryan. "She and Mitsuki had worked out this scheme to steal you away from the other Globals. Now she's got to explain how she royally fucked up."

As Ryan sat there, waiting for a deal to be cut that would either kill him or move him to a different prison, many of the things that he had seen and heard over the past few hours were starting to come together in his head, and the considerable load of bullshit had begun to fall out.

"My value to these Globals of yours is precisely what?" he asked Damm. "Do they really expect me to help them colonize my world?"

"You win the prize!" the mercie said. "Hand our Mr. Wonderful another Tater Cheesie."

Ryan wasn't amused. "I asked you a question. I need a better answer than that."

"Okay, listen close," Damm said, "because I'm only going to run this down once. Ever since the Big Shakedowns, there's been low-level conflict between members of the FIVE. They should never have privatized the fucking military, because all that accomplished in the end was to militarize the entire private sector. Every Global's got its own standing army to police and enforce economic operations. Even though the FIVE divided up the planet between them, made it all nice and legal with treaties, the sparks still fly when they get into each other's business. Bottom line, despite the truce, the agreements, each of the FIVE is fighting like hell to increase its market share. Mitsuki, being low Global on the totem pole, is extra-eager to move up.

"Problem for all of them is, there's nothing left here to divvy. Nothing but people and bacteria. We've poisoned or eaten everything else. Oh, we've still got plenty of rock, but like Jurascik says, you can't live on it for very long without going apeshit. The writing is on the wall for everyone to see: pretty soon the one-celled fuckers are going to win. And one hundred billion humans are going to lose."

It was a number too large for Ryan to comprehend.

"The CEOs on top of the heap spend all their time shuffling data," Damm went on, "trading the last few million containers of product back and forth, moving their cargo ships around the world, trying to make it look like business as usual. Nobody's buying it, though. What they *are* buying is you. The Globals have been planting the seeds for months on the tell-yous. In the past few weeks, they've been promoting the possibility of a mass exodus to a new and virgin world. Today, they stuck that knife-cut, one-eyed mug of yours on the sales package." The mercie grinned wolfishly at him. "Hope Lives, mother-fucker."

When Nara had completed her negotiations, she handed Damm back the comm device. "Mitsuki's agreed to all of it," she said. "They're making arrangements for the transport of you and your people, with the gear you requested."

"Hear that?" Damm shouted to the others. "What'd I tell you! We're getting the hell out of here!"

The mercies sent up a ragged cheer and started slapping one another on the back.

"It should take about two hours to get everything together," Nara said. "How long can we live in here?"

Damm said, "Long enough."

Chapter Seventeen

While Colonel Gabhart ran the software diagnostic on the missile's guidance system, through his helmet visor he continued to monitor the approach of five more Shadow people. Ten minutes had passed since the perimeter's distant sensors had picked up the intruders' presence, and had marked their cautious advance from the foot of the surrounding cliffs to the edge of the sorry little hamlet. Armed with crude, twentieth-century weapons and wearing no protective armor, the little band was hardly a test for his seasoned crew—except, perhaps, of their patience.

Which, under the pressure of the workload, was already starting to grow thin.

Before they could clear the missile and satellite for launch, the integrity of every mechanical and electrical system had to be checked, and every software program had to be error-proofed. There were no small mistakes here, only big ones. A screwup could mean an explosion on liftoff, or an inflight misfire of one of the three rocket stages, either of which would result in the satellite's complete and total destruction.

A catastrophic failure, which would mean delay.

Though the missile could be replaced within hours, its payload was altogether another story. To assemble and test a second satellite could easily take a month, assuming the job could be done at all. Conditions back home were deteriorating at such an accelerating pace that there was no guarantee the necessary technicians would be able to survive long enough to build it. Or if they did, that there would be enough power available to reopen the passage.

The people of Earth had already surrendered much for this cause, enduring hardship and agonizing death. That they had done so willingly showed the depth of their desperation. Pushing the timetable forward even a few days meant that hundreds of millions more would never live long enough make the crossing. Furthermore, a postponement of any kind at this point would most likely spark a global bloodbath, and a bloodbath was something the CEOs of FIVE wanted to avoid at all costs. Not because they gave a damn one way or another how many billions of surplus humans died. They were afraid that the chaos of an all-out revolt might threaten their own escapes.

Gabhart caught himself thinking dark thoughts, wondering if the Global CEOs really intended to bring the multitudes along, or if, after extorting them dry to finance and power the operation, the chief executives wouldn't close and lock the gate behind them.

As a rule, what FIVE extracted from humanity, it never shared in any meaningful way.

Past history aside, it was obvious to the colonel that only a certain number of people were necessary for the success of an Earth colony on Shadow World. If the Globals fulfilled even part of their grandiose promise and brought a tenth of Earth's humanity across, they would be transferring the population time bomb to a new location.

Gabhart had nothing but respect for the way Captain Jurascik had stepped up. She'd volunteered to escort the prisoner back home, even though the chances of her getting another trip to Shadow World were iffy, at best, given the power supply situation and the long list of important wannagos. He wasn't surprised by her action; he'd known for a long time that she was the toughest member of his team. He also knew if anyone could go fang and claw with upper-level management for a ride over and come out on top, it was Nara.

"How much closer are we going to let them get before we do something?" Ockerman said through the helmet-to-helmet comm link.

There was no mistaking the tension that crackled in the young captain's voice. "We'll take a break in a few minutes," Gabhart announced as he cued up the gridwork overlay to check on the intruders' progress. "Then you can—"

Inside his visor, one of the squares on the laser mine grid lit up. The ensuing chain reaction happened too quickly for Gabhart to follow: the four sides of that one grid square ignited the four squares around it, they ignited eight more, which ignited twelve more, and so on, to the periphery of his vision. The brilliance of the sudden flare of light wiped away the grid altogether. The colonel blinked in disbelief as the afterimage danced before his eyes. According to the battlesuit's display, every laser on the west side of the village had fired almost simultaneously, which was flat-out impossible, unless they were being attacked by an overwhelming force. He keyed up an instant replay.

A very disturbing instant replay, as it turned out.

The video showed a cluster of mines jumping up around a pair of Shadow females, then the site was struck by a tremendous blast of energy that overloaded the sensors. The recorded flash was so bright it made Gabhart groan. By the time the screen cleared of the overload, the mines were already lying on the ground. One female was down, the other was falling.

Both were clearly—and surprisingly—intact.

"Did you mark that surge?" Connors said. "EM ran off the fucking scale!"

"Toasted the mines," Ockerman reported. "They are no longer responding to input."

"Neither of those females is carrying a pulse weapon," Hylander said. "So where did that surge come from?"

Then someone shouted an obscenity at them, putting an end to the speculation.

Gabhart turned toward the sound. One hundred yards away, a lone Shadow man popped up from behind a pyramid of concrete rubble and immediately opened fire. The caliber registered on the colonel's visor. Nine millimeter. From a personal-safety standpoint, even more of a ho-hum than the 7.62 mm rifle rounds that had been thrown at them earlier.

The burst of automatic weapon fire kicked up a line of dust puffs between Gabhart and the missile truck. As quickly as it started, the shooting stopped. Six rounds fired. Gabhart looked at the side of the rocket and was relieved to see no evidence of bullet strikes.

Meanwhile the shooter, who wore a brimmed hat and eyeglasses, ducked back behind cover. Out of sight, he shouted his demand. In exchange for the safety of the missile, he wanted the return of the one-eyed man.

Through the helmet comm link came Ockerman's explosion of laughter. "Who does he think we are?" the systems engineer said. "Fucking CEOs? He's got Ice Nine for brains if he thinks we've got the power to make any kind of a trade."

"Maybe we've landed on the Planet of the Dopes?" Connors said.

"There's no way we can arrange a swap," Gabhart said, "but our Shadow friends out there can put the missile or the satellite out of commission with a single, well-placed bullet. When I give the word, kill them if you can, but make sure you drive them off."

The colonel keyed his external speaker and assured the shooter that their mission was peaceful.

The Shadow man responded by issuing his final ultimatum: if they didn't comply he was going to drill the missile with bullets.

"Do you believe the stones on this guy?" Hylander said. "He's asking to get his butt relocated up under his chin."

"Hey, Colonel," Connors said, "tell him the only 'dicks' that are going to do anything memorable around here are ours."

Gabhart did nothing of the kind. He had no intention of provoking a fight just yet. Instead, he told the shooter he needed until dawn to close the deal. Actually, he needed about twenty seconds—the time it took for his people to unobtrusively work their way into position.

The man in the hat didn't go for the stall. In a loud, clear voice he started counting down from ten.

As he broke into a run, the colonel switched over to helmet comm. "Get that fucker!" he growled. "Saw the bastard in two!"

Before he could reach his tribarrel, gunfire pounded the street from two sides. It came head-on at the missile, at 600 rounds per minute, and in widely spaced, single shots from the other end of the street. The hail of bullets sailed all around him. Ricochets skipped off the ground and rattled into the sides of the missile truck.

Cursing, Gabhart swung the laser rifle to his shoulder. As he did so, the autofire stopped, but the aggravatingly slow, single shots persisted at his back. The colonel didn't take the time to hook up the weapon to the optics of his battle suit, but laid the rifle's open sights on the pile of rubble that Hat Man was using for cover and squeezed the front trigger. A petawatt of pure energy turned the moisture trapped inside the material to nuke-heated steam in about a femtosecond. With a solid whack and a big puff of dust, the chunk of concrete exploded.

Hat man had cover, but not for long.

The colonel quickly detonated three more slabs of concrete, forcing the shooter to abandon his hide. The man ran like a bush bunny, very low and very fast across the rubble field. As he zigzagged from one cover to the next, because of the poor shot angle, the colonel was unable to take him out.

Gabhart lowered the weapon and two more single shots boomed from the rear. The bullets made hollow thunks as they struck high on the unprotected side of the missile. When he turned, he saw a pair of dark slashes in the rocket's bottom stage, about six inches apart, just below the thrust ring. There were three other dents as well, clustered above the second stage's stabilizing fins.

As much as he wanted to scream at that moment, he didn't. There was too much to do. He quickly checked the map grid to make sure their attackers were in full retreat, then ordered his people back to inspect the exterior of the missile and its payload for other damage.

With all of them on the job, the survey took less than ten minutes to complete and when it was done, the colonel asked the systems engineer for a damage report. "Give me the good news first," Gabhart told him.

"No worries on the second stage," Ockerman said. "I think we're looking at some minor repairs to the guidance controls, which we can make in a few hours. But I don't like those two rips in the first-stage booster. It's possible we've got something more serious going on inside there. From the position of the damage, we could even have a small breach in the main engine housing."

No one said a word.

They just stared at the twin slashes in the missile's white skin.

An engine breach could mean a fuel leak, and a fuel leak meant disaster.

The door to Shadow World might have just slammed shut.

Gabhart broke the heavy silence. "Okay, let's not panic, just yet," he said. "Let's get the damaged outer panels off the bottom stage and see what we're really looking at."

HER HEAD REELING, Mildred raised herself on an elbow.

The canyon around her reverberated with the sounds of gunfire and explosions. As she tasted her own blood in her mouth, she had no idea what had happened, except that she had been leveled, blindsided, and that Krysty lay unmoving, sprawled across her legs.

The redhead's prehensile hair hung as lank and limp as string. For an instant Mildred thought the woman was dead. With a sinking heart, she squirmed out from under Krysty's weight and checked for a pulse at her throat. It was there, weak and thready. What scared her worse was the state of Krysty's pupils, which were so dilated that her emerald-green eyes looked almost black. She was still alive, but only just.

Mildred quickly examined her for evidence of a wound and found none. Krysty's skin was pale and clammy to the touch; she showed the signs of having suffered an overwhelming traumatic shock.

About the time Mildred finished her exam, the gunfire stopped. She caught a flicker of movement across the rubble field to the north. It was Doc, Dean and Jak, circling away from Moonboy's city center. The attack had been a bust. Time to bag it, girl, she told herself.

After stuffing Krysty's side arm into a pocket of her fatigues, she wrestled the unresisting woman into a fireman's carry.

Though Mildred had a stocky build, with powerful legs, it was a tough job lugging Krysty over broken ground. She hurried as fast as she could after her companions, but she couldn't catch up with them.

She was unwilling to call out for help, for fear of drawing an attack her way. Burdened as she was, she knew she'd make an easy target.

Mildred had carried Krysty across a quarter-mile of ruination when the redhead let out a soft groan. When she continued to complain on every step, it was clear she was coming around. Mildred carefully set her down behind a toppled light post.

"Come on, Krysty, snap out of it," she said, gripping her shoulders in both hands and giving them a shake. "Open your eyes."

When the woman did so, Mildred examined her pupils again and found them nearly back to normal.

"Releasing a big burst of power like that," Krysty said, "made me weak as a kitten."

"It nearly did more to you than that," Mildred replied. "So it was you who walloped me like that? I thought I'd been run down by a truck."

"The lane was mined. Didn't see it until it was too late. I just reacted, I guess. Sorry, Mildred."

"You don't have to apologize for saving my life. We've got to move, now. Can you walk by yourself?"

"I think so."

THEY CAUGHT UP with the others behind a heap of boulders at the foot of the ridge, near the spot where they'd made their descent.

"Until Dean looked back and saw you coming," J.B. told them, "we thought you were dead." He held a bloody handkerchief to the side of his face.

"Nearly were," Krysty said.

"We never even got a shot off," Mildred confessed. "Did you do any damage?"

"Don't know for sure," J.B. answered, as he let Mildred take a look at the slash high on his cheek. "We didn't stick around to tally up the score. But I think we must've hit something vital or they'd already be on top of us."

"Either that," Doc said, as he completed the laborious reloading of his revolver's cylinder, "or our best efforts made no impression on them at all, and they simply cannot be bothered hunting down such insignificant annoyances."

"Well, one thing's for sure. We can't tell beans from down here," J.B. said. "Got to climb back up the ridge if we want to recce. Better hurry up before it gets too dark to see."

By the time they regained the summit and were back in position overlooking the main street, the visibility had dropped in a big way. A world of vibrant color had been reduced to harsh black and shades of gray. By the light of the stars and a three-quarter moon, they could just make out shadowy figures moving in the darkness around the rocket and gantry. The black-armored strangers apparently could do their work by the available light, and they did so in silence.

When J.B. had seen enough, he signaled for a retreat from the edge of the cliff. Back behind the ridge-top pinnacles, with the others gathered around him, he said, "They could just be prepping the missile for launch. No way to tell whether we hit it, or if we did, if we hurt it any."

"Back to square one, then," Mildred said.

"Square zero," J.B. corrected her. "We've got no options left. We just proved that we can't blackmail them into giving us Ryan back. We can't hurt them, but they can chill us whenever the mood strikes. Because they won't give ground down there, we can't force our way close to where that hole appeared and try to go in after Ryan. It doesn't look good for him."

"There's got to be a way," Krysty said. "My Gaia power worked against those bastards' machines. Mebbe I could use it to take them out, too."

"You've already used yourself up," Mildred reminded her. "You try that again, and all you'll succeed in doing is killing yourself. And that won't help Ryan out of the trouble he's in."

From the deep shadows of the canyon below, two engines started up. One, they all recognized. It belonged to the black aircraft.

"We might be on the verge of some trouble, ourselves," J.B. stated.

Chapter Eighteen

Major Oswaldo Lujan slithered over mounded heaps of bacterial slunk, and under the trailing edge of a massive slime curtain that hung suspended from a ceiling lost in pendulous greenery. For Lujan, the oppressive environment and the biohazard battlesuit he wore brought back memories of his early years as a soldier. Not unpleasant memories, either. Though he had been trained for infantry combat in the Slime Zone, he'd never gotten a chance to use the skills. The Consumer Rebellion, which was the only war he had ever served in, had been quashed long before it could move onto this slick horror of a battlefield.

The Slime Zone was a living desert; instead of sand, there was bacteria. Most soldiers couldn't handle the bleakness, the smothering dark and the ever-present threat of death. But Lujan appreciated the quiet and the emptiness, the peace—there was nothing like it left above condensation level. Between the galleries of slime that filled former city streets, with the aid of a suitable, high-intensity light source, a person could see for blocks and blocks, and best of all as far as the major was concerned, not see another single person.

After Lujan crawled into position opposite the rear end of the semi-trailer, he stopped and panned the scene through his helmet visor. The battlesuit's infrared sensor showed four lemon-yellow figures beside the hulking box on wheels. All were wearing rain slickers and boots, and antiphage bubbles. If they had body armor, it wasn't artificially intelligent. All of them carried the laser weapons that Mitsuki had provided.

He unslung his own pulse rifle, which was already umbilicaled to his suit. When he powered up the weapon's optics, the sights and range finder appeared in his visor, and the view behind them shifted as he swung the barrel onto the trailer and lined up the cross wires.

The distance to his targets was seventy-five yards. A piece of cake. One of the joys of sniper work with the tribarrel was that gravity wasn't a complicating factor. Because there was no bullet drop to compensate for, he could have just as easily hit the sentries in the eye from ten times as far away. Lujan picked his kill order, working from left to right.

That done, he turned up the gain on his external microphone, snuggled into the bed of slime and lined up the first shot.

Lujan wasn't by nature a trusting soul. As commander of the Mitsuki Tactical Unit, he had objected strenuously when his Global CEOs told him they were going to turn the abduction of the man from Shadow World over to a band of mercenaries led by a former Marine Corps sergeant. There were good reasons why Lujan himself couldn't be directly involved in the kidnapping. If Mitsuki were linked to the operation, it would bring down the united wrath of the other members of FIVE. But Lujan was convinced that using Damm and his crew was a big mistake, that based on their combat records they couldn't be trusted. Unfortunately, the CEOs didn't see it that way. They saw the insubordination, the failures to obey, the suspicious deaths of some of their commanding officers as the ideal background for members of a ruthless kidnap team—and the perfect cover for their own involvement. At Lujan's insistence, they had authorized him to monitor things from a distance, unofficially, and to take all necessary action if the situation called for it.

When the mercs bypassed the turnoff for their arranged hiding place, the major knew he'd guessed right about them, and that gave him no small sense of satisfaction.

It wasn't clear whether Mitsuki's deep-cover operative, Nara Jurascik, was in on the double cross or not. At this point, she might well be a hostage, too. She didn't interest Lujan, one way or another, because she had NCV—no commercial value. The only life worth anything inside the semitrailer belonged to the Shadow man.

Because he wasn't a trusting soul, weeks earlier Lujan had used all of his connections to get a look at the ultrasecret Shadow World transport manifest. Among other things, it contained a list of names, just fifty thousand in all, which was the nucleus of society that Mitsuki intended relocating to the other Earth. The seeds of humanity's future had been carefully selected by the CEOs. No way would they cross over without their families and their personal support staffs, without scientists and engineers, without serious offensive and defensive capability. Lujan had been deeply relieved, and gratified, to find his own name among the others.

When the mercs made their move in Gloomtown,

departing from the agreed-upon game plan, the major was following them at a discreet distance in one of six metal-tracked armored personnel carriers. Though they were slower than wheeled vehicles, he'd picked the tracked APCs because he thought the chase and skirmish would take place on the wreckage-strewn freeways—the personnel carriers could climb over just about any barrier they encountered. He'd guessed wrong about the freeways, but it still turned out to be a lucky break for his side. Wheeled APCs didn't provide good traction below condensation level. Tracked vehicles worked much better in the slime beds, and they were much quieter.

As Lujan put his finger on the front trigger of his pulse rifle, the six APCs were concealed in the pitch-darkness around him, ringing the semitrailer with laser cannon. He held the cross wires of his sights in the middle of his target's head. The man stood at the left corner of the trailer. Behind him, roughly at the box's middle, was a second merc. The other two sat on the bottom of the ramp angling down from the back of the trailer.

Being a sentry in the Slime Zone with no lights and only an Evac-Bubble for protection was grim duty, Lujan thought, then he squeezed the trigger.

There was no recoil, so he could watch the instantaneous result. He could hear it, too—the wet pop as the protective bubble depressurized and a six-inch bolt of green lightning passed through the man's skull. As the man fell, behind him so did a huge clump of downhanging greenery, which had been severed by the through-and-through.

Behind that clump, another dropped and another. The major tightened down on his second target,

the man at the middle of the trailer, and fired once.
When he heard the pop he was already swinging the
sights to the right. As he did so, he pushed the afterimage of a yellow figure collapsing from his mind.
Before the third man could rise from his seat on the
ramp, Lujan shot him in the forehead. Pop! The
fourth man, confronted, and no doubt animated, by
the sudden deaths of his three comrades, managed to
get to his feet.

The major had intended to make a final head shot,
but couldn't risk it because of the likelihood of another through-and-through that would alert his
quarry. The man's brain lined up almost level with
the floor of the trailer. Lujan dropped his aim five
inches and put the petawatt pulse through the bubble's canister and under the point of his chin. His
spinal cord neatly severed, the sentry buckled and he
slumped to the slime.

Immediately, the major keyed the signal to advance to the rest of his tactical unit. He didn't attempt to stand. One of the things he'd learned in
basic training was that it was dangerous to attempt
any serious fighting on foot in the Slime Zone. Sometimes the green slunk drifted six feet deep. It filled
elevator shafts and stairwells. A wrong step and a
person could sink down and never be seen again. To
move about safely over unmapped terrain, you had
to bring along your own secure walkways.

Behind him, his crew was busy unrolling yard-
wide lanes of ribbed plastic sheeting, first connecting
the ring of APCs, then advancing toward the tractor
trailer.

As Lujan waited for the walkway to unroll past
him, he scanned the trailer with infrared. The box on

wheels leaked light and heat like a lime-green beacon. Based on the slime growth on its roof and sides, he judged it hadn't been parked there for more than half an hour.

The scheme to hole up in the Slime Zone was ingenious; Lujan expected no less from a cunning bastard like Damm. Lucky thing for Mitsuki, the ex-Marine didn't really have the resources to pull off a triple cross. The tactical unit's audio sensors had isolated ten beating hearts inside the trailer. The major doubted very much that they had biohazard battlesuits for everybody inside. That kind of gear was even more strictly controlled than shoulder-fired laser weapons, as it offered a degree of invulnerability to the wearer. And the battlesuits couldn't be worn off-the-rack. Each suit had to be carefully tuned to the user's nervous system and reaction time—the black material was, among other things, a solid-state, microcrystalline computer. If the mercs inside the semi had protection from the hostile environment, it would have to be primitive at best—simple pressurized polymer suits to keep out the spores. Lujan was sure they had no real defense against lasers.

So killing them all wasn't going to present much of a problem.

The hard part was going to be getting the visitor out alive, if possible, which was what Lujan had been ordered to do. If it looked like the one-eyed man was going to escape and fall into the hands of FIVE or one of the other Globals, as a last resort, he was to be terminated with prejudice, and the kidnapping laid at the feet of the dead Damm and his crew, as had been originally planned.

The ideal scenario was a live recovery of the information source, with no one the wiser. With what the one-eyed man held in his mind, Mitsuki could maneuver to acquire the choicest pieces of Shadow World real estate, the richest deposits of natural resources, prime arable land, and even more important, it could gain control of strategic routes that would strangle the efforts of the other Globals.

All of the economic superpowers had paid dearly for the opportunity to move their operations off-world. It had taken most of the Globals' remaining material resources to construct and energize the transfer pathway. In order to finance this last desperate gamble, FIVE had been forced to tell Earth's one hundred billion at least part of the truth about the Totality Concept and its hope for human survival. This pacification was necessary because when the power was diverted from food processing, from water and air purification, millions of people had died—millions who weren't missed by the CEOs and who were replaced in a matter of hours by screaming, hungry newborns. Millions upon millions more had died when, at the peak of the drain, the power grids browned out, and the populace had gone mad. Recent history had taught them to be afraid of the dark. When the lights went out, bad things happened. Whole neighborhoods got walled in, the trapped multitudes were left to starve or to commit suicide by inhaling carniphages.

Lujan suspected that once the transfer of population began, all the gloves would come off. The treaties that held the FIVE together would be broken. A war would ensue on both sides of the reality passageway for control of the human future. No matter who won, one outcome was certain: society on Earth, which had been on the verge of consuming itself for decades, would take the final, irreversible plunge to extinction.

In his visor, the major saw yellow figures slowly unrolling plastic sheeting along both sides the trailer. When that job was complete, the members of his tactical unit used telescoping rods to reach high on the sides of the box and place limpet mines under the slime, on its metal skin. The precisely set charges would blow off the trailer's roof and peel back its walls to the floor.

As the demolition crew hurried back to the cover of their APCs, Lujan unclipped the remote detonator from his breastplate.

Damm would get no warning. Only shock, shock and more shock. Lujan was about to take his opponents from a place of relative safety and light into the deadliest of darks. A few moments of panic would give him the chance to pull the visitor to safety.

He enabled the detonator and put his thumb on the boom button.

Chapter Nineteen

In the glare of the trailer's overhead lights, the taller of the two female mercies hunkered down cross-legged on the floor and, right under Ryan's nose, started to fieldstrip her weapon. He couldn't help but notice the pair of tattoos on her pale wiry forearms. The one on her left arm said Buy or Die! 2034th MLAB. The one on her right, though it wasn't easy to read, said FIVE Forever. Her skin was blurred with furrows of waxy scar tissue; it looked to Ryan as if she had tried to scrape off the green, red and purple design with a serrated knife.

The mercie reached to the rear of the stock and dropped the wide, curving magazine into the palm of her hand. When she set it to one side on the floor, Ryan got a better look at its top. He saw nothing familiar there. No stacked rounds visible. Just a trio of silver stubs sticking up out of an upraised ring, which made him wonder if the thing wasn't a mag, after all.

She detached the entire trigger assembly by pulling a pair of small pins on either side of the pistol grip. After putting this encased unit aside, with a hard half twist she unscrewed the tribarrel and forestock, which also came away as a single unit. The removal of two more pins on the receiver below what appeared to be the fire control indicators allowed her to take off the protective housing that sat atop the buttstock.

Inside were many mysteries.

The female mercie lifted out a foot-long, flat-black cylindrical container that necked down at the end where it joined the barrels. It was connected to and rested upon a nest of thick, insulated cables. When this unit was out of the receiver, and hanging off to one side, it exposed a clear glass or crystalline block that had fibrous material laced all through it. After detaching the block from the interior of the receiver, she set it in her lap and with clips and wires hooked it up to a palm-sized LCD readout. Satisfied by what she saw, she wiped the ends of the crystal with a swab dipped in a tiny vial of some kind of solvent. She was careful not to touch the areas after she'd cleaned them.

Then the mercie snapped the weapon back together even more quickly than she'd stripped it. Her precise, seemingly automatic movements told Ryan she could have repeated the procedure blindfolded.

Damm noted Ryan's interest in the procedure and said, "Nothing like that on your world, huh?"

"Just the ones Nara and her friends brought with them," Ryan said.

"I guess the nuke war sort of put a crimp in your R and D," Damm said. "Don't suppose you could have gotten much farther than the neodymium-glass laser, which is probably fifty generations removed from what we've got now." The merc leader took the rifle from the woman, detached the magazine, and, to Ryan's surprise, handed the weapon over to him.

It was amazingly light and warm to the touch. No

more than three pounds without the magazine, he guessed. He shouldered it and found the fit, cheek to stock, very comfortable. The balance was even better; triple deadly, in fact. Slightly nose heavy, and quick on the point, which was just how Ryan liked his blasters.

He looked down the adjustable leaf rear and bladed ramp front sights. There were no dovetail grooves for a scope mount, which surprised him. He turned the rifle over and found a jeweled nub on the underside of the flash-hider. It faced the same direction as the muzzle. The back side of the little diamond's housing ended in a thin tube that ran along the join of tribarrels, and disappeared into the front end of the buttstock. To Ryan, it looked like part of a laser-targeting device of some kind.

Up close he could tell the dark-blue barrels weren't made of steel, but of some densely layered, polymer fabric set in clear resin. He could see its weave when the light hit the surface just right. He guessed it provided better heat dissipation and longer wear than steel.

"What you've got there is state of the art," Damm said. He pointed at the lump of scar tissue on his chin. "A near miss from a rifle just like that one gave me this beauty mark. Another couple of inches and it would have taken off my head."

"Why two triggers and three barrels?" Ryan asked.

"Front trigger is for single shots," Damm told him, "the back one is for bursts and sustained fire—controlled by those selector switches on the side of the receiver."

Ryan checked out the switches. One of them

pointed to the white letter *S*. It could also point to the red letter *F*. He figured it had to be the safety. The other switch determined the pulse length.

"The tribarrel configuration focuses individual laser beams a few micromillis apart on the target," Damm went on. "Get a kind of harmonic chain-saw effect that way. Big-time atomic disruption, which magnifies the temperatures at the point of impact, and the beams' cutting power by a factor of a hundred thousand or so. You've got to make sure of your background when you touch off one of these. The pulses can travel a long, long way before their energy's used up."

Looking at the blaster, Ryan couldn't help but ask himself why Damm was telling him all this. Because he was bored? Perhaps. Because he felt they were on the same wavelength? Fellow outsiders, freebooters, soldiers for hire? Less likely, but could be. Or was it because it didn't matter a piddling rad-blast *what* he showed him? Ryan decided that had to be it. With what lay outside the trailer, Damm knew that he wouldn't grab one of the rifles and try to escape. There was nowhere for him to run.

He shouldered the pulse rifle again. It made him think about J.B. and how much he'd love getting his hands on something like this, which made him wonder for the hundredth time if his companions had made it to safety, and if he was ever going to see them again. One thing he was pretty sure of—they wouldn't be coming over here to rescue him. He had to assume he was on his own. And whenever the opportunity to get away appeared, if it appeared, he had to be prepared to make the most of it. In the meantime, he had to soak up the information he needed to get back to Deathlands. For starters that meant learning how to operate the strange weapon he was holding.

He glanced up at Damm, who smiled at him.

There was nothing sneaky in back of the eyes.

No bastard-evil intentions hidden behind a grinning mask.

Ryan knew he'd probably have to chill the scar-faced mercie, and possibly Nara, too, if he wanted to escape. He didn't have a problem with that, but there was nothing personal in it.

Ryan smiled back. He decided to keep asking questions until the mercie stopped answering them. "How many shots is that mag good for?"

"You mean the power cell," Damm said. "It'll fire continuously, sustained beam, for fifteen minutes without a replacement. That's a lot of single shots and bursts, by the way."

Then the merc held his hand out. The meaning was obvious.

Ryan gave the rifle back to him.

Damm passed it and the power cell back to the woman merc, then he said, "As I understand the early reports, you've got no standing armies worth shit on the other side, no operational aircraft, no laser-proof fortifications. Bombed yourselves back into the Stone Age, more or less."

"More or less."

Damm looked mighty pleased. "Then it should be no sweat for fourteen combat vets and a couple of APCs to take over a nice chunk of your world," he said. He turned to Jurascik and said, "Nothing over here to hold a candle to us. Just like old times, Nara.

What do you say? We could easily make it fifteen vets."

From her seat beside Ryan on the crates, the blonde shrugged.

"At least think about it, Captain. The smart move would be for you to put in with us. You might as well act like you were part of the triple cross all along. It's the only way you're ever going to get a return trip to Shadow World, now. If you think Mitsuki's going to reward you after this, you're kidding yourself. Even if everything works out and they get Mr. Wonderful back, they don't reward screwups. They fry screwups."

"That's already occurred to me, Damm. And I've been meaning to thank you for getting me killed, you greedy fucking asshole."

"Hey, I'm just trying to take care of my own crew," he countered. "It's a safe bet nobody else will. Would you have done it any different if you'd been in my shoes?"

"Yeah, I'd have found a hideout that smelled better," she said. "Under the plastic, there's green shit all over the sides of your van. I've been passing the time watching it grow."

Ryan saw the creeping spread of bacteria on the van's tires, wheel wells, the places where it had splattered up during their passage.

"As long as we can keep it off the engine's air intakes, it doesn't matter," Damm said. "It isn't growing inside the passenger compartment yet."

"What is this Consumer War you're always talking about?" Ryan said.

"Rebellion," Nara said. "We don't dignify the campaign by calling it a war."

"Why's that?"

"The term 'war' implies two sides of roughly comparable strength," Nara said. "Maybe even some kind of code of conduct."

"The trouble started not long after the Globals linked up to form FIVE," Damm told him. "They decided they weren't getting the max return out of their marketing programs, that relying solely on advertising pressure from the tell-yous was a big mistake. So they dropped the Mr. Nice Guy routine. They started setting quotas and telling people exactly what they had to consume, when and how much. Of course, that was back when there were still things to buy, even if it was mostly crap.

"You bought your assigned quota of goods and services, based on a percentage of your annual income, or you got a visit from the Bureau of Resource Allocation's termination squad. Usually the t-squad came in the middle of the night, executed the offender on the spot and, for good measure, took out everyone else in the residence. The purchase quota kept getting pushed higher and higher, until it was around ninety-eight percent of gross income. Essentially all consumer spending is at discretion of FIVE, depending on what surpluses they had and what stuff they want to move. People finally got fed up."

"Everyone was hit hard by the policy," Nara said. "When the revolt started, it had all the makings of a worldwide revolution. Unfortunately for the consumer side, they didn't have battlesuits or pulse rifles. And there was no army to protect their interests. The military had already been privatized for twenty years. The armed forces subsidiaries were wholly owned by the Globals. After a couple of weeks of one-sided slaughter, keeping two percent of what you earned sounded pretty good to just about everybody.''

"Losses to the consumer side in that time period were twenty-eight million," Damm said. "And it was actually probably triple that because no one ever counted the people walled up in their neighborhoods and left to starve. Our side lost a few hundred thousand, mostly due to accidents unrelated to combat, and to friendly fire—'' again, he pointed to his chin ''—which also gave me this puppy.''

"Some factions at FIVE wanted to keep the war rolling for another month or two," Nara said, "to try to make a real dent in the population, but the foot soldiers got sick of the killing and put down their weapons.''

"In return for our services," Damm said, "and in exchange for our battlesuits, we received two weeks' worth of MREs, a new set of fatigues, one pair of resoled boots and this handsome campaign ribbon.'' He flicked the dirty bit of multicolored silk pinned to the strap of his battle harness. "Then we were told to go below Level 100 and stay there. Until something nasty and dangerous like this needed doing. Something the Globals didn't want to get back-splashed on them.''

Ryan shifted his seat on the hard crate. Sweat was sticking his fatigues to the backs of his thighs. There wasn't much room to move in the trailer, not with seven people, all their gear, and a parked van. And Nara was right about the ungodly stink inside their plastic envelope. The aroma of unwashed human bodies mixed with ammonia and fuel fumes. Uncomfortable. Cramped. Overcrowded. The trailer was like the mercies' world in miniature. Ryan could sympathize with their desire to get out.

Then, over the continuous noise of the air pump, there was a soft thunk high on the trailer wall.

Damm didn't have to tell everyone to shut up. Someone quickly turned off the air pump.

Another thunk, this time on the other side of the box.

Damm's crew moved as if they had rehearsed the drill a thousand times. Without a word, they stripped the plastic sheeting from the van, picked up their weapons and, pushing Ryan and Nara ahead of them, climbed through the vehicle's rear doors. Damm remained outside for a few seconds, bent over the plastic crates along the wall, then he climbed into the van.

The mercie leader paused beside Nara and showed her the two detonators he had in his hand.

"Can I assume you're with us now?" Damm asked.

"No choice," the blonde replied. "It's 'Buy or Die' time."

Damm gave her one of the detonators. "Hit it on the count of five, after mine goes," he told her. As he moved forward to the driver's seat, he said, "Everybody batten down. This ride could get a tad rough."

He hit the high beams, then the ignition button. As the van's engine roared to life, Damm dropped it into gear, stomped the gas pedal flat and pressed the detonator.

With a blinding flash and rocking boom, the trailer's rear doors blew off their hinges. The van shot forward, lurching through the fireball and down the ramp.

As they hit the ground, Ryan got a glimpse of the APCs ringing them. For an awful instant he thought they were going to take crossing lanes of fire, but Damm was too fast. Before the APCs could shoot, he squirted the van, engine howling, through their perimeter.

Beside Ryan, Nara stopped counting under her breath and pressed the detonator with both thumbs.

A fraction of a second later they were slammed from behind by a concussion so awesome that it made Ryan lose consciousness. The moment of relative peace was short-lived. He was jarred awake again as the blast-lifted rear end of the van crashed back to the ground and the impact drove his stomach into his throat.

Ahead of them, sheared by the power of the blast, uncountable tons of hanging slime dropped from the ceiling. Damm swerved around the newly made hills of wet slunk and ground his way through the intervening valleys. All four wheels spinning, the van threw up a rooster tail of green bacterial slime that splattered over the back windows. Behind them, the enemy APCs vanished in darkness.

Even so, Damm didn't back off on the speed. He drove like a maniac, forcing the van on an erratic, yawing, churning course around and over the obstacles. Though they had escaped the death trap, there were no cheers from the mercies.

Ryan thought this was strange. Then all became clear.

A green lance as thick as a man's body slashed past the right side of the van. If the light was blinding, the heat was worse. In a fraction of an instant, it blistered and bubbled the armored window glass. It turned the van's metal wall to liquid. One of the mercies sitting ahead of Ryan let out a shrill scream, and kept on screaming.

Ryan looked over the seat back and saw the guy was stuck to the wall. His shoulder had been leaning against it; his flesh and bone had melted along with—and into—the glass and steel.

Before the pursuit could fire again, Damm cut the wheel hard over and sent the van in a wild, sideways skid.

Chapter Twenty

Satisfied with the main rotor's rpm, Captain Ockerman released the skid clamps. As the gyroplane
jumped off the trailer and into the night sky, he addressed the passenger sitting in the contour chair directly behind him. "We're out of here, Pedro," he
said through the helmet comm.

"Oh, baby." Hylander groaned at the rapid ascent.

Ockerman smiled at the pull—a sudden three g's
of gravity squashing his backside into the seat. Yeah,
yeah, it was *good*.

In the cargo pouch at the waist of his battlesuit,
the FIVE systems engineer carried a tiny memento—
a single, flattened .44-caliber lead ball.

He had pried the crude projectile from deep inside
the first stage of the missile. After penetrating the
exterior skin, the bullet had plowed through a nest
of control cables and smashed one of the guidance
servos, coming to rest harmlessly against the outer
housing of the main engine. Fortunately, there were
double and triple backups of all critical systems, so
even though they'd lost a servo, no serious damage
had been done. The control cables were easily and
quickly respliced. It had taken more time and effort
to fill and smooth out the damage to the exterior
panels, which had the potential for causing dangerous
air friction and fatal drag at escape velocities.

The whole repair process, from start to finish, had wasted just forty minutes. With the missile now safely transferred by crane onto its gantry, only two technicians were required to monitor the remaining diagnostics, which were all automated. The colonel, in his infinite mercy, had decided to let his systems engineer, his biologist and his geologist all take a little recess, while he completed the prelaunch work with Bennett, the lieutenant who'd driven the missile across from Earth. In another four hours, they'd have the missile fully prepped and in countdown mode. Liftoff was scheduled to take place a little after dawn the following day.

Because they couldn't risk another attack and perhaps some more serious damage to the launch vehicle, once the repairs were finished Gabhart had given Ockerman, Hylander and Connors the green light to hunt down and eliminate the potential threat.

It was an assignment that warmed the cockles of Ockerman's heart.

He took the airship up to three hundred feet and banked a turn for the canyon mouth; once there, he swung 180 degrees and hovered. The anonymous village spread out below him was tinted in various unnatural shades of green, blue, orange and yellow, depending on the relative intensity of radiant heat.

"There goes Connors," Hylander said. "Man, is he honking!"

Ockerman's infrared sensor displayed a yellow Captain Connors driving a green ATV out of town at high speed. Like Ockerman, Connors ran without lights, relying on his battlesuit's simulations to find his way through the dark.

After adjusting the parameters of his visor's infrared scan, Ockerman cranked up the magnification to ten power and zoomed in on the ground. The gyroplane's forward-looking sensor could detect temperature differentials on the soil surface of less than one-one hundredth of a degree. Variations that slight were meaningless without a computer search for specific patterns of difference, patterns that could be expected to be left behind when six people were running for their lives.

Finding their footprints was almost too easy.

Even after more than half an hour, there was enough of an elevated heat signature for the system to isolate them. Ockerman located one set of tracks and followed it until it joined three others. At the base of the cliff, the four sets of prints were joined by another two.

"Connors," he said through the helmet-to-helmet comm link, "I have all of our targets heading up the south side of the ridge, about half a mile from the canyon entrance."

"Got any direct visual on them?" Connors asked. "If so, you'd better feed it to me."

Ockerman magnified his view field even further, holding the gyroplane steady as he scanned a greenish-blue landscape of craggy pinnacles. After a minute or so he said, "Pedro, I got nothing. What about you?"

"I can't see them," Hylander said, "but I can see the chute they climbed to reach the summit."

"Yeah, I mark that, too. Are you getting the video feed, Connors?"

"Roger that. I'll drive around to the other side of the ridge and cut off their retreat. From the map sim, it's going to take me a while, though. Maybe fifteen minutes, depending on the terrain I have to cross."

"No worries," Ockerman said. "In the meantime, we'll try to locate them and give you their exact bearings. I'll wait until you're in position before I make my first run." With that, Ockerman signed off.

The systems engineer tensed his lower back and his right biceps simultaneously. The gyroplane responded with a gut-wrenching, five-g loop.

Taken completely by surprise, his passenger could only moan.

As much as Ockerman enjoyed developing the complex artificial intelligences used in military weaponry, he liked the no-limits, hands-on stuff even better.

This dog loved to hunt.

Under a three-quarter moon, with the airship's sensory enhancements, its complement of lethal weaponry, its speed and maneuverability, there was no doubt about it. He was Shadow World's ultimate predator.

If the opportunity came his way, he had no intention of sharing the action with Connors.

"Ockerman, you're killing me back here," Hylander complained after he found his voice.

"Toughen up, Pedro. This is the AirCav."

"If you make me puke inside my suit…"

"What a fucking Grandma!"

"Let's just find the bastards and get the job done."

"Yeah, but with style." Ockerman gave his body a little twitch. The assault gyro juked upward as if about to pull another balls-to-the-wall, overhead 360. Ockerman didn't complete the maneuver; he didn't have to. The juke was enough to wring another highly satisfying groan out of Hylander.

The mission they were on was twofold—to preemptively stop the Shadow people from making another hit on the missile, and to recover as many live subjects as possible for Hylander's tissue studies. Part of the biologist's mission was to evaluate the health danger the indigenous population presented to migrants from Earth. FIVE's CEOs were concerned that the natives could be carrying infectious diseases that newcomers had no defenses against. It was conceivable that in order to make Shadow World safe for colonization, military units were going to have to isolate the existing human population in internment camps, or simply exterminate them.

Either way, it was a job for the AirCav, Ockerman thought.

In the back of the systems engineer's mind, he knew that no matter how Hylander preferred his test subjects, it was up to the man in the command seat whether the prey got captured or killed. Colonel Gabhart and Hylander could monitor what he was doing in the air, even see what he was seeing through his visor, but they couldn't remote-pilot the ship, or keep him from using its laser cannons, if the mood struck.

Ockerman's mood at that moment was for a wipeout.

A total fucking wipeout.

Hanging at summit height, he turned on the airship's laser-guided microphones, which provided pinpoint audio surveillance. Within a narrow field of search, he scanned for the rattle of gear, for footfalls, for coughs. As he listened, he realized that he was holding his breath, even though that wasn't necessary.

"Hey, Ockerman!" Colonel Gabhart said through the comm link, "I hope you're not contracting wood on us up there. Your blood pressure is flying higher than you are. You'd better start breathing through your nose, or you're going to blow an artery."

"Roger, that, Colonel."

Ockerman shut down the air-to-ground comm link, let out a howl and turned another five-g aerial somersault. After that, he had to briefly shut off his link with Hylander as well. The yelling hurt his ears.

It had been a long time since Ockerman had flown in an actual combat situation, and the action he'd seen had been very limited. Most of the fighting in the Consumer Rebellion had taken place inside the megalopolises, street to street, building to building. Assault gyros couldn't operate at their full potential in the enclosed, high-density, ultraurban environment. Shadow World, on the other hand, was made to order for them. It had wide-open spaces. No flight ceiling. No ground-to-air missiles.

A bell tone sounded in his helmet, indicating the computer had completed its search pattern without scoring a hit. He opened the comm link to his passenger; Hylander had settled into a sullen silence. Ockerman shifted the gyro's position to take in a new section of ridge. The onboard computer did the rest of the work, precisely aiming the laser mike within the assigned grid.

The sensor picked up a brief clatter of sliding rock.

Ockerman zoomed in with the infrared on the identified area. Everything was greenish blue. There were no halos of yellow behind the outcrops, outlines of humans in hiding. No sign of animals, either. He decided it had been a natural event, caused by the erosion of the bedrock.

The bell tone chimed. Search pattern complete.

Ockerman turned the airship another ten degrees of arc and resumed the scan. Almost at once, the laser mike picked up a human voice at a decibel level that was no more than a whisper.

The voice gasped, "Oh, shit."

"Famous last words," Ockerman said.

J.B. FELT AS IF HE WERE staring down a mutie mountain lion or grizz as one hundred yards away, a black specter hovered against the backdrop of stars. Even at that distance, its propeller blades were going whup-whup-whup inside his chest.

If he could see the plane, he knew it could see him.

A machine like that had to have a whole lot of technology that could search out people. Since blasterfire seemed to have no effect on the craft, there was no point in wasting it.

They had one hope of surviving the next few hours, and it was slim, at best. What they needed was hardened shelter, someplace that would stand up to the laser cannons. But finding it in the dismal halflight with the aircraft in pursuit was going to be difficult.

Turning his back to the machine, he spoke softly to the companions, "Retreat. One file. Tight. I'm point."

Assuming they'd already been spotted, there was nothing to be gained by a stealthy exit. J.B. burst from behind the outcrop and charged full tilt, boots thudding across a stretch of open ground. He ducked between the ridge's tall spires and kept on going. At his back he heard the grunts and curses from the others as they fought to keep up. Despite their best effort, they were slow-moving targets, and their escape route was entirely predictable, dictated by the impassable spires of rock.

Over the sounds of their desperate retreat, J.B. could hear and feel the propellers' insistent beat. The aircraft hung behind and above him, watching, waiting, perhaps fine-tuning its elevation and angle to take the perfect chill shot. J.B. expected to die before he reached the top of the chute on the other side of the ridge.

No shot came.

He paused for breath at the drop-off. Over his shoulder he saw that the aircraft hadn't advanced. The pilot was toying with them.

On the plain in the distance below, moonlight turned mud lakes silver, and clouds of steam rose into the night sky, carrying with them the smell of hot sulfur. J.B. looked over the edge. Thanks to the dim light, the drop didn't seem so bad. Of course, it didn't matter how it looked. They had to make the jump, anyway.

Suddenly, the sound of the aircraft changed. When the Armorer looked back, it was no longer there. The prop noise faded as the now-invisible ship swung away from them, circling and then crossing the ridge to the west. Once the aircraft cleared the ridge, it arced back in their direction.

More head games, J.B. thought.

"He's going to nail us when we're in the chute,"

he told the others. "We've got to hit the ground running."

J.B. screwed his hat as far down on his head as it would go, then hurled himself over the edge. As he flailed his legs to keep his balance, the wind rushed up at his face, ripping at his glasses, screaming past his ears. He hit the ground all right, but not running. As he landed on the soles of his feet, his knees caved in from the force of the impact, and his butt smashed down on the gravel in the chute.

He shook it off as best he could. There was no time to really pull himself together. He had to get out of the way or be crushed by the others jumping after him. As J.B. shoulder-rolled down the slope, he felt the whoosh and heard the grunt Mildred made as she crashed to the ground. Then he was up and running. He couldn't wait to make sure everyone else made it down because that would have blocked the escape route.

After three or four strides, his run became a slide, and his slide was on the verge of becoming another fall. He jammed the buttstock of the M-4000 into the loose rock, using it as a rudder to control his wild descent.

At the bottom of the chute, the grade flattened and J.B. came to a skidding stop. Mildred bumped into him a moment later, followed by Jak, Dean, Krysty and Doc. The experience had turned the old man a whiter shade of pale. Eyes tightly shut, Doc kept shaking his head and mumbling to himself. It was a miracle that no one had broken an ankle.

Barely breathing, they listened, straining to screen out the rumble of volcanic lakes and hissing steam vents. Overhead, now lost in the dark, the rhythmic beating of the aircraft came at them from the south.

"Let's move," J.B. urged.

Because he had no choice, he led them through an obstacle course of boiling hot springs, over ground he knew had to be undermined. They ran on a thin crust of earth that could give way under their combined weight, plunging them to a terrible death by scalding.

"Don't break. Don't break. Don't break," he muttered with every running stride.

They reached and rounded the muddy shore of an infernal lake, and as they raced on, they kicked through a scatter of shattered bones, pelvic girdles, ribs, vertebrae. There were paw prints, as well. Lots of them, jumbled and pressed deep into the muck. The heat along the shore was so intense that the sweat dripping off J.B.'s face, off his chest, and pouring down the middle of his back had no cooling effect. He felt as if his clothes were going to burst into flame.

When he looked up, a black shadow passed across the stars, cutting off all hope of their retreat. J.B. slowed, then stopped. He stood slope-shouldered, his blasters hanging useless in his hands. The companions closed ranks around him, facing the oncoming aircraft. Rumbling caldrons to the rear spit drops of boiling mud on their unprotected backs.

It was the least of their worries.

Silhouetted against the blue-white moon, the aircraft slowly turned its weapons pod toward them.

Chapter Twenty-One

As the van skidded through the slime, Nara threw an arm around Ryan's neck and pulled him to the floor.

Then everything flashed green.

Though Ryan shut his eyelid, the blaze inside his head was brighter than any sun. Brighter and closer. For a terrible, interminable instant, the doors of a nuclear blast furnace gaped wide, and Ryan stood naked upon its hearth. The heat, like a head-to-foot body blow, hammered Ryan into the floorboards. Then it was gone. He lay beside Nara, every muscle in his body quivering and jerking from the shock.

He lifted his head and saw they were still sliding sideways, but they were no longer riding in an enclosed van. In the space of a heartbeat the roof above them had vanished, along with the upper third of the side walls, rear doors and windshield. The tops of all the seats were likewise cut through. Ryan pulled himself up to his knees, then onto the edge of the bench seat.

Five heads popped up in front of him, three mercie men and a woman, and Damm behind the steering wheel, fighting to regain control. On the seat directly in front of him, the guy stuck to the wall no longer had a head to pop up. Like the roof and walls, it had been vaporized. Scorched black from shoulder to shoulder, he spit and crackled like a smoldering log.

Ryan swiveled and looked behind him. The torsos and legs of two mercies sat rigidly on what was left of the rear seat. More headless wonders. Their clothing and flesh were fused to the smoking pillow of black slag at the new, lowered top of the seat.

He squinted as a battery of floodlights from the APCs in pursuit swept over the van's interior. Whoever they were, they weren't interested in taking or recovering prisoners.

"Get them off us!" Damm shouted over his shoulder as he steered out of the skid.

"Tribarrels won't stop them," Nara shouted back. "Just slow them down!"

As Nara struggled to regain her balance and pick up her weapon, Ryan grabbed a pulse rifle from the floor. How well had he learned his lesson? It was final exam time. He thumbed off the safety and squashed the rear trigger. It locked back with a tangible click. Instantly, the weapon throbbed in his hands and burst after green burst shot through the middle of the rear door. Trigger still pinned, Ryan reached over the receiver and twisted the other control switch all the way to the right.

The laser weapon screamed.

A solid line of green connected the tribarrel's muzzle and the van door. With a single, backhanded swipe, he chopped away what remained of the van's rear doors, clearing them to the floor. Then he fanned the gallery ceiling behind, slicing free fifty feet of slime drape.

As it crashed to the ground, the headlights of the lead pursuer abruptly winked out.

The other two APCs veered wildly to avoid piling into the buried vehicle. It slowed them only for a second or two, then they were back on course. And closing ground.

"Do something, Damm!" Nara cried as she shouldered her weapon. "Before their weapons systems lock us in."

Over the blinding glare of headlights, an even brighter light flared. When he saw the green flash, Ryan averted his eye and shielded his face.

The van lurched forward and up, suddenly weightless, suddenly airborne. The laser cannon had hit low this time, taking out all the wheels. The van dropped hard onto its bare suspension, and its momentum sent it spinning across the beds of slime.

There was nothing Ryan could do but hang on and hope. Between his boots, the floorboards looked like lace. Melted lace. Bacterial slime, scraped free of the ground by the van's undercarriage, was forced up through the holes, sieved into a mass of thrashing green worms.

With a crash, they slammed sideways into a building wall, the impact cushioned by a pad of bacterial growth twenty feet deep. As Ryan bounced off the inside of the van, the slime curtain above broke loose from the ceiling and slopped down onto the roofless van. He was buried under a terrible wet weight. Choked by the stench of ammonia, he struggled to get free.

As Ryan pushed out from under the slunk, Damm was pulling Nara to her feet. He had a satchel slung over one shoulder. "This way!" the mercie leader said, vaulting the van's ruined side wall.

On Nara's heels, Ryan hopped down into the green slop. Already he thought he could feel something strange going on inside his lungs, a kind of chill, deep down, and a heaviness that made it hard for him to draw breath. He hoped it was just the power of suggestion. But he felt a noticeable strain in his chest and an accompanying weakness in his legs as he fought through the piles of slime to catch up with the blonde.

In the glare of the oncoming APCs' headlights the bleak, softly shrouded landscape before him stretched on and on, as far as he could see. If those lights went out, he knew he would be instantly, irretrievably lost.

And shortly thereafter, very dead.

Unseen, gauzy curtains of slime slicked over Ryan's face, his nose, his lips. An acrid, evil taste filled his mouth. He spit as he ran, and as he spit, he fought to keep from puking. Sticky moisture, from the humid air, from the mounds of slunk he stomped through, had seeped through his clothes and onto his skin.

At least he wasn't the last in line.

Perhaps because their infections were more advanced, the other mercies were struggling to keep up. Leading the ragged file of seven, Damm headed for the only source of light other than the fast-closing APCs—a dim, greenish rectangle at ground level.

Floodlights from behind swept over them, and almost in the same instant they were hit by another cannon pulse. Ryan felt the wave of heat above his head and to the rear. He heard a sizzling sound, then a scream cut off short.

When he glanced back he saw the man behind him was gone, turned to vapor along with tons of bacteria.

Another cannon pulse slammed the wall ahead of

them. Though momentarily blinded, he kept on running; there was no stopping now. As he sprinted through the billowing steam cloud, the stench of frying slime enveloped him.

Ahead of him, Damm vanished into the rectangle of paler green, then Nara. He hit the foot of the ramp and skidded on the thin layer of water that was sheeting off the concrete.

Above was more light.

Above was hope.

Gasping for air, Ryan charged up the incline. There was no mere chill in his lungs now. There was burning cold and a tangible, sloshing weight with every step.

He was drowning.

He wanted to cough, but he couldn't let himself. Once he started, he knew he'd never stop.

Behind them, he could hear the roar of the APCs' engines. No way could he outrun the pursuit. Certainly not uphill, on foot, with lungs half-full of bacteria.

Forty feet up the ramp from Ryan, Damm slowed long enough to unsling the satchel from his shoulder, pull a lanyard inside and drop the bag on the ground.

As Ryan dodged around the obstacle, he could hear the hissing of the fuse inside.

Damm cried back at him, "Run! Run!"

Run was all he could do.

There were no turns to hide behind, just an uptilting expanse of straight and narrow.

Though it felt as if he were dying, Ryan drove himself onward. The resounding clank of metal tracks on concrete filled the tunnel, as did the light from a bank of headlights. The APC driver gunned his engine and shifted into low gear.

Ryan had gone no more than twenty steps farther when he was slammed by a giant hand, flattened on the streaming pavement by a single blow while above him, chunks of hot metal sang off the walls. Shaking his head to clear it, Ryan scrambled to his feet.

The lead APC lay on its side, blocking the middle of the tunnel. The track on its left side had been blown apart. Fire boiled up from inside the passenger compartment. A pair of undamaged headlights cut tunnels through the spreading smoke.

Nara was already moving, if stiffly. Blood leaked in a trickle from her nose and ears.

Damm grabbed Ryan by the arm and pushed him up the ramp after her. "We've got a little bit of space," he said. "We've got to make the most of it."

He said nothing about the other three mercies, the ones who had been bringing up the rear, the ones his satchel of high-ex had blown all to hell.

Damm gave Ryan another shove. "Go!" he said.

The one-eyed man headed for the wall of fog that lay across the tunnel, fifty yards ahead. Behind and below them, powerful engines roared and there was a grating sound as one of the intact APCs tried to push the overturned vehicle out of its way.

Ryan felt as if he had a couple of bags of wet concrete in his chest, dragging him down. He could barely lift his feet, and he wasn't the only one who was slowing down. With the fog still a good distance away, Damm and Nara were fading fast, too.

None of them was going to make it, he could see

that. Before they reached cover, before the APCs even got close, they were going to collapse and die.

Unable to go another step, Ryan put a hand against the wall, bent over and vomited green slime. Nara was right there, by his side, helping him back up. As he straightened, Damm gave him a hard shove, pinning his back against the wall.

Ryan opened his eye and saw that the mercie had something gripped in his fist. Protruding from the heel of Damm's hand was a bright needle, as thin as a hair, and three inches long. He wielded it like a killing dirk, in a downward stab.

There was no way Ryan could deflect the blow.

He gasped as the full length of the hypodermic pierced his chest, driving in to the hilt. He gasped again as Damm thumbed the plunger home, as fingers of fire squeezed his wildly beating heart.

THE LIGHTS WENT OUT for Major Oswaldo Lujan, and as they did, a stunning impact hurled him against his shoulder harness. Plunged into darkness inside his APC, all of his external sensors blacked out, the major unleashed a ferocious string of profanity. He'd been buried under a mountain of slime by a sweep of laser fire from the kidnappers' van. Still cursing, he rocked the APC back and forth, shifting from forward to reverse, grinding a little more breathing room, and a little more, until he could finally reverse his way out from under the smothering heap.

With his optics cleared he saw two of his APCs already diving into the darkness ahead. The other vehicles had been caught in the trailer's explosion. Overturned and buried by slime fall, they were out of the picture. How much explosive had gone off, he could only guess. The blast had collapsed the ceiling on top of the crater where the trailer had once sat. There was no sign of it or the tractor that had pulled it.

He should have guessed the bastard would pull something like that, Lujan told himself as he roared after the others. The mercie had a history of desperate escapes that bordered on the suicidal.

Laser-cannon fire lit up the terrain ahead, and as Lujan approached the mouth of the tunnel ramp, he saw that there was still plenty of opportunity for him to make amends. The ruined van sat empty, covered in drapes of slime. The man from Shadow World and his surviving kidnappers were on foot.

Lujan checked the elapsed time since the trailer explosion. Three minutes. Inside the black helmet, a fierce smile lit up his face. Add three minutes to the time the mercs had already spent in Slime Zone and what you got was torpor, fading rapidly into death.

One way or another, the story was going to end real soon.

Throttle pinned, Lujan fought to catch up with the other two APCs before they reached the tunnel. It was impossible; they had too big a lead. He had just entered the foot of the ramp when somewhere above the bomb blew.

The tunnel was lit by hard white light and rocked by an awesome thunder crack. A fireball devoured the lead APC, rolled over the second vehicle and kept on rolling down the ramp. The major met it head-on, and it passed right over him.

More surprises from Damm.

Lujan's route was now blocked. He waited until the second APC shoved the burning hulk far enough to one side for him to scrape past, then he drove around the wreck. He stopped when he saw all the bodies strewed facedown on the ramp. The mercs had been killed by their own explosive. Between the bodies and the condensation layer there was only wet concrete.

"Out!" he ordered four of the APC's six-man crew. "I want to know if Shadow Man is among them. Double time!"

From the driver's seat, he watched as his men hurriedly turned over the corpses.

"Not here, Major," the report came back. "He must be up ahead. Damm's not here, either."

Lujan gunned the APC's engine, and, without waiting for the men to climb back inside, started clanking up the tunnel. When he accelerated away from them, toward the condensation layer, his crew realized he wasn't going to stop. The other APC pulled around the wreck and followed the major's lead, rushing for the wall of mist. Lujan's crew had to jump on the outside of the trailing vehicle or get left behind.

Chapter Twenty-Two

Dr. Huth faced the conference room's video screens and the assembled CEOs of FIVE. As he looked from screen to screen, he saw that they were all very upset, even infuriated with him. They demanded an explanation, knowing in advance that no explanation from him could suffice.

He angled his body so the overhead camera could pick up the scorched back of his lab coat and the wad of bloody bandage at his nape, and transmit said injuries to those who glared at him.

The CEOs' expressions didn't change.

If he expected any sympathy for a close brush with death, he was looking in the wrong place. Huth was glad to be behind the secure walls of the Totality Concept's complex and at least momentarily out of the reach of FIVE's tactical units.

In the meantime, the best defense was often a good offense.

In this case it also happened to be the truth.

"This incident wasn't in any way my fault," he said emphatically. "I didn't organize the transportation or the security for Ryan Cawdor. You people did. I didn't advertise the potential of Shadow World on the tell-yous for weeks, nor did I participate in the decision to plaster Cawdor's face all over the megalopolis. You did. I didn't plant the seeds for what happened today. You did.'' He paused to let the weight of his accusations sink in, then he said, ''All I am guilty of is surviving the attack.''

''Are you quite through, Dr. Huth?'' asked the auburn-haired woman from Omnico.

He wasn't through, but her disinterested and impatient tone of voice made him reconsider an extension of his rant. Obviously he'd scored no points with the frontal attack. If he continued, he might be making things even worse for himself, although it was hard to imagine that.

''Good,'' she said after he closed his mouth. ''Now, kindly rerun the abduction scenario for us.''

Huth nodded, relieved to be on solid factual ground. ''We'd stopped on the freeway because of the carniphage sirens,'' he said. ''Without warning, we were rammed, then explosives were set off under our vehicle. The explosions disabled the APC and set it on fire, so we had to abandon it. I never saw any of our attackers. I never saw what happened to Ryan Cawdor or Captain Jurascik or the security team after they got out of the vehicle. As I made my own exit, the APC was hit by a rocket. And I received some thankfully minor injuries. Do you know what happened to the others?''

''We found the bodies of some of the security force in the middle of the freeway,'' the CEO from Invecta said. ''The man from Shadow World and Jurascik remain missing. They vanished without a trace. We are still interviewing the few witnesses we have managed to gather up, but from all accounts they saw about as much as you did.''

''I think we have to assume,'' the man from Mitsuki said, ''that Ryan Cawdor is going to be held for ransom. There's no other reason for his having been taken by force like this."

Of course, Huth thought, there was at least one other possible reason, and they all knew it. Cawdor might also be being held to gain advantage, one Global trying to get the jump on all the others by accessing on an exclusive basis the information in Shadow Man's head. To speak the words, to make the public accusation, was to let ten thousand devils out of their box. It was something none of the chief executives were prepared to do at this point.

The white-maned man from Hutton-Byrum-Kobe asked, "Has anyone received a demand for payment?"

For a long moment no one replied. The CEOs just glared into the vid cameras.

Huth wondered if, out of sight of the lenses, they were digging their fingernails so hard into their palms that they were making them bleed. Or stabbing themselves in the thighs with blunt letter openers. He sincerely hoped so. If any of them had received a demand, they would never admit to it to the others. And they would have already paid the ransom.

Gladly.

"I have received no such demand!" said the woman, slapping her desktop with an open palm. Though her head moved, her hair didn't. It was as stiff as spun fiberglas.

"Nor have I," added the man from Questar.

One by one, and with equal vehemence, all of the CEOs replied in the negative.

"Perhaps the kidnappers are keeping quiet to put additional pressure on us?" the man from Invecta said. "So we will jump at their first offer?"

"That's ridiculous," the white-haired man said. "They have to know FIVE is ready to pay anything to get him back."

"He could be dead," the CEO from Questar said. "Killed trying to get away, or in an accident. There could be nothing for them to ransom."

"With an attack this well-planned and executed," the woman said, "I seriously doubt that an accident of any kind would be allowed to happen. And if he was killed on purpose to prove some political or economic point, we would've found his body along with the others."

"There's nothing we can do about the situation until we are contacted by the kidnappers," the man from Mitsuki said, "and of course, keep each other fully apprised of any developments."

"What about advertising the kidnapping on the tell-yous?" the CEO from Questar said. "We could offer a reward for the safe return of Shadow Man."

"That would definitely get him killed, if he isn't already," said the white-haired man.

"We have to face facts," the Mitsuki man went on. "Regrettable though it is, it might not be possible for us to recoup our investment in this man. We have to remember that he isn't irreplacable. After we make the crossing, we can capture another informant. Any number of informants."

"And you're saying...?" the woman prompted.

"That writing off our first specimen is always a viable option."

While the others considered this, Huth could imagine how hard the bushes were going to be beaten to find Ryan Cawdor. Looking into the icy faces of the CEOs, Huth had a moment of crystal clarity. He knew that one of them had done it. Out of stupid, ham-fisted greed, one of them had done it. He wanted to shout in outrage; he wanted to weep. But he knew better. By the tight, fixed expressions of the CEOs, he knew that all of them knew it, too.

What this meant, in terms of the survival of Earth-born members of the human species was simple.

They weren't going to make it.

Everything that FIVE had pulled together in order to open the passage and make the exodus possible was going to fall apart once the Globals started accusing one another of betrayal. To operate the system, it took huge contributions of nuke power from each of the economic giants, contributions that would be withdrawn when critical treaties were torn up. At some point, hours, maybe days away, the shit would surely hit the fan. The armies of individual Globals would battle for control of the Totality Concept complex. But by then it wouldn't matter. No one else would be making the crossing. Ever.

"May I offer a suggestion?" Huth asked.

"Please do," the man from Hutton-Byrum-Kobe said.

"Let's not jump to any conclusions about what is going on here, yet. Let's sit tight for another few hours. If there's been no word from the kidnappers by then, a decision on a plan of action will have to be made."

There were nods all around.

The strategy was comfortingly familiar: When in doubt, freeze.

Huth had bought himself a tiny window of time.

ON HIS BACK inside his coffinlike, executive-grade sleep cubicle, the director of the Totality Concept's most advanced research program sorted his worldly possessions. From the storage bins along the left-hand wall, he took his spare pair of socks, his two alternate pairs of underwear and a pair of plastic jogging boots. All of these he stuffed into a rucksack.

The bitterness that filled him at that moment was most terrible. His had been a distinguished career in science, a lifetime devoted to the pursuit of knowledge, to rationality, to the betterment of his species. At the top of his form, the peak of his game, he had had a success beyond imagining, beyond compare: he had discovered the true salvation of humankind, sanctuary for the desperate billions.

And it had all come down to this.

Huth felt as if he were standing alone on an immense sandy beach, under an empty sky, watching the ominous shadow of a tidal wave loom on the horizon.

He had no intention of meekly waiting for the wave to break.

From an overhead compartment he took his only warm coat, a quilted nylon flight jacket, his navy-blue knit cap, and a pair of insulated gloves, and put them into the backpack.

That part of the packing was simple. His collection of worldly goods was pathetic. He counted himself lucky he hadn't been born a CEO. The choices would have been so much more difficult.

What was infinitely harder under the circumstances was deciding what scientific equipment, if any, to take with him. Therein, perhaps, lay the biggest tragedy of all. Ninety-nine-point-nine percent of the gear he relied on in his daily work would be worthless on the other side of the rift. It only functioned thanks to a global support network of power sources, of other gear, and an elaborate social and economic system of other scientists, industry and government.

Even if he could power the equipment, without the social and economic system his results would be meaningless. What did the quality of uranium ore in Bolivia matter if there was no way to refine it, if there was no way to use it once it was refined? Under such conditions, applied science would have the same effect as a tree falling in a deserted forest.

Which was the exact opposite of what FIVE had planned.

In the history of humankind on either world, only a handful of times had such technologically advanced and primitive cultures collided. Huth, off the top of his head, could think of only a single example, when twentieth-century explorers made contact with the Stone Age people of New Guinea. Though there weren't thousands of years of development separating the two parallel Earths, thanks to the juggernaut of scientific progress, there might as well have been.

That gap was destined to remain, despite Huth's genius, insight and monumental effort.

Anticipating the consequences of an unstoppable population explosion, he had shifted the focus of Operation Cerberus, originally devoted to purely military experiments in time travel, to resource acquisition, using the trawl technology to try to exploit the past and the future for needed raw materials. Based on the success of the famous Theophilus Tanner studies, he had reasoned that if it was possible to trawl a live human being from a century back, it might also be possible to trawl the necessities of life.

Unfortunately, this turned out not to be the case. Because of a law of diminishing returns, it was impossible to rob Peter to pay Paul. It took more energy to bring resources across the barrier than could ever be recovered from them.

During one of the experiments, Huth had caused the passageway to materialize by accident. At first he wasn't sure what he had discovered. Robotic probes sent across the rift and then retrieved showed the atmosphere on the other side was breathable. Rock samples displayed the same characteristics as those found on Earth. DNA tests of the plants and animals the robots brought back proved they had common ancestries with life on Earth. And the mutation rates gave Huth an idea of the relative age of the two planets; it told him that they were in fact the same place, in different universes.

When a plan to shift resources along the passageway, to essentially refuel Earth by strip-mining Shadow World also failed for reasons of energy conservation, FIVE decided to move people to the resources instead.

Of course the massive shift in population described in the tell-yous was nothing but claptrap. Nine-tenths of humanity was redundant by any standard: biologically unnecessary for the perpetuation of the species; economically unnecessary because there was nothing for them to do, no living for them to make; socially unnecessary because they were uneducated clones of one another.

Eat, breed, die: that was all they were any good at.

As Huth slipped out of his cubicle and turned out the light, he thought how hard it was to have sympathy for people that selfish.

Chapter Twenty-Three

Sagging back against the tunnel wall, molten lava filling his chest, Ryan could only watch as Damm and Nara took turns stabbing each other in the lungs with similar, long-needled hypodermics, teeth clenched, eyes pressed shut as thumbs pressed the plungers home. A grim performance, and one that he didn't understand. Having murdered him, were they committing suicide, rather than be captured?

After administering the injections, Damm and Nara jerked out the hypos and dropped them on the ground.

"Feel better?" the mercie said, pulling Ryan to his feet and urging him onward.

Cawdor was unable to reply.

"Well, you should start to in another few seconds," Damm told him. "Come on, we've got to make it into the fog or we're dead."

With every step he took, Ryan could feel the tremendous weight lifting from his chest. Whatever Damm had shot him up with, it worked like a charm. By the time he reached the wall of mist, he was jogging without pain and breathing almost normally.

As he stepped inside the edge of the fog, a roar of engines and clank of tracks made him look back. Behind them, two APCs were in full pursuit. He saw four figures in black armor run across the tunnel and climb on the side of the rearmost vehicle, scrambling to stand on its fenders.

A hand gripped his wrist and squeezed. It was Damm. He had hold of both Ryan and Nara, and he drew them deeper into the mist, leading them over to the right side of the tunnel. Visibility was no more than a foot. The air was dripping wet. Ryan had to stifle the urge to cough.

"We'll take out the second APC," Damm said as the clanking grew ever louder. "The one with the crew hanging on the outside."

"Won't they be able to see us coming?" Ryan said.

"They can see about as well as we can," the mercie told him. "The condensation layer screws up all their automated sensors and the comm systems, too. We've only got one chance at this, so don't screw up."

Invisible in the fog, Damm caught Ryan's right hand, turned it palm up and firmly put a pair of flat, two-inch diameter disks into it. "They're slap charges," he said. "Butt simple to use. The material has an adhesive surface that only sticks to a battle-suit. The disks work no matter which side comes in contact with the target. The side that sticks is the side that kicks. All you've got to do is slap that puppy between the shoulder blades of a guy in a battlesuit and throw him off the APC. You got two to deal with, I got two to deal with."

"Anything else?"

"Oh, yeah," Damm said, "after six seconds, you might want to duck."

"What about me?" Nara asked.

"Go through the APC's rear doors and make yourself useful inside."

"How many men are in there?" Ryan asked. He had to speak up in order to be heard. The clanking noise was really getting loud; he could feel the concrete shuddering through the soles of his boots.

"Could be three. Could be as many as six. Important thing to remember is, we've got to be done and in control of the situation before the APC comes out on the other side of the fog. Otherwise, that bastard in the lead will find out what's up and be able to block our only way out."

The track and engine noise peaked in volume. Ryan thought he could see a faint, moving glow in the middle of the tunnel. Perhaps from headlights. Perhaps it was just his imagination. There was no question in his mind that he had to throw in with Nara and Damm. They had saved his life twice in the past five minutes, and from the looks of things, they were about to do it a third time.

Not ten feet from the wall against which Ryan stood pressed, the first APC lumbered past, a phantom in the fog. When the moment came, he was going to have to find the second one by touch. When he'd last seen them, the men in battlesuits were standing on the long, flat fenders that stretched the length of the wag, and covered the tops of each of the twin tracks.

As the lead APC moved on up the ramp, and the second vehicle entered the mist, Ryan heard Damm's hoarse whisper to Nara through the wall of white.

He said, "Buy or Die!"

Ryan remembered seeing the same words tattooed on the now-dead female mercie's forearm. A war cry, he thought. For his own part, Ryan was tired of being pushed around, held prisoner, chased, poisoned and threatened with horrible death. It was time for more than a return of threats. It was time for a little serious payback.

Ryan put one of the flat disks between his teeth; the other he held ready in his left hand. As the clanking rumble peaked, Damm gave Ryan a shove toward the middle of the tunnel.

Right hand outstretched like a blind man, Ryan lunged into the cottony mist. His fingertips brushed a hard, greasy surface. Above him, he could make out the dimmest of black shapes gliding past him. He stopped and let the edge of the APC's fender slide under his hand, keeping his palm in contact with it until the fender curved away and bent around the back of the vehicle.

Blinking the moisture out of his eye, Ryan saw a black boot about eight inches from the tip of his nose. He lunged up and grabbed. His fingers slipped over the smooth armor plates, then dug in under the edge of a belt or harness. With a mighty heave, he jerked the stunned man off his perch and crashed him down hard on the concrete. Ryan maintained hand contact until after he'd stuck the charge in the middle of the man's back, then he turned and ran through the fog for the rear of the APC.

From the other side of the tunnel there came another crash.

Two down, Ryan thought as his outstretched hand touched something flat and solid, something decorated with rows of rivet heads. His searching fingers found a handhold on the frame beside the right rear door. Grabbing it, he pulled himself onto the fender and stood. He leaned forward, looking for the shape of a helmet, but seeing only more vague shadows of black mixed with the swirling mist.

Twin explosions came from behind, one after the other. Muffled and sloppy wet.

The shadow he was staring at moved slightly to the right.

Ryan jerked back involuntarily, not having expected to come nose to nose with the enemy. Recovering at once, he snapkicked the man's outside shoulder, feeling the solid impact, then the give under his boot sole. As the man turned, Ryan hurled himself on his back and drove him facedown on the fender. He took the shaped charge from between his teeth, slapped it in place and rolled the man off the fender and into the mist. Ryan didn't see him hit the concrete, but he heard the clatter.

Seconds passed, then two more explosions rattled off in quick succession, again muffled and wet. There were no flashes in the mist behind, but Ryan felt the wind as fragments whistled by.

The APC suddenly swerved under him, and he had to hang on or be thrown clear. It was hard to tell for sure in the fog, but the wag seemed to be angling for the left-hand wall.

As Ryan reached the rear doors, they banged back and he got the briefest glimpse of a black figure hurtling out of the compartment, over the bumper and onto the ramp. As he piled into the APC, there was another explosion from behind and a spray of shrapnel peppered the outside of the doors.

Inside the wag, the fog wasn't nearly so dense. He could see Nara struggling with a black-helmeted man half again her size. She had him facedown on the floorboards of the passenger compartment with an arm pinned behind his back. He was kicking and thrashing his free arm. If he was yelling inside the helmet, Ryan couldn't hear him over the clanking of the tracks.

In the front, the driver was looking over the back of his seat, steering with one hand, likely torn between trying to race the wag out of the fog and abandoning the steering wheel to help his weapons system engineer before it was too late.

Damm reached in between Nara and the guy she was holding down and affixed the antipersonnel mine. As he jerked the man toward the rear doors, he told Ryan, "Get the driver!"

The one-eyed man rushed through the passenger compartment and wrenched the driver clear of his seat. As he dragged the man backward, Nara slipped behind the wheel and eased off the speed. Damm pushed Ryan aside and lifted the man in black armor to his feet. In the helmet, the driver was two inches taller than the scar-faced merc.

"Don't kill me," the driver pleaded in a scratchy, metallic voice. "I never did anything to you."

"We're coming out of the mist, Damm," Nara said over her shoulder. "I can't hang back here much longer or it'll look suspicious. It's too late to frag the guy."

"Let's see your face, you cowardly tac unit bastard," Damm said.

The helmet cleared, revealing a pale-faced man with a buzz cut.

"You did bad things to my crew back there."

"That was orders," the driver said. "I was just following orders."

The sheath knife came away from Damm's har-

ness in a blur almost too fast to follow. The mercie
slid the double-edged point in under the third breastplate from the top. Fighting frantically, the driver
tried to pummel Damm as he searched and probed
beneath the plate with the knife tip. The mercie
didn't seem to mind the full-force blows he was receiving to the face and head; if he did, he didn't show
it. He kept searching until he found what he was been
looking for.

A weak spot beneath the plate.

The driver stiffened as the gleaming blade slipped
into him about an inch and a half.

"They were all good fighters," Damm told his
captive, "the kind a man wants at his back. Hard to
find a crew like that these days." He pulled the driver
closer to him. "They died without begging anybody
for mercy. There was no begging in them."

"Please, no."

"Time to pay the piper," Damm said. He pressed
his nose against the outside of the helmet and snarled
into the man's face. "And I am the fucking piper!"

With a scraping sound, the long knife slid in to
the hilt. Damm held the man skewered until the kicking stopped, then he let the heavy battlesuit crash to
the deck. He put his boot on the breastplate and
wrenched his knife free.

Ryan noted the location of the entry wound, for
future reference. He figured there had to be a small
opening, or an unprotected area beneath the overlapping plates.

Ahead of them, the fog thinned, then parted. They
could see the back end of the other APC as it clanked
up the ramp, which was now dry. The air temperature
took a big drop, so much so that it made Ryan shiver.

"Oh-oh," Nara said. "I got a blinking light on the comm unit control panel. Our compadre up there is trying to hail us. Probably wondering why none of the suits in this can are responding."

"Let him wonder awhile longer," Damm ordered.

As Major Lujan's APC lumbered toward the wall of mist, his weapons system engineer turned to him and said, "Sir, shall I saturate the area with cannon fire? I can program the batteries to scrape them off the walls."

The idea was appealing, but impossible for Lujan to authorize. Even the lowest-power laser pulses wouldn't stop at the intended targets. They would take out anything between the APC and the mouth of the ramp, and then continue on to blow a few more holes in Gloomtown.

There was nothing to be gained by stirring up the mob.

"Forget the cannons," the major said. "If they're in the fog, we'll flush them out." Then he passed on the no-fire order to the driver of the APC bringing up the rear.

It was the last communication between the two vehicles before Lujan entered the condensation layer. The moment the mist closed in around him, except for the interior and exterior lights, which weren't computer-controlled, all of his electronic systems promptly crashed. Navigation. Surveillance. Weapons. Everything went stone dead.

He held the steering wheel steady in his hands, trying to keep the vehicle on a straight course. The width of the fog barrier varied from minute to minute, and there was no way to tell how long they were going to have to drive blind. The longer they traveled, the more likely they were to gradually veer off course. At any moment, the side of the APC could start grinding against one of the opposing walls.

At least they couldn't get lost.

As Lujan drove out of the fog and his headlights speared the darkness ahead, he expected to see one of two things. The mercs and their hostage would be either facedown on the concrete, having succumbed to the lethal effects of the agrobacteria, or they would be visible, easy targets running up the tunnel ahead.

As he looked out through the APC's view slit, neither scenario greeted him. To the limits of his headlight beams, about three hundred yards ahead, the tunnel before him was empty.

Lujan stared in disbelief.

All of his arrays were still down. He couldn't hear anything but the clankety-clank of his own tracks on the ramp. He continued to advance until one by one his sensors came back on-line. Then he used them to search beyond the range of his headlights. Not that he seriously thought they could have gotten that far ahead. He scanned all the way to the tunnel's end with infrared and found nothing.

"Shit!" he said, as it finally dawned on him. "They're still in the fucking fog!"

He keyed the comm link to the APC following behind. "I've got nothing ahead of me," he said. "I think we might have driven right past them."

When he got no response, he figured their systems were still rebooting.

After a moment, he tried again. "What's going on back there? Did you see anything in the fog?"

Still nothing.

There was no room for the APCs to turn around on the ramp. The easiest and quickest thing to do, if they had to go back and search the fog for bodies, was to exit at the top of the ramp, turn around in Gloomtown and return. They could go back through the tunnel side by side, with their wheels rubbing the walls, if they had to.

"Can you hear me?" Lujan demanded.

All he got was static.

What the hell, he thought. As long as they kept following him up and out, that was all that mattered.

As he approached the head of the ramp, he drove over the bodies that had been thrown down the tunnel. He met with much less resistance this time, having made the heaps more compact on the way down the ramp. The APC topped the rise and roared out into the crowded street.

In the haze of plastic smoke and flashing light from the tell-yous high overhead, masses of milling, dirty-faced people sullenly gave ground. They knew the APC wouldn't stop or turn to keep from running them over. Those who couldn't run, those who appeared, prostrate on the street, when the forest of legs swept apart, Lujan made no attempt to avoid.

Some of them were alive, if barely.

Alive enough to scream as they were crushed.

The major tried the comm link again, and again he was frustrated. Behind him the other APC was pulling out of the ramp tunnel.

"Bailey," he said to the lone crewman seated in the passenger compartment, "hop over there and pound on the door. Tell them we're going to head back down the ramp and grid search the fog. Keep your pulse rifle on maximum, in case a gloomer wants to pick a fight.''

To his weapons system engineer, the major said, "Stay alert when the doors open."

The gunner nodded. As the cluster of cannons came to life, swiveling, searching for targets, the mob fanned back, opening up a clear path to the other APC.

After Bailey ducked out the rear doors, Lujan followed him on infrared as he crossed over to the other APC and beat his gauntleted fist against the front of the hull.

"I THINK WE'RE GOING to have to do something," Nara said. "He's not going to go away."

The next round of thuds over her head was even more insistent.

Then from outside, an amplified battlesuit voice said, "Open the rear doors. Got to talk."

"He wants in," Damm said.

"The second that other APC finds out it's us in here, it's going to open fire," Nara said, "which means we've got to be moving and firing first. And that leaves Ryan to handle the guy outside."

"Got it covered," the one-eyed man replied. "Just give me another one of those little mine things."

Damm reached into a pouch on his combat harness and passed him a shaped charge.

The pounding shifted to the rear door. "Come on, hurry up and let me in," the crackling voice said. "The natives are restless, and it's starting to get a little hairy out here."

"It's gonna get way hairier," Ryan said.

He opened one of the doors just a crack. When

the guy outside stuck his armor-gloved fingers in the gap to grab the edge, Ryan caught him by the wrist, kicked the door open and jumped out beside him. A hip check knocked the man off balance, and he fell forward onto the APC's rear deck, with the toes of his boots still on the pavement. Ryan straddled the soldier and pressed his chest against the man's back, trapping his hips against the top of the bumper.

"See this?" Ryan said, holding the explosive disk under the guy's black helmet. "It's for you."

Then he slammed the charge to the guy's back, hauled him to his feet and pushed him out into the street. Behind Ryan, Nara gunned the APC. He grabbed for a handhold and stepped up on the bumper as she clanked away.

The man in the battlesuit screamed through his speaker for help, frantically trying to reach the disk on his back, running a mad, zigzag course for the other APC. The way he was swinging his arms, it looked as if he were being attacked by a swarm of invisible hornets. The mob found the sight comical; they laughed as they pointed at him, not understanding—or caring—why he was in such a state.

Over the top of the APC's passenger compartment Ryan saw the battlesuit flash in the middle, a clear white light passing all the way through it. There was a wet bang, and the battlesuit was severed in two. The lighter of the two sections, the one with arms and a head, skittered some distance across the pavement.

Fragments of the sheared body armor sprayed out in a wide circle, chopping down the nearest spectators like a scythe. Some clutched minor wounds; others were facedown and never going to get up.

Despite the injuries its members had sustained, the mob loved the show. It was much better than the tell-yous. Rarely, if ever, did they get freewheeling improvisational entertainment. Cheering, they swarmed in to collect souvenirs. Unlike the lethal wounds served up by laser weapons, the slap charge produced a messy chill. With hands dripping gore, the crowd fought over detached plates of armor, a boot, a tri-blaster with a shattered receiver and delaminated muzzle.

Nara had traveled about thirty feet when Damm touched off the APC's cannons. Bolts of green light flashed across Gloomtown. Like ground-level, horizontal chain lightning, it slammed into the side of the other APC, making it torque around on its tracks.

Because the vehicle survived the attack and wasn't instantly cut in two, Ryan figured it had to have some kind of defense against its own brand of weaponry. Anticipating a return of fire, he dived back inside the passenger compartment. And just in time.

The APC's interior hull glowed green for an instant, and in the same instant, the heavy vehicle was shoved hard to the right. Its tracks screeched as they scraped across the concrete. Not buckled to a safety harness, Ryan went flying into the illuminated wall, and it was like hitting the side of a blast furnace. As he bounced off the searing hull, caustic smoke erupted from the cables and pipes between the I-beams. The APC continued to grind along the pavement as if pushed by a giant, angry hand. When the vehicle came to a stop, it was tilted slightly off to the left.

"We lost a track!" Nara said, grinding the gears as she tried to maneuver with the one that remained.

Ryan pushed up from the floorboards. Driven by a single track, the APC was turning in a very narrow circle.

"Out!" Nara cried. She jumped from the driver's seat and yanked the visor off Damm's head. "Out or we're cooked!"

"WHAT'S WRONG with Bailey?" the gunner said. "Has he lost his frigging mind?" He had no more than gotten the words out when the man running toward them was blown into halves. Behind the two-part corpse, the other APC was moving quickly away.

It was only then that Major Lujan realized the people he hunted weren't in the fog.

"Shoot the APC!" he cried. "Shoot them!"

Before the gunner could obey, laser pulses slammed the side of the vehicle, jolting it sideways. Lujan flattened the accelerator and shouted, "Burn 'em! Burn them, goddammit!"

The weapons system engineer opened fire on the fast-moving vehicle. The sustained beam of the laser cannons let out a banshee howl. A foot and a half in diameter, the solid, lime-green ray sizzled across the crowded street, chasing after the other APC.

Beyond the rear end of the target vehicle, stretching as far back as the building facades, were masses of tightly compressed humanity. The full-power cannon blast melted through them as if they were made of candle wax. All the way back to the façades, people died, their bodies not merely bisected, but exploding horrendously as the liquids inside them instantaneously reached fusion temperature.

Lujan couldn't hear the shrieks of agony over the cannon's wail.

It was too late to do anything about the mess, even if he'd wanted to.

The gunner cut an arc of absolute destruction through the assembled multitudes, killing in the space of a few seconds God only knew how many people. His unbroken stream of fire sawed through the ground floors of a row of distant buildings, causing their upper stories to collapse.

Then he found the target.

The laser lit up the side of the APC, shooting a shower of green sparks in all directions. The facing drive track snapped, and its two-foot-wide treads went flying. With the APC disabled, the weapons system engineer finally eased off the cannons' trigger.

"I got them!" he cried. "They're dead meat!"

Lujan watched the smoke coiling up from the side of the wounded vehicle, watched as its driver tried to move away and instead clanked around in a feeble circle.

"Finish them," the major ordered.

There was a terrible roar to Lujan's left and something jarred the outside of the APC, jolting him hard against his seat harness. It wasn't the roar of cannon. It was the roar of human voices.

Thousands upon thousands of them.

The major realized with a start that he hadn't been watching the mob; he'd been preoccupied. He immediately gunned the engine. The transmission strained, but the tracks wouldn't move. Somehow they'd been jammed. The crowd noise was so loud he could hardly think.

Sensing his own impending destruction, Lujan shifted madly back and forth between forward and reverse gears, trying to dislodge the obstacle and break the tracks free. The APC shuddered, then began to rock as hundreds of people threw their bodies against its side. Hammering on the hull, they tipped the vehicle onto its right track, then the edge of its right track. With a sickening crash, it toppled over onto its side.

Lujan unbuckled himself at once and scrambled over the back of his chair. "Pulse rifles!" he shouted at the gunner, who was still seated. "We're gonna have to fry our way out of here!"

Snatching up a laser weapon from the floor and thumbing its fire selector to full power, the major rushed for the rear doors. Before he could reach them, the APC took a tremendous hit, delivered not by massed human hands but by massed high explosive. The shock blast sent him flying helmet-first into the ceiling of the passenger compartment, knocking him out.

When Lujan regained consciousness, he was on his back on the pavement outside the APC. There was a sharp pain in his rib cage every time he tried to sip air.

Backlit by the tell-yous, a head leaned over him. Its long hair and beard were twisted into a corona of greasy spikes. The major caught the glint of the thick goggles that covered the man's eyes. He saw the black plates of an armor vest and a pair of muscular arms, bare to the shoulders, and covered with a mass of interwoven, dark tattoos.

"Wake up, Lujan," the man said. "It's time to die."

The major recognized the voice.

It belonged to Thrill Bill.

Chapter Twenty-Four

Ryan leaped through the passenger compartment doors to the street, one hundred yards from the mob surging over the other APC. Unarmed, enraged people hurled themselves against it, first rocking, then overturning the lethal machine. The sight was so awesome, so unexpected that it made him freeze. Then he was struck by an overpowering stench.

Not burning plastic, this time.

Burning people.

Ryan looked around and saw the swath of slaughter created by the other gunner's sloppy aim. He had never imagined, not even in his most hideous mat-trans jump dream, that such a battlefield could ever exist. For five hundred yards, there was nothing but mounded dead, a rolling landscape made up of charred body parts, steaming like freshly turned compost. On either side of the arc, there were survivors. People sat on the ground clutching melted faces, and the stumps of scorched-off limbs.

Damm and Nara joined him outside the APC.

"Oh, fuck," the mercie gasped as he took in the carnage.

Nara's eyes widened. In her hand the pulse rifle began to shake uncontrollably.

As a huge crowd began to close in on them from all directions, Ryan raised his own weapon to his hip and prepared to fire. He looked into faces full of fury, faces that didn't care if they died so long as they got the chance to pull a nice big chunk out of him.

"Ryan, don't fire," Nara said. She let the tribarrel slip from her fingers and drop to the concrete. "It'll only make things worse."

"Captain's right," Damm said.

Ryan wondered how in the name of hell things could get any worse. Going against his gut instinct, he laid down his rifle, too.

Predictably, the mob surged over them at once, kicking and punching. On the other side of the street, there was a loud explosion. Ryan was too busy to pay much attention. He fought back as best he could, returning blows whenever it was possible, managing above all to keep from being pulled to the ground where he could be stomped.

Then somebody in the mass of swinging fists yelled, "It's him! Stop! It's him!"

The man standing in front of Ryan was winding up with a four-foot length of metal pipe, preparing to knock his head off his shoulders. The guy held up on the swing, a surprised look spreading over his face. Surprise quickly turned to delight.

"It *is* him!" the would-be batter cried. He pointed the end of his pipe at the tell-you screen hanging from the ceiling high above them. "Hey, everybody, it's the Shadow Man!"

Ryan looked up at his own image, magnified hundreds of times.

The people nearest to him turned and started shoving the others back. Damm and Nara were both down on the pavement; the mercie had covered her with his body. Ryan helped them up.

As he did, the crowd began to stomp and chant: "Thrill Bill! Thrill Bill! Thrill Bill!"

Down the street, Cawdor could see the mob parting by the overturned APC, parting before a wedge of sec men. A tall, ramrod-straight figure strode behind the wedge. When the man waved his hand, the crowd sent up a deafening wave of cheers. On either side of the tall guy, Ryan could see the tops of black helmets and a bunch more sec men. Two men in armor were being herded along like cattle.

As the tall man came closer, Ryan could make out his features. They didn't inspire confidence. The spike-haired and spike-bearded guy stopped an arm's length away. Behind the thick goggles strapped to his head, a pair of hard gray eyes sized up Ryan.

"I didn't think you were real," the man said. He reached up and twisted the tip of one of his beard spikes, drawing it into an even tighter point. Then he looked over at Damm and Nara. "You're running with a bad crowd, Shadow Man. Those two will get you nothing but roasted."

"Hey, Bill," Damm said, grinning. His teeth were smeared with red from a cut inside his mouth.

Nara stared and said nothing.

"I would've thought you already had enough blood on your hands, Captain," Thrill Bill said to her.

"I didn't mean for this to happen."

"Heard that song, done that dance," the warlord said. "We got business with Major Loo-jan, then we'll deal with you." The warlord turned to face the mob, shot his fist up in the air and shouted, "Vengeance!"

The bellow of approval made Ryan wince. Automatic-weapon fire rattled, sprays of bullets sparking off the street's concrete ceiling.

The warlord headed for an undamaged façade ahead. Ryan and the others found themselves pushed along behind by a legion of sec men. The shouts of the surrounding crowd were so loud they rattled his insides.

Thrill Bill stopped at the building's entrance, which consisted of four glass panels, the middle two of which were sliding doors. Beyond the transparent wall, bathed in weak light, the foyer was packed, nearly shoulder to shoulder, with more excited people.

Thrill Bill waved for the pair of tactical squad unit survivors to be brought forward and lined up before him.

He reached out and rapped a knuckle on the helmet of the shorter of the two. The black tint drained away and a man's face appeared. Blood leaking from his nose painted his upper lip and chin. His dark eyes were narrowed to slits.

"Oswaldo," Thrill Bill said, "you fucked up."

The major was defiant. "My orders were to rescue Shadow Man from Damm at any cost."

"Mitsuki has always been real generous when it comes to other people's suffering," the warlord said. "They are thinking about the bottom line, same as you."

"I don't think so," the warlord replied. He gestured toward the field of dead. "I don't think me and Mitsuki are on the same page. You picked the wrong place to fuck up, Lujan."

"If you kill me, you know there will be reprisals."

"If I don't kill you, there will be reprisals. Where, oh, where is the profit in that?"

Thrill Bill signaled the bodyguards with a jerk of his hand. "Take these Global humps inside."

Lujan and the other man were shoved through the doors and into the foyer, where they suffered a rain of wild blows and kicks. They would have been knocked down, but there was no room for them to fall. Ryan, Nara and Damm received much better treatment from the people inside—they were only spit upon and cursed. Prodded by sec men, they were made to follow Thrill Bill through the foyer and into a stairwell packed with more humanity. Then they were forced to climb the flight leading up. It wasn't easy. They had to squeeze by the three or four people sitting on every step.

At the first landing, Thrill Bill paused. He ordered his guards to proceed up to the next floor with the Mitsuki prisoners. "You know what to do with them," he said. As the men in armor were pushed up the packed stairs, the warlord turned to Ryan and said, "While those two are being dealt with, I think the rest of us should sit down and have a little chat."

The landing's door opened onto a windowless hallway, lit by a row of bulbs strung along the ceiling. The sight of more mob didn't surprise Ryan; he was starting to expect it. When the sec men cleared the people away from a doorway, Ryan saw a wide band of greasy dirt along the walls where countless hands had brushed. Thrill Bill opened the door, and, after ordering his guards to wait outside, waved Ryan and the others into the room.

It had a few furnishings—a couple of battered couches, a mattress and bed frame. Along one wall was an arsenal of blasters. Not just laser weapons, but the sort of thing Ryan was used to handling in Deathlands: standard military, stamped-receiver, mass-produced automatic rifles, stacked boxes of metal-jacketed rounds, armored breastplates and helmets. There were also open plastic crates of grens and antipersonnel charges. What the room didn't have was people. There were just the four of them.

The warlord closed the door behind him, then pointed at the opposite wall. "Stand beside the windows, please," he said.

They overlooked the street below. Ryan looked down at a sea of bobbing heads, too many to fight, and to the right, a fan of bodies.

Too many to move.

Loud, jangling music erupted from the rear. When he spun, Thrill Bill was smiling at him. The sound was coming from a small black box on the floor beside the bed.

"The people in the hall outside will be listening at the door," the warlord said as he stepped closer to them. "A little white noise will give us some privacy."

Then he faced Damm. "Okay, Sarge, let's hear the story.".

"Mitsuki hired me to snatch Cawdor away from FIVE," Damm said. "Me and the captain decided to pull a double cross on Mitsuki by taking him for ourselves. We planned to hold on to him until we scored safe passage to Shadow World."

"Mitsuki sent the tactical unit after you?"

"Looks like they didn't trust me," Damm said. "Now we're fucked in a great big way."

"Not an exclusive club anymore." Thrill Bill

looked at Nara. "Never seen you so damned pale. What is it? All those dead folks out there giving you a flashback, Captain?"

Nara glared at him, then said, "Yeah, I never could stand the sight of blood."

"Funny, that's not how I remember it." Thrill Bill adjusted the frayed khaki strap that held his goggles in place, then he changed the subject. "You've been over to the other side, Captain. Is it half as sweet as the tell-yous claim?"

"Sweeter," she told him. "Space to breathe. More animals than people. Trees. Even birds. I saw birds, Bill."

"Sounds like heaven."

Ryan was sick of the banter, and the delay. He stepped up toe to toe with the warlord, close enough to see the fingerprints and grease smears on the lenses of his goggles. "I want out of here," he said. "Back to where I came from. Back to Deathlands. If you can't help me get there, you're going through that window, hair spikes first."

Thrill Bill threw back his head and laughed. "Your vid doesn't do you justice, Shadow Man. You got style."

Ryan tensed, preparing to do just what he'd promised.

"What a minute," Damm said, inserting an arm between their opposing chests. "Maybe we can work something out."

"I'm listening," Thrill Bill said.

"Come with us," Damm stated. "Otherwise you'll rot here with everybody else."

The warlord reached inside his armor vest and produced a red plastic tag. He showed it to them proudly. It had the number 79 printed on it. "Already got my ticket, Sarge," he said. "I'm going over in the first wave with the CEOs."

"You might as well save some time and cut your throat right now," Nara told him. "The lottery is a hoax. FIVE isn't taking anybody below Level 100. Never had any plans to, either."

Thrill Bill looked at her. "You wouldn't shit me, now, would you, Captain?"

"Have I ever shit you, Bill?"

The two stared eye to eye for a long moment.

Then the warlord examined the ticket. "Guess I knew all along it was too good to be true." He ripped the ticket in two and tossed it over his shoulder. "Fucked by the CEOs again," he said.

"Fucked for the last time unless you hook up with us," Damm said.

Ryan glowered impatiently at the warlord.

Thrill Bill twirled the tip of one of his hair spikes. "You three stand zero chance of reaching the Totality Concept complex. FIVE's got the biggest army on the planet, and you can be sure it's going to be protecting the CEOs' escape route."

"If you hang around Gloomtown, you're going to starve to death," Damm reminded him.

"Maybe Bill wants to stick around and see his flock out," Nara said. "Very noble of him."

"What, you don't think I'm capable of something like that?" the warlord said. "You think it's beyond a former dog soldier grunt like me to go down with the ship?"

Nara shook her head. "I know you're up to it. I think it's a pointless gesture. You can't do anything for the people outside this room. You can't make their dying any easier. You can only save yourself."

As if to underscore the remark, screams loud enough to be heard over the din of music came from the room above.

A dark form plummeted past the window to Ryan's right. As he turned to face the glass, another body dropped from above. The crowds outside roared their approval.

"That'll be Major Lujan, on his way out," Thrill Bill said. He pushed between Ryan and Damm and threw open the windows so they could all lean over the sills.

One story below, the mob was closing in on two men in armor lying crumpled on the street.

A few feet from the building's facade, a pair of gray ropes swayed. Wet, glistening, gray ropes. On closer inspection, Ryan thought they looked more like empty hoses. Only they were twisted and kinked. Stretching over the window frame, he reached out a hand to touch one.

"No, don't," Nara cautioned.

"You-hoo!" someone shouted down at him.

Ryan craned his neck around and looked up.

The sec men leaning out of the windows of the floor above waved at him. They had bloody knives in their hands.

Not hoses, Ryan thought. Guts.

Before Thrill Bill's bodyguards had thrown their prisoners out the windows, they had nailed their intestines to the sills. The weight of their bodies had made their innards uncoil as they dropped, and when the weight came down on the ends of the tether, guts ripped free. That this had partially broken their fall was no mercy. With stomachs torn halfway through the missing armor plates on their chests, they were set upon by a swarming, angry mob.

"There is no truth, but some small justice," Thrill Bill said

"So, what's your answer?" Damm demanded. "Are you in or out?"

"If I can get us into the complex," the warlord said, "you can get us across to Shadow World?"

"No, but *he* can," Damm said.

Thrill Bill stared at Ryan.

"FIVE will take him back dead," the mercie said. "It's either that or the alliance is going to fall apart. But they would prefer to get him alive. Once we're inside in the complex, we can use him to bargain for transport."

Ryan had already picked out the weapon he wanted. He darted away from the window, stooped and swept up a submachine gun with a stick mag. He flicked the charging knob and leveled the blaster at them. "I think I'll find my own way back," he said. "And you can forget about tagging along. You're never going to leave this room."

"Easy, Ryan," Nara said. "We're not going to sell you out and leave you behind. I owe it to you to get you back where you came from. You don't deserve to die here."

"We're all getting out, Cawdor, or no one is," Damm said.

The mercie's words were still hanging in the air when the building was rocked by a blast that rained ceiling plaster on them.

Ryan looked out the window and saw black APCs pouring out of the ramp that connected to the levels above, fanning the street with lines of green fire.

Chapter Twenty-Five

Jak Lauren wasn't watching the sky as the aircraft closed in; the shores of the boiling lake held dangers, too. Dangers just as near.

Over the bubbling mud and the beat of the propellers, he strained to locate the sound he had just heard. Despite the sweltering heat, the muted back-and-forth yap-yap had made his blood run cold.

There it was again.

A signal.

Not human.

Jak kicked one of the bleached bones at his feet, a thigh bone from a wild boar, probably. It was sheared at both ends. To do something like that, an animal had to be triple big, with sharp teeth and powerful jaws. Long bones only cracked under tremendous pressure.

The other companions stood transfixed by the aircraft swooping out of the night sky. Jak alone watched their backs.

Along the shoreline in the dim distance, bursting through clouds of sulfurous steam, the teenager saw dozens upon dozens of red eyes just like his, bobbing a foot or two above the ground. Jak caught flashes of the moonlight reflected off yellow fangs, and over the steady rumble of the boiling pools, he heard their exalted yapping.

"J.B.!" he cried as he raised his .357 Magnum Colt Python and thumbed back the hammer.

The creatures weren't fleeing in a panic before the noise of the propellers, and they weren't short, unless you compared them to a buffalo. The pack of mutie coyotes ran with their necks bent, their heads lowered to catch the scent. As they loped around the curve of shoreline, now that their prey was in sight, they were deadly quiet, like shadows on all fours.

"J.B.!" the teen shouted again, and opened fire.

The big handblaster barked and bucked against his two-handed grip. A single coyote at the front of the bunch screamed and twisted in agony, throwing itself into the air. The pack kept coming. Jak fired again, crumpling the lead coyote, who tumbled under its onrushing followers, causing them to stumble and yelp, and leap out of the way.

"God's truth," Doc groaned as he looked away from the gunship, over his shoulder at what was coming toward them, "we are well and truly in the soup!"

J.B. spun and fired his 12-gauge. As he pumped the slide, he shouted, "Chill the bastards. Get them before they're on us or they'll rip us apart!"

The companions turned their backs on the hovering aircraft and unleashed a torrent of blasterfire at the onrushing horde. Death from above was no longer their primary concern. Though they dropped coyote after coyote with volleys of well-aimed shots, there seemed no end to the pack. And the twice-normal-size creatures could cover twenty feet in a single bound. Before they knew it, the beasts were in among them, circling, leaping, snapping at their faces.

Mildred seized the hairy throat of an attacker, jammed the muzzle of her ZKR pistol into its open maw, and blew its brains out the back of its skull. Before she could throw the creature aside, another had her by the seat of the pants, shaking its head wildly, trying to pull her to the ground. The coyote dragged her backward, down to one knee. It released her and lunged, open-jawed, for her unprotected nape.

Jak's right arm moved in a blur. His leaf-bladed throwing knife hit the coyote in midair. It was hurled so hard that the point drove in one eye socket and out the other. The coyote landed on Mildred's back and tumbled off, all four legs kicking weakly.

Ringed by dead coyotes, Krysty dumped a cylinder of spent casings into the dirt, and reached for her last, full speed-loader.

His shotgun empty, unwilling to use his Uzi in such close quarters with his friends, J.B. swung the M-4000 by its barrel, beating back the snarling animals that feinted and lunged at him, seeking the chance to go for his throat.

"Enough!" Doc cried, dropping his LeMat and unsheathing the sword from his cane.

The old man waded into the churning mass of waist-high devils, slashing left and right with the blade. He gave no thought to piercing hearts or bowels; there were too many for that. His goal was to draw them away from his companions, to inflict as much pain in the shortest possible time and thereby drive off the creatures.

Pain, he gave them. In spades.

The point of finest Toledo steel opened their flanks and split the hide of their backs. The mutie coyotes tried to get at him, circling around and around. Doc's blade trimmed a set of ears tight to a skull, opened a second grinning mouth beneath the first. Every lunge of dog beast, he parried with cold steel. And for every lunge, a beast paid dearly.

At last, the coyotes lost heart and gave up. Yapping, the badly dinged survivors slunk off with their tails between their legs, their behinds low to the ground. Every few yards they looked back over their shoulders to make sure they weren't being pursued by the two-legged demon in the frock coat.

Exhausted, bloodied, their weapons empty, the muddy field of battle strewed with dead foes, the companions once again turned to face the waiting aircraft.

"Morituri te salutamus," Doc said, sweeping a deep bow with his sword outstretched.

"What'd he say?" J.B. asked, his eyes locked on to the barrels of the cannons that held them pinned.

"Those who are about to die, etcetera, etcetera," Mildred said.

THERE WERE NO SECRETS between crew members of an assault gyro. When Captain Ockerman closed in on the group of Shadow people, his passenger knew exactly what he was planning to do.

Inside Hylander's visor, a single, red sight ring encircled all five of them. When Ockerman fired the cannons, nothing within the red ring that was made of flesh and blood would survive.

"John!" Hylander said. "Don't do it!"

Ockerman held his fire, but not because the guy sitting behind him told him to. "Would you look at that!" he exclaimed.

Along the shore of the mud lake, Hylander saw what so excited him. A scrambling patch of movement, bodies, legs, gaping mouths.

Animals.

Multicellular animals.

Hylander's heart leaped into his throat. He was a biologist, but the only living multicellular animal he'd ever seen was another human. The beauty and grace, the speed left him speechless. These were creatures born to kill, creatures who acted as a team to bring down their meat.

"Predators," he managed to say. "Pack hunters. Some kind of mutated wild dogs. Or maybe wolves. Can't tell from up here."

"There go your precious tissue samples," Ockerman said as the pack swept in around the Shadow people.

Pilot and copilot watched spellbound as the humans defended themselves against overwhelming odds. The combat was intense and at impossibly close quarters.

Hand to fang.

When the man unsheathed his sword, Ockerman let out a whoop. "Look at that bastard hack! They've got him surrounded and he's kicking their butts!"

It was only after the wounded animals turned tail that Hylander realized his own pulse was pounding, his hands trembling inside their gauntlets. He had never witnessed anything so exciting. A battle of near equals. And not over something abstract like consumption quotas. The battle was to keep from being eaten alive.

Hylander caught himself wanting to be down there

on the ground with them. No armor. No sensors. No laser. Just raw muscle and sharp steel.

Inside the red targeting ring in Hylander's visor, the swordsman turned and bowed to them.

The biologist's jaw dropped at the remarkable gesture. It yielded without yielding, showed both respect and contempt.

It said, "On my terms, you would not win."

"Awesome!" Ockerman exclaimed.

To Hylander's relief, the pilot switched off the weapons array and hit the paralyzing mist instead. Ockerman sent a cloud of knockout gas billowing over the six. It took about ten seconds to put them down. None of them tried to run. They stood together as unconsciousness overcame them, and fell across one another.

"Better call Connors and tell him where your meat pickup is," Ockerman said.

Hylander tried the comm link and got no reply. "That's strange," he said. "The ATV should be well within range."

"Maybe there's some interference from the ridge," Ockerman suggested. "When he comes around the backside, you should be able to raise him."

He set the gyro down a safe distance from the lake and they both got out. Ockerman opened an external storage compartment and pulled out a net woven of heavy plastic cord. While he spread the net on the ground in front of the assault gyro, Hylander walked toward the heaped human forms beside the volcanic lake.

The biologist gave them hardly a glance. He was much more interested in the animals that had attacked them. Up close, he recognized them from pictures he'd seen. Such creatures hadn't existed on his Earth for more than fifty years. They were definitely coyotes, but of tremendous size.

Hylander stooped over one of the dead animals. He smoothed his gauntleted hand over its fur and decided that wasn't good enough. He pulled the glove off and touched the coyote with his bare hand.

Amazing.

Still warm.

The fur was dense and soft over the powerful muscles that lined the shoulders and back. He peeled back the lips and examined the teeth. The canines were like curving ivory daggers. The tongue pale-purple. The nose soft and wet. The eyes wide set, and large. It had been a complex, highly intelligent and perfectly adapted organism.

Hylander gently laid the head back down and then looked up from the corpse, across the moonlit landscape.

"I thought you wanted to take samples from these people?" Ockerman said as he stepped up.

"Look at this." Hylander showed him the coyote's teeth.

The biologist couldn't read the other man's expression through the black helmet, but Ockerman immediately knelt. Without Hylander's suggesting it, he removed his gauntlet to feel the points of the fangs and to stroke the furry ears.

After a moment, the pilot straightened. "We'd better get on with it," he said, gesturing a thumb at the unconscious people. "Don't want them to come around before we get them bagged."

As they rolled the tall red-haired woman off the

top of the pile, Ockerman jerked his hand back in surprise. "Her hair moved! It's still moving! Would you look at that!"

Hylander watched the tendrils slowly retract.

"Correct me if I'm wrong," Ockerman said, "but hair isn't supposed to do that."

The biologist leaned closer and touched a tendril with a gloved finger. It sprang back into a tight coil.

"She's mutated," Hylander said. "Her hair's actually got nerves and muscle tissue. Really bizarre."

"Shouldn't we terminate her right here?" Ockerman said. "If she's got that kind of radiation damage, why drag her all the way back to the camp? If we're going to kill her anyway, why not do it here, while she's out cold? We can leave her body for the coyotes to eat."

Hylander knew that protocol said that was what they had to do.

But the men who had made up the rules were in another universe.

"No, the killing can wait," Hylander said. "We'll take them all back, as planned. I'll bet she's got some interesting genetics."

The two men took hold of Krysty's hands and feet and lifted her over to the open net. They handled each of the companions in the same way. When they had all the bodies stacked in the middle, they folded over the sides of the net. Ockerman cinched up the cable that ran around the edge, making a bag out of it. Then he connected the end of the cable to the mechanical claw on the underside of the gyroplane.

Hylander started to walk toward the aircraft's door, but stopped when he saw that Ockerman was heading back to the lakeside. The pilot bent down and started picking up the weapons the Shadow people had dropped.

"What are you doing?" Hylander asked.

"Thought the colonel might like to see this stuff," Ockerman said. He snatched up the cane and the fallen sword and took a couple of practice cuts in the air with it. "No sense in just leaving it all here."

Hylander gathered up a stubby submachine gun and a short-barreled pump shotgun. Then they lugged the stuff back to the gyro.

"Better give Connors another try," Ockerman said after they'd climbed back into their respective chairs. "Let him know that we're heading for base camp and that he missed the party."

Hylander still got no answer.

"Do you think the dumbfuck managed to get himself lost out there?" he said "He could've had an accident, maybe even gotten himself killed."

"Anything's possible," Ockerman agreed. "He could also have had a case of comm trouble and turned back, figuring there was no way to find us without it. Let's take the long way back, swing wide around the ridge, and see if we can pick him up."

CAPTAIN CONNORS WASN'T LOST and he hadn't been killed by mutie coyotes, or mutie anything else for that matter. When the assault gyro flew over, searching for him, he was sitting in the ATV, which he'd parked under one of the few overpasses still standing on Highway 15. He waited there with his eyes closed, leaning on the steering wheel, until the sound of the props faded away in the distance.

He hadn't even considered the possibility of deserting when he'd climbed into the ATV. In fact, the idea only occurred to him as he roared down the road out of the hammered little town. The mouth of the canyon opened up before him, and beyond it, the tilted plain sweeping down to the interstate. Overhead were the pinpoints of starlight and the cold white moon.

He remembered looking down at the fuel level indicator and seeing that the tanks were topped up. He remembered thinking that the vehicle had a range of close to a thousand miles, depending on how hard it was pushed.

Then it hit him.

For the first time in his life, freedom was within his grasp. Not the niggardly little range of choices offered up by his Earth. Beefie Cheesie or Tater Cheesie. Standing room on the sidewalk or in the stairwell. Cremation or mass grave. This was elemental, limitless.

As he'd driven through the gap in the ridge, out onto the plain, Connors had taken stock of himself. Like most of the other members of the team, he had people waiting for him on the Earth side—in his case, legions of relatives he felt no kinship to. Lovers he didn't love. Friends whose affection depended on what he could do for them. His career as a geologist had been reduced to looking for ways to turn rock into a hamburger that poisoned people more slowly. And worst of all, there was his military service, portions of which hung around his neck like a fifty-pound weight.

What he'd done in the name of FIVE during the Consumer Rebellion would never wash away. Those selfsame deeds had probably convinced the CEOs that he should be selected to make the crossing. By the butchery he had performed, he had proved his loyalty to FIVE.

And there was more butchery to come, an entire world to be subjugated and slaughtered.

Connors was by no means a coward, but he had nothing against the people who'd attacked the launch site. Their actions didn't anger him, and they couldn't hurt him with their outdated weapons. As he exited the canyon, he realized he didn't want to catch them; furthermore, he didn't want to have anything to do with catching them.

How long would it take FIVE to fuck up this place? he asked himself. One hundred years? Fifty years? If the mission was pure bullshit, why act like it wasn't? Why play the game? Life was too precious and too short to be spent in the service of a cause you didn't believe in.

When it occurred to him that he had the power to keep on going, that there was no one and nothing that could stop him from doing exactly what he wanted, it sent a chill up the back of his neck. The highway was visible as a straight line running across the plain below. No matter how torn up it was, he could traverse it in the ATV.

A thousand miles.

He could lose himself forever in this wild place, and when the ATV ran out of fuel, he could walk. And when the battlesuit's power source failed, he would abandon it.

FIVE would never find him. Who was he kidding? FIVE would never even look.

He thought about opening the comm link and saying goodbye, but he decided against it. Why complicate things? In time they would come to understand his reasons, if they didn't already.

When the gyro had landed back in the canyon, Connors started up the ATV and pulled out from under the overpass. He headed north because that was the direction of his home on the other Earth, and he was curious to see what it looked like. As he drove off, he thought, stick a fork in me. I am done.

Chapter Twenty-Six

A second burst of laser cannon sent Ryan, Nara, Damm and Thrill Bill to their bellies on the floor of the warlord's apartment. Succumbing to a wave of impossible heat, the windows facing the street imploded. The bolt of green screamed through the room, lancing the air three feet above their backs. If he could have, Ryan would have tried to rip the floor apart to escape the blistering inferno. But he couldn't move his arms or his legs, he was paralyzed by heat shock.

When Ryan opened his eye, he saw that the room's front wall had a fifteen-foot section missing. Windows, windowframes, wall studs, exterior sheathing, all were gone, and flames licked up from the sheared edges. Behind him, the opposite wall had a similar chunk taken out of it. The corridor beyond was on fire and people were yelling. From outside, he heard different kinds of explosions.

Moving closer to the breached wall, he saw the smoke trails of shoulder-fired rockets as they shot from the windows of buildings on either side of him. The missiles exploded with authority among the APCs clustered at the mouth of the ramp. The armored vehicles absorbed the direct hits and immediately returned green fire.

"This is insane," Nara said. "What are those assholes at Mitsuki thinking of? This is going to start another Global shooting war.''

''Take a closer look, Captain,'' Thrill Bill said. ''That's not Mitsuki down there. It's FIVE. And they want their boy toy back. The first place they're going to come looking is right here. They know where I live. It would be best if we beat feet before the ground troops start piling out of those APCs. Help yourself to ordinance, as much as you can run with. We won't be coming back for more.''

Ryan slung the submachine gun over one shoulder and grabbed a nylon rucksack. It looked to him like all the conventional weapons fired the same round— a rimmed, .40-caliber full-metal jacket. He stuffed his pack with extra stick mags for the subgun and power packs for the laser rifle. In an open crate were more of the disk-shaped AP mines. He took a big handful. He also took a half dozen grens. Some were frags, some flash-stun. By the time he picked up one of the laser rifles from the floor, he was seriously weighed down.

Thrill Bill waited while Damm and Nara struggled into the straps of their own overstuffed rucksacks. The warlord wasn't taking anything extra, just a pulse rifle. ''Got my own pack mules outside,'' he said.

They pushed out into the chaos of the hallway. A sheet of flame had crept up the walls and was licking across the ceiling. The thick smoke made it very hard to see what or who was underfoot. There were many dead, and their bodies had been ruptured by the intense heat.

Thrill Bill shouted for his sec men. A half dozen stumbled forward, dazed, drenched with blood that wasn't their own. "We're evacuating the building," he told them. "I'll break trail for us."

Ryan fell into step behind the warlord. As they ran down the corridor, the throng of confused and frightened people flattened against the walls, giving them room to pass. Over the tramp of heavy boots, Ryan heard the sounds of battle raging out in the street. It was growing even more intense.

"How long can your people hold out?" Ryan called to the back of the warlord's head.

"Until the last man falls," Thrill Bill said. "They know that surrender isn't an option. It's suicide."

The hallway was jolted by a terrific blast that sent the warlord and Ryan crashing to the floor. As they pushed up to their feet, there was another grinding roar.

"They've hit the main armory," Thrill Bill said. "We've got less time than I thought."

Before he followed, Ryan looked down the hall the way they'd come. All the civilians packed along its walls were falling in behind the last of Bill's sec men, a crush of people running for their lives.

The hallway before them ended in a T. Thrill Bill went left. There were open doors on either side of the corridor. Between the heads of the people standing in the hallway, Ryan could see inside the rooms. Mobs of pale, frightened faces stared back at him.

About fifty yards ahead, the hallway they were in was crossed by another. As the crowd melted back to the walls and they approached the juncture, from around the corner, to the right, Ryan caught flashes of bright green light, and over a multitude of screams from that direction, what sounded like bacon sizzling.

Thrill Bill slowed, then stopped well short of the intersection. He waved over a sec man carrying a heavy backpack, reached inside and took out a big handful of slap charges. "Out of the corridor," the warlord said. "On the double!"

The commands were meant to apply only to his own crew. No way could all the folks standing along the walls fit into the adjoining rooms, which were already full.

The civilians watched, as did Ryan, while Thrill Bill chucked the explosives down the middle of the hall, scattering them all the way to the crossing.

"Move!" Thrill Bill cried.

Ryan, Damm and Nara forced their way through one of the open doorways. As the one-eyed man wedged himself into the packed room, the unlucky souls in the hall behind him realized that their cause was lost and took off in a panic, running ahead of the advancing troops. Ryan looked down at the face of a little boy held by a woman, probably his mother. The kid's rosy cheeks were crusted with dirt and sores. He smiled up at Ryan.

Not because he was offering hope—there was none—but because he was returning kindness, the one-eyed man smiled back.

Then he heard the tramp of running boots, more screams, and he could see green light flaring down the hall outside. The FIVE troopers had rounded the corner and were stomping over the slap charges.

Ryan could imagine the devices sticking to the soles of the soldiers' boots like great wads of chewing gum. How long would it take to realize what they'd stepped on? How long would it take to strip them off?

Three seconds?

Four seconds?

The mines discharged in a tight string, rattling the walls and floor, and sending the people around Ryan staggering for balance.

"Let's go!" came Thrill Bill's shout from across the corridor.

Ryan exited the room and stepped into a charnel house. Blood dripped from the blackened ceiling, and the floor was awash in it. The broken bodies of FIVE troopers and Gloomtown residents lay mingled on the floor. Their legs blown off at the hip, some of the soldiers still thrashed, shrieking behind their black helmets.

There was no time—or inclination—for mercy bullets.

Thrill Bill jumped over the bodies and Ryan followed, moving past the perimeter of the mines' blast zone to the join of the connecting hall. The warlord didn't pause at the corner, he threw himself across the gap. Ryan did the same, and as he jumped, he glimpsed more figures in black rushing down the corridor toward them, trampling over the piles of dead and dying innocents, those already well serviced by the legions of FIVE.

Damm, then Nara, leaped across the hallway. Ryan caught the blonde as she cleared the gap, then pushed her ahead of him.

Another pair of sec men made the jump without drawing enemy fire. But the next two who tried to cross were hit by a half dozen beams at once. Their bodies knocked sprawling in midair, they came down ten feet away, in pieces.

Hissing.

On the other side of gap, the warlord's sec men hesitated, wanting to make the jump, but afraid to try. With the pulse rifles massed down the hallway to the right, to cross the corridor was death by firing squad.

Thrill Bill shouted to them, "Stay there! Don't try to follow us! Just keep them off our butts!"

Ryan and the others had only moved a short distance down the hall, when they heard the sounds of furious fighting from the juncture behind them. The warlord's sec men were doing their best to obey his final orders, to defend his back against all comers.

Then, above the grinding tumult of battle, it sounded like a hundred teakettles were blowing their tops.

"They're cutting through the walls with sustained fire!" Damm told the warlord. "They'll have your men flanked in no time."

"Run!" was Bill's reply.

To keep up with the tall warlord, Ryan had to break into an all-out sprint. High-kicking down the hall, they took a dogleg to the right. Twenty feet down, on the left side of the corridor was the first closed door that Ryan had seen so far. It was also locked. Thrill Bill quickly opened it with a key.

Once Ryan was inside it was clear why the warlord was concerned about security.

The room was a bunker.

Its left rear corner, the one that faced down the long hallway they'd just fled, was heavily fortified. The wall itself was defended with plates of the same black material as the battlesuits. Sandbagged in place, the armor ran from the floor halfway up the wall. More black plates extended from the ceiling, leaving a gap in the coverage of about a foot. It wasn't a firing port, yet; the wall on the other side was still intact. The gap in the armor ran ten feet along the middle of the wall—roughly the width of the corridor. There was plenty of room for four pulse rifles to line up along it.

"Know how to use one of those?" Thrill Bill said to Ryan, pointing at the air-cooled light machine gun that sat on a tripod at the far end of the firing port.

In front of its pistol grip was a huge drum magazine. Ryan checked the round counter. The thing was loaded with 2500 rounds. The barrel had a massive recoil compensator, but nothing else unusual.

"Yeah, I can use it," Ryan replied, "but why would I want to bother? Bullets won't penetrate that armor they're wearing."

"You've got a lot to learn about battlesuits," Damm said.

Down the hallway, the sounds of fighting died away, but the screaming continued.

It wasn't a good sign.

Thrill Bill pounded on the wall's black armor with his balled fist. "Under the plasterboard of the walls, the floor and the ceiling, the hallway out there is lined with this stuff. It reflects the battlesuits' defensive pulses. If you pack a lot of suits in a confined, reflective environment and then put them under heavy fire, things get all fucked up in a hurry. The defensive pulses from one suit are read as offensive attacks by the others. They counteract and cancel each other. In other words, what we have out there is a shooting gallery. I want you to open fire when I tell you to and don't stop firing until I give the all clear."

Ryan hunkered down behind the machine gun, found the actuating handle and chambered round number one. Then he looked at the blank wall that filled the firing port.

"Better turn your heads," Thrill Bill said. "I'm five seconds from blowing that wall."

The warlord had a small detonator in his hand, and was staring at a video monitor that showed a view of the hallway, looking down from ceiling height. Ryan watched the monitor, too. After no more than a couple of seconds, men in black appeared in the distance.

Fifty or more, Ryan thought.

The troopers at the head of the line fired their weapons, cooking the people still trapped in the hall, then booting the corpses out of the way.

"We got them!" Thrill Bill said, tripping the switch.

With a whomp, the front of the wall blew out into the hall. Before the plaster dust cleared, Nara, Damm and the sec men had their tribarrels shoved through the port.

"Fire!" the warlord shouted.

The range to the troopers in the front of the pack was less than forty feet.

Ryan pinned the machine gun's trigger. As the weapon roared to life, its buttstock rammed hard against his shoulder. He fanned the front-runners with hot lead, sending an unbroken string of brass hulls clattering against the wall to his right.

On his left, the others cut loose with pulse rifles cranked up to the max. If he hadn't already lost the eye on that side, he would have had to close it to keep from being blinded by the green glare. The whistling noise of their sustained laser fire was deafening.

For a fraction of a second the battlesuits' defenses seemed to hold. The four men in the lead continued to advance as their armor deflected the incoming fire. The full-power laser beams veered off their chests and into the side walls, only to veer off again when they struck the concealed armor sheathing. Over and over, the beams deflected off armor and reflected off walls, only to strike armor again farther down; laser light zigzagged the entire length of the hall, turning it into a screaming green inferno. Ryan poured a torrent of slugs straight into their black helmets; it sounded to him like the machine gun was putting out better than a thousand rounds a minute, but the men in black kept coming.

Then, as Thrill Bill had predicted, it all fell apart.

So many rounds, so little space.

The row of black helmets shattered under Ryan's hail of lead, the armored bodies were flicked aside by probing lances of green.

The pressure of their concentrated firepower peeled back the point of the attack, melting men, rattling them inside their armor. As the targets disintegrated and fell away, Ryan adjusted his aim, reaching farther and farther into the corridor.

If the sustained lasers were largely bloodless, the conventional military rounds he fired were anything but. They blew through the black chest plates and exited the other side, taking with them plumes of red mist.

There were no screams audible over the whistling of the laser rifles. There was no return of fire from the opposition.

Thrill Bill had laid his trap well.

Ryan was still firing into the bodies heaped at the far end of the corridor, when the warlord shouted, "Clear!"

Ryan let up on the trigger. When he looked down, the magazine's round counter showed twelve bullets remaining.

Nothing moved in the hallway but smoke and fire. The haze of burned cordite from Ryan's weapon mixed with the clouds rising from the piles of dead. Fire raced along the great rents in the plaster that the pulse rifles had made.

Nara viewed the carnage on the other side of the firing port with stoic silence.

Damm was less subdued. "We cut them bite-sized!" he said, slapping palms with the sec man next to him.

The warlord didn't join the celebration, either. Already at the door, he was waving for them to follow. "Come on, there's a lot more where they came from," Thrill Bill said. "We've got to move."

As Ryan picked up his gear, Damm said, "How many of those mantraps have you got, Bill?"

"Not nearly enough to handle what FIVE's throwing at us. We've got to get clear of Gloomtown, and fast, or they'll box us in."

"Gloomtown is a sealed level," Nara said. "The only way in and out is controlled by FIVE."

"The only *official* way out," Thrill Bill corrected her.

In the hall outside, the warlord turned left and fell into a steady hard jog. Ryan noticed that the people in the corridor had stopped trooping after them. They were drawing way too much heat. It was safer to lie on top of one another in the side rooms, and pray that when the lasers sliced through the walls, they took out only the people piled above.

After a series of alternating right and left turns, the warlord stopped at another locked door. He opened it, then reached inside and hit a light switch. Ryan could see a long flight of metal stairs. Deserted stairs. The light was too dim at the bottom for him to be able to make it out. The stairwell was lined with red-brick walls, which looked ancient, and the mortar crumbled at the slightest touch.

"After you," the warlord said.

When they'd all entered and descended a few stairs to give him room, Thrill Bill stepped in. He shut and relocked the door from the inside.

Ryan saw him take a compact, tape-wrapped package from a niche in the wall. He wasn't sure what it was until he saw the man connect it to the door's top hinge. Booby trap.

"A wake-up call," Thrill Bill explained.

At the bottom of the stairs the floor was concrete. Ahead, was a narrow, low-ceilinged tunnel, lined with more of the decaying brick. As they advanced, overhead they could hear muffled sounds of explosions, the growl of engines and the clanking of tracked vehicles maneuvering on concrete.

"We're under Gloomtown," the warlord said.

They trotted for another five minutes, following the tunnel as it wound underground. The walls on either side were featureless. No doors. No windows. But occasionally, there were breaks where sections of wall had either collapsed from age or been broken in on purpose. In the weak light from bulbs strung along the ceiling, Ryan could see into the cramped little rooms beyond. They were empty but for piles of dirt on the floor, and massive, rusting, I-beam supports that crisscrossed the interior space.

It was at one of these unremarkable breaks that Thrill Bill called another halt. He stepped through the large hole in the bricks, then ducked under the crossing I-beams and moved to the far wall.

Ryan, Nara and Damm watched him from the tunnel side of the break.

"I hoped I'd never have to use this," the warlord admitted, as he bent and started to push the top off a heap of dirt.

"Use what?" Damm said. "I don't see an exit."

Ryan noticed a pair of iron hooks screwed into the mortar at about chest height.

Thrill Bill exposed the lid of a plastic crate. He opened it and took out a flashlight, which he set aside. The crate yielded two more tape-wrapped parcels, which the warlord hung by loops of cord to the exposed hooks. He stepped in front of the parcels and something beeped.

"Outside," he said, scooping up the flashlight. "We've got ten seconds to get to cover."

Ryan and Nara ran for half that time, then crouched against the base of the tunnel wall.

A thunderous explosion avalanched the already breached walls and sent a roiling wave of pulverized brick dust sweeping over them. Thrill Bill jumped up and led them through the choking pall and over the rubble. The man-size hole he'd entered was now wag-size. Only the crisscrossing iron beams had kept the room from caving in.

The warlord's torchlight cut through the dust and played over the far wall, where there was a yawning gap in the bricks. Behind the hole there was concrete block, and it, too, was blown apart.

Thrill Bill climbed through the breach and waved the others after him. Ryan stepped over the broken wall and into another empty, windowless room.

When they'd all crossed over, the warlord played his light over their faces. Nara looked grim, resigned.

"Come on, Captain," Thrill Bill said, "it's time to bury some ghosts."

He led them through the door in the wall opposite. There were no lights in the hallway beyond, which was also concrete-floored. They moved in a tight file behind the warlord, staying close to their only source of light. Sheets of cobwebs draped the tunnel; in places they hung from floor to ceiling. The trail-breaker used his pulse rifle's muzzle to slash a path through them, and his spiked hair and beard were soon decorated with long gray streamers.

The door Thrill Bill was looking for opened onto a stairwell that smelled of dust and mildew. Ryan followed Nara and Damm up the dismal shaft, which had landings and switchbacks spaced every fifteen steps.

Ryan had counted eight flights, when something crunched and skittered not far above. They all stopped as the warlord swept his torch over the steps leading to the next landing.

The light revealed human bones, bleached white. They lay in a jumble from wall to wall.

Thrill Bill reared back and booted a skull hard, ricocheting it off the wall and sending it clattering down the steps into the dark. "One of yours, or one of mine, Captain?" he asked.

Nara said nothing.

"Don't be shy about taking credit," he said as he resumed the climb. "Plenty more where that came from."

Thrill Bill wasn't exaggerating. The stairwell was a tower of the dead. The landing above was piled two feet deep in bones; it was only the beginning. The staircase above was choked with them.

In short order, the skeletal remains ceased to be surprising or alarming to Ryan, and became merely annoying. But they couldn't be completely ignored. A misstep and a slip while carrying a heavy pack could mean a bad, even a fatal fall.

"What is this place?" he asked, when they paused on a landing.

"Free-fire zone in the rebellion," Damm replied. "We're three street levels above Gloomtown."

Thrill Bill opened the door at the far end of the landing, and they stepped out into an enormous, open area plunged in darkness. It felt like the slime galleries below, only without the slime. The warlord's flashlight revealed a street like the one Ryan had seen in Gloomtown, complete with mob.

But there was a difference.

In this case, the mob was dead.

Long dead.

Acres of bones appeared in the flashlight's beam. So many that at first, Ryan couldn't believe what he was seeing—thousands upon thousands of skeletons, in every direction the light shone. They covered the sidewalks and the street. They lay inside the ground-floor buildings. Up against the facades, they were heaped ten deep in places.

Tremors in the pavement under their boots, earthquakes from the explosions in Gloomtown, caused skulls to slide, here and there.

"Been awhile, huh, Captain?" the warlord asked. "I know it sure takes me back."

"Shut up," Nara said.

"Haven't you always wondered what it looked like in here, after we walled all these people in? Wouldn't you like to have been a bug on the wall when the last one death-rattled and it got really, really quiet?"

Nara said nothing.

"Tell me you don't ever think about this," Thrill Bill said.

"I think about it every day."

"Well, now you can put a face to it." The light searched the white mounds, picking out a skull here, a skull there. "How about this one, or this one? Or this one over here?"

"You're puke, Ransom. Unadulterated puke."

"We both did what we did, and we got paid for it. I guess that makes you pretty much puke, too."

"I'm not proud of it."

"Neither am I, Captain. It might surprise you, but beneath this well-polished exterior is one very miserable dude."

"These people are beyond help," Ryan said impatiently. "We should go, and quickly, before the troopers catch up."

"Cawdor's right," Damm said.

"Yeah, I guess so," the warlord agreed. "Nothing's quite so disgusting as a couple of old soldiers weeping over their atrocities. What do you say to a truce, Captain?"

"Why not?" Nara replied.

With Thrill Bill in the lead, they worked their way across the avenue of death, kicking a path through the bones, and going around when the bodies were piled too high.

"How did they all die?" Ryan asked Damm.

"They breathed in carniphages," the mercie said. "Most likely they did it on purpose. They had shelters to hide in. They didn't use them. From the bullet holes in some of the skulls, it looks like a few of them got impatient and shot themselves. Maybe they thought it wouldn't hurt as much. None of these people offed themselves before they were two-thirds starved and dying of thirst. FIVE cut off the water supply, too. Carniphages cleaned up all the skeletons, nice and tidy."

"What'd they do to deserve it?"

"They didn't surrender fast enough to suit FIVE's CEOs," the warlord said over his shoulder.

Thrill Bill took them to the middle of the street. He pointed his light at the ground and said, "There it is."

In an area surprisingly clear of bones was a circular metal plate about three feet in diameter.

"Help me move it, Damm," the warlord said as he passed the flashlight to one of his sec men. The mercie bent, and the two of them struggled to shift the plate out of the steel flange inset into the surface of the street.

"What are you doing?" Nara asked.

"This is how we get out," Thrill Bill told her.

Nara looked dubious.

The job done, Thrill Bill took back his flashlight. "We aren't the first visitors to this place, Captain. A while back, our friends from Population Control dropped in to see what kind of job their one-celled pets were doing. Guess they must've been really pleased. Anyway, the PCS boys came in and went out via the main sewer line.''

"How appropriate," Nara said.

Thrill Bill put the flashlight between his teeth, eased through the opening feetfirst and started down. The light from the hole got dimmer and dimmer as he descended, and with each succeeding climber more and more of what little remained was blocked.

By the time it came for Ryan to bring up the rear, he could hardly see the opening. After locating the steel rungs inside with the toe of his boot, he backed partway down the pipe. As he was the last one to enter the manhole, it was his job to pull the grate back in place. This he did, though it took some effort, hampered as he was by the pack and two shoulder-slung blasters. Below him, something faintly flickered and he could hear boot soles scraping on rungs.

He couldn't see the hand-and footholds, so he descended by feel, one careful rung at a time. A light played over his back as he climbed down the final twenty feet. The vertical feeder pipe he was in emptied into a much wider, horizontal channel, a corrugated steel cylinder about ten feet in diameter. The others stood clustered to one side, around the only source of light.

"We'd better hurry," Thrill Bill said. "The guys who're after us know about this, too." Then he set off down the sewer pipe.

Still at the rear of the file, Ryan sloshed through the stream of evil-smelling liquid that was running down the center of the pipe. The footing was damned slippery, and in the bad light there was no telling exactly what kind of nastiness a person might be slipping on.

They had traveled a short distance when, behind and way above them, Ryan heard the sound of steel scaping concrete. Someone was dragging back the sewer grate.

He stopped long enough to dig into his pack for a few slap charges. As he resumed walking, he dropped them at intervals behind him, tossing them into the sluggishly moving water, where they couldn't be seen. When he had dispersed them all, he ran to catch up with the others.

As he chased after the bobbing light ahead, he wondered if the mines would "stick and kick" if they were submerged. He'd rejoined the others, and they had put another fifty yards of sewer behind them when something went whack far to the rear.

One whack became seven, in a row.

Thrill Bill instantly shut off his light.

"It was me," Ryan told him. "I dropped some mines back there. Thought it might slow them up."

"You thought right," Damm said. "They're dead slow, about now."

"There'll be more of them," Thrill Bill stated as he switched the light back on. "You can bet on that." He picked up the pace.

After another fifty yards, the channel rounded a bend and Bill's flashlight found another row of rungs.

"This is it," the warlord said, shining his light up the vertical pipe.

Ryan looked up and couldn't see the top. The rungs just faded into darkness at the edge of the light, about two hundred feet up.

"It's a long climb, so let's get cracking," Thrill Bill said. He started up the pipe first.

Damm went next, then Nara. Ryan moved in behind her and the two sec men came last.

They climbed much farther than two hundred feet. Ryan tried to keep track of the rungs, but he lost count. Above them, there was a familiar roaring noise; it came in waves. The higher they went the louder it got.

Finally, Nara stopped climbing ahead of him and he had to stop, too.

His curses muffled by the flashlight in his mouth, Thrill Bill shouldered aside the grate that blocked the top of the pipe. Weak yellow light bathed them. Ryan recognized the sounds, which he'd heard earlier. They came from high-speed traffic.

Holding on to his rung, Ryan leaned to one side, trying to see around Nara and Damm. He glimpsed Thrill Bill as he stuck his head out of the opening, and ducked it right back. A roar passed over the hole and a gust of gritty wind whipped their faces.

"Shit," the warlord groaned. Then he popped his head up again. After a pause, he scurried out.

Ryan had the problem pretty much figured out by the time it came his turn to exit the pipe. So it wasn't a big surprise when he poked his head up over the rim of the drain and saw a fireblasted ten-ton wag bearing down on him at a hundred miles an hour. He dropped back down; it was either that or get beheaded.

What he'd seen verified his suspicion. The manhole opened smack in the middle of fifty lanes of freeway.

Ryan raised his head again, checked the oncoming

traffic, and seeing he had a good chance, jumped up and out. The sec man behind him thought he had an opportunity, too. Ryan saw him scramble halfway out of the hole, then a burst of green light from below swept through him like he was made of mist. The sustained beam gouged a hole in the freeway tunnel's concrete ceiling, showering Ryan with fat yellow sparks.

He instinctively reached for the man's outstretched arms and caught him by one wrist.

"No!" Nara shouted. "He's dead. Leave him."

Ryan pulled on the man's wrist, and there was no weight to him. Nothing remained of him below the waist. When Ryan let go, the weight of the sec man's pack drew him back toward the hole.

As the one-eyed man turned away, the sec man's torso slipped down the pipe and vanished.

Nara had already abandoned the scene. She was running across the lanes of traffic to the big pileup of wrecked wags where Damm and Thrill Bill waited. Ryan measured the distance and timed his dash. He'd crossed three or four lanes when he realized the oncoming drivers were speeding up and changing lanes in an attempt to cut him off and run him down. He sprinted the last forty feet, and even then had to make a panic dive to the pavement to keep from being clipped.

As Damm helped him to his feet, the wags zooming past honked their horns.

Thrill Bill was rummaging around in Nara's pack. He took out five grens and a couple of slap charges. He handed each of them a gren and kept a pair for himself. "Throw when I do, where I do," he told them, then climbed the twisted heap of steel.

After a moment or two, he shouted down, "Got a big pack of vehicles coming on the right. Four lanes deep. This is it!"

Ryan yanked the pin and let the grip safety plink off. When he saw Thrill Bill underhand his grens toward the approaching wags, he did the same. All five grens rolled to a stop in the middle of the four lanes of traffic.

As the grens popped off, Ryan pulled back to cover behind a crushed sedan. Shrapnel spanged the side of the wreck and skipped off the tunnel's ceiling. The explosions were followed by a squeal of tires and the crash of metal and glass.

The new pileup was massive.

Thrill Bill jumped down from his perch and ran. "Come on!" he shouted to the others. "Before they get away!"

Ryan chased after him.

The four wags in front were tipped on their sides and starting to burn. The ones behind were wedged together tight, and crumpled fore and aft. Ryan saw the drivers slumped over their steering wheels.

Thrill Bill kept running, past the rows of totaled vehicles. He stopped alongside the driver's door of a sleek maroon minivan at the back of the pack that appeared undamaged. The driver, a man in a blue blazer, shirt and tie, took one look at the hair, the beard and the pulse rifle and decided he wanted no part of the warlord. All the van's windows started to fill with black from the bottom up. They were made of armor.

Before the guy could put the wag in reverse, Thrill Bill slapped his hand against the driver's window.

When his hand came away, there was a two-inch disk stuck to the surface.

Ryan dived for cover behind one of the wrecked cars. As Nara joined him, he saw the driver's door fly open and the driver bail out. The door locked back on its hinge, and the man sprinted away from it. He got about as far as the rear bumper.

The explosion blew off the door, and armor shrapnel nailed the driver in the middle of the back. He hit the concrete on his face, bounced once and didn't move again.

Thrill Bill jumped in through the doorless opening and unlocked the other doors. The tint was dropping from the windows as Ryan and Nara piled in the back, with Damm in the front passenger seat. With a screech of tires, the warlord reversed the wag, then shot forward around the obstacles.

He seemed to know where he was going, and what he had to do to get there. With the accelerator floored, he slashed across the lanes of traffic, cutting between the speeding wags. Miraculously, Thrill Bill hit only one other wag, smacking its right rear bumper as he swerved past. The impact sent the other vehicle into a lazy slide that turned into a 360, then another, then another. Ryan saw the car slam into a twisted pile of wreckage. As orange flame billowed, Thrill Bill shot up an off-ramp on the right and the finale was lost from view.

The ramp ended in the merging lane of a higher-level freeway. Thrill Bill eased over three lanes to the left and stayed there. The wind through the open doorway was whipping his hair around and making its spikes untwist into long, greasy curls.

"Check that," Damm said, pointing at a tell-you coming up fast on the right.

Ryan saw his own face again, again enormously enlarged, but this time with the words Find Me. Go In The First Wave!

"FIVE's getting downright desperate," Damm said.

"With a reward like that on your head," Thrill Bill said to Ryan, "maybe you'd better keep it down."

Ryan slumped lower in his seat.

After another ramp leading upward, and another merger with a higher freeway, Thrill Bill announced, "We're almost there."

He stuck his head out the open doorway and looked back. Then, with hard jerks of the wheel, a lane at a time he began cutting into the gaps in the unbroken flow of traffic, working his way gradually past the middle of the freeway. He was a dozen lanes from the left-hand wall when he slammed his fist on the dash and said, "Shit! Shit! They've already got it sealed off!"

Ryan looked out the windshield. Five hundred yards ahead, the far left lane was blocked off by black APCs. Ground troops in battlesuits stood behind the barricade.

"That was the entrance to the Totality Concept complex," the warlord said as they whizzed by. "And those were FIVE's APCs. No way are we getting in there."

"Do they expect us?" Ryan asked.

"They expect trouble," Nara told him. "The CEOs are trying to protect their tickets out of here. By defending the TC complex with a jointly manned force, FIVE can keep any one Global from rushing in and taking it over. And they all have to be worried about their own upper-level managers. Probably figure the lot of them are going to go berserk when they find out how short the passenger list really is.''

"What are we going to do, Bill?" Damm asked.

"Go up another way," the warlord said, "and try to break through from the outside."

"You mean, on top, through the roof?" Damm queried.

"What other choice have we got?" Nara queried. Then she leaned between the front bucket seats and asked, "Ransom, how are we going to get into one of the other complexes?"

From the console beside him, Thrill Bill picked up a flat, black object about two inches square and showed it to her. "This van's previous owner was a midlevel executive at Hutton-Byrum-Kobe. This is the key to the front door."

The warlord moved into the far left lane and slowed. They slid along a solid concrete wall until it bent farther to the left, leaving a narrow shoulder for him to pull onto. A sign painted on the concrete said HBK. The shoulder ended abruptly in a blind wall. Thrill Bill stopped the van and pressed the key. The entire wall slid back, exposing a long, narrow room. Ryan recognized it as the interior of a wag-sized elevator.

"First things first," the warlord said as he leaned out the van's doorway with his laser rifle. He fired left-handed, a single pulse that melted the sec videocamera mounted high on the wall at the back of the car. Then he got out, stepped into the elevator and fried the camera on the facing wall.

Thrill Bill then pulled the van into the elevator and parked. The door slid shut behind them, and immediately the elevator lurched, groaned and started upward.

"We can't stay in here," the warlord told them. He climbed on the roof of the van, reached up and pushed open the trapdoor in the ceiling of the elevator. He pulled himself through the hole.

Ryan was the last one up, and Bill shut the trap after him. The light was dim, supplied by a single, caged bulb atop the frame that contained the car's spinning gears and pulleys. The stained, concrete-lined shaft sped past them as they rose. Ryan saw a second set of cables swaying on the other side of the shaft. Over the sound of their elevator's motor, he could hear a grinding, rushing noise from above.

"We've got another car coming down from the top," Thrill Bill said. "When it passes by, we've got to jump onto the roof."

"You've got no plan whatsoever, do you, Ransom?" Nara said.

"I plan to keep on living."

The concrete box above kept dropping, and they kept rising to meet it. Ryan wondered when they would catch up to it after they jumped. Would it be thirty stories down, when it had finally come to a stop?

But the falling elevator came to a halt one floor below them.

Bill stepped across the four-foot gap between the cars. Damm, Ryan and Nara stepped after. They landed so lightly on the roof that no one inside could have heard them.

After a moment, the car's doors closed and it started dropping again.

In the weak light Ryan could see that Thrill Bill was grinning from ear to ear. "We ride down," he said softly, "then take the car back to the top of the shaft."

The elevator stopped again, and the doors opened. Ryan could hear footsteps as people exited. More people got in, then the car resumed its descent.

After a long drop, the car stopped again. This time, after the passengers got out, the doors stayed open longer. When they closed, the car didn't move.

"It's got to be empty," Damm said.

"I'll hit the button," the warlord stated.

Ryan pulled open the trapdoor for him, and Thrill Bill jumped down. A second later, the car started up with a jolt. The warlord reached up, and Ryan and Damm grabbed his wrists and lifted him back to the roof. After which, they closed the trapdoor.

As they flew upward, the bottom of the wag-sized car came into view. It was still stopped.

"Hasn't moved," Ryan said.

"They're probably searching the van," Nara said, "trying to figure out what happened to the driver."

"And their security cams," Damm added.

"Keep low as we pass it," Thrill Bill warned them.

The crossing of the cars was over in a second. In that second, Ryan saw the other trapdoor swing open, and then they were past.

"Did they see us?" Damm asked as he straightened.

"Weren't looking our way," Ryan told him.

"There should be an I-beam up there," Thrill Bill said, pointing high overhead. "Yeah, there it is."

Ryan craned his head back and saw the light at the top of the elevator shaft—a light and the beam beneath, growing rapidly larger and more distinct. The beam was no more than a foot wide and it spanned forty feet of shaft, wall to wall. Ryan had to step aside or get squashed under it as the car stopped at the top floor.

"Get on," the warlord said, throwing a leg over the beam.

As Ryan climbed on, something clanked inside the elevator and the car dropped away.

The four of them sat perched over an abyss. The ceiling was ten feet above their heads.

"Now comes the tricky part," Thrill Bill said.

Chapter Twenty-Seven

A communal groan went up as Dr. Huth finished his remarks. The scientist looked over the throng of researchers whom he supervised, a sea of lab coats. Oh, so put upon, he thought. The way they rolled their eyes and let their jaws fall open in horror.

"This is asking too much," the stout man standing before him said. Above his beard, Dr. Wisehart's face was deeply flushed, the dark eyes full of genuine anger.

It seemed even his closest associates, his academic peers, were appalled at his request.

Huth opened his arms in a helpless gesture. "If it was up to me, I wouldn't put you through it. I know how tired you all must be."

"Does FIVE?" Wisehart demanded.

"FIVE doesn't care," someone farther back in the crowd shouted.

"Not about anything but results," another scientist said.

"Look," Huth said, trying to quiet this uprising from his most skilled and most important workers, "we are on the verge of a great undertaking. We have to follow orders. We have a duty to fulfill. We have to trust FIVE. The building has been sealed. No one will be allowed to leave until we have completed the job."

The protests were even louder.

"There are plans in progress that you aren't aware of," Huth told them.

"So fill us in," Wisehart said.

With what appeared to be great reluctance, the research director of the Totality Concept proceeded. "I have received information on the most recent developments that none of you are privy to. Because of these developments, it is imperative that we alter the existing schedule."

"You'll have to be more forthcoming than that," Wisehart said.

"As many of you know, we have been running continuous simulations on a duplicate of the satellite's flight control system. A precautionary measure. Unacceptable failures started to show up about an hour ago."

"That's not our fault," someone yelled. "We pulled both units off the shelf."

"That is correct. Omnico built them," Huth said. "No one is blaming you for the problem. But we have to do something about it before the Shadow World satellite goes into orbit. That means we have to beat the scheduled launch."

"What you're asking of us is impossible," Wisehart said. "We need more time to align the power grids and stagger the energy transfers, or we'll end up permanently blacking out half the planet."

"Believe me, I understand the danger," Huth replied. "You don't have more time. It's as simple as that. This has to be done or we will lose the satellite. The fourth opening of the passageway has been bumped forward by six hours." He looked at the wall clock. "I make that 5:38 a.m."

"But Dr. Huth—"

"We are wasting precious minutes," the research director said. "Stop your whining and get on with it!"

With that, Huth stepped down from the dais and waded through the packed conference room.

As he looked from face to face, he grew more and more confident that the decision to go alone and tell no one about it had been correct. He couldn't trust any of them. Not with something as important as this. If he had given the information to a select few, even old colleagues like Wisehart, they would have wanted to bring others along, wives, children, lovers. They would have insisted. Perhaps even tried to blackmail him into getting their way. The word was certain to get out, and when that happened the whole complex would fly into a panic and the situation would no longer be containable. FIVE would promptly step in and stop him.

And that would be that.

When he'd really thought about it, about which of his peers deserved to come along, he came to the conclusion that all were unworthy of the gift. So he decided not to share it with any of them. After all, the passageway was his creation. It was only fitting that he be one of the last to use it. There was a possibility, though remote, that FIVE would get another shot at opening the rift, but by the time that happened he'd be long gone on the other side.

In the same vein of not letting the cat out of the bag, Huth had decided that it would be a bad idea to start mat-transing expensive scientific equipment onto the passageway jump pad, or worse, packing it into an ATV and then materializing that on the pad.

That would fall into the area of a dead giveaway. The only instruments he was taking along fit easily into the side pockets of his lab coat—a microcomputer, wafer thin and the size of a playing card, and an equally small electron microscope. He patted his pockets to make sure they were there as he weaved his way through the crowded halls.

Out of necessity, he was leaving the bulk of Earth's technology behind. It wasn't such a great tragedy, after all. There were advantages to being self-contained. Huth planned on becoming Shadow World's only philosopher of science, on roaming the pristine landscape, working with his mind, with his skills of observation, as had the earliest practitioners of his art. Like them, he carried in his head the scientific method, a tool powerful enough to attack any problem. Unlike them, he had the Twenty-Five Theories, which linked all available knowledge.

The bulkhead door leading to the jump area was mobbed with scientists. Most of them had nothing better to do than stand around and wring their hands. There were excess scientists, too. Pushing his way through the mass of lab coats, he entered the bulkhead door. He stopped in the middle of the metal catwalk and looked down, watching the army of technicians, hard at work. Hundreds of them. From tiers of scaffolds, they serviced the canyon of electronics that enabled the rift to open.

He crossed the catwalk and stepped onto the concrete platform. Between the plate above his head and the plate under his feet, the passage would form. And then it would be time for a fond farewell.

"Dr. Huth," a feminine voice said at his back.

He pointedly ignored the interruption.

"Dr. Huth?"

Irritated, he whirled.

The petite brunette took a step back, eyes wide. "This just came back from DNA retyping," she told him. "You said you wanted to have it as soon as it was processed." She held up a stoppered glass tube. In it was a single, intensely blue human eye.

"Yes, yes," he said, taking it from her just to shut her up. "You can go, now." He slipped the tube into his pocket and immediately forgot about it.

Chapter Twenty-Eight

Thrill Bill used his flashlight to point out a screened, three-by-three-foot rectangle set just under the shaft's ceiling on the wall opposite. "Where we've got to get is over there," he said.

There was a twenty-foot gap between the beam they sat on and the wall, and it was another eight feet up to the vent.

"Tricky is putting it mildly," Damm said, "considering that none of us can fly."

Nara was just as upset. "How did you expect us to get across?" she asked the warlord. "Even if we didn't have all this fucking gear, there's no way we could jump that far."

"I was hoping you'd have some suggestions once we got here," Thrill Bill said.

Nara looked down at the seemingly endless drop and shook her head. "Oh, man…"

Ryan swung his leg over the I-beam, straddling it as he pondered the problem.

"We could wait until the next car comes up," Damm said, "jump down through the trap, and search the top floor for another way into the vent shaft."

"If we did that, we'd alert the security force," Nara said. "They'd seal us in, and we'd never get off the floor alive."

The four of them sat in silence for a long time.

Ryan didn't speak up until he had the whole thing figured out and was pretty sure it would work. "I've got an idea," he said. "First thing, let's get rid of that screen."

He unslung his pulse rifle, put the selector switch on sustain and fired from the hip. The pencil line of green struck the corner of the grate, instantly melting it. Ryan followed the perimeter of the opening, cutting away the metal mesh, which dropped away into the dark.

They all held their breath, waiting for it to hit bottom. After thirty seconds, Ryan gave up. He decided either the sound had been so faint that they'd missed it, or the shaft went to the bottom of the earth.

Ryan adjusted the blaster's beam to the slowest pulse. Then he said, "What we need next are some foot- and handholds."

"I think he's got something," Thrill Bill said delightedly.

Ryan took a one-handed aim and began blasting a series of holes in the concrete at the far end of the beam. It took him several tries to figure out how many bursts it took to make a proper niche, one that was deep enough without being too wide.

Once he had refined his technique, he started manufacturing a line of holes about a foot apart at shoulder height above the beam. He cut them all the way to the corner of the shaft, then across the facing wall, angling slightly upward to meet the vent opening.

When he was done, he swung the laser rifle back toward the end of the beam and started burning out the footholds. He bored them about five feet below the first set. Because they had to accommodate the toes of their boots, he made them both deeper and wider than the ones above.

"I knew we'd come up with something," Thrill Bill said when the process was complete.

"Going to be a bitch scuttling around that wall carrying packs and weapons," Damm said.

"Well, we can't leave them here," Nara snapped. "We're going to need them in the complex."

"Look," Thrill Bill said, "I'm not carrying anything but my tribarrel. We can shift the loads around and make things a little easier for everybody."

It took them a while to decide how to divide the weaponry. When they were done, Ryan said, "Since it's my idea, I get to go first."

Nobody gave him any argument.

Ryan pushed to his feet and tightrope-walked along the beam to the wall. He put his hand flat against the cool concrete and measured the distance to the first foothold. No point in putting it off, he thought. He reached out with his right hand and slipped his fingers into the niche, then he cautiously extended his right foot.

The first step off the beam was the toughest. All his weight came down on his right toe, and he had to dig his fingers in hard to keep his body from being pulled over backward by the pack.

"Balance is a little funny with the weight on my back," he told the others. "Seems okay, though. I'm going to take it nice and slow."

He moved methodically along the wall, first hand, then foot, hand then foot. He had to concentrate not just on grip, but on relaxing his hand and arm as he reached out, otherwise he was sure to cramp up. And a cramp was the ticket to a very long fall.

When he reached the corner of the shaft, he paused, one foot braced on either side, and shook out the tension in his fingers. The facing wall was a little more difficult, as he had to pull himself up to take each slightly higher step. When he reached the vent opening, he unslung the pulse rifle and subgun and chucked them into the hole. Then he grabbed hold of the edge and pulled himself inside.

"All right, Shadow Man!" Damm said.

The vent duct ahead of him was dark. Ryan pushed his weapons down the passage. With difficulty in the narrow space, he shrugged out of his pack and kicked it out of the way, after the blasters.

"Go ahead, Captain," Thrill Bill said. "You're next."

The blonde traversed the narrow beam, then crawled around the inside of the shaft. She moved much faster than Ryan had, though not recklessly. She took fewer pauses to shake out her hands. When she reached the vent, Ryan grabbed her weapons, then he grabbed her by the pack straps. As he pulled her in, he had to back up to get her legs inside.

"That was hairy," she gasped, nose to nose with him. "I don't think I've ever been so scared."

"You did good," he told her. "Real quick, no hesitation."

"I had no choice," she said. "I was afraid my arms would give out if I took too long."

Nara squeezed past him and moved deeper in the passage.

Thrill Bill came around next, then Damm, who moved very slowly. The mercie was drenched with sweat when Ryan lugged him into the vent opening, but he was smiling.

Thrill Bill passed Nara his flashlight, and with her in the lead, they crawled on hands and knees another thirty feet.

"Got a vertical turn in the shaft," she said over her shoulder.

They paused while she examined it with the light.

"It's a straight shaft that runs about six feet up," she said. "It's got a cap on it. Looks like our exit. I'm going to melt it off."

Nara rolled to her back and aimed her pulse rifle up the shaft. Green flashed as she sheared off the ventilator cap. She scooted back out of the way as molten drops of metal rained.

"That's got it," she said, then rolled back to her knees and stood in the vertical duct. Her boots disappeared as she climbed up and out.

Thrill Bill followed her. Ryan moved forward, then stood in the narrow passage. From the cutaway vent cap, Thrill Bill reached down for his pack and blasters. Then Ryan pulled himself out through the opening.

Overhead there were no stars. The sky was covered by a thick blanket of clouds tinted yellow by the strings of lights on the sides of the huge concrete cones that surrounded them.

"They're cooling towers," Nara said, anticipating his question. "Cooling towers for the nuclear power plants."

Ryan looked around. They stood roughly in the middle of an acre of flat roof. It was like a plateau. Red warning lights glowed in all four corners. Similar lights stretched off into the distance. As he turned, Ryan saw a solid mass of enormous rooftops, all of various heights and shapes. The chaos was unbroken by canyons; the buildings were built against one another. In all directions the city appeared to reach the horizon line. The smell of petrochemicals made him choke.

"How far is it to the Totality Concept complex?" he asked.

"Not too far," Thrill Bill said, "but it's too dangerous to try and make the crossing in the dark. We could trip an alarm and have FIVE on our backs in no time."

"He's right," Nara stated. "It's best if we go after first light. It's not more than a couple of hours away."

They all sat down on the concrete roof by the ventilator and waited for the sun to come up. After a while the wind started to pick up and it got bitterly cold. There was no shelter. When Nara leaned against Ryan, he could feel her shivering through her thin lab coat. He put his arm around her shoulders and drew her closer.

"Thanks," she said, looking up at him. "I'm about frozen."

"No problem. It's warming me up, too."

The blonde snuggled in, getting as comfortable as she could. After a moment she said, "Ryan, don't worry. We're going to get back. We're going to make it. We've got to."

Ryan didn't reply. It was a waste of breath. He closed his eye, lowered his head and tried to rest.

Chapter Twenty-Nine

Krysty awakened with wrenching pain in her right shoulder. Her arm was twisted and pinned under her side, and her cheek rested in the dirt. It felt like something was stretched over her face and head. Above a line of collapsed roofs, above the black wall of the ridge, the sky was beginning to lighten, fingers of pink clawing through the lavender. She knew at once that she was back in the ville of Moonboy, but she didn't remember making the trip. There was a steady hissing noise, too loud even for mutie snakes, she thought.

She was aware of a warm, heavy weight on top of her. Whatever it was, it was snoring softly. Krysty tried to move forward, out from under the pressure, and found she couldn't. Something that was stretched over her head prevented her. With her fingers, she felt the mesh of a net.

She closed her eyes and tried to remember. The effort made her head spin, and she thought she was going to be sick.

Then she heard footsteps. Turning her head as far as she could, she saw four black figures moving across the street. They stopped in front of a huge shape silhouetted against the morning sky. When she saw the missile, and the steam jetting from its base, Krysty's confusion began to lift.

She remembered trying to rescue Ryan, and failing. She remembered fleeing with the companions over the ridge to the shore of the mud lakes. She remembered the battle with the coyotes and facing down the gunship.

There, her memories ended.

Whatever the men in black had done to her, she was now trapped.

With her free hand she felt around above her, and caught the snorer by the ear. From the frames of the wire-rimmed glasses, she guessed it had to be J.B. She gave his ear a hard shake.

"Uhhh," J.B. moaned in protest, but he didn't wake up.

She shook him harder.

"Easy, Krysty, or you'll tear the damned thing off," a voice behind her whispered. It was Mildred. "And he won't even feel it. He's still narcotized, dead to the world."

"Where are you?" Krysty said.

"Sort of behind you, and turned sideways. Is this your calf?"

"Ow."

"I thought so."

"What about Doc?"

"I'm facing his boots."

"My back must be turned toward him. I can't see him. Jak and Dean have got to be on top of J.B."

"Did they take all your weapons?" Mildred asked.

"I've got nothing I can reach. Probably got nothing, period."

Krysty felt for her Smith & Wesson. It was gone. "They got my blaster, too."

"Man, this net cord is tough stuff," Mildred said. "It's way too thick to bite through."

"I could've snapped it," Krysty said, "if I hadn't already used up my powers."

"Have knife," said a soft voice from above.

"Jak and Dean, are you okay?" Krysty said.

"I'm okay, Krysty. My head hurts, though," Dean replied.

"Cramp in foot. Ache in head. Have knife. They missed it. Had it hid inside my sleeve. Cut net."

"No, wait," Krysty told Jak. "Not yet. Not until J.B. and Doc wake up. We can't make a move while they're still unconscious."

"I wake J.B.," Jak said.

From above there came the sound of a muffled blow, followed by another, then another.

"Fireblast," the Armorer groaned. "I'm awake. Stop smacking me."

"Can you reach Doc?" Mildred asked.

"Reach him?" J.B. repeated. "The old geezer's fogging up my glasses."

Krysty felt a shuddering movement above her.

"Hey, Doc," J.B. said, "wake up."

Then there was the sound of another slap.

"By the Three—"

The old man's exclamation was shut off by Dix's palm. "Easy, Doc, just be quiet."

It was getting lighter by the second. Krysty could now see the figures clearly as they walked around the foot of the gantry. She also noticed something much closer that she hadn't been able to see before. About fifteen feet away, over against the ruined curb, stood the squat black cube on wheels. Beside it was the canister that dispensed the flesh-eating foam. That didn't bode well.

"Okay, Jak," she said, "use that blade."

"Cut top out of net. We slip away."

The pressure of mesh against Krysty's head gradually lessened, then the weight pinning her to the ground lifted. J.B. helped Jak peel the net down, so Krysty and the others could get free.

They had no more than straightened when a harsh male voice barked at them, "Stay right where you are!"

It was too late to run. Two of the armored figures held them covered with light blasters. A third walked casually over to the curb, picked up the canister and shrugged into its harness straps. The fourth hung back, watching.

J.B. ignored the three-barreled longblaster pointed at his chest and demanded of the figure closest, "Are you bastards human? Or are you rad-blasted mutie cockroaches?"

"Okay, let's detint," the figure said.

Krysty watched as the black helmets turned clear. They were all men, between the ages of thirty and forty. The one with the canister wore a red, bill-less cap.

"You've got human heads, anyway," J.B. said, leaning forward for a better look. "Do the suits come off?"

"Of course."

"How about the heads?"

"We don't have time to play with them, Colonel," said the other rifleman. "We're set to launch in T-minus four minutes."

"Put the launch on standby."

"Colonel…"

"Do it."

The rifleman turned away and headed for what had to be the makeshift missile control center—a table pulled out of one of the gaudies with whitecoat electronic gear stacked on it.

"We were going to let you live until after the launch," Gabhart said. "Now you've given us no choice. We can't have you running around loose while we're trying to get the missile away. We've got to take care of you before we proceed."

Out of the corner of her eye, Krysty saw Jak move. With a flick of his wrist he sent the leaf-bladed knife spinning toward the colonel's throat at a speed almost too fast to follow. Three feet from the target, the blade was slapped away by an invisible hand, and it dropped harmlessly to the dirt.

"I thought you said you searched these people for weapons?" the colonel said.

"Sorry, sir," the man with the canister said. "That kid had so much metal sewn into his clothes, there was no way of telling what he was carrying. The only way to make sure he was unarmed was to strip him naked. Pedro didn't want to do it. Neither did I."

"Where's Ryan?" Krysty said to the man in charge. "What have you done to him?"

"Ryan? You mean the guy with the eye patch? He's long gone. I wouldn't count on seeing him again in this life." The colonel waved the fourth man forward. "Hylander," he said, "go ahead and take your samples now."

The guy with the walrus mustache stepped over to the squat cube and from behind it took out a gleaming silver apparatus. It had a pistol grip and a latticework, cylindrical frame. He gripped a small knob at the frame's opening and gave it a pull.

Krysty was standing close enough to see the razor-sharp inner ring slide back and lock in place.

"Are you sure you want him to do this, Colonel?" the canister man said. "If we just tie them up again, they can't interfere with the launch."

"We've each got our own jobs to do, Ockerman," the colonel said. "Part of Hylander's job is to analyze tissue samples for disease vectors. It's important work, or FIVE wouldn't have asked him to do it. They need the information if they're going to protect our people after they arrive."

Something behind the armored figures caught Krysty's attention, a vague shimmering in the middle of the street, like heat waves, rippling, only it couldn't have been—the sun was barely up. Then the shimmer began to rotate, and she saw the glittering motes within, spinning faster and faster.

Chapter Thirty

After daybreak Ryan got a good look at his surroundings. This Earth needed the night to make it seem less hideous. By day, he could see that the roofs of most of the skyscrapers and high tower blocks were splintered and caved in. The top stories, visible above the canopy of skyline, were cadaverous wrecks. Windows were broken out, and scorch marks from ancient fires blackened the outer walls.

And the megalopolis didn't reach to the horizon in all directions. When Ryan moved to a far corner of the roof, he got a glimpse of what lay on the far side of the nuclear cooling towers: strip-mine terraces for as far as the eye could see; huge rusting skeletons of extraction machinery; monster wags designed to haul hundreds of tons of rock lay overturned and abandoned. Nothing was green. The only colors were the red of the dirt and the gray of the concrete.

As they prepared to leave the rooftop, Damm asked the warlord, "What's the plan after we get in the complex?"

"Since the captain knows the place so well, I was hoping she'd have some suggestions."

"Yeah, I do," Nara said. "We should forget about trying to make a deal with the CEOs and head straight for the passageway to Shadow World. Fight our way in if we have to. Based on the firepower

FIVE's been throwing at us, I don't think Ryan's much of a bargaining chip anymore. They might have already written him off. Once we're inside the chamber, we've got a lot more options to work with. If FIVE won't trade for Ryan, it's going to want to keep its equipment in tiptop shape. We can barricade ourselves in, do a little minor damage to show we mean business, then bargain for a trip out of here."

"Puts us on the offensive," Thrill Bill said. "I like it."

"It might even work," Damm agreed.

When Thrill Bill started to lead them from rooftop to rooftop, Ryan realized he'd been right about waiting until dawn. There were sec devices on every roof. The warlord knew how to outfox them, though. Another reason not to try the move at night was that some of the crossings were on ledges no wider than a handspan. They followed a complicated route, dictated by the irregularity of the buildings' shapes and the differences in their heights. They had to climb down before they could go up, and vice versa.

After they'd been moving awhile, Ryan caught the now-familiar sound of rotor-driven aircraft approaching. Thrill Bill waved for them to take cover behind an upraised ledge. A squadron of black airships passed overhead, moving the same direction they were.

"Those were FIVE's assault gyros," Nara said. "Probably reinforcing the Totality complex."

"I never promised this was going to be easy," Thrill Bill said.

Ten minutes later, soaked with sweat, Ryan peered over a roof ledge that overlooked their destination. Three of the black ships had landed on the enormous, flat roof below and men in armor stood around a little outhouselike hut in the middle of the space. Beyond them were rows of raised skylights.

"That hut is one way in," Thrill Bill said.

"I hope you've got a second choice," Damm told him.

"Yeah, but there's a problem. If we don't take care of those guys now, we're going to have to face them later, once we're inside. I hadn't planned on going in quiet. When we make our big entrance, the noise is going to make them come running."

"No way can we kill all those troopers down there," Nara said. "If we try, we'll never get in the building. We have to use surprise and speed. Break in no matter how much noise it makes."

"Yeah," Ryan said, "and let them take us out if they can."

They circled and came around the structure from the far side, hopping down from an adjoining building. That roof was much bigger than the one on the HBK tower. Ryan couldn't see the aircraft or any of the black-armored men.

Thrill Bill led them to the rows of elevated skylights, then turned and started to run parallel to them. He seemed to know where he was going. He slowed after a few hundred feet, then stopped.

"What do you think, Captain? Shouldn't this about do it?"

"There's no way we can get any closer from up here."

"Everybody dump out your packs," the warlord ordered. "Cracking this baby is going to take some serious explosives."

Ryan took a look at the skylights. They were made of the same stuff as the black armor.

The warlord cobbled together an assortment of mines, grens and blocks of plastic explosive and built a sort of pyramid on top of one of the skylight panes.

"Put the rest back," Thrill Bill said.

Not that there was much to put back. Ryan had four grens and one slap charge left. The latter he slipped inside a front pocket.

"That should do it," the warlord said as he finished the fusing.

"And if we're standing too close, it'll do for us, too," Nara stated.

"Better move over a couple of rows to the side, then."

The explosion was nothing if not spectacular. A billowing orange fireball sent a fountain of black shards high in the air. The stuff hadn't stopped falling when Thrill Bill charged out from cover. He didn't hesitate a lick, jumping through the big hole he'd made, feetfirst.

Nara did the same, then Damm. Ryan jumped last. He didn't know for sure what he was jumping into, because nobody'd bothered to tell him, but he didn't expect to deadfall twenty feet.

He landed on the seat of a conference room chair with his boot soles and it crashed apart under his weight, breaking most of his fall. If he was surprised, the people in lab coats standing around the conference table were stunned.

Damm had fallen on three of their colleagues, inflicting serious damage to them and none to himself.

"Out of the way!" Thrill Bill yelled at the room full of scientists. To emphasize the urgency of the situation, he cut loose with his pulse rifle, sending a superheated green slash through the air above their heads that brought down the ceiling light fixture and half the opposing wall.

The scientists hit the deck, pronto.

"Follow me!" Nara shouted.

Ryan fell in behind her. He was ready for anything, but he soon realized it was a case of the same old, same old. They jogged through hallways choked with noncombatants.

"It's Shadow Man!" they shouted as he ran by.

Some of them surged forward with outstretched arms, trying to grab him and pull him down. Their expressions of eagerness and delight melted away when he charred a bit of ceiling above them. It took a snap-kick in the face to dissuade the really serious grabbers.

They encountered no sec men until they approached the entrance to the passageway. Nara stuck her head around a turn, then quickly pulled it back.

"There must be at least ten of them standing in front of the bulkhead door about seventy feet down the hall," she said. "No point in saving anything."

"Yeah, let's use it all," Damm said.

They set out all their grens on the floor. After they divided them up, it worked out to six apiece, mixed frag and flash-stun.

"Will these hurt them?" Ryan asked.

"Blast concussion should knock them all out at the very least," Thrill Bill said. "No way battlesuits can handle this much concentrated high-ex."

Ryan started to pull pins with his teeth. When the others let their grip safeties plink off, he followed suit. He had three grens in either hand, fuses burning, when the hallway lights dimmed.

And then went out.

DR. HUTH STOOD on the edge of the catwalk with his fingers crossed. Unscientific or not, he needed all the help he could get. He would have sacrificed a live goat to Beelzebub, if such a creature had still existed. The whole operation was a house of cards. The intricate, Global power interlacings had to hold long enough to establish the passageway; then he needed a really big surge to kick open the door to Shadow World.

The second hand of the big clock on the wall behind him swept past the twelve. It was 5:38 a.m. Right on schedule, the vast room was jolted by a violent shudder.

One of the technicians working the operating system monitors along the wall behind him said, "Blackout in five, four, three, two, one..."

Huth gripped the catwalk rail as night fell and a hurricane was born. Gale-force wind plucked at his lab coat, and he had to hold on with both hands.

Over the howl of the wind, another technician was screaming out more numbers, counting down the time until the complex's battery backup power kicked in.

Light returned to the grim, low-ceilinged chamber.

And as it did, the room was rocked by a tremendous explosion. Concrete dust rained on him. Right away, Huth knew it wasn't the thunder of the passage opening. It came from the hallway behind him. More explosions, and a blinding white light flashed through the window of the bulkhead door. For a sickening instant, the catwalk teetered, and the vibration through the rails was so violent that it made his hands go numb.

First thing he thought was that it had to be one of the Globals, trying to seize control of the passageway. The second thing he thought was that he had to get to the door.

Bar the door.

Huth dashed across the catwalk. When he looked out the scorched glass of the bulkhead door, he saw the one-eyed man charging at him. Cursing his numbed fingers, he fumbled with the lock.

RYAN DIDN'T WAIT to toss the grens, and neither did the others. With six second fuses burning, to hesitate was to die. Ryan took a step out into the pitch-black hall and chucked his grens at the far end.

Twenty-four grenades landed among the sec men guarding the bulkhead door. They heard the clunks on the floor and felt impacts against their armor as the grens hit and bounced off. By the time the lights came up two seconds later, and they saw what lay all around them, it was too late.

The first explosion was really a dozen grens popping off at once. It dropped the hallway ceiling, blew out the walls and blew the sec men through the walls and the ceiling. The explosions that came after that were pure overkill. They propelled already flying bodies farther down the hall.

"They're powering up the passageway!" Nara said. "Let's go!"

Ryan charged out ahead of her. Through the plaster dust he could see a head on the other side of the door's window. He threw himself against the barrier and it gave, slamming back.

The man behind it went flying.

Ryan didn't give him a second look. He held the door open as Nara and Damm ran past.

Thrill Bill had to have slipped on a body because he was still halfway down the hall. "Go on, go on!" he cried as he dashed toward Ryan.

The one-eyed man gave the warlord covering fire, but it was impossible to control the whole corridor. From the opposite end of the hallway, green flashed. Thrill Bill screamed, and a blast of light sizzled past Ryan's hip, narrowly missing him.

Thrill Bill crashed down, just outside the doorway. Ryan grabbed him by the shirt. "Come on, stand up," he said.

"Can't do it. My legs…"

When Ryan pulled him through the doorway, he saw the terrible injuries. Thrill Bill moved, but his right leg didn't. It was severed at the hip. His other leg dangled by a thread. Ryan shut the door and locked it.

"Never had any luck," Thrill Bill said.

"Come on, Ransom, you can make it," Nara yelled as she started across the catwalk. "We can carry you."

"I don't think so," Thrill Bill said. "I'm dead meat, no matter which side of the passageway I'm on. If I stay here at least I can do some good. Get some payback. Give me your tribarrel for a backup. I'll keep them off you."

Ryan passed him the weapon, then gave his shoulder a squeeze.

"Pleasure knowing you."

"It's mutual, Shadow Man."

Ryan crossed the narrow bridge. With Damm's and Nara's help, he managed to push the end of the catwalk off the pad. It didn't tumble into the canyon as they'd hoped, the other end was held by hinges. The catwalk dropped to the vertical, crashing into the opposite side of the abyss, and hung there.

Nara turned and ran for the tornado materializing in the middle of the pad. She vanished; Ryan dived after her. He didn't see the maw this time because he had his eye closed, but he felt the thunder down to his toes.

Chapter Thirty-One

Across a wide, lush meadow framed by tall evergreens, Ryan saw the glowing lights of the crude log cabin. Warm. Yellow. Inviting. They said "home."

Home at last.

When he saw his companions step out onto the porch, smiling, he broke into a trot. Krysty ran out to meet him, her beautiful hair flowing down around her shoulders. They kissed, and her lips were softer and warmer than he had ever thought possible.

Then the others rushed up. Dean, Jak, Mildred, Doc and J.B. They took turns embracing him and slapping him on the back.

"Come on inside, Ryan," the Armorer said. "We got quite a meal laid out in honor of your return."

They took him through the wooden door. Beside the hearth was a table set for seven. On it was a huge haunch of smoked roast boar, pots of yams, stewed greens, jugs of dark ale, crusty bread.

"Sit at the head of the table, dear boy," Doc said, as he sharpened a carver on a steel. The old man attacked the juicy haunch, slicing it into thick slabs.

Soon they were hard at it, laughing, eating, drinking.

After the apple pies had been vanquished, as the brimming ale jug went around a last time, a sudden pall fell over the table.

Ryan looked at his friends and saw the growing unease on their faces.

"What's wrong?" he asked.

J.B. waved him off, scraping back his chair. He started to get up, then slumped back down. He seemed perplexed.

"I feel decidedly queer," Doc admitted. He stuck out his tongue and wiped it on his white cloth napkin. He gawked at the result in horror. "Look! Look at this...."

The napkin was green where he had touched it to his tongue.

Mildred fell into a kind of fit. She clutched both hands to her throat and made sounds as if she were slowly strangling. Her eyes bugged out of their sockets, then thin trickles of green started to leak out of her nostrils.

Dean was bashing his forehead against the end of the table, over and over, as if he were trying to beat in his own brains.

Jak was gagging, green fluid gushing from his eyes.

"What is it?" Ryan said, jumping to his feet.

J.B.'s swollen tongue protruded from between his teeth; it had become too big for his mouth to contain. Green slime drooled down his chin.

Then Krysty slumped forward onto her plate.

He pulled her up at once. When he saw her face, his heart nearly stopped. Beads of green dew dotted her cheeks and forehead. Her eyes were wild and staring, and they wept green tears.

"Was it something we ate?" Ryan cried, sweeping the remains of the food off the table and onto the floor. "Why aren't I sick?"

Krysty's mouth moved; no sound came out.

He put his ear close. Her breath smelled shockingly of ammonia.

"Krysty, why am I the only one who isn't sick?" he repeated.

She inhaled a deep, slow breath, summoning her strength. Then she said, "Because you brought it with you...."

She died in his arms a moment later.

As Ryan threw back his head to scream his outrage, the room began to spin.

HIS EARS RINGING with thunder, Ryan crashed onto his hands and knees. He dropped his head and began to heave. A tiny, detached part of him was aware that Nara and Damm were close by, and in the same condition that he was. He also knew they were surrounded by armed men in battlesuits. He saw his friends standing huddled to one side. He wanted to jump up and go to their aid, but there was nothing he could do. He was helpless in the throes of nausea. Over and over, the spasms gripped him.

Unstoppable.

When they finally calmed, he knelt there, forehead lowered to the ground, strands of vomit swaying from his chin.

"Well, I guess I was wrong about your never seeing this one again."

Ryan recognized the voice. It belonged to the colonel. He raised his head from the dirt, put his hand to his stomach and pretended to retch some more. As he did, his fingers dipped inside his pocket for the slap charge he had squirreled away.

Ryan waited, because he knew he was weakened, and that he would only have one chance.

When the colonel stepped a little closer, Ryan threw himself at the man. He grabbed him by the shoulder, turned him, then locked a forearm across the bottom of his helmet.

The other black-armored men started to close in immediately.

"What exactly do you think this is going to get you?" the colonel said with a laugh. "You can't hurt me."

"Mebbe I can't, but this can."

Ryan showed him the AP charge, holding it right in front of his nose. Then he said to the others, "Lower your blasters or this guy's head is going to disappear."

"Cook him," the colonel said.

"Sir, I think he means it," Hylander said.

"And I think he's bluffing. Take him out!"

"No, don't!" Nara cried as she struggled to her feet. "I know him, Colonel. He will kill you."

The colonel shrugged. "I'm expendable, Jurascik. Just like any of the others. Just like you. The mission will go on without me. And that's all that matters."

"There isn't a mission anymore," Nara told him. "On the other side, it's all falling apart. Right now, FIVE is probably already at war with itself. There's not going to be an exodus from Earth. Not of a million, not even a thousand."

"She's right," Damm said. "The only people who are going to come across after us are a handful of CEOs and Totality Concept bigwigs. The rest of the hundred billion is as good as dead. My guess is, the bastards have arranged it so no one else can follow."

"Things could come together again," the colonel said. "Sometime in the future maybe."

"You've got to face facts. There's not going to be a next time. This is the final gasp."

"I know that's a possibility—"

"Colonel, I wouldn't joke about something like this," Nara said. "Believe me, it's done. It's over. I saw it. For better or worse, as it now stands, we six are the sole survivors of planet Earth."

As the truth slowly settled in, Gabhart seemed to sag in Ryan's grasp. He loosened his hold on the man's chest and said, "I want you other three to put your weapons down on the ground, then take three big steps back from them."

After they'd obeyed his order, the companions moved in and picked up the strange blasters.

"Now, out of those armor suits," Ryan said. "All of you. Help them, Damm."

Under their high-tech gear, the soldier-scientists of the parallel earth were less than impressive. They looked undernourished, and they wore threadbare jumpsuits. The toes of all their white polyester socks had holes in them.

When they were out of their armor and seated on the ground, Ryan released the colonel. Krysty immediately rushed over and gave him a hug.

"You did it, Ryan!" she cried. "You came back!"

Standing beside Damm, Nara watched as they kissed tenderly. When their lips parted and Ryan glanced over at her, the blonde shook her head sadly. "Something told me you were taken," she said.

"I can't believe this is happening," Gabhart said, as Damm removed his chest plate and tossed it aside.

"They were so close to making it all work, and it would've worked."

"Don't know about that," the mercie said. "The same mentality that fucked up the planet in the first place was in charge. If you look at it that way, what happened isn't any big surprise."

"You really think they're coming over here?" Ockerman said from his seat on the curb. "The scum-sucking CEOs, I mean."

"I think they're probably going to try," Ryan answered.

"You can *bet* they're going to try," Nara said.

"What are we going to do with their missile?" Hylander asked. "There's sure no point in launching it. Without the technology to use it, the satellite's nothing but orbiting junk."

"Why don't you send it back?" Ryan said.

Hylander frowned. "What do you mean?"

"I mean, launch it back through the passage, before the damn thing shuts for good."

They all looked at the tornado, still dimly visible, hovering in the middle of the street.

"As I understand it," Ryan went on, "even though the gate's closed on the other side, stuff from here can still get sucked back the other way. That's how Nara and I got pulled in."

"Do you have any idea what would happen if we launched the missile into the passage?" the colonel said.

"Enlighten us, please," Doc said.

"For starters, it would take off the top thirty stories of TC complex."

"I don't have a problem with that," Ryan said. "Does anybody else?"

The companions all shook their heads.

"Sounds good to me," Hylander said.

"Hey, I'm up for it, too," Ockerman said. "Give the bastards back their techno-rubbish and hand them their heads at the same time."

"Why don't you sit down for a while, Colonel," Ryan said, "and let your boys see to the details?"

Gabhart sat heavily on the curb, his head in his hands.

With Krysty by his side, Ryan watched as the crew turned the mobile gantry, then carefully lowered the nose of the missile until it lined up with the shimmering bit of space in the middle of Moonboy.

"We left the countdown at T-minus four," Hylander said.

Gabhart raised his head. "Once you reinitiate the sequence," he said, "we'd better all move to safer ground. There's no telling what will happen."

They took cover behind the collapsed porch roof across the street.

When the numbers fell to zero, orange flame fifty yards long whooshed from the rocket's tail nozzles. That was all that happened for a few seconds. Then when sufficient thrust was built up, the clamps fell away, and the missile surged forward.

The hole in space gobbled it.

And when the tail fins vanished, the canyon resounded with a solemn thunderclap that announced the end of a world.

Chapter Thirty-Two

The door hit Dr. Huth so hard that it knocked him off his feet. He hurtled backward onto the computer workstations along the wall and bounced to the floor. With laser fire zipping into the room from the hall, he lay on his side behind a pair of ergonomic chairs and pretended to be unconscious.

When he heard the intruders, captained by the one-eyed man, struggling to dump the catwalk, he lifted his head slightly. What he saw made his heart sink. The wounded man with the beard sat guard by the door, cutting off any hope he had of dashing across the catwalk. Pushed by Cawdor and the other two, the bridge to survival scraped off the edge of the pad and dropped, slamming into the wall on his side of the canyon.

There was nothing Huth could do.

He had to stay there, biting his lips, while the trio made good their escape, perhaps stealing his only chance to do the same. After the third thunderclap, Huth jumped to his feet and snatched up one of the chairs by the backrest. He rushed at the legless sentry, swinging the chair high overhead.

The bearded man glanced over his shoulder as Huth brought the chair down. The metal wheels and undercarriage smashed into his head. Huth swung again as the rifle dropped from the man's hand. The crunching impact jolted all the way to his shoulders. He raised the chair a third time.

The sentry slumped to the floor, his face badly gashed and spurting blood. Huth tossed the chair aside, snatched hold of an arm and dragged the unconscious man to the edge of the chasm. Without a moment's hesitation, he kicked the body over the side. He didn't watch it fall.

"We can still make it!" he shouted at the technicians cowering on the floor. "Help me pull the catwalk back up!"

His staff slowly stood, but made no move to join him.

Huth picked up the laser rifle the sentry had dropped and menaced them with it. "You've got a choice—help me or die!"

They decided it was in their best interest to help.

Raising the catwalk again wasn't easy. A rope had to be fastened to the bottom end to gain additional leverage. Even then, it took all their combined strength to lift it. Once they had slid it back across the gulf, Huth ran to the other side. From the shimmering air in the center of the pad, he could see the passageway was still intact. The gate to Shadow World, however, had most definitely closed.

"I need more power!" he shouted at the technicians.

"But, Dr. Huth," one of them protested, "if we try to energize the gate again, we'll blow every grid on the planet."

Huth was in no mood for trifles. He leveled the tribarrel at the tech and squeezed the trigger. The man jerked backward, arms flying up as a bolt of green pierced his chest; behind him, a second before he crashed into it, a computer monitor exploded in a shower of sparks. The body rolled off the front of the workstation and dropped to the floor.

Someone pounded on the other side of the bulkhead door. Huth turned and saw a black helmet peering at him through the glass. A gauntleted hand waved for him to unlock the door.

"More power!" Huth repeated.

The technicians worked frantically to make it so.

An angry voice boomed from the intercom speaker set in the wall. "Dr. Huth," it said, "this is FIVE security. Open the door and stand down the procedure. You have not been authorized to draw power."

The lights dimmed to nothing.

As they came back up, the amplified voice said, "This is your final warning! Open the door!"

Huth had no intention of doing that. The glittering tornado had appeared on the pad. He dropped the pulse rifle and started to run for it. Behind him there was a whomp as the security team blew open the bulkhead door.

"Stop where you are!" a voice shouted. "Stop or we'll fire!"

Sprinting, Huth had fifteen feet to go. He dived for the spiraling column of air, but had the sickening realization that it was too far away, that he'd never make it. He hit the concrete on his belly, and in anticipation of being burned, he covered the back of his head with his hands. As he did so, something rolled out of his lab coat pocket and clattered onto the pad. He clutched for it without thinking.

Huth stared at the glass tube in his hand. In it was an intensely blue eye. At this moment of his final defeat, Ryan Cawdor stared back, mocking him.

Then the room rocked, as the lips of reality split, then gaped. Chunks of the ceiling rained around him and over his head, the tip of a white cone, six feet across, appeared out of nowhere. With a terrible roar the huge missile unrolled above him.

There was fear, pain, then blistering, yellow-white oblivion.

Epilogue

Sitting on a chair he'd rescued from under one of the fallen porches along Moonboy's main street, Ryan watched Mildred throw more scraps of wood on her cook fire. She'd already fed everybody once, and was starting in on seconds for those who could handle them.

There was nothing quite like fresh mesquite-grilled rattlesnake, he thought, raising the jug to his lips and taking a long swallow of air-temp beer. Especially when the steaks were as big as a man's head and three inches thick. Get that crispy charred crust on the outside and inside everything stays nice and moist. Kind of like chicken, with the texture of fish. He burped softly and set down the jug.

Jak had taken Hylander and Ockerman over the ridge to collect their morning meat. Hunting in the cool light just after daybreak was the ticket when someone was after reptiles, no matter how big. Once the desert started to heat up, snakes and their like got up a full head of steam.

The men from the other Earth hadn't taken their pulse rifles along on the hunt. Ryan had been pleased when they took up the weapons dropped by the dead cannies instead. They'd abandoned the tribarrels, along with the battlesuits, in a pile in the middle of the street. There was no need for either in Deathlands, nor for jump mines, which the colonel had promptly decommissioned.

While Mildred cooked seconds of snake, the companions and the visitors sat together around the fire, drinking up the remaining stores of Moonboy's green beer.

They'd started out talking amiably enough, like two groups of travelers who'd met on the same stretch of road and decided to share a meal. Gradually, the colonel and his crew had drawn back from the conversation. Now, when they spoke, it was to one another. Ryan figured it was starting to hit home to them what they'd done, and that what they'd left was gone forever.

The gulf between the earths was too wide to jump in a few hours, or a few days, or even a few years. The memories and regrets would stay sharp, just under the surface. He figured the colonel and his crew would be saying goodbye before long, and going their separate ways.

Nara caught him staring at her. She smiled sadly, then looked away, poking at the fire with a long stick.

Krysty came up from behind, slid her hands over his shoulders and leaned close to his ear. "When are you going to tell me what happened between you and that woman?" she asked.

Ryan rose from the chair and turned.

"I need to know how jealous I should be," Krysty said, searching his face.

He put his hand on her chin, gently pulling her mouth onto his. He kissed her tenderly for a long time before he drew back. Krysty's eyes were shining. As he took her hand and started down the path between the vacant shanties, he said, "I'll tell you all about it, after we make love."

A jungle threat...

STONY MAN™ 46

Hostile INSTINCT

The Stony Man team is called in to stop a disenchanted Congolese man from taking over a jungle region in central Africa. He is setting himself up as dictator and wields a great deal of power...including several vials of Ebola virus that he stole from a lab!

Available in April 2000 at your favorite retail outlet.

Take 2 explosive books plus a mystery bonus FREE

Journey back to the future
with these classic

DEATH LANDS ®

titles!